DESERT ISLAND DIARIES 1

# Destiny at Dolphin Bay

# DIANA DELACRUZ

Heart Ally Books
Camano Island, Washington

Published by:
Heart Ally Books
26910 92nd Ave NW C5-406, Stanwood, WA 98292
Published on Camano Island, WA, USA
www.heartallybooks.com

ISBN-13: 978-1-63107-037-2 (epub)
ISBN-13: 978-1-63107-036-5 (paperback)
Library of Congress Control Number: 2021937024

2 3 4 5 6 7 8 9 10 11

For the Family S. M. You know who you are.

*Hardships often prepare ordinary people*
*for an extraordinary destiny.*
–C. S. Lewis

# MAP of CHAUQUELÍN ISLAND

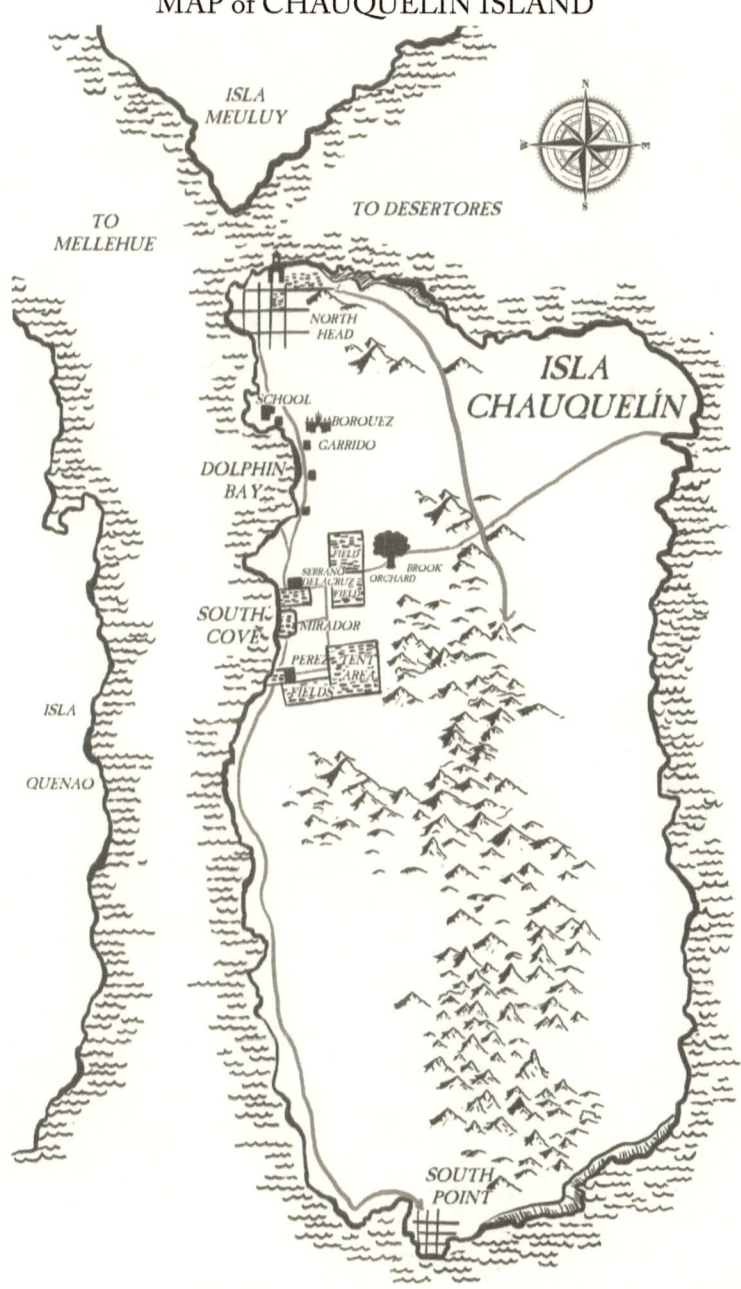

*Chiloé Islands, Chile*

*Day 1, January 31*

*Lucky that Martinet Martin didn't assign me to write about what I <u>liked</u> in Chile, since I could list that on one hand so far. But the first thing I've <u>learned</u> here is that nothing's ever as good as you hope or quite as bad as you fear. I don't know what I expected when Linda called Chiloé a group of islands in the South Pacific. Tahiti? You can always dream. But whatever I imagined, it wasn't this.*

Anyway, put a good face on bad karma, that was my philosophy. A week ago, visiting my missionary sister didn't even register on my radar, and here I was warp-speeded to a galaxy far, far away. The final frontier...

Nah. Blame the mashed-up plotlines on my reeling head, but it looked more like a rerun of a sixties sitcom—in the uttermost fringes of the earth. I threw a smirk at my sister as I trudged after her and my nieces down a pier jammed with fishing tubs bobbing low in the water. "What is this, some kind of *Gilligan's Island* set? A three-hour tourrr..."

"You're Ginger and I'm Mary Ann?" Linda shifted her toddler, Rachelle, on her hip and pointed toward one of the grungy boats huddled along the crumbling concrete jetty. "There's our version of the *Minnow*, Melissa."

The name *Última Esperanza* sprawled across the peeling hull in wine-red streaks. Oh, perfect. If that boat was my Last Hope, then I was going down, for sure. A horde of sleazy fishermen jostled between the other vessels, hauling beer crates and baskets of bug-eyed fish and other creepy crawlers. I scrunched my nose at the stench. Shrill alien voices scraped across my nerves.

How would I survive a whole month in this Chilean backwater? I'd die if I had to hang around longer than that. Even if it did mean my last hope of temporary escape from home. And maybe my parents' last-ditch hope of reforming me. Not going to happen. I'd had enough of squeezing into their mold. God knew I didn't want to hurt them *more*, but why couldn't they just leave me alone?

Sure, I was grateful to Linda. The invitation to visit her family couldn't have come at a better time, and the travel plans had worked out fast. Just six days after Martinet Martin suspended me from Mt. Washington Christian Academy, I'd boarded a plane to South America.

Figured I could do a lot worse than Chile in February.

Only now, doubts swamped me.

At least I had my big sister. Floundering in this tidal wave of unfamiliar faces and accents, I hung on to her encouraging smile. Though why Linda chose a white cotton blouse and lime-green print skirt—I kid you not—to clamber aboard a grubby boat mystified me. Didn't she know the 1990s had arrived? The Iron Curtain had fallen; Star Wars had sprung to life. But even in this last decade of the millennium, the Chiloé Islanders seemed to lag fifty or a hundred years behind the rest of the world.

No question, though, Linda shone a beacon of cool elegance amid the filth. I grinned at her. "You got it wrong. Ginger was the redhead. At least you're not wearing high heels. Are we the 'fearless crew'?"

"Yep, but relax, ours is the next launch down." Linda grinned. "You were looking a little skeptical at the *Última Esperanza*."

The wooden craft moored beside the *Last Hope* glared an immaculate canary yellow, trimmed in black and white. "Okay, that's a bit less scary, I take back the scowl," I said. "But *Ambassador*? Sounds way too grand, Lin. Better go with *Minnow*. Except it's bad luck to change a ship's name, isn't it?"

"One thing we *don't* need around here is more superstitions. But ambassadors for Christ is the idea, you know."

*Right*. I rolled my eyes, heaved my bulging canvas bag onto the mold-caked dock, and tore off the fleece jacket I'd layered on. Linda had warned me that Chiloé might turn cool, even in midsummer. Not that it was tropical-humid, but still, I hadn't expected this heat wave.

Or a lot of other fine points. Like the total shabbiness of the seaside hamlet where Linda and her husband, Cole Peterson, lived. Like getting hauled off to *another* island before I'd grabbed a nap or even caught my breath from all the traveling. Like the slime underfoot or the reek of diesel fuel, rotten wood, and seaweed. Bottom of the globe, bottom of the barrel. Bottom of my bucket list, too, though my parents hadn't laid out many options.

I'd painted the trip as an early spring break to my friends back in Baltimore, but this miserable village dock felt more like the end of the world than any top vacation destination. So *not* my dream of a holiday cruise—

Someone plowed into me from behind and all but toppled me across the bag at my feet. "Ow!" Bracing myself with my fingertips, I shot a glare after the klutz.

A heavyset man with a grizzled beard bushing from a sweaty red face gripped the armful of boxes he carried and barely spared me a glance. Never mind an apology. He bellowed something at a dilapidated craft named the *Akina* and shoved his cargo to a sailor on board.

Seriously, they were loading Christmas lights? At nearer Valentine's Day? These people couldn't even get their seasons right, let alone the century.

"Sorry, people aren't usually that rude here." Poor Linda didn't have to offer excuses for the jerk, but she did.

"Rude man," echoed her five-year-old, Reba, and slipped her hand into mine.

A gust of wind fragrant with salt and pine scuttled off the ocean, making the red-white-and-blue Chilean flags billow from the row of masts with a synchronized snap. My eyes watered in the brisk breeze. So maybe Chiloé wasn't Hawaii, and this was no five-star boardwalk thronged with beautiful people. But it smelled, even looked, a little like the coast near my grandmother's cottage in Maine.

Only I'd never stay there with Grandma Rose again.

Nothing could bring her back. She'd intended for us to make this journey together, and now I had to fumble along however I could. And it was my own fault.

Blinking tears, I swept my gaze back up the pier. "So this is it, huh? A thumbs-up for the scenery, at least. While the gang back home's shoveling snow, I'll be sunbathing."

"I—I wish that was true." Linda winced and set two-year-old Rachelle onto the salt-pitted dock. "I have a confession to make—two, actually."

*Uh-oh.* I blew a stream of air up over my flushed cheeks, fluttering damp bangs. "What's the deal then? You already said you were kidnapping me to visit friends of yours on another island. Like, an even *more* remote paradise?"

"Chauquelín, it's called. But—there's more to it than just visiting."

I chewed my lip. "So the boat *might* sink before we make it back?"

"Hope not." Linda's dimples quivered. "But we're staying for a week or ten days. To hold tent meetings. Believe me, I didn't plan things this way when I invited you here. But a few days ago a young couple Cole met recently came by and begged us to visit their home island."

Gaping, I blurted, "What, you mean, like a *revival* thing?"

A pair of dirty gulls flapped down the pier and squawked their protest, too. I should have known Mrs. Paragon-of-Perfection would con me into something like this. Had Linda even conspired with Mom and Dad? Pack the idle kid sister off for a month of hard labor disguised as educational tourism?

"Not quite like that," my sister said. "The Pérez family are new Christians, and they want to share with their neighbors. Though not everybody's sympathetic. Some famous local *machi*—like a shaman, a-a witch doctor—just returned from…I don't know…but he's causing quite a stir…" She slid the clips out of her burnished-copper hair and tucked them back in. "Anyway, we don't get such a wide-open door very often, so Cole feels we should go."

A weird prickle snaked down my back. "But...*now*? I thought it was summer vacation here."

"That's the point. While the weather's still good. Winters can be brutal."

I sighed. "Okay, right. Makes sense, I guess." I could hardly blame Linda when she was trapped in the middle.

But it also meant I had to go wherever my hosts dragged me in this strange country. I thought I could go with the flow, but this meant wading pretty deep. Who would've imagined? Ten years ago, when my family went missionizing without me—the baby of the Travis clan got in their way—I'd have been thrilled to tag along. Now that I couldn't care less, I was hog-tied on a mission trip.

Already my Great Escape had backfired.

"I'm sorry we're whisking you off to the boondocks before you've even had a chance to see the town or anything," Linda said. "I promise we'll tour the capital later in the month—"

"So I don't need to unpack my tanning oil and sunglasses yet?" I tried to show a brave face. Do the right thing, for a change, instead of whining. The Petersons had a pressing reason for hustling me off the bus from the mainland and pausing at their home in the village only long enough for me to repack a bag.

"And we'll celebrate your fifteenth birthday in Santiago," Linda said. "Do it up big like the—"

"Oh, would you quit apologizing." I had an idea—I'd make myself useful. "How about I wash the dishes and babysit Reb and Rachelle while you and Cole rescue the perishing? Call it community service." *Just don't try to suck me into your mission-ary stuff.*

"Sounds like a deal to me." Linda smiled as she twirled prancing Reba back from the edge of the dock.

Guilt gnawed at me. I hated my snarky suspicions. Linda and Cole and their two little girls had welcomed me—on short notice—and treated me with nothing but kindness. Just... why did my oldest sister have to be so perfect...so churchy?

Compared to Linda and her fabulous hair, I always felt as pale as a spring bud next to flaming fall foliage. As dull and pathetic as the moon at noonday. Ginger and Mary Ann, all right. Oh, not just because my plain blond hair never flowed in a sleek waterfall like hers. But I was the oddball among the six Travis siblings, the one who didn't belong. Misfit Melissa. I couldn't even begin to measure up to their shining standards.

*Qué será, será.* For now, while things cooled off at home and school, I'd do my penance, let the dust settle, and more or less play along with Linda and Cole. Get in, get out. Have fun, go home, quick and painless as possible—that was the strategy.

I nudged my bag forward a couple of inches with the toe of my sneaker. "You said *two* confessions?"

Linda's face pinched. "Um, yeah. Mom and Dad called last night, and it's not good news, I'm afraid."

My chest tightened. They'd already settled everything for my stay in Chile. What else could there be to talk over? I pretended to groan. "So what now, you're gearing up to deliver their I-hope-you'll-take-time-to-reflect-on-your-wayward-life-before-you-come-home speech?"

My parents' snap agreement with my getaway plan had already tipped me off that the trip to the Chiloé Islands was more of an exile than a get-out-of-jail-free card. Or maybe a bribe to come clean about the whole incident at school. They suspected I was holding something back—that the spiked-oranges episode wasn't all my fault. And they were spot-on. I'd covered for my friends, taken most of the rap.

But honestly, what did Mom and Dad think? No way was I going to snitch on my friends. I'd die first.

"Dah, duh." Little Rachelle tugged on my arm and pointed to her daddy on the *Ambassador.*

My lanky, straw-haired brother-in-law towered at the deck end of a crude plank walkway between the dock and the boat. Hard to imagine any man less like the skipper of the *Minnow* than Cole. "You girls ready?"

"To walk the plank?" I grimaced and hefted up my heavy bag again.

"We can discuss this later, Melissa." Linda handed Rachelle across the precarious bridge to Cole. "After we get underway, I'll put the kids down for a nap and then we'll talk."

Linda sounded more like Mom in full-blown worry mode than my usually cheerful and bossy big sister. But after helping Reba over the walkway, she pirouetted and scampered across like a gymnast along a balance beam.

*Huh.* If my prim-and-proper sister—pushing thirty and in a skirt, no less—could do that, I wasn't about to be left behind. Clutching my bag, I drew in a breath and wobbled across.

A little less graceful than Linda. Maybe a lot less. Oh, what on earth was I doing here? Sure, nobody'd forced me to come. I'd voluntarily jumped out of the pressure cooker back home, and this backward place was about as far from Maryland as I could possibly go.

How much was that worth putting up with? When I longed to get away, I didn't mean to another planet. My plans didn't include virtual time travel either. Was I doomed? Fate—cosmic payback, or whatever—just wouldn't stop chasing me.

But what could I expect when I'd killed my grandmother? Yeah, it was an accident, not some premeditated horror flick. I wasn't even there. But I should've been.

So I was responsible for her death. Even if nobody knew except me and God.

That first wretched mistake.

My friends could believe this was a cool vacation. My parents might sigh in relief and pray I'd be sorry and "smarten up." And my sister might hope I'd come to Chile to help her save the world. I didn't have to wonder what God had sentenced me here for.

Did Ginger and Mary Ann get a bad feeling about boarding the *Minnow?* I took another deep breath. *Okay, I can do this. For a month. Just a month.*

2

As I settled onto the deck of the *Ambassador*, my head throbbed. Had I ever zigzagged between such mixed feelings in my life?

On one hand, adventure beckoned. And then it seemed all wrong…without Gran. I'd chosen fun with my friends over keeping her company last summer. Now I had to pay the piper.

A deafening engine growled from the open mouth of the stern, so I slouched against the low wall of the forward hold and tucked my arms around jeans-clad knees. The whole reverse-seasons thing hadn't sunk in until now. It was hot today, even on the ocean.

A light wind caressed my face as I tilted my nose toward the sun. While Linda settled my nieces for their siesta, I shaded my eyes against the water's glare and tried to shift my mind into neutral.

Moss-green bluffs slid by, smudged in the distance. Ahead down the channel, mountains floated in a violet haze over the far-off mainland. The Andes looked like a sandwich—rippling slices of snowy tips between sky and sea.

I should get my camera for the Kodak moment, but I'd tossed my gear into the cabin. Didn't want to disturb the girls now. My notebook was still packed too, and—*oh, great.* I had a suspicion I might have left my books behind at Linda's house. Hardly surprising. Even though only a couple of hours separated winter in Maryland from summer in Chile, my brain still spun to catch up.

The flight to the Chilean capital of Santiago. An overnight bus ride south to the final outpost of mainland civilization. Then another bus-plus-ferry to the little town of Mellehue on Grand Chiloé where Linda and Cole lived.

After the long journey—and two nights in a seat—I could use a nap myself. Mabel Baker, Linda's elderly colleague, had chattered nonstop on last night's bus trip too. My eyelids drooped.

But I tensed the instant the cabin door thudded open and shut. Linda joined me in the prow, perching against the edge of the hot zinc roof.

"I knew that wouldn't take long." She didn't notice that I pretended to be asleep. "The kids got up at the crack of dawn, and they'll probably be up late tonight, too."

I gave up, stretched my legs out, and pried my eyes open. The sunlight on the water dazzled.

Linda fiddled with the tie-belt of her skirt. "So…how are Mom and Dad?"

*Here comes the sermon already. Not-so-slick workup to the topic, Mrs. Missionary.* I squinted at a looming headland. "The same. They drove me all the way to JFK and saw me off. Greatly relieved, I'm sure."

"What do you mean? Mom's usually reluctant to let one of her chicks head off alone for the first time."

I stifled a yawn. "Oh, she clucked enough about it. All the mother hen stuff. But too bad my plane wasn't hijacked to Cuba. Convenient load off their minds."

"Melissa Rose Travis, what an awful thing to say. I'm sure they don't feel like that at all."

"Yeah, well, nobody needs to tell me I'm the black sheep of the family. In deep disgrace at the moment." I scowled at the mountains that hovered on the horizon. Like an army of rugged giants, they seemed to guard against any possible escape from Chile. That was my life—forever fenced in, trapped wherever I went. "Kind of a disappointment after my five virtuous brothers and sisters."

Linda bent toward me, her green eyes round and luminous. "That's what you really think of us?"

"Oh, I salute you all." I twisted to my feet and flopped beside her on the roof. "Then there's me, the family embarrassment."

Not that I was proud of that. I was sorry they were ashamed of me. But not sorry for being myself. I was *not* going to play the saint just because the rest did. Maybe my parents could make me attend Christian school, but they couldn't make me drink the sappy Kool-Aid.

"Don't you think you're overreacting a bit?" Linda said.

"If *you* think they shipped me off to the 'mission field' as a reward for good behavior, then you're overestimating Mom and Dad's mellowing in their old age." I stared her down.

"Maybe being the youngest *is* kind of hard." Linda popped up and clung to a steel cable at the tip of the bow, rocking on her sandals. Her hair danced in a flourish of cinnamon-colored waves behind her. "Tough act to follow."

Icy sea spray hit my ankles and gave me goose pimples. I shivered in spite of the heat. "Believe me, I'm not even trying."

The spray drizzled over her freckled face while she studied me for a second, then dropped her gaze. With the toe of her sandal, she scuffed at the pitch that patched a crack between the deck boards. "So…what exactly happened with you at old Mt. W.?"

"You don't mean they haven't told you the dirty details?" I leaned back on one elbow.

"Just bits and pieces. I want to hear *your* version, Meli."

"I got bounced for a month, that's all." The wind swept my hair into a tangled cloud about my head. I caught it and concentrated on taming it into a side braid.

"But isn't this the second time this year? You've lost quite a bit of school."

"I made all my credits last semester, I can do it again. Nothing wrong with my grades, so their big punishment will hardly put me behind at all. No great loss, just vacation time."

A twinge of regret stabbed me. I'd miss the school music festival. But as long as I made it for the drama finals…and I'd be home again well before then. "I do have to write this corny essay on 'What I Learned in Chile' while I'm here, so I won't laze around completely." I snickered.

"You were suspended, but you still have school assignments?"

"Yeah, go figure." I scratched at a spot of salt on my jeans.

"But *why*? I mean, I've heard the *what*…the drinking and partying and all. But on the bottom line, why would you—?"

"Why did I do it?" I finished for her. I bit my bottom lip and closed my eyes.

*Because I'm not your clone.* That boring school smothered me, everything Linda and her type stood for. I only wanted the chance to be myself. Make my own decisions.

No point going into it all, though. Linda would never understand. I tried to sound flippant. "Oh, Mr. Martin called it 'attitude.' Guilty as charged."

"I see." My sister's tone went quiet and flat, like a pond smoothing out after a stone plunks into it and sinks.

*Did* she see? Not likely. "I really don't care what that old goat of a principal thinks."

"I wonder if you'll care—" Linda broke off. The wind snatched her voice and carried it away like the hollow echo in a deserted classroom.

The boat—launch, they called it—gave a sudden thrust to starboard. Now headed south, it skipped over the swells as we chugged along offshore of an island—our destination, I assumed. I couldn't help giggling as the motion tickled my stomach.

"Never mind, we'll talk about it later," Linda said. "We're almost there now. How'd your Spanish hold up on the trip down?"

"Hold up? It was on hold. I didn't have a chance to practice a word with Mabel there. She even tried to translate *Coca-Cola* for me." I refrained from grumbling about the forty years' worth of South American missionary anecdotes my travel companion had subjected me to on the bus trip south.

Linda chuckled. "Maybe Mabel was a bit too helpful."

"Never mind, I'd have freaked without her. How long *does* it take to become fluent in Spanish?"

"Only the rest of your life." She winked, her lips twitching. "But you could make some progress even in the short time you're here, though, if you're willing to use what you know. And don't let mistakes discourage you from trying again."

"Ha, never fear. If I did that, I'd never open my mouth all month." I waved a hand toward the onshore vista. "So what's this place like, anyway?"

The hills above the sea unrolled in a haphazard patchwork quilt of lush greens and golden browns. Dark stands of trees made a vivid contrast with the fields of ripe grain and the emerald meadows. Here and there, houses dotted the land-scape in flashes of brick red, patina green, and driftwood gray. Gran would've liked it. All through the voyage, I'd dreaded washing up on a deserted isle. But a place sort of like Maine, even wound back a hundred years, couldn't be all bad.

"I've never been here before," Linda said, "though Cole has. Chauquelín's supposed to be one of the most pagan islands in the archipelago. There's a twenty-dollar word for you, *archipel-ago*. Means a group of islands."

"Looks gorgeous, even if it's not Hawaii. Hey, what are those—they aren't—oh, wow, dolphins!"

A real Flipper show glued us both to the deck railing. Several of the creatures—an entire pod, maybe—played leap-frog just off the launch's port side. They breached in and out of the creaming wake, soaring, diving, racing with the boat. For almost ten minutes, the black-and-silver silhouettes romped alongside the *Ambassador*. Then, with a chorus of throaty barks and ticks, they charged away toward another island west across the channel.

"Must've located some lunch." I released a pent-up sigh. "Wow. I just love them. Did you hear the Baltimore Aquarium's opening a new marine mammal pavilion later this year? I can't wait to go." When I was six, Gran had taken me to the aquar-ium as a consolation prize while the rest of my family went off on one of their save-the-world missions. I'd been crazy about the place ever since.

"The Chilean dolphin's called a *tonina*," Linda said. "We see them a lot around here. Don't even have to visit the aquarium."

"That's so awesome. My friends will drool with envy when they hear." At least, I hoped they would. This cool experience deserved writing home about. I gave a snort. "Something else for my 'What I Learned in Chile' essay, too."

"Um, yeah. Right." Fidgeting with the belt of her skirt again, Linda inched along the narrow deck toward the cabin. "I'd better rouse the girls."

The launch's motor geared down a notch and eased to a dull rumble. Our two-hour voyage—*not three, Gilligan*—came to an end. Straight ahead lay a peaceful cove and a boulder-strewn beach, glittering in the sunshine. Definitely no white sands or swaying palms. Still, a lot better than February slush in B'more.

Cole, his close-clipped curls bleached white against his sunburned face, dashed onto the deck, dropped an anchor, and ducked back into the cabin to cut the engine. On shore, two boys in shorts and flip-flops hopscotched from stone to stone and tossed pebbles into the pools left by the last high tide. A skinny leprechaun of a man shouldering a hoe and a rosy-cheeked woman piggy-backing a little girl also picked their way toward us.

So we'd landed on Chauquelín. Hanging out on this island had to be better than enduring the school grind or loafing around home listening to Mom's lectures. But tent meetings? *Get a life.* The language might turn out the least of my hassles this week.

It occurred to me then that Linda hadn't even mentioned what Mom and Dad had called about. Either it wasn't as important as she'd insinuated—or it was worse than I could possibly imagine.

3

One by one, Cole loaded our fearless female crew into a row-boat to make the short glide to the beach. When the boat struck the shallows with a scrape of gravel, he leaped out and dragged it ashore with the leprechaun's aid, both men sloshing through crystal-clear water in tall rubber boots. Then Cole lifted the children out while Linda and I jumped onto the shore. My duffle bag only got partially wet in the maneuver.

Cole made the introductions. Our host, Ramón Pérez—the leprechaun—grinned like a scarecrow under his crooked wool hat. Seriously, wool? He must be cooking. Despite his scrawny frame, his biceps bulged as he skidded the rowboat over the rocks to tie it on higher ground. His equally robust wife, Virginia, had a glowing complexion and curly black hair bobby-pinned behind her ears. Her limp red polyester blouse, drenched with sweat, clashed with her rose-pink peasant skirt.

"Just call me Gina." She hugged me. "I'm so glad to meet you, Sister Melissa."

*Sister?* Did I look like a nun? Whatever. At least her soft country accent was easy to understand. So maybe the woman

18

could stand a shower and a toothbrush, but her greeting was so sweet that my eyes prickled.

The Pérez children shared their parents' bronze skin and solid limbs. The toddler, Anita, raced Rachelle up the beach. The boys pumped my hand and kissed my cheek with polite solemnity, then nudged Reba to show off a boat they'd concocted from a wooden shingle and a tin can. The toy launch floated down a brook that trickled into the sea.

"Come on up to the house for tea." Gina linked her arm through Linda's.

"I'll help you unload afterwards, Don Colin," Ramón said as we started along the road above the beach. It was little more than a trail of hard-packed earth and shells.

"Great." Cole wiped a layer of peeling skin along with the perspiration from his brow. "Got a mountain of stuff. We'll need some extra hands."

"Julio and Joelín were worried you wouldn't make it today," Gina said. "They're so excited about the Bible classes for the kids, they've already invited half the island."

Linda laughed. "Makes our work easier anyway."

The Pérezes' house—I assumed—floated on a green hillside overlooking the cove. Cedar shingles, faded to glossy silver-gray, cloaked the square, two-storied cottage. In helter-skelter English style, a huge flower garden framed the house in a riot of color. Above double front doors, a crescent moon–shaped balcony skirted the second-floor gable end, and…a black-clad woman, her hair like a bank of fluffy snow, hunched over the railing. She peered hawk-eyed at our approach. Seriously, only missing a conical hat.

But we bypassed the path of crushed shells leading up to the house. "That's not it?" I asked Linda.

"They're our nearest neighbors," Gina said. "Luisa Guzmán and her daughter, María Angélica De la Cruz. Both widows. Angélica's two boys went to school in Mellehue last year."

"Not the Serrano boys?" Cole said. "They're from this island, I know."

Ramón nodded. "Sí, Nicolás and Marcos. Good young fellows, a bit cocky, but they help their mother plenty. You met them in town then, Don Colin?"

"I referee some soccer from time to time."

"Didn't Nicolás come to the youth meetings at church, Cole?" Linda said.

"Yeah, came with Tito Bahamonde a few times toward the end of the school year. Good at ping-pong. Always very quiet, though." Cole winked at me. "These guys would be about your age, Meli."

"Charmed." Bother, the last thing I needed—a couple of backwoods bumpkins competing to impress me.

We detoured off the main path onto a narrow track that wound uphill through a tidy field of potatoes. Amazing they could even plant anything on land this steep. But when we arrived at the Pérez yard, I couldn't hold back a gasp. Mud oozed to the very front doorstep of a low, teal-blue cabin. My white sneakers would never look the same.

Squawking chickens flapped in every direction. As we passed a shed where tools and sacks of grain were stored, I heard a pig snuffle in a crude pen nearby. In another thatched shack, meat and fish dangled on ropes from the rafters, drying in a haze of smoke and flies. I wrinkled my nose and coughed.

Gina threw open the front door into a dank cave of a room, a living area of sorts where the reek of garlic and mildew mixed with a kerosene-scented floor wax. Painfully neat, the furniture consisted of two chairs and a settee of stiff bamboo, piled with lumpy, garish, flower-print cushions. Flattened cardboard cartons carpeted the red pine-board floor like scatter rugs. Presumably to protect the wax job?

Our hostess waved us through into the kitchen. "Sit down by the stove while I reheat the kettle." She slid a soot-smudged aluminum kettle to the center of a decrepit cookstove.

Gingerly I took a seat on the grimy cushioned bench that bordered the stove. Filth encrusted the stovetop. The rust-eaten chimney pipe belched smoke. Conversation flowed on around me, but I couldn't concentrate on the Spanish any longer. My head pounding, I could only gawk zombie-like around me.

In contrast to the living room's humble spotlessness, the kitchen floor had rarely seen a broom, let alone wax. Burnt matches wedged between the boards. In a murky corner stood a precarious open cupboard, crowded with chipped cups and plates, grease-caked tins, and jars of crimson sauce—hot peppers? Nearby, a lone faucet dripped over a dirty porcelain sink. The oilcloth table covering looked sticky enough to be made of flypaper.

The oldest Pérez boy, Julio César—what a goofy name—shooed a nosy hen out to the yard and shuffled back to Cole's side. He made no attempt to clean up the hen's contribution to the nasty floor.

A creepy sensation, like spiders, crawled up my back. I shuddered, hoping no one picked up on it.

I could barely touch the generous slices of homemade bread that Gina offered me. When she handed Linda a cup of tea, I stood up. Gag, three spoonsful of sugar, and—*instant?* My stomach churned.

"Uh, sorry, I'm not too fond of tea at the best of times." Lame, but I knew I couldn't choke anything else past the lump in my throat. I had to get out of this squalid kitchen before I upchucked. "I—I think I need some fresh air. Maybe I could watch the girls outside for a while, Lin."

Linda frowned and nodded. "The men will get our tent stuff soon and we can set up camp, okay?"

I was supposed to spend ten days in this dump? A tragicomedy show, all right. It made the Fells Point slums back in Baltimore look like upscale Guilford. I kind of liked our host family, but how could nice, decent people live in…such degradation? Oh, I was ashamed of my snobbiness, but my nose was going to be permanently scrunched.

Gulping deep breaths, I lurched into the backyard and slumped against a rustic fence woven from twigs. The children ran and shrieked with the dogs and the chickens, oblivious to the mud spattering their clothes. I couldn't help smiling as little Rachelle waddled, squealing with delight, after a dusty-feathered goose.

That's when I noticed him—a teenager chopping firewood on the far side of the yard, near one of the outbuildings. Noticed, such a dull word. More like I was *arrested*.

The lean-muscled boy in faded cutoffs and a navy T-shirt worked steadily, his movements lithe, almost relaxed. As if he relished the exercise, swift and streamlined as the dolphins. So alive…with the easy energy of a kid at play, and the strength and skill of a man. Only the glistening wetness of the coffee-brown hair plastered to the back of his neck hinted that the task required any exertion.

He raised a golden forearm in greeting, and I waved back, hiding my smirk at the smear of mud on his right cheek. He couldn't be much older than I. Once again, he hefted up the next chunk of wood, balanced it on a rock-hard stump, and split it in three or four effortless strokes, stacking the sticks with the others inside the shed.

He never once stopped to rest. For a while, I lounged against the fence and watched his rhythmic swings, humming to myself under the ring of the axe on the block. I was fascinated by a Rambo guy chopping wood? Sheesh, was I hard up.

The men strode into the yard again. Ramón made a beeline for one of the pasture gates. "I'll hitch the oxen up right away, and we can—oh, there's the Serrano boy, Don Colin." The pom-pom on his wool hat tilted toward the young woodcutter.

My brother-in-law turned to me. "Have you met Nicolás? No? Don't be shy then. Aren't many teenagers around here, so you might want to get along with him for the duration." He grinned and steered me around the edge of the mudflat.

So he was Cole's soccer friend from the next house.

Nicolás Serrano paused and extended a hand to Cole. "Hope you had a good trip to Chauquelín."

"Thanks, I just hope the weather holds for a bit," Cole said. "Nicolás, this is my wife's sister, Melissa Travis. She's visiting us from the States for a few weeks."

Close up, he reminded me of one of those hot Latin singer sensations: the olive complexion, the deep-set eyes that flashed like topazes. His clasp firm, he took my hand, leaned, and kissed my cheek. "*Encantado*, Meli…Melissa. Do you speak any Spanish?" A quick smile, showing even white teeth, brightened the dark tan of his face.

*Encantado.* Had he just said enchanted—charmed—with every indication of meaning it? The old-fashioned courtesy of his Chilean manners astonished me, but his pronunciation of my name, May-lee-sa, definitely *charmed.* I dug out my best smile and accent. "*Un poco.*"

"I speak a little English, too, so we will manage. Don Colin, you need help unloading your launch?" He thrust the axe head into the chopping block. "I could stop at the house and get my brother, too."

"Then maybe a game of soccer afterwards," Cole said.

Nicolás's eyes lit up as he sauntered after Cole toward the lane.

*Soccer, huh? I like soccer.* Maybe the local yokels wouldn't turn out so boring, after all.

4

"I feel like part of a circus crew," I said to Linda, only half joking.

The two of us were trying to organize the chaos of boxes and barrels in the camp setup. The men and boys had already made several trips via oxcart from the shore to this large, flat meadow above the Pérez home. Cole and the Serrano guys drove in a circle of stakes for the enormous tan canvas tent and strung lines for electric lights to be powered later from a gas generator. A sound system, a film projector, a dozen wooden benches, a port-a-potty stowed behind a curtain, a tiny gas cookstove on a folding table, and a metal trunk full of dishes all furnished the grassy space under the Big Top, as I'd christened it.

Linda laughed, a gurgle like a fountain. "Are you a clown and I'm a monkey? As long as Reba doesn't use the power cable for a trapeze." She opened a box of groceries and then paused. "Oh, let's not unpack everything now. Gina invited us back for supper, so we won't need any of it until morning."

*Oh, thrilling.* I hoped tea-syrup wasn't on the menu again. The heavy bread still rolled around like a bowling ball in my stomach. I sidled closer to my sister. "How can they live like that, Lin?"

She plopped down on one of the slab benches and studied me—again, lips pressed together. "If you mean the shabbiness… you just have to understand these people."

"Understand what? Shabby's one thing, this is something else." Sheesh, their *house* smelled as mildewy as this old canvas tent. I wrinkled my nose. "Just because they're poor doesn't mean they have to be dirty."

"I know." Linda heaved a sigh. "Honestly, I struggle with it too. I've only lived in Chiloé a few years, myself." She plucked a handful from the grass carpet at her feet. "I wonder what kind of housekeeper I'd be, though, without conveniences of any kind, without even some of the most basic resources we take for granted. Sometimes they have to choose between soap or food, you know."

I bit my lower lip and scraped the muddied toe of my sneaker along the ground. "There's always water."

"Yes." Linda let the blades of grass filter through her fingers. "But the islanders in general haven't had much education. Most of their neighbors live in similar conditions, or worse. They don't know any other way. I think Ramón and Gina try hard, considering their background. They even have indoor plumbing of sorts."

"And a television set in the kitchen. What's with that? I thought they didn't have electricity out here."

"It's run off a car battery they recharge in the village. But you should see some of the other places, Melissa. Of course, a few live better, too, depending on their financial situation or experience of the outside world."

"How…how did you say you met this family?"

"They attended tent meetings like the ones we'll be having here while they were visiting Gina's folks on another island just before Christmas. As far as we know, they're the only believers on this island. Pretty dark and needy place." Linda stood as Rachelle burst through the tent door-flap, wailing, and picked her up. "Gina's a hard worker, and she's so hungry for Bible teaching. She and Ramón practically begged us to come here when they passed through Mellehue last weekend, so I hope we can at least encourage them this week, if nothing else. It's a bit spur-of-the-moment. Normally we'd enlist a support team for this sort of thing."

I held out my arms. "Give her to me, she's finally warming up a little. And did I hear you call her Keli? How'd she get *that*?"

"Rachelle translates to Raquel, which evolved into Keli for short."

"Got it. And Cole is Don 'Cole-in' here?"

"That's how some people pronounce Colin in Maine too, you know."

I brushed Keli's red-gold hair off her flushed face. "Looks like I may not see Reba again till the end of the week. New friends trump the old aunt every time."

"Seems so." Linda chuckled. "Maybe *your* new friends will trump the old sister, too."

"Don't count on that." My smile turned into a grimace. "I'm it here, right? Your support team."

"Afraid so, sis. Sorry about that."

"I'll survive. Pretend it's summer camp in Maine. Better than shoveling snow in B'more." If I kept telling myself that, I might even believe it.

"What was supposed to be wrong with your attitude, anyway?" Linda grinned as she blotted Keli's face with a paper towel.

I dreaded returning to the Pérezes for supper, but by eight o'clock I was starved enough to rate the meal as tasty: a thick soup they called *carbonada*, followed by a heaping plate of rice, whole potatoes, and slices of smoked pork. More of the dense bread, and this time, real coffee, blended with dried figs, which mellowed the taste, Gina told me as she poured boiling water through a tiny cheesecloth strainer at the table. Maybe they weren't much for housekeeping, but these Chilote islanders believed in hearty meals.

Close to nine o'clock, Linda prodded her girls. "These two need to get to bed. It's been a long day, and lots more activity tomorrow."

"Got a few minutes to kick the ball around, Don Colin?" Nicolás Serrano asked. He and his younger brother, Marcos, were invited for supper, too, after their work rowing our baggage ashore from the launch and hauling it all uphill. They ate, plates in hand, squeezed with the Pérez boys onto the bench behind the stove.

"Guess we have another hour or so of light," Cole said. "Where, then? In the meadow? What about it, Ramón?"

Cole straddled Keli over his shoulders. Ramón carried Reba piggyback. At our campsite in the high field, Cole grabbed a soccer ball from the Big Top and headed out. In the smaller, sky-blue nylon tent the Petersons would sleep in, I helped the children get into their jammies.

"Yeah, yeah, I'll read you the new storybooks in the morn-ing," I told Reba. "I promise. I've got a couple in Spanish, too."

Linda knelt on a foam mattress on the tent floor. "I'll lie here with the kids for a few minutes, so they'll settle down. Are you into playing ball with the guys, Meli?"

Already engrossed in their game, they looked set without me. I shook my head, pretending indifference. "Uh…not this time. I'll just watch, I guess."

"If you want to read or whatever in the other tent, I'm sure Cole would light the kerosene lantern for you."

I grabbed up my spiral notebook and stretched out in the doorway of the Big Top. The guys had set up a pair of decaying logs as goalposts at opposite ends of the meadow. Cole and Marcos teamed against Ramón and Nicolás. Quite evenly matched, too. Cole had played college sports, and Ramón probably worked out every day in his fields. But the boys were younger and incredibly agile.

The two of them flew fleet-footed as deer through the slick grass, now slipping and skidding, then in a burst of footwork racing halfway down the field with the ball, hair rippling in the breeze. Long-legged Marcos might be half a head shorter than his older brother, but he was a lot taller than me and only thirteen, I'd heard at supper. Not as dark as Nicolás, he had apple-red cheeks and pale eyes—gray, maybe. Both cute guys, in their different ways.

I breathed deeply. Crushed underfoot, some kind of mint mingled with the green smell of grass. Eucalyptus from the woods wafted on the crisp wind, along with evening sounds—barking dogs, bleating sheep. Like in Maine, an undercurrent of waves whispered from the beach.

I wrote nonstop about "What I Learned in Chile" until the light faded: *Chile is like the West Coast of the U. S. turned upside down…*

The temperature dropped with the sun in this South American Alaska. Too chilly for any tropical paradise. Shivering, I scrambled up to get my blue fleece hoodie from the tent. Earlier today, I'd figured it was a waste of luggage space, but I needed it, after all. I fished around in the bag for my Walkman. Cross-armed in the doorway, I slapped on the earphones and blocked out the shouts and thuds of the soccer players. How could they still make out the ball?

Below the hillside, the cove faced the sunset west. Puffs of cloud floated in the sky like copper-hulled boats sailing in a sea of fire. I watched, a knot in my throat, until the flames burned out and left only the stark lumps of surrounding islands in a coral glow.

Dusk stole over me. The whole surreal place segued into the lost memory of a dream, the watery reflection of a faraway landscape. These Chiloé Islands of Linda's were so lovely—and so ugly at the same time. The contrast of fabulous beauty and appalling poverty, crowded side by side, made me feel a little dazed.

Already the time here stretched out in a blur. An endless day. Would I have to spend the next week—or month—the way I had today, stuck on the sidelines, dumbstruck and horrified, or else ignored and bored? Destined, as usual, to play the unused cup in the family cupboard.

Maybe there was something to be said for kicking around home.

No! I preferred any kind of monotony in this island to the punishment of one-sided tea talks with Mom.

But fate had conspired against me, for sure. First, the banishment to Chile—veiled as a holiday invitation, of course. Then, as soon as I arrived at temporary refuge in this far corner of the globe, Linda's little bombshell—her surprise confession about their missionary agenda on Chauquelín.

If any more twists popped up in the plan, I'd—

# 5

*Day 1, continued*

A voice at my elbow startled me. "We left you out, no? I am sorry."

The soccer game had broken up. I turned to Nicolás Serrano, yanking off the earphones. "Never mind, it's, um, really peaceful here. I was sort of enjoying it."

"Don Colin said I could take you down to the bay for a while." He pulled his T-shirt up and wiped his face. Even in the indigo shadows, he glistened all over with sweat. "If you like—would like—to go."

"Now?" I said incredulously.

"Go ahead, if you want." Cole drew aside the flap of the big tent. "I'd be glad to another night, Nicolás, but an old guy like me has to rest sometime. Bet Linda fell asleep with the kids. I'll just light the lantern in here for when you get back, Melissa."

*Cool. A night on the town, haha.* Maybe managing Cole and Linda as my keepers would be a cinch, after all.

I stumbled down the hill with the Serrano brothers. Lucky jail bust, but still, a late-night jaunt with two strange guys? I felt a little skeptical, but Cole appeared to think it harmless. He'd even lent me a flashlight for the hike.

A lot better than brooding about my problems in the tent, anyway.

Maybe I just needed to relax and enjoy myself while it lasted. Even Linda had said something about having fun while I was here, though her idea of fun and mine were probably galaxies apart. Whatever, this presented a welcome distraction for now.

Falling dew made the grass slippery until we reached the well-trampled shell pavement. The three of us headed north on the road that apparently traced the shoreline of Chauquelín. Just what kind of quaint island amusement did Nicolás Serrano have in mind? Something *really* exciting was probably too much to ask for in this deadbeat locale. I only hoped "down to the bay" didn't mean grubbing for worms for a fishing trip.

When we reached the lane that wound to his home, the younger boy, Marcos, turned uphill again.

"Not coming, Marc?" Nicolás asked.

"No, Cahuel, I am—how do they say in English? I am beat tonight. I wash and to bed." He yawned and cocked a mischievous grin. "Also, I do not play the violin."

I lifted my eyebrows. "What's the violin got to do with it?"

"Nothing," Nicolás said. "He is just an idiot little brother, no?"

A three-quarters moon hung over the water, flooding the shore with milky light. The yellow oars in Cole's rowboat, tied up above the high-water mark, shone like glow sticks, but

Nicolás skirted around it. "Isn't this where we're going?" I asked.

"It is another *caleta*—what do you call it? Another cove just across the peninsula there." He pointed out a rocky curve of land jutting out ahead and cut a path toward it.

"And? What's there?"

The moonlight made weird shadows in the hollows of his face as he grinned. "*Amigos* of mine. Wait and see."

When I tripped among the stones, he took the flashlight and towed me across the beach onto a dim but even trail. The path bisected a strip of woodland that smelled of damp pine and eucalyptus. Silently I moved behind him. *Like in a bizarre dream.*

In just a few minutes, we stood on the shore of a larger cove, a bowl of liquid silver. Nicolás clicked off the flashlight. "This is Dolphin Bay." His voice quivered, as though he held back some emotion. *Anticipation?* "If they come tonight."

"Who?"

"You will see. Sit here and watch, Melissa."

What was the big deal here? More mystified by the minute, I perched on the edge of a flat bench the size of a loveseat, a niche gouged into an outcropping boulder. He kicked off his sneakers and tossed his T-shirt beside me. Then, humming a quick lilting melody that echoed over the water, he walked into the sea.

At first he treaded through the gravelly shallows. Then he shot into the depths with a swish like an arrow from a bow. He swam underwater without disturbing the smooth-as-glass surface with the slightest ripple. *Wow, champion swimmer.* My neck prickled as curiosity gripped me. What on earth was this extraordinary guy up to? The water had to be frigid, even on this summer evening. For several moments, I lost sight of him.

Then I heard a series of odd blowing sounds, followed by a hoarse squeal. Nicolás's head burst from the water with a shout of laughter, and beneath him the dark, sleek body of a large fish. At once I knew it must be a dolphin. I gasped as a second dolphin leaped high into the air, its great fluke waving, and arched back down beside its mate in a cascade of jewels. A third and fourth surged up behind.

Energetic splashing and whistling now pierced the quiet bay as the group of playmates swam and dove, flipped and twirled in a froth of water, the satin figure of the boy one with the dolphins. Sometimes Nicolás clung to the back of the largest of the pod, as if he were taming a bronco. Then a flick of the creature's tail catapulted him into the air, and he flew across the horizon like a shooting star, a streak of gold against purple foil. The others encircled and nudged him, then dashed away in some marine version of a game of tag.

My gaze never wandered from the scene. If only I dared brave that icy sea to join them. If only it were daylight, at least, so I could see them more clearly. So it wasn't Baltimore nightlife—it rated way better. This was my kind of fun, like those long-ago visits to the aquarium with Grandma Rose.

If only Cole's rowboat were closer. If only I'd brought my camera...

I had no idea of the time while I watched, riveted, but the water acrobatics must have lasted for more than half an hour. At last the creatures glided out of the bay, back to the open sea. Their barks and clicks dwindled into the distance.

I sighed. If only my life held that kind of joy...that kind of freedom to be myself...

Nicolás thrashed back to shore, spinning water like a top. I ran to meet him, clapping and shaking his crumpled T-shirt like a cheerleader's pom-pom.

"That was quite a show! For an audience of only one, at that."

"Did you like it?" His smiling face glittered with wet diamonds in the muted white light. "They are great, no?"

"Wonderful. So you're some kind of dolphin whisperer, huh? But aren't you cold?"

He used the T-shirt as a towel and slid it back on. "Are you? We can head back now if you want."

"No, no, I meant you—the water…"

He shrugged and grinned. "It is not bad. Just getting out again."

I returned to my stone banquette. "How long have you been doing that, swimming around with those dolphins—*toninas*, right? They seem to know you pretty well."

"It started this summer, just before Christmas." He took a seat beside me as he retied his shoelaces. "I was sitting here—right here—playing my *guitarra* and singing a little—"

"You play the guitar? Me, too."

He looked over, eyebrows raised. "Cool. We will play together sometime then."

"Yeah, maybe. Go on, about the dolphins."

"So I noticed them swimming around in the cove. You often see *toninas* in the channels here when you travel by launch, but I never knew them to come so close to shore before. It was a warm evening, so I thought to have a swim and see if they will let me get close to them."

"And they did."

"Síp."

*Sip?* That was like the Spanish version of *yep?* "So it's fairly recent then. Kind of thrilling."

"I started to come here most evenings. Sometimes they come, sometimes not. After a while, I understood—it is the music they like." From his jeans pocket, Nicolás pulled a round object threaded onto a length of yarn. "So now I use this. A sort of clay flute called an *ocarina*. If they are not here, I play a tune and they respond. Usually."

"But you didn't have to use it tonight."

He grinned. "But I did. Underwater."

"And they only come in the evening?"

He nodded. "Or early morning. They have come close a few times in the afternoon, but they are more *cauteloso*—more afraid..."

"Cautious."

"Sí, when there is much activity or noise."

"Marcos usually comes with you?"

"Almost always. Other than him, I introduce my dolphin *amigos* to only a few special people. My mother and sister."

"Oh..." *And he invited me.* "So you have a sister, too?"

"Valeria is ten."

I bit my lip. "Thank you, Nicolás. *Gracias* for bringing me."

In silence, we relaxed against the stone loveseat, as if we were sitting on a rock's lap. The tide crept in, stroking the pebbled beach. I was watching the tide come in? *Lame, but...*

The stillness began to weave its enchantment. The very hush of the air tuned my ears to the music all around. The wind murmured a lullaby, rustling the eucalyptus leaves and pine branches on the hill behind us. The steady lick of the waves, the random screech of a gull, in the distance the tinkle of a brook as it ran to the ocean—everything integrated in an immense orchestra of land, sky, and sea.

Until a note of discord jarred. The grind of footsteps approached on the road. I whirled, startled, as the blinding light of a lantern shot toward us.

6

"What are you kids doing here?" the intruder's gruff voice demanded from behind the lantern's glare.

The stench of stale sweat, sour beer, and kerosene assaulted my nostrils, but I could see only the outstretched arm of a short, dark form, topped with a wool hat. My breath cut in rapid jerks.

But Nicolás acted calm and cool as the cove waters. "Sitting."

"Eh, Nico! Didn't recognize you, boy." The man's tone moderated. "Shouldn't you be getting on home? It's almost midnight. Your poor mamá will be worried."

"My mamá knows where I am, Don Juan."

An annoyed sound—part cluck, part growl, part sigh—escaped the raspy throat. "*Chu*, I keep telling Angélica you boys need a man's hand. More every day. Run along now, boy."

Nicolás also made a low sound of disgust, but he stood up. "Let's go, Melissa."

As we retreated toward the path back across the peninsula, crunching through the stones, I whispered, "Who...who was that? You know him?"

"Juan Bórquez." Nicolás scowled. "A neighbor of ours. Also a distant relative of my grandmother."

"He...doesn't seem very nice." *Didn't smell too nice, either.*

"He is a good-for-nothing troublemaker."

"Why do you say that?"

"Oh, I don't know. I am not sure what he is up to, but it's not good." Nicolás tore a leaf off a nearby tree and chomped it between his teeth. The aroma of eucalyptus punctured the air. "He left Chauquelín long ago, and then last July he showed up here again. God only knows where he has been for the past twenty years."

"Was he, like, some sort of political prisoner?" I didn't know squat about Chilean politics, but hadn't I heard mention of recent tensions? They'd had an election or something?

"Maybe, but I doubt it." He snorted. "He came back flashing money and acting like he owned the whole island. Bought up property all over." He swung around and pointed back through a break in the trees, across to the northern end of Dolphin Bay. "Robbed *that* piece of land from a poor *viuda*—what do you say? A widow."

A half dozen ramshackle cottages were sprinkled along the shore road. With my attention on the bay earlier, I'd barely registered them. But beyond, a steep, wooded hill rose from the beach, and in a clearing near the top soared a three-story house, its gingerbread trim frosted golden-pink in the moonlight. How could I have missed this one?

"Looks a bit out of place here. What do you mean, he didn't pay the woman for it?"

"Oh, he paid…something…but not nearly what it's worth. He wanted only the land anyway, see? Bórquez demolished *her* house and built his own. The old lady moved in with her sister in the south of the island. But her son and his family really need the land—they live in that cottage at the foot of the hill."

I still stared across at the ginormous structure, a lord's chateau surrounded by a jumble of serfs' huts. It only lacked a backdrop of snowy mountains and a touch of Baltimore Formstone work—*job for Travis Masonry, Dad*—to resemble a miniature Neuschwanstein Castle. "I take it this Bórquez wasn't exactly king of the island when he lived here before."

"Had nothing but a shack no better than our grain shed. He never worked hard and wasted what he did have. At least, that is what my mother says. Now he has his own *lancha*—fishing boat—and half the carpenters in Chiloé finishing up that big fancy cedar mansion for him." Nicolás's right cheek twitched as he glanced down at me. "Don't think I am *envidioso*—jealous. But the man does not own the beach. He has no right to tell me what to do. But he—"

A spear of light stabbed into our eyes. Bórquez, a stout troll figure sporting a rat's-nest beard, now stood atop the stone bench Nicolás and I had just vacated, pumping his lantern up and down.

"Wait a minute," I said. "That guy—he practically ran me down at the dock in Mellehue. Rude doesn't begin to describe it." Sheesh, the stink alone had almost knocked me over.

"Not surprising," Nicolás said.

"He—he can't see us here, right?" We stood just under the shadow of the trees that blanketed the peninsula. Nicolás hadn't turned Cole's flashlight back on yet.

"I'm sure he thinks we are long gone. Otherwise he would not do that silly dance on the rock." Nicolás peered out to sea, north of the curve of headland dominated by the Bórquez mansion. "Almost like he is signaling to someone. And look, a couple of *lanchas* are coming in."

Both fishing boats cut their lights as they slid around the headland, but not before I saw that one was larger than Cole's *Ambassador* and the other a bit smaller. The drone of their engines throttled almost immediately, too.

Nicolás grunted. "That small one is Bórquez's, the *Angélica*. Don't know the other one."

What was the name of the launch I'd noticed in Mellehue? Not the *Última Esperanza*, but something feminine and foreign sounding. "Not…the *Antonia?*"

He shrugged and wheeled around. "Wonder what that devil is up to now? Probably bringing in something else for his castle that he does not want us commoners to see. I would walk down there and watch just to spite him, except—"

I snatched his arm. "Wha-what's that?" A gauzy shape, silver-washed in the moonlight, flitted down the hill from the Bórquez mansion. Floated among the trees like a random bubble on the breeze. Silly goose pimples popped on my skin. "It-it's not a—"

"What, a *fantasma?* A ghost?" Nicolás grinned at me. "Never fear, the White Lady of Chauquelín is a harmless one. She sometimes wanders in the woods or along the shore."

Was he serious? I didn't think so and tried to make light. "Somebody's laundry blew off the clothesline?"

"Or let loose on purpose." He resumed our pace across the peninsula.

"So why *don't* you stay here? You said he had no right to make us leave."

"It makes less trouble for my mother if I stay out of his way."

"He spoke as if he knows your mother, like fairly well."

"He knows her all right. They are third cousins, something like that. He had the *impertinencia* to name his launch *Angélica*, after her. But I wish…"

"What?" I said.

"I just wish he would stop *acosando*—bothering—her and my grandmother." Nicolás kicked a shower of pine needles into the air. "He keeps trying to *persuadir* Mamá to marry him. As if that would ever happen."

"The new house is the dowry, the bride price, huh?"

"Or bait." He twisted his lips. "He wants to impress us with how much we need him. Only we're not that *desesperados*."

Not that desperate, huh? I *did* feel for the predicament of this guy and his family. So friendly, so frank, and so…poor.

"Melissa, you are understanding me okay?" he said. "Hit me if I speak too fast. I try to use the English I know, too."

We'd communicated the entire evening in an alphabet soup of languages. Except for some missing contractions, his English was pretty amazing for a country hick. I wasn't about to admit my head was swimming with the effort in Spanish. "Yeah, okay. Go on, Nicolás. So your mother won't marry this guy?"

"She would never even consider it."

"Why not? I mean, aside from the obvious." *Like the Jabba-the-Hutt looks.*

We emerged from the peninsula woods onto the shores of the southern cove, where Cole's *Ambassador* drifted at anchor. The road gleamed like marble tile underfoot.

"There is a history," Nicolás said. "He always chased her, even years ago, until she left to work in Santiago. For another thing—" He shivered for the first time that evening.

"You'd better head home, it's getting pretty cool," I said as we passed the path up to his house. "You don't have to walk me all the way to the tent door, you know. I don't think I could get lost from here."

"Compromise, okay? I will take you as far as Don Ramón's yard." He grinned, and then sobered. "It's not the cold, anyway. It is Bórquez. I do not trust that guy. People say his mother was a—a—the word is *witch*?"

My jaw fell slack. These days, the notion of witchcraft sounded like a crazy fairytale, overblown imagination. A thrill of dread told me I was a long way from Kansas—er, Maryland. "A witch!" I whispered, licking my lips as the blood drained out of my face. "You don't mean…seriously?"

"A lot of that in these parts." He'd laughed off the ghost story, but not this. "Not much in the open anymore, sure. But sometime, you ask your *cuñado*—you say *brother-in-law*? I bet he knows about the Righteous Province, as they call it."

"But you think this—this Juan Bórquez is mixed up in—witchcraft?"

We veered off the road to climb the hill toward the Pérezes' farmhouse. "He pretends to *avivar* some of the old island *tradiciones*—to return?"

"Uh…to revive traditions?"

"Exactly. He tries to revive the customs forgotten for fifty years or more. My *abuela*—my grandmother—she's always very superstitious, and she thinks it's wonderful."

"I can't imagine why, if he's been hassling her daughter so much."

He raised his palms. "It is the way she is. With Bórquez, I think it is just a *fachada*—a front for—something else. He has some power over Abuela, though. Look, Señora Linda is waving from the tent door."

*Mother hen.* I groaned. "Now she'll want to gab for hours. Probably woke up and got her second wind when Cole went in." *And been waiting up for me ever since.*

"*Hasta mañana*, Melissa." Nicolás handed me the flashlight, gave a casual salute, and took off downhill in a sprint.

So I admitted, the island of Chauquelín definitely wasn't boring. Dolphin shows, mysterious villains, good-looking guys…

More than that, I knew I'd made a friend. Even though… Nicolás was nothing like any of the guys back home.

And he said I'd see him again tomorrow. Everything about this island visit just changed for the better.

7

I'd hoped Little Mama had got all the big-sisterly guidance counseling out of her system earlier, but no such luck. I might as well settle in for a long-haul chat. Linda lifted the kettle from the hot plate and poured hot water over some waxy green leaves.

"Really thoughtful of Nicolás to show you around a bit," my sister said. "Want a cup of tea? It's *boldo*. Makes you sleep like a log."

I waggled a finger. "Give me a break. I don't do any more tea than I have to."

"Since when? You were practically raised in Mom's tea shop." Linda took a sip from her mug, sighed, and sank onto a bench. "Melissa—"

"What? Look, I know our family has this tea-bonding fetish, but I'm not into it, okay? Seriously, we should've been Chinese."

"Chileans do a lot of herbal teas, too. Coffee, then?"

"Instant, right? Do you have cream?"

"Um, powdered milk."

"I'll pass. Speaking of tea, Mom sent you part of Grandma Rose's teacup collection. It's packed in my other suitcase, the one I left at your house, so when we get back to civilization... But I was looking for some music tonight" —I knelt and groped through my canvas bag— "and found this Bible."

The tattered black leather cover almost slipped off the binding when Linda took it. "Grandma's Bible." Her voice sounded awed as she traced the spidery handwriting crammed on the front flyleaf.

"We—Mom and I—have been sorting through her stuff," I said. "Thought you should have it."

"Thanks, it can't be easy for either of you." Linda squeezed my arm. "Maybe you should have this. Especially since you were with her right at the end."

*That's what you think.* I'd ducked out on her—the person who loved me most. I should've been named Melissa *Stinkweed* Travis. Blinking, I squatted again to stuff the disheveled contents of the bag back inside. "No, no, you keep it. One of the last things she...talked about...was visiting you here. Besides, she had a bunch of Bibles."

"Meli...I have to tell you something, and maybe this isn't the best moment, but...I've already put it off too long."

"So tell me," I said coolly. *Here comes the lecture I've been dreading all day.* "You feel obligated to replay Mom's speech? Shoot, get it off your chest."

"Yeah, well. I've got to break some news to you, and it's not easy—for me *or* you."

I made a face. "What, they won't let me go home unless I arrive in sackcloth and ashes?"

"I think they'll be glad to have you home in face paint and feathers, actually. But...there's a bit of a problem. Apparently the school board met the night you flew here, to reevaluate your case, and they decided that your suspension's…permanent. At least the rest of this year."

I sucked in a sharp breath. *What!* I was sure Amanda and Jared—my crowd's ringleaders in the spiked-oranges affair—would take their share of the blame. The lion's share. At least, they'd implied they'd set the record straight with the school authorities. It wasn't fair—

But wait, I had other friends at Baltimore City College. I lunged across the tent, flapping my arms. "Yes! I can finally go to City! I tried to talk Mom and Dad into it last summer, and I know they don't want me there, but now there's no option."

"They've been checking into some options."

"I won't be homeschooled!" I wanted to stamp my foot like a child but resisted. "They can't lock me up like that. I'd rather die."

My sister leveled her green laser-gaze on me. "Would you rather lose the entire school year?"

"What!" I dropped to the bench beside Linda. "What…do you mean?"

"For whatever reason, City won't transfer some of your courses from Mt. Washington. Sure, you can attend there, but you'd basically be putting in time until next fall. Ditto for most of the other public high schools. And Mt. W. is being very particular about what they'll accept as alternative studies when and if they take you back."

"Some other Christian school then?" *Anything* was better than Home Ec with Mom.

"Doubtful they'd accept you at this late date in the year. But…there *is* homeschooling."

I groaned. Twiddling my thumbs for months at City would be preferable. *If Grandma were still alive, I could even have studied with her.* But if Mom and Dad and Martinet Martin thought I was going to come home begging and swear on the Bible to be a good little girl from now on, they could think again. I wouldn't do it.

*Pinch me, wake me up from this horrible dream.* Had my friends tricked me, let me take the whole fall? Tears stung my eyes. Blinded, I pitched over to the tent doorway and leaned into the whipping of the hilltop breeze, gulping it to the back of my dry throat. My stomach churned. I needed to clear my head, needed a drink, and not Linda's pathetic tea, either.

I was the one out of options, about to suffocate. My life was sinking away from me to the rock bottom of the bay.

My back to Linda, I said, "There's always reform school, too."

"You don't mean that, Meli. But brother, I do feel like your probation officer, having to tell you this. It's been eating at me all day." She joined me in the doorway and wrapped an arm around me.

I hunched my shoulders but didn't shake her off. I didn't need Mrs. Perfect's sympathy. Still, my sister was only trying to be kind. Trying too hard, maybe—but acting as the shock absorber between our parents and me didn't put her in a comfortable position, either. And she'd given me some time to chill before dumping the bomb.

So Linda had known all this even before asking me for my own account of the school situation. Why did she bother? The sweet little missionary probably considered her baby sister practically a juvenile delinquent.

"Well," I said. "Not much use working on 'What I Learned in Chile' now, is there?"

"Oh, don't give up. I'm going to pray about it. I have faith God will provide some solution." Linda swigged down the last of her *boldo* tea. "In the meantime, let's enjoy this time we have together."

Exactly what I planned to do here—enjoy myself. Forget everybody—parents, teachers, even my fair-weather friends. "It could be worse," I said. "I could be home watching reruns." *And enduring Mom's heart-to-hearts over tea and crumpets.* "Instead I got a front-row seat at Sea World tonight, for starters."

Compared to the moonlit marine pageant, Amanda and Jared's stupid escapade took on a dishwater hue, anyway. Lame, lukewarm, full of garbage. On the other hand, Nicolás Serrano was an original, at least. *Refreshing.* Who cared if he was a peasant from the sticks of Chile? I hardly knew him—yet—but he was way cooler than Jared's sidekicks.

"By the way," Linda said, "we've got a guitar. Do you think...?"

*Chauquelín Island*
*Day 2 – February 1*
*Would it impress the higher powers at school if I dou-bled the word count on the essay? I spent most of the night writing instead of sleeping, but the snail's pace in this metropolis didn't exactly run me off my feet the next morning.*

My sister had moxie, I gave her that. Somehow she talked me into playing choruses for her children's class, so that afternoon

I ended up in the tent with a guitar tucked under my arm. I'd even agreed to teach a Bible verse during the evening meetings, too. *Temporary insanity.* Or maybe just a sudden absurd desire to please my big sister.

The Big Top buzzed with children, close to thirty by my last count. They quickly caught on to the three songs Linda introduced, but my sister was going to have her hands full keeping order, even with Gina's help. Rachelle—Keli—was napping, so I decided to stick around for the lesson and craft time. Lend a hand with crowd control, at least.

Amid the confusion, one pretty little girl drew my attention. Her apple cheeks and willowy form marked her as the Serrano boys' sister, though the fair complexion, nut-brown hair, and angelic features resembled Marcos rather than Nicolás.

I handed the girl a workbook. "You're Valeria Serrano."

"I know who you are, too." She beamed. "The *gringa* my brothers met yesterday."

I winced. *Gringa* could mean anything: *I'm a foreigner, I have blond hair, or my Spanish rots?* "I'm Melissa Travis. Not the gringa, por favor."

Valeria only flashed me an adorable smile. "My mamá wants you to come for tea." Then she dove for the dish of colored pencils.

*Tea again? Oh, charmed.*

By the time Linda dismissed the class, it was four o'clock, tea hour on the island of Chauquelín. From the tent doorway, I saw Nicolás and Marcos striding up the hill as I waved goodbye to the children scattering in all directions from the Pérezes' field.

"We finally finished splitting Don Ramón's wood this afternoon." Nicolás switched the axe he carried to the opposite shoulder. "Melissa, my mother would like to invite you to tea and meet you. Señora Linda..." He shifted a hesitant glance to my sister.

"That's fine, Nicolás," Linda said. "Your mother mentioned it this morning when I went to invite your sister to the class. I'm sure Melissa would love to go. Cole and I will take our turn another time."

*Ah.* He wasn't so much asking Linda's permission as apologizing for not including her in the invitation. I shook my head. These super-polite Chileans.

"What time is the meeting tonight?" Marcos asked.

"Seven thirty. You boys coming? Your mamá wasn't sure."

"We will be there." Nicolás wagged a bronzed arm to his sister, who stood framed in the trees overhanging a north corner of the field. "Let's go, then. We will all come back together later, Señora Linda."

As Marcos sprinted in Valeria's direction, I raised my eyebrows to Nicolás. "Where are they going, then?"

"To our house, by the high path. It is shorter than the shore road, and there's a nice place in the woods you must see."

He set off at a comfortable saunter. I fell into step beside him in the worn footpath at the edge of the field. After the dimness of the tent, the midafternoon sunshine dazzled but the breeze felt fresh.

"Right here." At the shady spot where Valeria and Marcos waited, Nicolás pinned up the heavy branches of a drooping pine with his free hand.

We all filed through onto an almost-hidden forest trail. Instantly, another world, hushed and cool, surrounded us—all sun, wind, and noise shut out. The air hung moist and fragrant with resin.

I paused to inhale deeply. "Umm, it's beautiful and cozy."

"Come and see from El Mirador." Valeria tugged at my arm, then pranced a few paces ahead.

"That means 'the lookout' in English," Nicolás said. "There is a *vista*—a view, sí?—of the islands all around. It's my favorite place on Chauquelín."

"At least," Marcos said with a grin, "it *was*, until Cahuel discovered Dolphin Bay. Now El Mirador is only a distant second."

Nicolás smiled. "Probably right."

Despite our language limitations, a sort of easy friendship had sprung up between me and these Chilean kids. I scuffed along the path, drinking in the lush greenery and rich, earthy smells. The spongy carpet of needles and wood chips almost bounced beneath my feet. Maybe I'd been too sophisticated back in Maryland to appreciate such…simple pleasures. *Maybe I was never quiet—or bored—enough.*

Nicolás propped his axe against a peeling tree trunk, then sprang a few feet ahead and into the air and snapped off a small branch of eucalyptus. He munched a leaf and offered me one.

I wrinkled my nose, grinning. "Yuck, nasty. Very *malo*, *amigo*."

"*Refrescante*." He shouldered the axe again.

"Here we are." Marcos pointed out another path to the left, narrower and more overgrown than the one we were on.

*Practically a jungle.* I arched my brows.

Nicolás chuckled. "It is only a few meters in. And no thorn bushes, I promise. At least, I cleared the worst away last week."

We plowed through the choked brush of blackberries and bamboo and in another minute came onto a green half moon clearing atop a ridge that overlooked the whole channel below. I stopped short and caught my breath at the sweeping panorama of sea and sky. Sunlight traced a crinkled pattern on the silver sheet of water, like a window of cathedral glass. The neighboring islands glowed like emeralds set in the crystal.

"That's Quenao, due west." Beside me, Nicolás pointed straight ahead. "It is the biggest island close to here. Then Meuluy a little to the north, and Chuque on the far horizon."

Along the shoreline to the right stretched a finger of rock-strewn beach—the peninsula I'd crossed with Nicolás last night. A pair of fishing boats left frothy trails in the water as they chugged from the southern cove into Dolphin Bay.

"The wind is up now." Nicolás sighed. Was he upset? Or maybe just contented.

I turned my gaze on him. "You love it here on your island, don't you?"

"I didn't always, but now…sí, I do. And no one is going to take…" His voice slipped away with his thoughts. A shadow crossed his face, deepening the tan.

"Take what, Nicolás?" His mood swing puzzled me.

His restless gold-brown eyes narrowed on the two boats bobbing north around the peninsula. "Look." He jutted his chin out and elbowed his brother. "Bórquez's *Angélica* and that mystery launch that sneaked in with her last night."

"What's that *sapo* doing now? Snoopy toad." Marcos shook his head and swung away.

"That's what I want to know. They are sailing from the south this time. And Don Juan Bórquez does not sail for fun."

"Mamá is making *empanadas de manzana*, Nico," Valeria said cheerfully.

Nicolás roused himself from his somber thoughts and smiled. "Then we definitely do not want to be late, eh Vali? Let's go."

We headed back through the brambles to the forest path again. A short hike brought us to an open field smothered by a honey-colored blanket of ripening grain. As we cut along its lower edge, Valeria plucked a stalk and tucked it behind my ear.

"The wheat matches your hair." She giggled. "You are *la primera persona* I ever met with *real* golden hair."

From a center furrow that parted the field in two, a steep trail angled downhill. Conversation dwindled as we maneuvered the incline. Rather, *they* maneuvered. My legs quivered like jelly just trying to stay upright. I felt like a clumsy cow beside these mountain-goat boys. Valeria raced on ahead, more like a squirrel.

We approached the Serranos' home from the back. Their yard resembled the Pérezes', except neater and drier. Nicolás tossed his axe into a shed and led me around to the front entrance of the silver-gray chalet I'd admired the day before. Now the family who lived here piqued my interest more than the alpine architecture.

I followed Nicolás up the stairs to the carved double doors and into an old-world cottage straight out of a fairy tale.

# 8

The intricate panels of weathered cedar opened into an immaculate hall paneled in pine beadboard, like I'd glimpsed in Linda and Cole's home in Mellehue during the few minutes I'd spent there. To my right, a wooden staircase wound to the second floor. Under a long mirror to the left stood an oval table made of a light wood I didn't recognize, crowned by a crocheted doily and a ceramic pitcher of dahlias and calla lilies. A fluffy wool rug spread over the buffed floorboards, like a dollop of cream-cheese frosting on gingerbread.

Out of sight at the opposite end of the hall, a kettle lid clanged over the murmur of voices. Then Valeria skipped forward, her arm draped through that of a petite, dark-haired woman.

Nicolás did the honors. "Mamá, here is Melissa. My mother, Señora María Angélica De la Cruz Guzmán."

Linda had cleared up my confusion about the mouthful of names just that afternoon when Valeria signed her name as Valeria Serrano De la Cruz. Apparently, everyone in Chile had two last names, the paternal name first and then the maternal one. Married women always kept their original surnames. If they used their husband's name at all, it was tagged on as a courtesy. *For the essay...*

"How lovely to meet you." Señora María Angélica spoke in a soft, melodious voice. "Your sister visited here this morning, and you are like her."

*Like Linda?* I gaped. *Señora, you've got to be kidding. I am not!* Somehow I muddled through the correct words and motions of greeting. María Angélica De la Cruz had dainty hands. Incongruously rough, they carried a faint—though not unpleasant—whiff of floor polish and apples.

Curious, I looked at her closer. Obviously Nicolás represented a taller, masculine version of his mother—Marcos and Valeria must have inherited their father's coloring. The Chilote woman moved with the grace of a ballerina in her periwinkle wool dress. Her hair, glossy brown without a hint of gray, coiled about her head in a single thick braid that emphasized a fine-boned face and deep-set tawny eyes. Brunette Little Mermaid-meets-Princess-Leia, but still, she was...as exquisite as a doll.

A wheezing sound startled me. In the kitchen doorway, a tiny, bird-like woman appeared. *Must be the kids' grandmother.*

And surely this was the same old woman I'd seen inspecting the *Ambassador's* arrival from the balcony of the house the day before. Today her scraggly white hair was bound under a black headscarf. Leaning on a bamboo cane, she wore a stained apron and rubber boots that half swallowed her, but the dark eyes in her seamed face missed nothing.

"Mamá!" María Angélica scurried to her mother's side. "There was no need for you to get up. We were going to bring our guest into the kitchen in a minute."

"Chu, Angélica, I can manage." The older woman grunted and brushed her daughter aside as she hobbled toward me, puffing asthmatically.

She, too, shook my hand, and...*whoa*. The rancid odor billowing from *her*—a stew of sweat and garlic and stale grease—made me gulp back a wave of nausea. It reminded me of the old man's porch when I'd tagged along with my brother Dan on his paper route years ago. I did the same now as I'd done then—held my breath.

The Serrano kids towed me into the kitchen. Valeria leaned in with a confidential air. "Abuela Luisa is having a bad day. She gets asthma and colitis attacks sometimes."

I'd mentally geared myself to encounter another squalid Chilote kitchen, but this one was as spotless as the hall. Despite the afternoon's heat, the varnished pine walls projected a light, bright atmosphere. A collection of kettles on the black cookstove had all been scoured to a metallic gleam. The delectable aroma of baking pastry wafted from the oven.

The grandmother shuffled to a seat on the cushioned bench behind the stove and took up a hand-held wooden spindle. Señora María Angélica transferred steaming brown turnovers to a tray. Valeria spooned dried herbs into a round silver cup. Marcos stoked the fire with another stick and shut the draft, while Nicolás slipped out the back door to an adjoining lean-to and scooped up an armload of wood for the fireside basket. I watched. The useless one, as usual.

Their mother gave me a shy smile. "We shall have our tea in the dining room today, I think. It is cooler and more comfortable there."

"Coming, Abuela?" Valeria asked.

"Not now, later." The old woman never lifted her sharp black eyes from the spindle. Steady as one of the Muses, she twisted creamy white fleece from a bulging sack into a smooth strand of yarn.

The Serrano kids exchanged glances and led me into a combination living/dining room that, like the Pérezes' living room, seemed as neat as a stage set, as though they only used it for company. An image of my Baltimore home—the state-of-the-art stereo, sleek sofa, plush carpets—darted through my mind and contrasted with the outdated furnishings here. Still, the place was scrubbed to a glow and brimmed with country charm.

Bowing heads of hollyhocks and blue hydrangeas peeked through sparkling windows at their reflections in the polished floor. An open fireplace, swept and cold at present, dominated one corner, and in the other hung a shelf with a small crucifix and a row of plaster statuettes. Posters of haloed saints and virgins papered the walls. The table in the center was set with a bowl of shell-pink roses on a crisp drape of white linen.

"Sit down, please." Nicolás drew out a chair for me and then sat opposite.

His mother poured hot water over a sprig of leaves in matching china cups for herself and me. Was that Limoges? Even my fancy-pantsy mother rarely used the delicate French pieces she'd inherited from Grandma Rose. The fine porcelain struck me as an unlikely luxury in this homespun room.

"The kids prefer *mate*." Señora Angélica indicated Valeria's metal cup of herbs.

Valeria added water from a miniature kettle and a spoonful of sugar. She sucked the brew through an embossed metal straw and made a face. "Ugh, the first one is always bitter."

"Let me help then," Nicolás said. "We will let Melissa try it too, when it's a bit milder."

"How did the class go?" Señora Angélica asked.

"Great," Valeria said. "Tía Linda is a good teacher. I'm going back tonight."

"Perhaps we can all—Mamá!" Señora Angélica jumped up. "Come, sit down with us if you want."

The old lady observed us from the doorway, still twirling her spindle. "No, no." She ambled away again.

*And I thought* my *grandmother was quirky.*

I enjoyed the family tea party, except for Grandmother Luisa's periodic spying from the doorway. Señora Angélica's overreactions made me feel jumpy, too. Why was the woman so nervous? Was she *afraid* of her mother? Though the kids ignored the spectacle, I had the impression much more was going on here below the surface.

However, the food was luscious, "island gourmet," as Marcos dubbed it, laughing. Even the real mint tea tasted good. I'd never tried anything like the *sopaipillas*, flat deep-fried biscuits spread with butter or purple *maqui* berry jam. Then came those mouth-watering turnovers, filled with apple-sauce. *Maybe I should get the recipes for Mom.*

"The apples come from our own orchard," Señora Angélica said. "If enough are ripe, Nico, you boys should get out the press and make cider while these folks are here."

"Ready for your first mate?" Nicolás passed me the cup with the straw, which the kids had shared among themselves.

Wrinkling my nose, I accepted. The green herbal tea was horrible—no other word for it. But the cup held only three or four sips, so I played the good sport and sucked it dry, while the kids looked on expectantly. "Tastes like grass," I said.

They howled.

While the boys hustled upstairs to change out of their work clothes for the tent meeting, I helped clear the table. The grandmother slipped off her dingy apron and untangled a black shawl from the hook beside the back door.

Valeria glanced over from the plates she was rinsing. "Where are you going, Abuela?"

"To the meeting." Her dried-apple face shriveled further into a scowl. "Here I am, an old woman hardly able to move around, but I must make Angélica happy. I can see she is dying to go."

María Angélica's cheeks drained, leaving her face the pasty color of cold turnovers. "But Mamá, I am glad to stay home with you. I can attend another evening, and one of the children will stay then if you are not well." Her slender fingers fumbled as she knotted the top opening of a plastic bag of leftovers.

"Don't bother yourself, Angélica. I will go if I must suffer all the way." She thumped toward the front door.

But Nicolás blocked her way. Now in gray pants and an open-necked white shirt, his tall figure loomed immovable. His jaw tightened, but the corners of his mouth turned up. "Abuela, you wait while I hitch the team. Then I will take both you and Mamá in the oxcart. You do not have to walk." He gestured toward me. "You better go ahead with the kids, or your sister will wonder what happened. I will be a little late."

Nicolás had mentioned a customs revival last night, but Cole's revival meetings must have offered the biggest entertainment in Chauquelín since the advent of television. Nearly the entire population of the island packed the Big Top.

I'd figured repeating John 3:16 or some verse like that with these islanders couldn't be too challenging, but by the time Nicolás ushered his mother and grandmother to a side bench, I wondered. The verse of the day, "All we like sheep have gone astray..." hit the nail, right enough. The stuffy tent smelled like a sheep pen. About to gag, I scooted to the back as soon as I finished my part and edged out the doorway into the cool hilltop breeze.

Nicolás stepped out behind me. "Sorry to send you back with the kids, but I figured if Abuela insisted on coming, I should help her get here." He tipped his chin toward the team of gangly oxen harnessed to a rough wooden cart. A pair of benches sat in its bed.

"What's with your grandmother anyway?" The woman seemed like a batty old bat to me, yet he'd gone out of his way to cater to her whims.

"Oh, *bueno*, she's not that well. But—" He frowned and spread his palms. "I think she is not as sick as she pretends sometimes. She only wants Mamá by her side all the time, and she tries to make Mamá feel—what do you say? *Culpable.*"

"She feels guilty? Why?" I knew what that was like. *Poor Señora Angélica.*

"Because she was not here—she lived in Santiago—when her father, my Grandfather De la Cruz, died. So Abuela was alone then." He glanced inside the tent. Cole was standing up to speak. "I should go back in. Just wanted you to know I did not *abandonar* you on purpose. You are leaving?"

Why should he feel personally responsible for me? But it was kind of him. "Uh, no, just getting a breath of fresh air."

He ducked back in. How much longer could I loiter out here without drawing Linda's attention? I'd rather miss as much of the preaching as possible. Maybe I could pass the time by adding to "What I Learned in Chile." Had I learned anything yet?

Sure, already. Last night I'd learned a bit about the behavior of dolphins. This afternoon I'd observed some rare plants in their natural habitat. I reckoned I'd seen historical agricultural practices in actual use too. I'd sampled new foods yummy enough to write home about. And I'd noticed a chasm of contrasts between two households less than half a mile apart.

I'd also discovered I could progress awfully fast in Spanish when I was forced to use it all day long. And another thing—after tea with the Serranos, I saw that poverty was no obstacle to beauty and hospitality.

That was a start. Whether it would impress Martinet Martin was debatable, but…

Maybe I'd better squeeze back into the tent and catch the tail end of Cole's sermon for good measure.

## 9

*Day 3 – February 2*

*The next evening, Nicolás came to the meeting alone and even later than before. Maybe trouble brewing...*

"Where's the rest of your family?" I asked him afterwards.

He scowled. "Abuela is on the warpath. Don Juan Bórquez visited her this afternoon with his superstitious propaganda, and now she refuses to let anyone in the family attend your meetings anymore."

*My* meetings? I ignored that and repeated with a twitch of my lips, "She *refuses?*" The old lady seemed more fragile than a withered leaf.

"Don't laugh. The old folks rule in these islands, you know, and my abuela's domineering. She bullies my mamá something terrible. Valeria cried and cried to come, but no way."

"So how did *you* manage to escape?"

"I just left." He shrugged. "Let them think I went to Dolphin Bay, as I usually do. Even if they realize I came over here, *no importa*—I will still come. *Las amenazas* of Bórquez do not scare me." He tilted his chin.

"What kind of threats, Nicolás?"

Jaw clenched, he watched a woolly clump of lavender cloud scudder across the pale face of the moon. "I don't know exactly, I admit. He probably told Abuela that the old island gods would take revenge if we follow this new *gringo* religion. Or something like that."

*Day 4 – February 3*
*The next morning at breakfast, I broached the subject with Linda and Cole.*

"The grandmother takes all this seriously." I stirred sugar into my hot milk. Café con leche was the only way to stomach this instant coffee. "But Nicolás didn't seem impressed."

Cole stretched his long legs out in the now-flattened grass inside the tent. "He's a pretty independent guy, Nico is. Being raised mostly outside the island, I suppose he hasn't swallowed the Chilote law of the elder too well."

"He wasn't brought up here on the island? He acts like a native to me."

"He's probably learned to fit in well enough. Had to, to survive, I suspect. But as I understand it, he was born in Santiago. Lived there until his father's death about three years ago. The dad was a *carabinero*, an officer of the national police force—a major, I think. He was shot by a terrorist during a street riot."

"Oh," I muttered. *Sheesh, nobody told* me. Asking about his father hadn't even occurred to me. And if he'd grown up and gone to school in the capital, no wonder he spoke fair English.

"Well, if Nicolás isn't intimidated by Señora Luisa and this Bórquez fellow, his mother certainly is," Linda said. "She sent us a note last night to cancel the plans for tea there this week. Best not to come right now, she said, as her mother was all upset and had even hung a wax amulet at the door."

"What does that mean?" I asked.

"It's a charm against witches," Cole said.

"So what? You don't mean she thinks we…"

He nodded.

"That's positively Dark Ages. She's off her nut! Nicolás told me the other night that that Bórquez crony of hers was maybe involved in witchcraft. If she's on a witch hunt, she'd better take a closer look at *him*."

"Bórquez. Is he the owner of that three-story house just north of here?" Cole asked. "Extravagant new place, with a batch of mean dogs around. Short, stocky man with a beard?"

"Sounds like him, all right," I said. "He knocked me over at the dock in Mellehue."

"That was him?" Linda's sleek copper eyebrows lifted.

"He wasn't too friendly when I stopped by there yesterday morning." Cole drained his coffee mug. "Said he was the *fiscal*, like the trustee of the local chapel. Told me in no uncertain terms to get lost." He shook his head. "I've heard of a sort of Chilote cultural revival in some of the remoter islands, where the *mayores*, the older folks, feel that modern life has made too many unwelcome inroads on their traditions. But I wasn't aware Chauquelín had hopped on the bandwagon."

"Does that mean going back to old superstitions like even witchcraft? Nicolás said you'd know about that."

Cole chuckled without humor. "I know only as much as an outsider looking in can. But yeah, in some cases it means exactly that, I'm afraid—a return to pagan practices. Or rather, a grotesque combination of popular religion with ancient spirit worship. Some call it Christopaganism. It can have a powerful influence on susceptible people."

"Sure brings home the wrestle-not-against-flesh-and-blood idea." Linda sighed. "Oh, dear. Here I thought things were going so well. I wonder if Valeria will be allowed to come to the kids' class now."

But Valeria attended as usual that afternoon. "I told Abuela that Señora Linda was teaching stuff I have to know for religion class at school this year." She winked at me.

I smothered a giggle. The clever little liar knew how to get around her cantankerous grandmother after all.

*Day 5 – February 4*
*Nicolás also continued to show up without fail.*

"When are you going to invite me back to Dolphin Bay?" I asked him after the Sunday evening service.

His face lit up. "You want to? Why not now, then? I am on my way down."

"I'll ask my brother-in-law to lend his rowboat."

"Good, but—do you swim a little?"

"Who from Baltimore doesn't swim? But that freezing water…" I made a face. "I'll think about it."

Half an hour later, we hiked down the now-familiar hillside trail. Nicolás lugged the oars Cole had lent and I carried the flashlight. After another hot day—as the islanders called it—the night air hung humid and still.

"There's no wind." I held up a licked finger.

"You are right, that *is* rare around here. Maybe your best night for a swim. I bet the water is beautiful."

"Oh, I bet. *Refrescante*, right? Wicked."

"*Wicked*, what is *wicked?*"

"Like, so good it's bad, *entiendes?* Get it?"

He laughed, his dark hair ducktailed over his polo-shirt collar. At the shore, he ditched his socks and sneakers and scraped the rowboat over the coarse gravel and into the shallow water. Then he plucked me up and deposited me onto the plank seat of the boat, eased it offshore, and hopped in himself.

The sea slumbered, serene and motionless once again. Like a distorted glass, it flickered with the candlelight of the stars. I studied the sky while Nicolás locked the oars into position and spun them around.

"Where's the Big Dipper?" I asked.

"The Big Dipper?" He looked confused and then amused. "Oh, but this is the bottom of the world, Melissa. You cannot see it from here. We do have the Southern Cross though. Over there."

"Oh. Of course, the Southern Hemisphere." *Idiot.* I was glad the dark hid my blush. "Nothing like showing my *ignorancia*, right?"

"Not at all. Someday maybe I'll visit your country, and *imagínate* all the mistakes I will make then, eh?" He maneuvered the rowboat north around a dragon's backbone of jagged rocks at the point of the peninsula. "Are most people in the States evangelical Christians like you and Don Colin and Señora Linda?"

"Are most people—*Christians?*" I blurted. Was he kidding? "Hardly! This island may be two hundred years behind my home, but in some ways it's more Christian."

"What do you mean?"

"Oh, well…" I searched for the words to express myself, but Spanish made the topic doubly difficult. "At least it seems peaceful here, I guess. In our city, there's so much crime and evil. Maybe the United States used to be a Christian country, Nicolás, but now most people who claim to be Christians are, well, like here—just *religious*. It doesn't mean much of anything."

"*Superficial*…in name only, then. Underneath, people are all the same."

"You got it, man."

"Then what makes you people different? A different kind of Christianity?"

He was persistent, I'd give him that. Why wouldn't he back off with these questions I had no clue how to answer?

We floated now along the southern edge of Dolphin Bay, a contrasting stage of stark white light and inky black shadows. A pungent breath of eucalyptus trailed across from the evergreen woods of the peninsula at our backs.

"No, I think Christianity is the same," I said finally. "Maybe the difference is whether a person practices what he says he believes. Whether the Bible is just a good book or whether it's your guide for life." *Where did that come from? Get a life, I sound like Linda.* To my relief, movement slithered in the middle of the bay. "Look, here come the dolphins!"

He stripped down to his trunks. "Coming?"

I dipped a finger into the water and shuddered. It made Maine waters feel like Florida. "Uh, I don't know."

"Aw, *vamos*." He nodded at my T-shirt and shorts. "You dressed for it, no?"

Like him, I wore a swimsuit beneath my clothes. "Yeah, but...that was just in case."

Nicolás cannonballed out of the rowboat, throwing up a geyser of cold spray after him.

"Hey, watch it!"

My polar-bear friend surfaced several yards away, laughing as water streamed down his face. "But you were prepared for it. *Por si acaso.* Just in case, you said." He edged closer and splashed another wave my way.

"Lay off." I must have sounded more feeble than grumpy because he baited me again. "That does it! I'm getting you!" I kicked off my shoes and leaped in after him, clothes and all.

The initial shock of the water disoriented me for a moment. Gasping, I kept thrashing until my limbs thawed and my blood zinged with energy. Then one of the dolphins nudged me. I forgot about revenge-dunking Nicolás.

Outgoing and frisky, four of the pewter-gray creatures drew close enough to pet. The skin on their blunt noses felt like moist velvet. Though full of razor teeth, their mouths curved in permanent smiles.

"They don't seem to mind my being here." Treading water, I stroked a rubbery flank.

"No. They trust you. Because of me, maybe." Nicolás wrapped his arms around a white-bibbed throat, and they turned a double somersault together. Then reversed the routine with a double backflip.

He showed me how to grasp their dorsal fin. The dolphins took turns towing us in circles around the bay. They glided around and between us like silver wraiths, dipping beneath the surface of the water, then soaring into the air again as though playing a game of peek-a-boo. Sometimes they shot almost upright on their tails before plunging under again.

Next it was keep-away as they pushed Nicolás and me with their heads and chased each other away from us, as if we were beach balls. Whenever our rowboat drifted, they made it part of the game and bunted it toward shore. Now a pool of moonlight-frosted foam, the cove rang with hoarse dolphin barks and clicks and our watery human laughter.

*What a blast.* I'd never forget this evening as long as I lived. I could hardly tear myself away but, finally exhausted, I paddled back to the boat and drifted along with one arm draped over its side. Nicolás soon joined me as the pod headed out to sea.

"So," he said, "how's the water? Wicked?"

"Totally. But I'm glad you *persuaded* me to get in."

A roguish glint in his eyes, he boosted me into the rowboat. "Good, because I intended to tip the boat over next."

"You'd want me to scream for help from your hospitable Señor Bórquez across the way there?" I glanced up at the mansion that overlooked Dolphin Bay from the north. It was veiled in complete darkness this evening. "The old king crab never came down from his castle to chase us off tonight. How come? We made twice as much racket as last time."

He shook his head, glowering in the same direction. "He does not care now, his launch is gone. I saw it leave from the village dock this morning."

"What, you think he didn't want us around when his ship came in the other night?"

"Just a bad feeling I have." Nicolás waved both arms and yelled to a couple of men in wool hats on shore, shoving another rowboat off the beach.

"There's not exactly a shortage of neighbors around here," I said.

"No-po, that's for sure. That is Don Ramón, you know, and Don Jaime Garrido. It was his mother who sold most of his inheritance to Bórquez." Nicolás grinned. "They are probably going fishing now. How do you feel about gutting *pejerreyes* for tomorrow's lunch, Melissa?"

# 10

*Days 6–9*
*The days fell into a routine...*

My sister and brother-in-law spent the mornings visiting homes throughout the island while I made good on my promise to babysit Reba and Keli and cobbled together a simple meal for us all—sometimes pasta or packaged soup, more often salad fixings from Gina's garden or homemade bread piping hot from her oven. A sack of razor clams Ramón dropped off one day, along with instructions on how to cook them, turned out even tastier than the little *pejerrey* fish.

Most afternoons I helped Linda and Gina with the children's class and afterwards had a few hours of free time before the evening meeting. I soon knew the immediate area quite well. Sometimes the Serrano boys and I played a pick-up game of soccer with the children leaving for home and teatime after class. Sometimes we just hung out. More often, the boys invited me on a ramble through the woods or a hike along the winding shore, where something beautiful or interesting popped up around every bend in the path.

This island of Chauquelín was the National Aquarium-meets-the-coast-of-Maine-meets…what, Endor from *Star Wars*? My head whirled. I sure felt like I was on another planet as I joined Nicolás, and often Marcos as well, on their evening jaunt to Dolphin Bay for the rest of the week. I swam with the dolphins, learned to make silly blowing noises and use the ocarina well enough to call them, played piggyback and fetch with a piece of driftwood. Along with the El Mirador lookout, it became my favorite haunt on the island.

One day—Tuesday? I lost track of time—we wandered through the few dusty alleys of North Head, Chauquelín's one real village, and up to a bluff that commanded the northwest point of the island. When Nicolás told me that the picture-postcard wooden chapel at the crown of the hill had been declared a world-class heritage site, I asked to take a peek.

Inside the primitive church, I shivered in the mildew-scented coolness. Robed images lined the shadowy walls and a handful of time-blackened benches huddled near the altar at the front, but mostly it yawned like a dark, dank cavern. *Wow, pure Gothic spooky.* I fled back into the sunshine again.

Thursday the boys arranged to kidnap me for the entire afternoon.

"You sure it's okay?" I asked Linda after lunch. A tower of empty mussel shells heaped in a wooden bowl between us. "I mean, you've got more kids attending every day."

"We're pleased with the interest here, in general." Cole drained a glass of apricot juice in one swig. "So are Ramón and Gina, of course."

"I insist," Linda said. "We'll manage. Gina's neighbor, Vanessa, might be able to give a hand, too. The Garrido children's mother, remember them?"

I frowned. "Uh, vaguely." *That mousy little girl who sticks to Valeria like a barnacle, right?*

"So go and enjoy yourself. Even if Chauquelín isn't Hawaii."

"Oh, rub it in. I'm not lamenting that anymore." Secretly—since I had to serve the duration of my sentence *somewhere*—I wouldn't have traded places for anything. Not that I would've admitted that to anyone back home. Not to my friends, because it wasn't their type of fun. And definitely not to my parents, because they didn't think I should have fun, period. "But—you two didn't put the Serrano boys up to entertaining me here, did you?"

"They've certainly taken you under their wing, haven't they?" My sister smiled. "But not at all, cross my heart. It's all their own initiative."

Natural enough, I supposed. They lived close by, and they were around my age. But it *was* nice to be liked for myself instead of for my family, for a change. They accepted me at face value, and here I had no image to keep up, so we were cool—easy—with each other.

I barely had time to rinse the dishes before Nicolás and his brother materialized once again and whisked me off on another tour of their magical kingdom.

We hiked into the dense hinterlands and along a high ridge that formed the backbone of the island. Thank goodness, I was in a *little* better shape than a week ago. A white haze swathed the rolling hills—the camellia-like flowers of the *ulmo* tree, Marcos told me. Their anise-and-vanilla fragrance almost overpowered the undernotes of earth and evergreens. Massive ferns and wildflowers, in shades of scarlet and deep rose and feathery white, grew in thickets. *Chilco*—Magellanic fuchsia—and baccharis, according to wannabe botanist Marc.

Crystal waterfalls plunged in leafy vales every few steps. The guys made a ritual of taking a thirty-second dip or dash in each one. I snapped photos—until I ran out of film. *Bummer.*

Hours later, we made it to the very southern tip of the island—the end of the road, if we'd followed the road. Marcos pointed out the parade of Humboldt penguins strutting on the beach far below us.

"So far from the Antarctic!" I said.

"As you see. They're not that uncommon around here."

Brown pelicans and black cormorants winged overhead. Squinting into the vivid aquamarine horizon, I glimpsed dolphins racing alongside a launch below. "What about the eastern side of the island? I bet you could get a good view of the sunrise over the mountains from there. If you get up that early."

"That side is mostly deserted," Nicolás said, "except for wood lots and sheep pastures. Nobody lives over there—no road and not much for good harbors."

"Great hideout for pirates in the old days, though." Marcos grinned. "And other stinky wildlife."

On the ledges that lined the cliff, dozens—hundreds, maybe—of sea lions basked in the sun. Their grunts assaulted my ears. The blubbery bodies, mottled red and gray, glistened with slime and steamed with a stench that rose upward in the heat.

Other than that detail, I wondered if I'd died and gone to heaven.

I kept filing away the sights and sounds of my "Desert Isle" adventures in the notebook I'd started the first day. Heaven forbid I should ever leak *some* of these jottings into my return-to-school essay, but all the experiences would provide good fodder for later. I could add to "What I Learned in Chile" the lesson that modern conveniences and chemical highs weren't all that essential to a great time. That statement ought to grab old Martinet Martin's attention.

And the bizarre thing was, I meant it.

*Day 10 – February 9*
*After Friday's class, the Serrano kids invited me for tea again.*

"Thought I was *persona no grata* at your place now," I said.

"No importa, we're going to the orchard," Valeria said.

I hoped my Spanish was improving as fast as their English. We communicated mostly in our own dialect of Spanglish, but they used more contractions now, and I understood a lot more Chilean vocabulary. At least they called me by name, as if I were an equal. Everyone else relegated me to *Señorita*, or worse, *Sister. Get thee to a nunnery!* Right, I'd already be doomed to a convent if our church had that sort of thing.

This time I waited outside while the kids ran into their house to pack a picnic. I figured their mother and eccentric grandmother were probably working around somewhere, but the yard slept, as quiet as the church cemetery in the village the other day.

A long crimson wax ribbon stirred in the breeze at the back door. I stiffened. *An amulet.* Just as Linda had commented, the blood-red streamer shook a warning to evil spirits. Bunk to me, but somebody here took the possibility seriously.

The hydrangea bushes, heavy with puffs of powder blue, crackled. Something scuffed and snuffled within the kitchen garden enclosure. Had the pig burrowed in? Maybe I should rescue Señora Angélica's flowers.

My hand on the woven-twig gate, I halted. *Voices.* The pig sure wasn't talking to himself.

"—all the herbal remedies we need right here, so no, thank you, Juan." That was Señora Angélica's voice, sweet as apricot nectar. And Juan—as in Juan Bórquez?

"Your mother may have been the midwife, but she's no healer like mine was. And neither are you, Gela. You cannot afford to be so snooty and proud anymore. You need my—"

"I need nothing from you. My boys—"

"Wander about the island at all hours. I'm offering to help—"

"Help! If you think, after everything you did to my family—" Her voice clogged and broke.

"What about how you snubbed *me*? Just because I was not the dreamboat moneybags like Serrano."

"*Mil diablos.* That's not why I left here, and you know it."

"I am not a penniless cripple anymore." Bórquez stomped his foot. "So if you think I'm going to stand for your insolence much longer, think again. I will have you this time, or—"

"Or what?" She sighed with a deep whoosh. "There is nothing you can do to hurt me anymore."

"That's what you think, my girl."

A moan tore from Angelica's throat. "If you dare touch my children, I swear I will—"

"Chu, *cálmate*, woman, I am no murderer. Unlike your hero husband. But I have ways of reaching you. I'll make you understand and come around."

"God help you." Muffled sobs laced her voice now. "You are a pitiful soul, Juan."

"That's what you always thought of me, no? But I have money now, influence around here. I'm not the clam digger you used to know—"

The kids banged out the back door. The voices in the tangled wilderness of the garden fell silent. Footsteps shuffled away. The audio drama snapped off.

Whoops, I'd been eavesdropping, but I was right about one thing. The Serrano household was like an iceberg, ninety percent below the surface. Kind of like me.

And Señora Angélica had left home to escape troubles. Like me, too.

A little dazed, I followed the other kids up the hillside path behind the house and into the woods.

Nicolás held a large Thermos in one hand and a guitar in the other. Between them, Marcos and Valeria carried a wicker basket containing four mugs, a single spoon, a round loaf of bread, a block of yellow cheese, and a plastic bag of sugar. Instead of turning off at the wheat field toward the El Mirador lookout, we headed left onto another foot trail. Quickly it twisted and led higher up the hill.

Trees crowded thick and bushy, bowing over our heads like a tunnel of jungle growth. The trail petered at the edge of a narrow brook that gushed in a miniature waterfall and tinkled on over pancake stones. We crossed the stream over this natural bridge and arrived at the orchard—a broad green glade spiced with the aromas of ripe fruit: apples, golden plums, blackberries, wild rhubarb, and others I couldn't identify.

Diana Delacruz

I gave the Serranos two thumbs up. "Delicious picnic spot. This is the brook that comes out on the beach where Cole's rowboat is tied up, right?"

"After it curves around the wheat field," Marcos said. "Empty that basket for me, Vali, and I'll scrounge up the food."

Sprawled under a heavy-laden apple tree, we feasted off the land. Valeria steeped mint tea with leaves she picked there, while the boys mounded fruit and nuts around us, broke the bread, and sliced the cheese with jack knives. I'd never eaten a more unique meal. Even the tea wasn't so bad.

"What's this fruit I don't recognize?" I pointed to a round black berry that resembled a polished bead.

"*Luma* berries." Abnormally quiet today, Nicolás seemed to brood about something.

"They come from that odd-looking tree there," Marcos said. "The one with the roots half sticking out of the ground and moss all over the trunk. We use luma for our best firewood too."

"It smells nice. Like cinnamon." Valeria's Cupid's bow lips were stained purple with *maqui* berry juice.

"And these?" I held up a palmful of small brown shells that looked like hazelnuts.

"*Avellanas,*" Marcos answered. "Chilean hazelnuts. Want me to crack one open for you?"

"They're the trees with the pretty white flowers." Valeria pointed them out. "The nuts are just ripening from last year."

"Not all the white-flowering trees are *avellanos*," Marcos said. "Some are *ulmo* and *tiaca*."

"And the trees with the reddish leaves? Isn't it early for the leaves to turn color?"

80

Nicolás roused himself. "It's not the leaves, it's the fruit. Gives the whole tree a red tint in the summer."

"You cannot eat that *tineo* fruit, though." Marcos grimaced. "What did you bring your guitar for, Cahuel?"

"Thought Melissa could teach me some of the songs she's been playing at the tent meetings." He appealed to me with a glance and lifted the guitar from where it was propped against the gnarled trunk of the apple tree.

"Vamos, Marc, let's get the apples Mamá wanted," Valeria said. The two meandered toward the opposite end of the orchard, swinging the basket between them.

Reluctantly, I accepted the guitar from Nicolás's outstretched hand. *Whatever.* I strummed a chord and yawned. "I feel so sleepy. Why don't *you* play something? A song of Chiloé?"

Shrugging, he took it back. His mind seemed to roam while his fingers and the strings made music on their own. The same hands which had deftly swung an axe a few days ago now picked out a musical repertoire with casual expertise.

I closed my eyes and listened to his clear, pleasant baritone. A peculiar emotion stole over me. I didn't understand all the words. But snatches about mermaids and witches, launches and shipwrecks, told me they were traditional island folk tunes. The melodies, both melancholy and lively, had me *encantada*.

My drowsiness evaporated. I straightened up and clapped with gusto. "Teach me!"

"Sure. I was in a folkloric music group at school. I know a lot of the island songs, and…" His voice trailed off, as if he'd lost his place in the script.

I cocked my head and arched an eyebrow. "Nicolás, what's up? Your grandmother giving you a hard time again?"

"No, no. Well, you might say that, only it's my *other* grandmother this time." He wrenched a rumpled envelope, addressed in delicate handwriting, from his jeans pocket and smoothed it out on his knee. "Mamá brought back the mail from North Head this morning. I don't think she even wanted to give this to me."

"Why not? It's from your other grandmother? Your father's mother, you mean."

He nodded. "She lives in Santiago. Where we *all* lived until...until my father was killed a few years ago."

"Cole told me about your father." I laid a sympathetic hand on his arm.

In his silence, bees buzzed over the hot mash of blackberry bushes and in the white lace of the *ulmo* trees. A languid breeze rustled in the highest leaves. The bird concert never ended: chirp, whistle, squawk, trill, peep. Soprano runs up a scale—*coo-cuck-a-chu-caoo*. Valeria's cry of "Over here, Marc!" shrilled across the meadow.

Finally I asked, "Is it more bad news about your family in Santiago?"

Nicolás sighed. "Not really. My grandparents have invited me to spend the last few weeks of the summer vacation with them in Santiago. Today they sent a check for my bus fare and so on."

His lack of enthusiasm mystified me. "Sounds super."

"No, it is not!" He slammed a fist into the ground beside him. Then he ripped the check from the envelope and tore it in two.

## 11

I gaped at him. "Nicolás Serrano! What'd you do that for?"

His jaw worked up and down as he heaved himself to his feet. Wetness glittered in his deep-set amber eyes. "*Perdón*, it is just—"

I raised my hands. "It's okay, you're not offending *me*. If you need to unload, go ahead."

He dropped back beside me, wiped sweaty palms on his jeans, and gazed toward the opposite end of the orchard. Marcos swung from a tree branch like a sinewy brown monkey while he pelted his sister with apples. She scampered around, catching them in her basket.

Nicolás spoke in a monotone. "In the three years since my papá died, my grandparents have had almost nothing to do with us. A few months ago, their other son and his wife separated, so they have decided maybe we are worth more attention. Well, I want nothing to do with *them* now."

Pain edged his voice despite the harsh words. I bit my lip as my own eyes pricked with tears. "But why? I mean, why did they ignore you for so long? There must be an explanation. You'd think after losing their son—"

"You might think so," Nicolás cut in, "but the Serrano-Larraíns of La Reina aren't ordinary folks. It's a long story, Melissa."

*Oops, bitterness there, for sure.* My own petite grandmother had been a classy French dame, but never a snob. I tried to offer an encouraging smile. "I have the time."

His lips tugged up at the corners. "I don't know why you should care so much."

"But I do. God knows you seem to need a friend right now."

"Sí, God. God knows." Nicolás plucked a handful of grass and sifted the bright blades through his brown fingers. "I'd like to believe that. Like you and your family do. But I don't know. God is so far away. And here we are, a bunch of animals surviving the best we can."

Bother, I'd never intended my careless reference to God to derail into another religious discussion. I came back with a light response. "Animals like sheep, you mean? Like in the verse I taught a few nights ago."

"Exactly. 'Gone astray and each of us turned to his own way.'" His thoughts stuck on the serious track. "What's that other verse? The one we had last night."

I picked up a leftover plum from the ground and inspected its wrinkled yellow skin. "John 3:16. 'For God so loved the world that He gave His only Son...' Everybody knows that one. I don't know why Cole chose it."

His riveting golden eyes widened. "Maybe everybody where you come from. I never heard it before."

My turn to be surprised. "Never? Well." Half embarrassed, I repeated the verse in full for him.

"That's it." Nicolás kneaded his chin. "But I don't understand it. I mean, sí, I comprehend the *words*, but it makes no sense. *Bucha*, seems too simple."

The…yearning…in his tone gave me a jolt of guilt. How could I let him go on floundering for answers that he so obviously wanted to hear? I felt a little awkward—okay, a lot awkward. *Make that hypocritical.* But fifteen years of Sunday school prompted my overflow.

"It *is* simple," I said. "A lot of people, maybe in this part of the world especially, have complicated the way to God. Sort of dressed it up in so many traditions and rituals that nobody sees how plain the Bible actually is. They're trusting in things like…an awesome church building, some promise from a priest or whatever, I don't know. When all you really have to do is believe in Jesus."

Head down, he drummed his fingertips against the tree trunk. "But we do believe in Jesus."

"The real Jesus? Or somebody's *idea* of Jesus?"

"What is the difference? What do you mean, the real Jesus?"

He wasn't trying to debate me, I knew that. But I also knew I wasn't going to get off with parroting pat answers to this guy's sharp intelligence. *My gosh, he honestly wants to know.*

How did I get roped into this again? Barely masking my annoyance, I blurted, "Well, He's not some everlasting baby in a nightgown, for pity's sake. And He's not the helpless victim forever hanging on a cross, like I saw in the church the other day, either. The real Jesus is the Jesus of the Bible, the Son of God who created all this." I flung my arm out to indicate the beauty of nature that surrounded us. "He's alive, not the figment of some artist's imagination."

I took a deep breath. *Melissa Travis, you are way out of your depth, girl.* Time to backtrack in this conversation. "It's all in the Bible. If you want to find the truth, the real Jesus, Nicolás…just read the Bible, okay?" *Oh, that's lame.*

He knew it, too. "The Bible is a big book."

"Then start with the Gospel of John. That's where that verse, John 3:16, is found." I twirled the plum in my palm and took a savage bite out of it. Juice dribbled down my chin. "Anyway, your long story?"

He stretched up again. "I'll tell you while we walk back."

"What about the other kids?"

"They can come behind with the basket. Valeria doesn't need to hear this. She does not remember much of it." He picked up the guitar. "So much for the music."

Once across the stone footbridge, he began. "Remember I mentioned the other night how Juan Bórquez was always chasing my mother? When she was a young girl—a bit older than we are now, I suppose—he harassed her so much that her father finally allowed her to go with a girlfriend to work in Santiago, just to get away from the island."

*He harassed her, huh?* The way he talked today, she'd insulted *him.* Not that I believed his sob story. "Bórquez didn't follow her to Santiago, did he?" I shuddered, imagining that disgusting hood stalking a lovely teenage María Angélica on the streets of the capital.

"Even if he did, chances of finding her in a city that size would be small. As far as I know, she never saw him again until recently." He pushed aside a low-hanging branch. "Mamá worked at several different places—maid work, you know, in wealthy homes—and ended up staying. Much against Abuelita Luisa's wishes, I'm afraid."

"Your mother's her only child?"

"Only daughter. Mamá did have a brother who died long ago. Eventually, she got a job with the Serranos—my father's parents—in the La Reina neighborhood of the city."

"The plot thickens. This is starting to sound like a variation of *Cinderella*. Your mother's that beautiful."

Nicolás's chuckle ran to more of a snort. "Sí, but this is no happily ever after version of the fairytale. Mamá studied evenings to finish her high school, and my papá, David, admired her—what do you say?—*determinación*, I guess, and started to help her when he came home on the weekends. He was in officers' training for the carabineros then—the Chilean police. So…they became friends."

"And fell in love."

"There was war in the Serrano household when his parents found out." Nicolás's gold-brown eyes flashed fire. He opened and closed his mouth twice before continuing. "Same as a lot of Chileans, they were pretty racist—proud of their pure Spanish blood. Even though they *liked* my mother—just not for their eldest son, see? But Papá was just as stubborn and proud as they were, in his own way. In the end, he and Mamá got married."

"Wow." I whistled softly. What was it Bórquez had insinuated about David Serrano? "Nicolás… was your father, like, involved in the coup here years ago?"

"He was a carabinero at the time, all right, but not directly involved, no. He and Mamá were actually on their honeymoon when it happened."

"Oh. Hmmm."

"Why do you ask?"

"Just…wondering. So after that, they called a truce?"

He shrugged. "You might say. I remember happy times with my grandparents in Santiago. They treated us all well, Papá saw to that. Maybe they even forgot—sometimes—that Mamá was a humble Chilote girl. At least until…until Papá was gone."

Shot by a terrorist, Cole had told me. I didn't pester Nicolás for raw details right now. "Losing him must have been a terrible shock to you all," I said.

"And without my father around, it did not take long for family relations to come apart. Oh, nothing so *drástico* right away. But over the next months… My uncle Daniel, Papá's younger brother, had recently married. My grandparents just turned to playing everything on his card, so to speak. They were not interested in us anymore."

I bit my lip. *Unbelievable.* How could anyone—least of all a set of grandparents—be so unfeeling?

"My mother was to receive a pension from the carabineros, but paperwork takes time here," he said. "In the meanwhile, she could not pay for our big house or the exclusive school we kids attended, so she was in a—a difficulty, no?"

"Gotcha. A bind."

"She did not wish to ask my grandparents for money. *Or* to offend them by going back to work. Then her father died, too, and Abuela Luisa begged her to return to Chiloé to help out. My Santiago grandparents probably thought that was good luck for them, to get rid of an embarrassment. We have hardly heard from them since."

*Good riddance of bad rubbish? How brutal.* Nicolás had lost not only his father, but almost his entire world in a single blow. "Must've been kind of weird for you, coming from the capital city to…a place like this."

We reached the edge of the wheat field. Nicolás threw out his arms to the panorama of vibrant greens and blues below. "Chu, no importa. Chiloé makes Santiago look like a dump—just metal, dust, and smog. Grandmother writes like we're in exile in Siberia. Ha! She doesn't know we came to paradise instead."

"But why did she contact you now, after all this time?" I asked. "I mean, maybe that's a good sign."

His jaw tightened. "They are only shuffling cards again. Like I said, my uncle Daniel's wife ran off with some Argentine *millonario* a few months ago. They had no children, so guess what? Now Grandmother Rosalía says she misses us. Well, I am not playing their game."

I cringed at the ominous finality of his tone.

*Day 11 – February 10*

*Nicolás didn't appear with Marcos to play soccer with the younger boys the next afternoon.*

"Oh, Cahuel—Nico left at noon," Marc said in response to my question. "Had to go check on our sheep, and that pasture is a long hike inland. I was going to keep him company, but he wanted to be alone. Cannot get his nose out of that Bible Don Colin gave him last night."

"Oh?" So that was it. *The guy's loco.* I'd noticed Nicolás approach Cole after the evening meeting.

"Abuela Luisa doesn't like it much. She already threatened to burn the Bible."

I shook my head in disbelief. "What did Nicolás say to that?"

Marcos shrugged. "Aw, you know how he is, Meli. He's always polite to her, but he does his own thing." He turned to kick off the ball.

*Bummer, no trip to Dolphin Bay tonight, then.* My friend had abandoned me for his sheep. And a Bible.

That complaint was unfair—he had to work sometimes. I might as well spend the evening polishing my back-to-school essay. Unless...

Hadn't I seen a *cantina* on the raggle-taggle outskirts of North Head? The scruffy village boasted almost as many bars as people. I'd sworn my best behavior to Linda, but what if I told her I was meeting Nicolás and snuck off?

Rocking Keli on my hip, I wandered back inside the Big Top. "Reba's in her glory, tending goal. You raised a good Baltimorean, Lin."

Linda sliced through a round loaf of Gina's fresh bread and added to the mound in a wicker basket. "Where are you off to with the boys today? I can't believe tomorrow's our final day here. It's gone fast."

"So then it's back to civilization, huh?" *Back to the real world.* Keli squirmed. I gave her a couple of bounces, set her down, and buttered a chunk of still-warm bread. "I think—"

"You know, Gina asked me today if you were going to school in Mellehue." Linda handed me a glass of juice. "And I said no, you only planned to stay for the summer. But it got me thinking. Maybe you could attend classes there for a while."

"Huh?" The bread stuck to the roof of my mouth. School in Mellehue? In a fishing village in Chile? A picturesque port of call, sure, but hardly more than an overgrown pit stop. Linda had pointed out the school grounds on the way to the town dock that first afternoon—Reba would start kindergarten there in

March—and the whole complex consisted of little more than an assortment of unpainted wooden-block buildings.

And if I stayed, I'd have to live with Linda and Cole, for more than a few weeks. My sister and brother-in-law's home seemed comfortable, but...no phone? Only *one* TV channel? Did they ever even listen to any music besides hymns? The villagers' concept of fast food was probably a run down to the beach at low tide for clamming.

Unfortunately, all that couldn't appeal much less than my current predicament back home.

*So Linda to the rescue again.* Why didn't my obsessed sister just abandon me to my fate? She'd helped enough by offering temporary asylum right now. I didn't deserve anyone's sympathy—and I didn't need it either, didn't even want it. All I wanted—

"Consider it, at least," Linda said. "You know the Serrano boys now. They come into Mellehue to board for school, so you'd already have some friends. There's still a few weeks to decide anyway, but it could be an option for you."

"But..." My voice fizzled. "But...will they take me as a student there?"

"We'll have to ask, but I think it's quite possible. Cole's acquainted with the school director, like the principal."

Was I coming down with a cold? My throat kept clogging. "And what about Mt. W.? Will *they* accept the idea if they're being so...so *picky* about everything?"

"That's another thing we'll have to find out, of course."

"Well...thanks, I'll think about it." I knew I didn't sound overly grateful. But go to school here in Chile? Could I even imagine it? The month—doable—would stretch into the foreseeable future.

Yet returning to Maryland remained my only alternative. What good had it done me to escape prison at home only to face a worse sentence when I got back? Six months-to-life… of solitary confinement, torture… It wasn't fair!

So I could choose between the devil I knew and the devil I didn't. Neither choice exactly appealed.

# 12

*Day 12 – February 11*

*What point in dragging out the decision, though?*

"I'm going to turn into a mermaid when I grow up," Reba said at teatime on Sunday. "What do you want to be, Auntie Meli?"

I grimaced over the breadbasket. "I think I'll opt just to be myself."

"Isn't it hard to be someone else?" Linda asked with a smile.
"It's a given."

Mrs. Perfect was either pretending or deluded. But before I could answer, Cole hurried into the Big Top. "Guess what, gang? I ran into Nicolás Serrano up the road, just as I was heading back here. Had a good chance to talk with him, and he has trusted Christ."

Linda set down a pitcher and gave Cole a hug, her jade eyes shining. "Why, that's wonderful news! Isn't it, Melissa? He's been such a good friend to you this week."

Cole emptied the last of the water into a glass and drained its contents in a single gulp. "Seems he read most of the New

Testament over the past couple of days. Started with the Gospel of John and went on from there. What a guy."

"He did?" I stared, butter knife poised in midair. "I don't think I've *ever* read the whole New Testament."

Nicolás's words came back to me. *The Bible is a big book, Melissa...*

*Then start with John,* I'd replied offhandedly.

*But he read the whole New Testament! Talk about going overboard.*

"Probably a lot of Christians haven't, even older people," Cole said. "But you might say that was what clinched it for Nicolás. He's been quiet—not the type to make an impulsive commitment—but I think he's given the gospel a lot of serious thought ever since he attended our youth group in Mellehue last spring. The Holy Spirit's obviously been working in his heart. Today he just...gave his life to the Lord."

"Every once in a while," —Linda released a sigh— "God lets us see the result of our seed sowing. Rebecca Peterson, don't you eat any more of that *manjar*."

"I'm thirsty," Reba said, licking the caramel spread off her fingers.

"I'm not surprised! Honey, I'll make your sandwich while you—"

"More water from the spring?" Cole grabbed up the bucket. "I'm on it."

Nicolás announced his faith decision at the tent meeting that evening. I didn't even have a chance to talk with him beyond a few words of greeting as he hurried off afterwards.

"It's your last night here," he said. "Sorry not to make a final visit to the dolphins, but I...I feel I must go straight home this time."

I nodded, choking back my disappointment. "I understand, amigo. But you're coming over to Ramón and Gina's clambake tomorrow, aren't you?"

"Planning on it."

"We'll be leaving right after that."

"Say good-bye then?"

As on other nights, I watched him dash down the hill in the twilight—a tall, slim figure with a rolling step, dark hair ruffling in the rising breeze. But tonight, he'd stepped out of character somehow. Unless I missed my guess, Nicolás Serrano had changed, and it was more than the collared dress shirt and tie he'd donned for the service. It was that *look* in his topaz eyes.

I'd seen it before, in the faces of people back home I considered fanatics and do-gooders. *Oh mercy, what have I done? He's got religion.* I couldn't picture Nicolás as a stuffed-shirt bore like that. Part of me was glad for him. *I am, seriously.* Yet I dreaded to see my cool new friend mutate into a religious nut.

His unhesitating stand in the tent this evening would remain stamped on my memory. Cole's closing words echoed in my head as well: "If a person truly believes, he will repent of his sins, make a firm commitment to Jesus Christ, and begin an about-face in his life..."

About-face, right. Here we'd really started to connect, and now he was taking off in another direction. Shivering in the tent door, I gazed after Nicolás until he was out of sight.

I had a decision to face, too, and soon. Not about Jesus Christ, of course, but about school and my return to Maryland.

Maybe half the reason I'd gotten so involved with the kids here was so I didn't have to think about my own life.

But the Petersons were leaving Chauquelín tomorrow to return to their town of Mellehue. I could either stay with them a while longer—no in and out in a month—or I could say *adios*, board a plane, and choose the lesser of a dozen evils back home. And I still didn't know which.

Late last night and again this afternoon, I'd written feverishly on "What I Learned in Chile." I inserted notes about the fishing, the crops, the scenery—I'd even tossed in a few intellectual zingers like *temperate rainforest* and *ecosystem*. I explained what I'd observed of Chilote culture—how the elders dictated every action and opinion in the family, how their religion consisted mainly of superstition and community solidarity. I praised the virtues of the simple life.

It helped to take my mind off my dilemma a little. I'd convinced myself that maybe a super-inspiring essay might persuade Martinet Martin and the Mt. W. C. A. school board to relent. But deep down, I admitted it wasn't enough. I was in denial. After everything I'd done, they weren't about to give me a second chance for a good long time, if ever.

This island had fooled me into believing that an exciting path might branch off around the next bend. A door would open. As Linda had suggested, God might rearrange my circumstances to bring about an unexpected solution of some kind.

But if I were honest with myself, why would He? I hardly gave Him a thought. Why should He care about me?

Time to burst my bubble, throw off the bewitching effects of my island escape pod. I felt like I was waking up from a dream. Not that it had been a bad dream, not at all. It just wasn't...*real*.

I took a deep breath. Maybe I should take a walk. The cantinas in North Head called, but I had to tackle the challenge of my grim reality. *Bite the bullet.*

By the time I'd meandered to Nicolás's lookout at El Mirador and back, I'd made up my mind to move on Linda's spontaneous school-in-Chile proposal.

After the initial shock, I'd pretended to take the whole kicked-out disaster in stride in front of my sister. But in reality, the bottom had dropped out of my life. I was busted—trapped—backed right to the edge of a cliff.

So, given the present run of bad luck, I supposed I could suck up life with the Petersons for a while. Linda was all right. She'd hesitated to break the news, even seemed sincerely distressed about it. Maybe she was on my side.

So I could attend school here and put off facing the music at home till the dust settled a little more. Sit out for a couple of months, keep my options open, and hope for the best. There *had* to be a way to go back to how things were. Amanda wouldn't let me take the whole rap. Surely not, now that it had come to this.

In the meantime, Chiloé wasn't such a terrible prospect. I always considered myself a city girl, but I *loved* this island. The dull side trip had turned out fantastic. So maybe this new, forced hand would flip a winning ace, too, who could know?

Just as I arrived at our campsite again, Linda crawled out of the small tent after putting the children to bed. She poked her head into the Big Top and surveyed the mess with a sigh. "If I wasn't so tired, I'd start cleaning up tonight."

"Where's Cole?"

"Ramón invited him down for mate and *sopaipillas*. I told him to go, it's our last night here."

"Why don't you join them if you want? I'll stay here and listen for the kids."

"Well…all right. Thought you were off to Dolphin Bay with Nicolás."

"He had to go home tonight. Linda…" My voice sounded shaky in my ears. "Would it really be okay if I opted to go to the Mellehue school for a while?"

"Of course." My sister smiled. "Your life will never be the same if you do, though, I warn you."

"Aren't you the mystic?" I rolled my eyes. "It's not as if I have much choice, anyway."

"I was hoping you'd want to stay." Still grinning, Linda drew a brush through her gorgeous hair. "Didn't want to pressure you, but seems like that would be a lot less boring than auditing at City College. Not to mention more worthwhile in the long run."

"I can't believe I'm saying this—probably you can't either—but I agree with you there. Just until things get straightened out…if all the powers that be will accept it?"

"I'm sure the director in Mellehue will be delighted to have you. Quite a novelty for the school there. I think I can get Mom and Dad on board too, and even Seth Martin might consider it. Your principal at Mt. W. is, uh, an old school friend of mine."

I opened and closed my mouth. *Sweet, if that's not a mega bit of clout.* Why hadn't she mentioned it before? I made a wry face. "I promise I'll behave myself in Mellehue."

"Naturally, sis." Linda's mouth pressed into a prim line, but I detected a glint of humor dancing across the wide green sea of her eyes. "I wouldn't expect anything less."

*If she only knew...* Ever since my first ramble through North Head, and especially the last couple of evenings without Nicolás, I'd wrestled the temptation to break my word and slip into the village.

But I hadn't. It might cramp my style, but I'd comply if it killed me. "Will language be a problem?"

"How about more an opportunity? You've made such good progress."

"What grade will I be in?"

"What they call *'segundo medio,'* I'd think. Roughly equivalent to tenth grade back home."

"But...I haven't finished ninth yet." Suddenly I felt stupid and shy.

"Doesn't matter. You turn fifteen next week, so they'll place you on that basis." Linda grabbed up a sweater. "I think that's the same grade as Nicolás. My, won't you be the star of the English class, Meli."

I groaned. "And the dunce of the Spanish class."

*Day 13 – February 12*

*As quickly as Cole and Linda and I could pack the gear in the morning, Ramón Pérez carted it by ox team to the shore.*

Nicolás and Marcos showed up to help with the reverse task of loading everything back onto the launch. When the work was finished, we joined Gina in her preparations for the farewell clambake on the beach.

Blistering stones, heated in a nearby fire, lined a deep hole in the damp sand of low tide. In a party spirit, we filled the pit under Gina's direction with layers of freshly dug clams and mussels, crabs, *longaniza* sausages, new potatoes and bread dough patties, broad beans and peas in their pods. Missing the lobsters and corn like in Maine. And no seaweed, either—Ramón sealed everything beneath gigantic wild rhubarb leaves they called *nalca* and a cover of sod squares.

My stomach growled the entire hour it cooked, but it was worth the wait. My sister's family, the Serrano kids, and their neighbors, the Garridos, all gathered with the Pérezes around the steaming pit for this marine finger food feast. *Who says this isn't the South Pacific?* Except for the menu, it could've been a Polynesian luau.

An all-you-can-eat buffet, too. Finally, I sprawled on the warm beach, digging my bare feet into coarse sand. Mounds of empty shells and lemon rinds ranged around me. How could the children keep running and squealing?

Nicolás squatted beside me. "Do you want to try to see the dolphins now?"

I moaned and made a face.

"Hey, I'm serious. You have never been out in the daytime. Cannot promise they will come either, but it's worth a try, no? Don Colin says he's waiting to leave when the tide turns, in another hour or so. So we have time to row over, if you like."

I took his extended hand and hauled myself up. "But no swimming today, okay?"

He threw back his head and laughed, patting his middle. "Not even for me."

Soon we drifted in Cole's rowboat in the center of Dolphin Bay. By day, the cove shimmered with emerald and aquamarine instead of moonstone, in a setting of sunshine-gold instead of silver.

"Your eyes are the color of the sea," Nicolás said. "Calypso, we call it here."

"Calypso, the sea goddess?" I couldn't resist teasing him. "You're getting romantic, amigo."

A faint stain of color brushed the tan beneath his eyes. "I can afford to. This is good-bye, no?"

"Aren't you going to school in Mellehue this year?"

He tilted his head, frowning. "Sí, but you will be gone by then…won't you?"

Of course he assumed that. It had been my original plan, and I'd been low-key about my complicated life back home during this island idyll. "Nope. I'm going to Santiago with Linda and Cole and the girls for a couple of weeks now, but I'm coming back. I'm gonna stay with them for a while."

"Oh." He kneaded his chin and grinned. "Then I take the poetry back."

"Too late, I have it on record."

He snapped a handful of water beads at me, but I could tell he was pleased that we'd see each other again. "I read the Bible like you suggested, Melissa."

I bit my lip hard. Avoiding his eyes, I swung my legs over the boat's side and let them trail in the water. "And did you find out what you wanted to know?"

"I found *Who* I wanted to know. For a long time now, I have been messing up my life—filling it with so many things, trying to hide the emptiness. But that's gone now. I have met Jesus, the real Jesus, like you said."

A fountain of tears sprang into my eyes as I looked across the bay at the reflection of the woods in the water. *Must be the sun's glitter.* I cleared my throat. "I'm glad for you, then."

"Oh, I have much to learn," he said almost humbly. "But for the first time in my life, I feel like I'm on the right track. Nobody, not Abuela nor Don Juan Bórquez nor anybody, can take that away from me." His chin jutted out.

I glanced up at the Bórquez mansion. The obnoxious mad bull hadn't harassed us at Dolphin Bay since the first night I'd come, but that didn't mean he was idle among the islanders. He could be hidden away in his castle right now, casting spells, making charms, devouring widows— up to no good, anyway, in Nicolás's opinion. "Is your grandmother *very* upset?" I asked him.

"To say the least. When I went home last night and told my family, she called me a disgrace. I'm a *canuto* now, you see."

"A canuto?"

"That's our Chilean term for an evangelical Christian. Not usually meant as a compliment, either." He dangled his feet in the water beside me. "But that is all right, it is water off a duck's back. Abuela *needs* me, to work her farm here. It's Mamá I feel sorry for."

"Why?" I dipped my fingertips into the ice-crystal water.

"She is caught in the middle. I can tell she—what do you say? She sympathizes with me. But she would never cross Abuela. And I am afraid Abuela will make her life miserable because of me." He paused and watched me sprinkle water droplets onto my sun-burned face. "Sure you don't want to cool off with a swim, Meli? Looks like this week of country life has been hard on you."

"Come on, I came from the middle of winter to all this saltwater sunshine. What do you expect?" I returned his grin. "To tell the truth, though, I've enjoyed this week in Chauquelín to the max. Thank you for helping to make it awesome."

"I'm glad. Maybe you will visit the island again sometime."

"You never know." *I hope so.* "What about you now? Why don't you travel with us to Santiago and visit your grandparents there before school starts?"

A shadow grayed his golden face. "No. I cannot go, not alone, and not with you folks. We start the wheat harvest next week. Ton of work to do." His tone was curt, his expression like a lifeless wax mask.

Maybe I shouldn't push the subject—it wasn't my business, after all—but what if something happened to his grandparents? *Like to Grandma Rose...* "Did you at least *answer* their letter?"

"No." He glared at me from beneath fierce brows.

"No growling, amigo." I laid an impulsive hand on his arm. "Would you give me her address, at least? I could look your grandmother up while we're in Santiago."

"What for?" His eyes burned as cold and glassy as the sunlight on the water. "Why are you so interested?"

I looked down and scratched at a stain on my jeans. "I—well, my only grandma—died a few months ago. I never knew the others." I shrugged and met his gaze again. "Someday you might wish...you'd sent her a message or something."

"Whatever." His rigid profile softened—a little—as he swallowed. "I will give you the address. But no message. I have nothing to say to them. You'll see what I mean."

"Maybe, but—there, Nicolás, the dolphins have come! Can you believe it?"

# 13

*Mellehue, Grand Chiloé Island*

*Days 14–15*

*I knew all along I'd have to clean up—read <u>censor</u>—these notes before they went to school. But at some point, I stopped writing for Martinet. I find myself writing more for Grandma Rose now, because this was <u>her</u> dream trip.*

En route to Santiago, we paused in the Petersons' time-capsule village long enough to unpack, do laundry, and pack up again. That gave me a couple of days to check out my new home.

Chiloé wasn't a tropical paradise; I'd accepted that. Still, reflected in the ocean's mirror, Mellehue was as picturesque as a postcard. And what Cole and Linda's saltbox house lacked in Baltimore pedigree, it made up for in coastal charm. From my bedroom window high on the outskirts of town, tin roofs corrugated like corduroy tumbled down the hill and nestled around the shore. Turquoise and moss green, garnet and silver. The neighbors below us had spread out fishing nets to mend in their backyard.

*But.* It was not only a one-horse town, it was a one-tele-phone town, too. Wednesday afternoon, Linda decided we needed to consult my parents before contacting the school, so we headed down the hill for errands and a phone call. I walked hand in hand with Reba while Linda pushed Keli in a stroller.

"Welcome to Mellehue City, Melissa." Linda's tongue-in-cheek was almost visible.

"Yeah, bustling metropolis. Compared to Chauquelín, anyway." We rumbled past the local medical outpost, the car-abineros' police station, and the teal-blue fire department. "I guess you're used to the place by now."

"Pretty much, it's been over three years since we came. But sometimes—" Linda sighed. "Sometimes I think I'll never get used to it."

That didn't sound encouraging.

We stopped first at the post office, tucked into a corner of the creaky-floored municipal building at the foot of the hill. A stack of mail awaited the Petersons in a dusty pigeonhole behind the desk.

"Nothing for me?" After this much time, Amanda had surely written.

"It takes a while." Linda waved a red envelope. "We're still getting Christmas cards."

We veered off to the right on Freire Street, where Linda paused to pay her light bill at Don Carlos's General Merchandise. Though the resemblance didn't stretch further, the store was more jammed than Macy's at holiday rush.

"It's the largest business in town," Linda said. "Everything from soup to nuts, literally. Tourist season now, too."

"Your Little Town on the Prairie has a tourist season?"

We cut back toward the village center along a potholed waterfront path. On the channel side, dilapidated shacks teetered on stilts over the beach.

"Classic Chiloé," Linda said. "They're called *palafitos*. Toilets flush twice a day with the tides."

I made a face. "Did I need to know that?"

"It stinks here," Reba said.

"You're telling me, kid. And no wonder."

Despite the assault of odors, the quirky architecture of the oceanfront street fascinated me. Halfway along, a rambling mansion, sided in white corrugated zinc and adorned with tar-black gingerbread trim, reigned over the port area. A round fake-stone tower squatted beside it.

"What, the Chilote version of B'more Formstone?"

"I guess." Linda grinned. "It's a lighthouse, actually."

"Looks like a—I don't know—a bunker?"

"Yeah. It's attached to the port captain's office, where we have to get our *zarpes*—permission to sail."

We zigzagged across the street to the town market and dock area. Wool-capped deck hands scurried along the pier toward the fleet of wooden fishing crafts at anchor, Cole's mission launch among them. Even though smartly kept, the *Ambassador* was built like most of the other boats moored here, even to its belt of old-tire bumper pads. Not inner harbor Baltimore, for sure, hedged with skyscrapers and choked with ships from around the world. These all looked the same.

A rusty tin roof covered the shell-carpeted open-air market. I threw a glance at the overcast skies. "Bet that place leaks like a sieve when it rains. Which it might do soon."

"Yeah, I'm thinking too," Linda said. "During the week it's only the fishermen's catch of the day here. On weekends it's packed."

"It's pretty busy today. Oh, right, tourist season."

"You want to check it out a few minutes?"

"I don't like the old ladies in here," Reba whined.

"Reba!" her mother said. "What a thing to say. Why ever not?"

"They always pull my hair."

"I'm sure they just want to touch it because it's pretty." Linda rolled Keli's stroller in among the rustic stalls. I followed with Reba, dragging her feet. My chatterbox niece wasn't much like me, but sometimes we agreed in our declaration of independence.

The market thronged with people buying and selling artisans' handcrafts as well as fresh produce from land and sea. Yellow, green, and red apples, purple-veined potatoes, and cabbages as big as bushes. Barrels of cider, sacks of toasted wheat flour. Cedar wood carvings and woven-grass baskets crammed with hand-knit dolls in Easter egg colors. Dried smoked clams and mussels and garlics the size of tennis balls dangled on reed braids. Piles of nubby woolen blankets, sweaters, and hats smelled like they'd just been sheared off the sheep. Stray dogs roamed, on the lookout for fallen scraps of *empanadas* or the foil-colored *pejerrey* fish that might slip out of newspaper packets.

I stooped to examine a tiny, sweet-scented basket with handles at each side.

"You like?" A wizened crone—Nicolás's Grandmother Luisa's twin—shuffled toward us. Reba made tracks for the far end of the maze of stalls. "Is tea box."

*Tea, wouldn't ya know?* I smiled as I dug out one of the bills I was getting used to from my jeans pocket. "Maybe for my mother."

"Sí, for you mamá," the old woman crooned in a sing-song accent. With a toothless grin, she reached out a hand as brown and gnarled as a twig and stroked my ponytail of spiral-permed curls. "Butter head." Then she made change and stuffed my purchase into a flimsy plastic bag.

When we continued our walk, the route curved gently uphill again at the village square. The timeworn Catholic "cathedral" dominated the north side of this plaza. Its shingles washed to the shade of driftwood, the immense church badly needed new window glass and other repairs, despite its status—according to a faded plaque—as a national monument.

Linda halted and knocked at the door of an age-blackened house. "The telephone office."

I would've thought she was kidding except for the dull mustard-yellow sign jutting over the door. A middle-aged woman in skirt, heels, and lipstick let us into a gloomy hall that seemed to double as lobby and phone booth. She dialed the number Linda gave her and clattered away.

"Mom?" Linda said. "Yeah, we're back in town..."

I lifted Keli for a break from her stroller and tried not to listen any more than I had to, but I was basically trapped. My usual luck.

"We'll be just fine—Oh, don't worry about that—I'll need a copy of her birth certificate—Oh, I thought maybe till the winter break in July—Well, they do trimesters instead of semesters here—"

*What?* Linda was suggesting I stay until the middle of the school year in July? Not to burst her bubble, but if I stuck it out six weeks, I'd deserve a medal. Two months, tops, before the drama competition back home.

My sister tapped me, took Keli, and handed me a receiver that weighed as much as a dumbbell. "She wants to talk to you."

"Are you on board with this, Melissa?" My mother's voice crackled from another hemisphere.

"Yeah, yeah…"

"And you'll be all right?"

"Chill, Mom."

"You be sure to help Linda, okay?"

I gritted my teeth. "Duh, I already help her. Quite a lot, as a matter of fact. What do you think I am?" *A useless, good-for-nothing child, that's what.*

"Just making sure…" *Yada, yada…*

But she never even touched on the school situation at Mt. W.

What did that imply? Back outside the phone office, huge charcoal buzzards flocked and cawed on the towering roof ridge of the church. A sinister tingle at the base of my spine made me shiver. "They waiting to move in for the pickings?"

"Nasty *jotes*," Reba agreed.

"Yeah, they're pretty disgusting," Linda said. "And here's the school."

Liceo Insular Nueva Galicia bordered the west edge of the plaza. As mediocre as I remembered, the cluster of one-story buildings sprawled out for half a block, boasting rain-grayed shingles and a patch of closely hacked lawn.

"Kind of plain vanilla," I said.

"Yep. Budget shortfalls, I'm afraid." Linda chewed her bottom lip as we wound up to Freire Street again. "Let's hit the bakery before we head home. We'll have tea before prayer meeting."

Prayer meeting? Wasn't there a limit to going with the flow?

# 14

*Santiago, Chile*

*Days 16–28*

*For the rest of the month, I ignored the edge of tension about attending school in Mellehue. At least, Nicolás would be there. But take one day at a time.*

The din on the Santiago street bus racked my nerves. At least Linda and I'd grabbed a seat instead of jostling in the aisle of this cattle car. The sun's orange glare only intensified the impatient blare of horns, the gunning of engines, the screeches and bellows and the nonstop hum of millions of people going about their lives. I'd heard the city's population cleared out in the summer, but you wouldn't notice. In a fleeting moment of nostalgia, I recalled the bell-like stillness of Dolphin Bay on the island of Chauquelín.

Above the clamor, I yelled to my sister, "Nicolás didn't like the dirt and smog of Santiago, but he never mentioned noise pollution!"

"Isn't it atrocious? Things should quiet down once we turn off Vespucio." Queen Serene as always, Linda peered through the press of standing passengers blocking our vision. "So how have you liked Santiago, otherwise?"

"Nothing quite like it back home, I'll say that. But it's just a city." I shrugged. "I *have* enjoyed the trip here, Lin. I—thanks for taking the time for me."

We'd spent two weeks in Chile's capital, celebrating my fifteenth birthday—Latin America's elaborate equivalent of Sweet Sixteen, according to Linda—by doing the tourist things my sister had promised. My memory bank overflowed with scenes. Cardboard shacks leaning next to palaces, mushrooming shantytowns huddled below majestic mountains. Ritzy department stores, colorful boardwalks and flea markets, and hole-in-the-wall cafés. We even made a couple of trips to the coast, and there I was sure I'd at last found the sultry beaches of the South Pacific—until I dipped my toes in the ocean. Another day we took a picnic lunch into the foothills of the Andes.

Cole and Linda seemed to believe in variety as the spice of life, so I experienced everything they could think of. Of course, that included several of their mission churches in the city, but never once got close to any stimulating nightlife. *Oh, well, gotta suck up the bad with the good.* After all, I'd pledged not to make any trouble for my sister. And the tranquil beauty of the Chiloé Islands wasn't such an unwelcome future to look forward to.

On our last stifling afternoon in Santiago, just this final visit remained. We'd tried to contact Nicolás Serrano's grandparents the first week, only to learn from the housekeeper that the Serranos had left for a few days at their summer retreat on the coast north of Viña del Mar. Then this morning, Rosalía Larraín de Serrano had returned our call.

"Goodness, the woman sounds almost frantic," Linda remarked after making the date with her. "They just got home last night, but she's anxious to connect before we leave."

Now, as the bus swung into the heart of the La Reina district, the homes and businesses themselves took on a superior look. Even the traffic roar toned down in awe.

"Definitely upper crust." Linda shook her ginger mane. "I can't understand it. From what you told me Nicolás said, I figured these folks for complete snobs. Which their class often is. But this woman certainly didn't *sound* that way on the phone. And I just can't conceive of their practically abandoning their own family to live hand-to-mouth in the islands."

"They didn't approve of Señora Angélica. To them, she was just the maid."

"Absurd and unfair as that attitude was, you could maybe understand it, given their culture and position. But the *grandchildren?*" Linda was incredulous. "I mean, blood ties run pretty deep here."

At the corner of Bilbao and Monseñor Errázuriz, we squeezed off the bus to air that was still heavy and unbearable. I retied my ponytail and wiped my forehead with the back of my hand. "Phew, I'll be glad to get somewhere I can breathe again."

"You and me both, sister, though we'd better enjoy the sunshine while we can. I hear it's rained in Chiloé ever since we left. Still can't believe what fabulous weather we had the whole time in Chauquelín. An absolute miracle."

I wiggled my eyebrows and grinned slyly. "Why are you so surprised? You're the one who believes God handles these arrangements."

We strolled a block and a half into a neighborhood of stately trees, immaculately groomed lawns, and elegant homes silent and aloof behind high wrought-iron fences. Keeping the world out? Or shutting themselves in?

The home of Nicolás's paternal grandparents, a three-story colonial at Monseñor Errázuriz 0767, gleamed with white stucco and oak trim. While Linda punched the bell at a black iron gate, I admired the picture-perfect beds of carnations and dahlias just inside.

I took a deep breath, suddenly—and unexpectedly—nervous. Why had I jumped in and volunteered to contact these snooty people? Sympathy for the grandma, yes, and probably more than a little curiosity.

When Nicolás mentioned his father's family was well-heeled, it hadn't impressed me much at the time. Now, newly aware of Chilean society's class-consciousness, I doubted whether a mere middle-class American teenager would know what to do or say. I glanced at Linda. Slim, stylish, and put together in her beige print sundress. *Of course.* My sister didn't always wear skirts, I'd discovered—sometimes she even slipped on a pair of jeans. But she was careful to fit in with whatever culture surrounded her, and Chilean protocol tended towards more conservative and formal than in the U. S. Linda did have good taste, I admitted grudgingly. Biting my lip, I squinted down at my sailor top and capris. Why hadn't she told me to dress up?

"Someone's coming," Linda said. "Too late to back out now. Probably the maid, though."

But it most definitely wasn't. A tall, apple-cheeked woman with perfectly coiffed, pale-gold hair approached in clicking heels and swishing skirts of apricot silk. "Señora Peterson?" Breathless, she punched a keypad at the gate.

"Yes," Linda said. "And my sister, Melissa Travis. How do you do…Señora Serrano?"

"Please come in." Nicolás's grandmother whisked us down a tiled garden path lined with citrus and avocado trees.

We passed through a lattice archway, draped with vines of translucent pink grapes, into an inner patio shaded by climbing bougainvillea and rose trellises. A glass-topped table and roomy wicker armchairs, plumped with pastel-flowered pillows, were arranged beside a kidney-shaped pool.

Señora Rosalía de Serrano motioned us to a cushioned seat. "It is so hot in Santiago, we spend most of our days out here in the summer. I am sure you will find it more comfortable than the house at this hour."

"It's an oasis in a desert," Linda said in her most gracious-lady tone. "You've been away for a few days, I understand?"

"Up to our place in Zapallar. Family friends were being married there over the weekend." She toyed with an embossed medallion on a thin gold chain at her throat and coughed. "When our grandson Nicolás did not arrive last week, we thought we might as well attend the wedding."

A uniformed maid set a tray with a sugar-dusted cake and a pitcher of iced coffee on the table. *Not tea, major novelty.* As the servant vanished back through the open French doors into the house, I glimpsed ivory drapes stirring in a gentle cross-breeze, and, beyond them, furniture upholstered in wine-colored plush.

"My husband, Manuel Ignacio, was called to an emergency at his office earlier this afternoon. He was sorry to miss you." Señora Rosalía's hands trembled as she poured and served the refreshments for us. "Now, which of you met our grandchildren in Chiloé recently?"

"Well—" we began together and then laughed. Linda gestured toward me. "Actually, we've both seen them, in the island of Chauquelín. But Melissa spent more time with the young people."

Our hostess leaned forward in her chair. "Tell me, how are Nico and Marco and little Vali?"

"They all seem very well, except for their other grandmother." I took a long sip of the iced coffee.

A flag of color swept across Señora Rosalía's face as she cleared her throat. "Ah, sí, the island grandmother...Doña Luisa." She seemed to find it difficult to speak the name.

What to say next? My conversations with Nicolás had led me to expect a cold, arrogant woman, not this clearly anxious-to-be-cordial one. Why was she so nervous? It didn't fit. Was Rosalía de Serrano putting on an act?

I twirled my glass in my hands. "It was really my idea to visit you, Señora Rosalía. My poor big sister's just along for the ride, humoring me and keeping me from getting lost, I guess. I'm not even sure myself what brings me here today. I just came to Chile from the States a few weeks ago and met Nicolás on Chauquelín then."

"My husband has known your grandsons for a while," Linda said. "They're fine boys."

Señora Rosalía's smiled, pathetically eager. "I am delighted to know that. We have heard so little of them since they left Santiago, you know."

I sucked in a breath. *Do I dare say it?* "But isn't that...your own choice?" *Not to say fault.*

Señora Rosalía drew back, a deeper flush flooding her cheeks. Her hand fluttered to her throat, her rosebud lips quivered. "Perhaps you could say that, my dear. We are poor letter writers, I fear." Her fingers shook as she plunked her glass on the nearby table. "But I hoped we could persuade Nicolás at least to visit his home here before school starts. Surely he must miss Santiago way down there in Chiloé."

"I...I didn't get that impression." How could I tactfully contradict the lady? "He...he told me he didn't want to go to Santiago."

She paced to the pool edge, her gaunt frame slumped. "Why not?" she asked in a low voice. "Did he say why not?"

I glanced at my sister. Beneath her golden dapple of freckles, Linda's face was pale and troubled. She raised her palms. Sweet, she didn't know how to handle this either?

A bird chirped in a branch close by. How could I hear anything so sweet and whisper-soft with the cacophony of the city so near? Another world, hushed and secluded, existed in here. The garden courtyard magnified even the tiniest sounds. The bird's trill became a siren, a rolling pebble echoed like a landslide, a ripple of breeze across the pool swashed like a waterfall.

Her back to us, Señora Rosalía's narrow shoulders heaved. I had to say *something*. But how could I describe to this weeping woman the contempt in her grandson's voice when he spoke of her? How could I blame her for the hurt in *his* eyes when she was obviously in pain herself? Yet Nicolás was convinced that pure selfishness motivated his paternal grandparents' sudden effort to mend their relationship.

All so confusing, and I'd tangled myself in the middle of it. Mom always accused me of being too impulsive, and for once she was right. I shouldn't have got involved.

"I think," —I measured each word— "that maybe…you can guess most of the reasons." I paused, horribly embarrassed, then plunged on. "Please, please don't think I've come here to grieve you, señora. When I saw that Nicolás was determined not to visit you, I talked him into giving me your address. I—I guess I felt sorry for both of you. I wish I could do something to help."

Señora Rosalía returned to the table and snatched up a lace-trimmed napkin to her face. "It's too late. I am afraid it is too late for help now."

Another moment passed, punctuated only by distant traffic, birdcalls, and her sobs. So much for dignity. "Forgive me for this outburst," she said finally. "I don't usually make scenes, especially not in front of my guests. But so much has gone wrong, and now this disappointment with Nicolás, too."

"Never mind," Linda said. "I think we understand."

"Please have another slice of the almond torte, my dears." She dabbed at her eyes. "It's an heirloom recipe, from an old family friend. My daughter-in-law, María Angélica, became even better at making it than I." She gave the faint trace of a smile, as if remembering happier times. Then her face crumpled again. "I made this one for Nicolás, thinking they probably cannot get marzipan down there. It was always his favorite."

I speared a piece of the dense, creamy nut cake with my fork. "Can I ask why you invited Nicolás just now, Señora Rosalía? I think it would be important to him to know that."

"We invited Angélica and all the children last summer. She turned us down, said it was too difficult to leave her elderly mother alone. Perhaps it is, I do not know. But she suggested Nicolás might travel up alone this year." She paused to pour herself another glass of coffee.

As if she needed anything to make her more jittery. It *was* delicious, though.

"So as soon as my husband set his vacation dates for this summer," Señora Rosalía went on, "we sent Nicolás a check for the bus fare. All for nothing, it seems. Oh *Señor mío,* our entire family has fallen apart."

"You mean—" Linda said.

"I mean, both of our sons." Her voice caught, ragged again. "We lost David, our eldest. Now it appears we have lost his family as well. And recently, the marriage of our other son, Daniel, broke up. Daniel quit his father's law firm, and we have not seen him for months, either. He is bitter, I know—we all are—because Francisca left him for an Argentine business-man. He calls them another Angélica and Bórquez."

Bórquez! My ears pricked up at the casual mention of the name. Cold gooseflesh rose on my arms in the oppressive heat of the summer afternoon. "Did—did you say Bórquez? You mean, Juan Bórquez from Chauquelín?"

"Of course, although how Daniel could compare Francisca and her lover with darling Angélica and that dreadful Chilote, I don't know. More coffee, my dears?" Señora Rosalía didn't seem to notice Linda's wide eyes and stunned expression. She kept rambling, frank but fuzzy, at least to me. "But that was years ago. I confess that scoundrel Bórquez threw this family into chaos at the time, but David adamantly refused to believe his obscene insinuations. Manuel and I eventually realized

Bórquez was nothing but a filthy liar. Anybody could see Angélica worshipped the ground David walked on, and Nico is obviously his father's son, for all he doesn't resemble David so much physically."

I could see Linda felt uneasy listening to such an intimate confession. Evidently Señora Rosalía assumed we knew more about the Serrano family's private affairs than we did.

My sister cleared her throat. "Is there anything—some message, perhaps—you'd like us to take back to María Angélica and your grandchildren?"

Nicolás's grandmother stood up again and clacked across the patio tiles. "I don't know. No. If our letter reached Nico and he did not wish to come, what more is there to say? Just tell him we are very disappointed and that he is welcome any time."

"Have you ever thought of visiting them in Chauquelín?" I asked.

The woman literally blanched. "Oh, I couldn't!" She clutched the back of a chair with one hand and the gold medallion at her slender throat with the other. Just short of crossing herself. "I traveled to Chiloé once as a young girl—such a miserable place. It poured rain nearly every day, and what—what would I do if they served me one of those slimy black *milcao* things, fried in pig fat? Besides, Manuel really cannot take that much time off."

Linda smiled—smothered a chuckle, more like. "Perhaps you'd be pleasantly surprised to find the Chiloé Islands more advanced in recent years. The climate can't be helped, of course, but in your daughter-in-law's home, I'm sure they'd under-stand if your stomach's a bit delicate."

Señora Rosalía dismissed the idea with a toss of her hand.

"I bet they'd love to have you," I said. "I had a great time with them. Nicolás showed me most of the island in the ten days I spent there. It's a beautiful place, Señora Rosalía. Seriously."

"Is my eldest grandson a complete Chilote then?" She compressed her lips. "Do you think he honestly enjoys life there? Even...*prefers* it?" The woman's eyes once again brimmed with tears. Earlier I'd pegged her kitten-soft gray eyes as exactly like Valeria's, but now the intensity of their gaze reminded me of Nicolás.

I shrugged. "Honestly? Yeah, he enjoys it. He loves Chiloé. I don't know about preferring it. Hard to say, you know? Nicolás isn't quite like anyone else, Chilote *or* Santiaguino."

"He *is* like someone else—his father, David."

Linda pushed back her chair. "Señora Rosalía, I think Nicolás may come to you in time. Keep in touch with him and perhaps God will change his mind."

"I pray so," she said.

"I'll pray, too. If we can do anything for you later, please contact us. Here's our address in Mellehue, where your grandsons attend school." Linda tucked a business card into Rosalía de Serrano's hand. "I'm afraid Melissa and I have to go now. I've left my husband babysitting our two girls, and we have to pack for the drive home tomorrow."

After good-byes at the dahlia-banked front gate, Linda and I headed toward the bus stop. "Some posh place, huh, Lin," I said when we were out of earshot.

"Oh, sure." Linda's tone plainly indicated she was unimpressed. "Par for the course in this neighborhood. But I couldn't help remembering that Proverbs says some poor people are rich and some rich people are poor. Not to judge unkindly, but that dear woman is absolutely empty."

Her words struck me like a dagger. *Obvious enough.* Past a lump in my throat, I echoed, "Poor rich woman, yeah, I know what you mean. She seemed nice, but what does she have except a fancy house?"

"I have the feeling" —Linda scraped her bottom lip with her teeth— "that most of the Serrano family's problems may be just the result of terrible misunderstandings and foolish pride. Probably right and wrong on both sides."

"Why do you say that?"

"So maybe the parents *did* fuss about the marriage at first. But I sensed that Señora Rosalía was fond of María Angélica—and crazy about the children. When her son was killed...I don't know, sometimes grieving people act illogically. Especially when it's the kind of shock such a sudden, violent death would've caused. People withdraw, become hypersensitive, maybe misinterpret others' words and actions. Even revert to old attitudes or behavior patterns that are wrong but comfortable." Highlighted with sunset, her auburn waves shimmered as she shook her head. "Perhaps the Serranos' own grief blinded them to María Angélica's needs and fears. Maybe *she* felt so alone that her old insecurities took over. Anyway, just thinking out loud."

"Hmm." Could the whole situation truly be the overblown result of groundless paranoia? Nicolás believed otherwise. "What about Juan Bórquez, Lin? Did you hear what she said about him and Angélica practically accused of having some affair?"

Linda frowned. "It sounds like he followed her here and tried to ruin her life by telling her in-laws ugly lies about her. But Señora Rosalía insisted that the possibility of Bórquez being Nicolás's father couldn't be anything but a lie. Whatever, I don't think we should have heard that gossip."

"I don't think Nicolás knows anything about it. He told me his mother never saw Bórquez in all the years she lived in Santiago." Even the mention of that scumbag's name was starting to creep me out.

What was I going to tell Nicolás about my visit with his grandmother?

# 15

*Back in the Archipelago of Chiloé*
*Month 2 – March 4*
*My first day of school in Mellehue began with a bang.*

I dutifully set my alarm for six thirty a.m. But before it had
a chance to ring, a tremendous crash jarred me awake. It felt
and sounded like a speeding car had slammed into the house.

Dazed, I sat up in bed. Again, a quick jolt and a boom
that reverberated like thunder through a cloudless sky. And
then silence.

At the opposite end of the hall, Cole and Linda's bedroom door creaked open. I tiptoed out to join them in the
second-floor family room. "What on earth was that?" I asked,
scouring sleep from my eyes.

"Seemed like a tremor." Cole was still buttoning his shirt
in the half-light of dawn.

"A tremor. You mean…like an earthquake?"

"Yeah, a minor one. Common enough around here."

"Should we get the girls up?" Linda said.

Cole tilted his head to one side a moment. "I don't think so. It's over, Lin. But that was the strongest one we've felt since we've lived here."

A bad omen? Not much point in returning to bed at that hour, so I had plenty of time to get ready for classes. Plenty of time to battle second thoughts about this adventure I was leaping into.

Miriam Barrientos, a Chilean girl I'd met at Cole and Linda's church the day before, had offered to meet me at the school entrance and accompany me to our classroom. One friendly face in the crowd, at least.

With Linda's good wishes, I left the house early and dawdled down Mocopulli Avenue. But at the intersection with Freire Street at the base of the hill, I stopped short in surprise.

Nicolás Serrano sprinted down the sidewalk toward me, a spiral notebook tucked under one arm. I hardly knew him in the pressed pants and navy blazer flashing an embroidered school patch on the breast pocket. A rim of white traced his freshly trimmed hairline. But I couldn't mistake that easy, springing walk.

The same warm, taffy-brown eyes lighted up in recognition as he approached. A broad grin creased his tanned face. "Melissa Travis! What a transformation—you look like a schoolgirl." He whistled and then greeted me with a Chilean peck on the cheek.

I grimaced down at my outfit. His reaction only confirmed my rebellious opinion of the shapeless navy jumper and ridiculous knee socks. "They told me this was the dress code."

"So you're really a student here, huh?" He fell into step beside me on the sidewalk and rubbed his chin, his eyes twinkling. "Seems like they could have spared you the school fashions for just a few months."

"Linda thought I'd blend in more this way," I said sourly.

"Blend in." He smirked. "Don't you believe it. With your hair and eyes, *amiga mía*, they would have to be blind not to notice you. What grade will you be in?"

"*Segundo medio–A.*"

"Same as me, good. I expect some help with my English homework."

His banter and candid pleasure at finding me a classmate relaxed me. I felt as if I'd run into a lifelong friend instead of a foreign boy I'd only known for a few weeks. Smiling, I asked, "Did you just arrive in town?"

"Last night on the passenger launch." Nicolás waved the new notebook in his hand. "I am not ready for classes to start this morning. And the señora in charge of our boarding house has been scolding Marcos and me for our unpolished shoes. Says we look like country bumpkins, imagine that."

I laughed. "Where do you board?"

"Just up the street here, before you turn toward the school. Valeria is here this year, too, in the girls' house down by the waterfront."

"Oh, that's nice. But I thought the Chauquelín school went up to sixth grade."

"That's right." He frowned. "The teacher quit last week. Things are bad on the island, Melissa—just everything. We have had bad weather for the harvest too. I almost did not finish the wheat in time to come in to school. As it is, Mamá must do most of the potatoes on her own."

"Why did the teacher quit so suddenly? And what do you mean, everything's bad?" We'd reached his residence at the corner—a quirky old house with a dozen awkward angles, peeling seafoam-green shingles, and luxuriant ivy crawling up the stone-slab steps and porch. A monkey puzzle tree writhed in the front yard.

Nicolás swung open the screechy wooden gate. "I have to get the rest of my things together, so I will tell you about it later. We have a soccer match after school this afternoon. Can you come watch, and then we can talk after that?"

"Not ready for classes, but you already know the soccer schedule?" I winked. "I guess I can come. I want to tell you about my visit with your grandmother in Santiago, too."

His open face distorted to closed indifference. His voice went toneless. "Okay then, after school. Don't forget."

I left him at the corner and met my acquaintance from church, Miriam Barrientos, at the picket fence in front of the school.

Miriam's eyes bugged, as round as pale blue moons. "You know Nicolás Serrano?"

"Yeah, from Chauquelín last month. Why?"

"Oh. Oh, sí, I remember Pastor Colin mentioned the tent meetings there." Miriam shifted her book bag. A large-boned girl with a face as white as a bleached clamshell, she wore her contrasting dark hair in a long fishtail braid. "I don't know about that. Do you think he's sincere? I mean, Nicolás Serrano is quite a hellion."

*Sheesh, what a nitpicker.* I jumped to Nicolás's defense. He was my first friend in Chiloé, after all. "What do you mean? I thought he was a great guy—fun, interesting to talk to. Why don't you like him?"

"Oh, everybody *likes* him. Only—he's really wild."

I bit my bottom lip in rising irritation.

"Sorry." Miriam laid a hand on my arm. "Don't misunder-
stand me. Nicolás is one of our best classmates, no? He's nice,
and sí, lots of fun. But he's always in trouble, never opens a
book. I-I just never thought he'd be interested—in God."

"Well, he is, amazing as that may seem," I said, only half to
Miriam. "I think he really is."

"Good, then." Miriam smiled. "If you and he are friendly,
maybe you can help him, you being the missionary's sister and
all." She turned to push open the glassed front doors into the
school.

Was she serious? I rolled my eyes and glowered behind
her back. If she only knew.

My original impression of Liceo Insular Nueva Galicia
didn't improve now as I compared it with the modern facilities I was used to in Baltimore. Miriam led me to a drab
classroom with bare, drained-yellow walls and whitewashed
lower windows. Colorless, but not quiet—it buzzed. Thirty or
so students greeted one another and wrangled over their seats.
Miriam introduced me to a flock of girls near the door.

One of them, a busty beauty in a purple velour track
suit, snorted and flounced across the room. Her full red lips
curved in a pout that spoiled an otherwise perfect satin-rose
complexion.

"How come—" I started to ask how she got away with
not wearing the cheesy uniform like the rest of us, when she
spiked me with a glare scary enough to frizz hair.

Flinging aside her black cloud of shiny corkscrew
curls—*real* spirals, unlike mine—she snuggled down beside
a beanpole boy I also remembered from church last evening.
The other girls stared after her and then glanced nervously at
me. *Class prima donna or what?*

"Never mind her." Miriam's voice thickened with disgust. "Delicia's just jealous. *She* saw you and Nicolás walking and talking like long-lost friends just now, too."

"So, what is he, her private property?"

Miriam giggled. "Doesn't she wish. But she at least has a claim staked, or so she thinks. The only reason she even *notices* Tito over there is because he's Nicolás's friend."

A murmur of agreement swept among the other girls as the clique broke up. The homeroom teacher arrived, and Nicolás dashed in behind her. From across the room, he winked.

# 16

Shell-shocked, that's what I was by the end of my first day in Mellehue school.

We students carted all our belongings from class to class in a backpack that got awfully heavy. No lockers, no desk space, no textbooks to speak of—we had to copy everything we studied from the blackboard into individual notebooks for each subject. Some of the teachers' handwriting was so different from the North American style that I had to whisper to Miriam for clarification of a word more than once. Before the end of the second period, my right arm throbbed, and I wheezed like Nicolás's Grandmother Luisa from the chalk dust.

Nowhere in the entire school did I see such a luxury as a map or a globe. Encyclopedias, who needed them apparently? The so-called library consisted of a pitiful collection of tattered volumes locked in a glass-front cupboard. Disappointing, since I'd practically grown up in the libraries of The City That Reads.

But when I went to use the bathroom, I forgot everything else. Revolted by the stench of urine and the scum-coated facilities, I backed out, gagging. I could wait. *Note to self, never venture near here again.*

At one thirty the high school dismissed for the day, and the younger children poured in for the afternoon session. I met Linda on the sidewalk as she dropped Reba off at the kindergarten annex for the first time.

My sister gave my arm a squeeze. "How'd it go?"

I sighed, letting my shoulders slump, and then waggled my eyebrows. "Putting an optimistic spin on it, something tells me I'm a long way from Mt. Washington Academy."

Linda laughed. "I want to hear all about it later. Left your lunch keeping warm on the back of the stove. Oh, and I just picked up the mail. This came for you."

"Thanks." *Uh, no thanks.* I recognized Mom's tidy handwriting on the envelope in my sister's outstretched hand. *Go ahead, make my day.* "Lin, I'd like to go over to the soccer game that's on this afternoon, okay? And by the way, do the kindergarteners have separate bathrooms? If they don't, we might all come down with hepatitis."

I trudged home. Nothing, not even a postcard, from any of my friends. *Bummer.*

As I lunched alone in the Petersons' deserted house, I chewed over the contents of my mother's letter. Mom tuned the first pages of her epistle carefully low key, full of trite news about the church ladies' retreat, the snowstorm that closed schools early one day, a shopping trip to New York with her new tea shop partner. But in the final lines, her tone switched:

*Your dad and I hope and pray that your time in Chile with Linda will help turn you around from this path you seem headed down. We're concerned about you, sweetheart, and don't want to see you ruin your life before it barely gets started. You have so much potential if you'd only let God change your heart...*

*Change me, huh?* Did Mom and Dad have *any* idea how much I'd longed for change? My boring life in Baltimore had dragged on, eternally the same. Even the negatives here at least offered a bit of novelty.

Indigestion churned in my stomach. I still simmered as I hurried to the rear of the church property and crossed the stream to the municipal soccer field via a narrow plank bridge. Why had fate cursed me with such a family? I wasn't sure how long I could put up with the Mellehue school, but it solved my parents' biggest problem—me—for a while, didn't it? Why couldn't they just drop the subject?

I clenched and unclenched my fists inside the big pockets of my blue hoodie. *I* was praying too, that my time in Chile would give me a break from the nagging at home. *Let me live my own life...for a change.* I just wanted to be left alone. Didn't I?

Candie Davenport had asked about me in church, my mother also mentioned. Candie, my friend since kindergarten, was more straight-edged than Linda, if that was possible. Just too square, too meek and too milk-toast. I'd outgrown her in the last year or so.

I felt a little sorry about it now, because, even though I'd pushed her aside, Candie never stopped being pleasant. Most of my new friends—even Amanda—evidently hadn't given me a passing thought since I disappeared off the radar.

Still, what did I have in common with a childhood play-mate anymore? Too-sweet Candie should've been Edward and Susanne Travis's daughter instead of me. Linda's little sister—yeah, they were sort of alike.

Linda and Cole were okay. Awesome, really. At first I'd hesitated to get too close, afraid they'd harass me like my parents. But Linda understood how I felt. She was pretty laid-back. She did her own job but didn't try to load me with guilt or turn me into another pious missionary in skirts like herself.

Though some of my classmates here, like Miriam, labeled me as the missionary's sister today. Were they in for a disappointment. Flattening my lips, I squashed into a seat on the packed bleachers of the open-air stadium.

I didn't see anyone I knew well enough to hang out with, but no matter. Mt. Washington Christian Academy had a soccer team too, and it was my favorite autumn sport. The match had just gotten underway. Nicolás scrambled in the thick of the action.

The crisp afternoon held a nip of fall in the brisk breeze and brassy blue sky. *Glorious.* By the time Mellehue won 3–2, I'd become a hometown fan. And I'd nearly cooled off about my mother's letter.

Near the end of the game, I noticed Delicia Treviño, the sassy class belle who'd snubbed me earlier, loitering at the edge of the field with another attractive brunette from her clique. *Seriously, if looks could kill...* I'd got that Delicia saw me—the gringa intruder—as a rival. The scowl she threw my way would've paralyzed me except for the excitement over Nicolás's winning goal.

As the crowd dwindled, Delicia pounced toward Nicolás. But he loped off and dropped, panting, onto the low bench beside me. "Hi."

"Hey."

He plucked a long stem of timothy grass and nibbled it. "No eucalyptus here."

I sniffed. "You always smell like a cough drop."

He roared with laughter, his teeth shining in his flushed bronze face, his deep-set eyes sparkling. "Better than fish or sweat, which are both more likely today."

"Congratulations, Nicolás, on that terrific goal." Purring like a cat, Delicia Treviño slunk up with her friend.

Nicolás blinked. "Uh…thanks."

"Why not come with Mónica and me over to the Chilote Corner?" She flashed a vivacious smile. "I am sure my uncle Moncho can find us something to celebrate with."

Nicolás's expression turned wary. "Not today, thanks."

"But you always used to go."

He shrugged, cool aloofness like a shutter over his face.

Her demure pout twisted into a sneer. "Well! It must be the canuto company you keep these days."

"Must be." He appeared as unperturbed as on that night with Juan Bórquez.

"It will not last long," Delicia snapped at me. As fluffy and friendly—*not*—as a chow chow dog, she spun on her heels and stalked away.

"Maybe I'd better beat it." I smirked. "Wouldn't want to come between you and your girlfriend."

Nicolás made a face. "She's not my girlfriend, and please don't leave."

"Your *ex*-girlfriend, then?"

He poked the timothy stem at me. "Not even that. I don't have any girlfriends."

"No? She's a pretty girl."

"Is she?" Nicolás stood, stretched, and faced me soberly. "Forget Delicia. You would not say that if you knew her at all. Besides, I already have a date today, with you."

"A date? Is that what you call this?"

"Melissa, you're cranky this afternoon." Like my big brother Dan, he took my arm and wheeled me across the field onto the web of rutted downgrade streets. "What's the matter, señorita? Too much homework?"

Abruptly the adjustments and emotions of the day hit overload. My veneer of composure cracked. In seconds, tears filled my eyes and spilled over. "Oh, what'd you say that for?" I bit my lower lip hard.

"Whoa, what did I say? I didn't mean to make you cry, Meli." He patted my shoulder as we reached the main part of town. "Come on, I better make good on this date business and buy you a Coke."

"Don't worry about it. I know you don't have money to spare."

"But I'm *rico*, I got my scholarship from *el presidente* today."

"The president. You mean…you don't mean the president of the country?"

"Who else? Though we will have a new one next week."

"How could *you* get a scholarship? They told me you never crack a book."

"Ha. I make pretty good grades and I'm a needy student." He grinned. "I think you have listened to too much gossip today."

"So it's not true, huh?"

"Maybe I cannot say that *none* of it is true, but any insults to my academic record… now that I would dispute. I admit I do not study a lot. I slept for the first couple of years after I came from Santiago."

"Is the school here really that far behind?"

"In some ways. Or maybe not behind, just different."

After a duck into Don Carlos's shop, we sauntered between the store and Mellehue's lone gas pump to the waterfront street as we shared a liter bottle of soda. The scenic views and bouquet of sea scents reminded me of my first day in Chiloé. A row of fisheries strung along the left side of the lane, each banked by snowy mountains of clamshells. Employees in rubber aprons loitered outside on their smoke break. One spanking-new processing plant advertised Treviño Enterprises in royal blue over the gable end. *Her* family's?

"So then, was your day really that bad?" Nicolás asked gently.

I shrugged. "Just...overwhelming, I guess. Everything's *very* different here, like you say. I'm going to become a hunchback carrying that book bag around, and...looks like I've made an enemy without even trying. *And* I got a letter from my mother."

"What's so bad about a letter from your mother? Like me getting one from my grandmother?"

I kicked a shell off the sidewalk. "About as welcome, believe me. She's always pressuring me. Wish she'd just lay off—"

I clamped my mouth shut, suddenly embarrassed to discuss my family and boredom with religion. Nicolás was a new Christian, after all. Maybe I'd been-there-done-that and opted out, but why disillusion *him*? If that was a little hypocritical, so what? I owed Linda and Cole that much. They'd worked hard in Chauquelín, and they'd been more than kind to me too. As long as nobody shoved too much holy stuff down my throat, they deserved my respect.

I cleared my throat and pointed to a floating platform of net-framed crates partially submerged in the water between

Mellehue and its island neighbor. "What're those things? They look like old-fashioned playpens."

"Salmon farms," he said. "Big business here now. We might get to tour one sometime—they recruit apprentices from the high school."

"Uh, not my career choice. But it's a cool idea."

The factories gave way to ancient multi-hued houses that opened directly onto the sidewalk, almost like the iconic row houses in my own hometown. Baltimore's dignified brick facades never sagged, though, and the stoops weren't made of rotting wood or this cheap, disintegrating cement, either. As I brushed by a wall of faded pea-green shingles, flecks of paint drifted to the ground. Or maybe it was mold.

Just before we turned uphill at the port captain's corner, Nicolás thumbed toward the shack-on-stilts across the street. "My sister boards at that *palafito*."

"Oh, yeah, you said she was here, too. Nicolás…I saw your grandmother, Señora Rosalía, in Santiago."

His guard fell over him like a gray blanket. "And how was she, *glamorosa* and busy as always? Maybe wept a bit?"

I stared. *Guess he does know his family pretty well.* "Um, yeah, but… I honestly think she was genuine. She was hurt that you didn't go to Santiago—and kind of lonely. I didn't meet your grandfather—he wasn't home at the time."

Nicolás's eyes narrowed to glittering slits. He said nothing.

"She said you could visit them any time. And oh, she sent you a marzipan cake—at least, half of one. We've got it for you at the house."

He crossed his arms and propped a shoulder against the slender trunk of one of the scarlet-flowered trees that lined the avenue—firebushes, or *notros*, Cole had told me. "A marzipan cake?" Nicolás swallowed. "That's nice of her, I guess. Haven't had marzipan since… since those days."

"She said it was your favorite." I knew I was babbling, happy that at last he seemed touched. "We were about to leave, and she was in such a hurry to bring it that she almost tripped into the dahlias by the gate, silk dress and all."

He seized my arm. "What? Did you say, 'dahlias by the gate'?"

"Well…yes. Why?" His vehemence, on the heels of weary indifference, bewildered me.

He closed his eyes for a moment. When he answered, his voice sounded flat and far away, as if he were reliving scenes in a distant time and place. "My mother planted the dahlias in that yard when she was a bride. Her favorite flowers."

"Big and bright. I remember her garden on Chauquelín."

He gulped. "The day my father was killed… My grandparents were having a family party that night, and we kids went over early while Mamá waited for Papá to get home. In the patio Grandmother Rosalía was talking to my aunt Francisca, Uncle Daniel's new wife. I heard—I overheard Francisca tell Grandmother that she detested dahlias, thought they looked so 'common and countrified.'" Nicolás paused, as if he couldn't find his breath. "A few weeks after Papá's funeral, *all* the dahlias were dug up and gone."

I bit my lip. I got it, those flowers symbolized for Nicolás the Serranos' rejection of his mother, all tangled up with the pain of his father's death. "The dahlias are there again," I whispered, trying to draw him back to the present. "And they were lovely."

He nodded and then shook his head, as though he couldn't comprehend it.

"What—what exactly happened to your father, Nicolás?" I asked. "I mean…I don't know the details."

"Shot by a drunk terrorist." A nerve twitched in his right cheek.

I knew that much already. For a moment, I thought he'd closed the subject.

Then he strode a few paces ahead and slugged back the rest of the Coke. "It was the last year before the Sí-No referendum, you know? When they voted the military government out."

I barely had a clue, but I nodded as we sauntered uphill again toward the Petersons'.

"The leftists called a big *protesta* downtown that day," he said. "The police expected trouble—we had an assassination attempt only a few months before—so my father went on the streets with his men. Things got out of hand, and this *loco* opened fire on my father's unit. Papá died in the hospital a few hours later. It—it was a terrible night."

His stark explanation pierced me to the heart. We walked the rest of the way to the house in silence. A sympathetic silence, not awkward.

"Is your brother-in-law home?" Nicolás asked as we approached the gate. "I'd like to talk to him."

"You haven't told me what's going on in Chauquelín yet."

"And that was my *pretexto* for taking up your whole afternoon. Oops." He slanted a sheepish grin.

No one else was home yet. Cole was probably out visiting parishioners, and I assumed Linda had taken Keli to pick up Reba from school. I plopped down in the yard and plucked at the weeds in Linda's flower plots. "My sister likes dahlias, I guess."

"They grow great here, that's why." Nicolás snapped off a couple of drooping hydrangea heads. "These aren't doing so well though. Rain saw to that."

"Yeah, a lot of bad weather, you said."

"Rained for two weeks after you folks left. Too much for harvest season. Put our whole island on edge." He grabbed a stick and dug at the grass choking the hydrangea bushes. "So Don Juan Bórquez tells everybody it's because *Diosmundo*—the earth god, Mother Nature or whatever—is angry."

"Angry about what, for pity's sake?" I couldn't help the tinge of sarcasm in my voice. "Getting too modern out in Chauquelín?"

"In a manner of speaking. Angry because so many people went along with the canuto religion recently."

"Are these islanders so superstitious they actually believe Cole and Linda's tent meetings affected the *weather*?"

"Some are." He shifted on grass-stained knees to meet my gaze. "But the thing is, this old wives' chatter only started after Ramón and Gina refused an offer from Bórquez to buy their land. They're getting the brunt of it right now."

"That's too bad." A finger of chill wind poked through my jacket, and I shivered in spite of the sunshine. "What about the school situation? The Pérezes didn't send their kids here to Mellehue? Their oldest must be a first-grader, at least."

"Síp, they will send Julio to Chauquelín-South. School at the other end of the island. It's a bit far, a good hour's walk, if you remember. But they think he's too young to leave home."

"They're probably right." At that age, I'd hated even staying with my grandmother for a few weeks.

"This business with the teacher, Señorita Marisol, happened from one day to the next." Nicolás's forehead knit with frustration. "She lived alone in a cabin near the school, along the road between Dolphin Bay and North Head. She would not say why, only that Chauquelín was not a safe place and gave her *nervios*. I have my suspicions about who gave her... the creeps, you say?"

"Bórquez? What, he's telling her she can't live so close to his castle grounds?"

"You might think that, no?" He gave the garden earth another stab. "Three other families that lived on Dolphin Bay agreed to sell their property to him last month—either bullied into it or needed the pesos. They've already left the island. And for us, the worst is—"

"He's not still chasing your mother, is he?"

"If he is, he's disappointed. But apparently he owns some land my grandmother's family has used for years. Juan Bórquez's great-grandfather gave the land to his daughter who was Abuelita's mother, something like that. But no proper deed was ever written up."

"So what'd he do, claim your grandmother's land?"

Nicolás's grimace deepened. "More subtle than that. He called on Abuela the day after you folks left. Very polite—he is trying to court my mother, right? But he's a sly snake. Announced he had plans for that land, what we call the north field, but since we had already planted it—"

"The wheat field?" I leaned an elbow back on the damp grass. "Planted! It was almost ready to harvest."

"Precisely. So he would graciously allow my grandmother the use of it this season for a small fee—two hundred thousand pesos, no less. Bucha, Abuela was angry. She shooed us all—Mamá too—out of the house, so I don't know what they said after that. But when he left, she was pretty quiet."

"I don't get it. If he wants to get in with your family, why turn them off? Did you end up paying it?"

"First thing the next day, Abuela sent me to the deeds office in Quenao, the next island." The nerve twitched in his clenched jaw again. "It's true, all right. The land is still registered as Bórquez property. We had to come up with the money or lose the wheat."

"Man, what a scumbag that guy is."

"At least we could pay it, for now," he said. "Sold our rowboat and most of the sheep. But as you say, the whole thing is odd. What does he want with our field? It's not shorefront property, like for his launches. No use for much except farming, and he doesn't plant the land he *has*."

"He's just digging at you, then." I held a handful of weeds in midair. "Nicolás, your grandmother in Santiago said something about Juan Bórquez that I didn't entirely understand."

He looked up. "What did she say?"

"Remember you told me your mother never saw Bórquez when she lived in Santiago?" *Press pause.* Did I have the right to spill that sordid gossip I'd kind of accidentally heard? On the other hand, wouldn't Nicolás want to know about the damage Bórquez's preposterous claims had done to his family years ago? I should warn him, yet...it wasn't my business to blab. "But your grandmother mentioned that he *had* turned up there and caused a lot of heartache for your mother once. I suppose you were just little."

"I doubt even Bórquez could have caused my mother more heartache than the Serranos themselves." He stood and stretched as the whole Peterson clan filed through the gate into the long lane. "I don't know. Marzipan cake is nice and all, but I almost don't want to give Abuela Rosalía the satisfaction of—of enjoying it. They dropped out of my life, and I don't need them now. Wish they would just leave me alone."

*Leave me alone.* His words echoed in my mind with uncomfortable familiarity. I wished my parents would leave me alone, too. A tense knot came back into my stomach as I returned Linda's wave.

Nicolás would rather make his own decisions, be his own person, than suck up to his Santiago grandparents or kowtow to Don Juan Bórquez. Or even to his little tyrant grandmother Luisa. He rebelled against being anyone's pet or puppet.

So would I. Even if I disappointed them, I refused to be forced into the family mold. I intended to choose my own path in life.

I had a feeling Nicolás was mistaken about the Serranos' motives. But I understood him.

Nobody had a right to make you what *they* wanted you to be.

17

*Month 2, continued*

*The autumn weeks marched along in alternating files of drizzle-gray and sky-blue. Like my mixed feelings about life in this time warp...*

A quintessential small town, the fishing hamlet of Mellehue moved at a pace somewhere between the rush of the capital city and the crawl of the outer islands. Everyone not only knew everyone else, but they also knew each other's family history for three generations back. They addressed their mayor by his first name and tolerated the town drunk, usually face down on a bench in front of the post office, with fond amusement. A constant flow of people—neighbors, students, and travelers as well as church friends—knocked at Cole and Linda's door, often from before breakfast until after bedtime.

The swiveled heads about town and gawking looks in school embarrassed me at first. As Nicolás had predicted, my blond hair and blue-green eyes hardly let me pass incognito in a place the size of Mellehue. But as the weeks wore on, people saw me as more of a familiar face and fixture, I figured. I felt less and less like an outsider.

It didn't take long to get to know Mellehue, either. After the first week, the town's sights became so commonplace I stopped snapping pictures. Many afternoons—timed to coincide with Reba's kindergarten dismissal—Linda and I strolled out with Keli to pick up the mail and buy a kilo of crusty mini-baguettes to go with the evening soup. Nothing second-rate about the so-called French *panadería*. The heavenly aroma usually had me drooling my way home. I learned from Reba to stash *manjar* nuggets—tubes of condensed-milk candy—in my pocket as an emergency snack.

After late school activities, Nicolás walked me home and filled the gaps in my education about town. Across the street from the bakery, and diagonal from his boarding house, loomed a charming three-story house, sleek in elaborate oak-stained shingles. I admired the place until I discovered it belonged to Delicia Treviño's fishing tycoon father. *Then* the Treviño mansion resembled Juan Bórquez's manor house on Chauquelín. And as Miriam had implied, Delicia was positioned to scrutinize the comings and goings of nearly everyone in town and of Nicolás in particular.

My new friend Miriam Barrientos's large family lived in a decrepit, mildewed home along the oceanfront, not far from the *palafito* that served as boarding house for the out-of-town schoolgirls, including Nicolás's little sister, Valeria. On both sides of that street, an uncanny number of seedy cantinas thrived. I soon located Delicia's Uncle Moncho's bar, The Chilote Corner.

After sixteen years of dictatorship, Chile's new president was sworn in amid televised fireworks and fiestas the second week of school. Dense as I was about politics, I couldn't help absorbing the buzz.

"What do you think about *el señor* Aylwin?" I asked Nicolás the next morning. "Your family's kind of military, right?"

"I'm glad democracy is back," he said. "Only…it is not the solution to everything, as some people believe."

"What is?"

"You know," he said. "Chile needs a change of heart more than a change of government."

*Oh, you know it. Sorry I asked.*

Though I never would've predicted it that first disastrous day, I enjoyed attending the *liceo insular* once I made a few friends and adapted to its idiosyncrasies. More or less. I'd *never* get used to writing my own textbooks or carting around a ten-pound book bag all day.

Studying in Spanish presented a challenge, too. I grudged having to work so hard at it, but I *was* determined. I made plenty of mistakes, both in speaking and in writing, but I refused to let that shut me up. My patient teachers and classmates helped me improve daily. *Slow but sure.* I aimed to show off a glowing report card from Chile to narrow-minded Principal Martin at Mt. Washington Academy.

I flung myself into a host of extracurricular activities as well. I'd never intended to get so caught up in the local pond, but nobody would let me hang on the sidelines. I joined both a floor gymnastics class after school and the charming folkloric musical ensemble, called Choros y Locos, that Nicolás had told me about in the summer. On Saturday mornings, I even motivated a group of girls to play *baby fútbol*, a Chilean version of soccer on a small field.

Sergeant Major Miriam—she made Mom, even Linda, seem like pushovers—balked at that idea. "It's too rough, Meli. Soccer was never meant for girls' bodies."

"Oh, don't be such a wimp, Miriam. I played it all the time back home. Field hockey too. We'll just be girls playing together, anyway. No guys."

"Good thing," Nicolás said. "What I remember from last summer, she might put some of the guys to shame."

"See, Miri?" His friend Tito Bahamonde chuckled. "Go on, it will be good for you."

Delicia participated in the girls' soccer club too, though since our initial hostile encounter, she only ever acknowledged me from a distance. Okay with me—who needed more friends like Amanda Ellis, anyway? She still hadn't written, and the drama finals were inching closer.

Once I mistakenly referred to Delicia as Delilah, and after that, the name stuck, in my mind at least. Like the devious woman who betrayed Samson, Delicia would've given *me* over to enemies worse than the Philistines without batting an eyelash. All because I was Nicolás's confidante, a threat to the petty status quo of her life.

But, to be fair, Delicia was a feisty soccer player, whether ally or rival.

My friendship with Nicolás grew to include a whole community of teenagers. Miriam had a good heart, even if she was a Miss Prudie, for sure. I also liked Nicolás's easygoing pal, Tito, the lanky string bean to whom Delicia had huffed the first morning in school. Tito, I learned, had first invited Nicolás to Cole's church youth group the previous spring. I rarely saw Nicolás's sister, but he and his brother Marcos often hung out together.

Most of the other guys called Nicolás "Cahuel," as Marcos did. I finally asked him what the nickname meant.

"*Cahuel* is an indigenous Huilliche word meaning dolphin." He angled a half smile at me.

"It fits you, then."

"I suppose, though Marc christened me that long before the dolphins of this past summer. Islanders use the tag for a kid who will not stay out of the water." He grinned. "That was me."

As Miriam had said, Nicolás Serrano De la Cruz was popular with *everybody* despite a reputation for mischief and mutiny. I heard some hilarious tales of last year's pranks. Other stories, such as the weekend carousing, failed to scandalize the missionary's sister, though I certainly didn't confess that to Mother Superior Miriam. But for a guy who carried so much responsibility at home, it was an odd deviation. Perhaps he was letting off steam. In that he was like me.

Even this year, he spent half a morning in the principal's office explaining why he'd sprinkled powdered sugar into the other boys' beds at his boarding house. He spent that afternoon hand-washing sheets. Another time, he was confined to his room for the weekend after filling the boarding-house señora's mate Thermos with *pisco*—a cheap, colorless brandy as common in Chile as water. Linda and Cole missed him at church, and *they* questioned him later about that episode.

"Sorry, Pastor Colin." He shrugged. "Delicia Treviño sent me the *pisco* after we won that game against Castro last week. I did not want it, honest, but I didn't want the other guys to get into it, either."

"For heaven's sake, why didn't you just dump it down the sink, then?" Linda's lips twitched.

"Should have, I guess." He ducked his head. "I couldn't resist trying to get the old crab sputtering. Bucha, never thought she would get *drunk* before she realized it."

I snickered into my sweater sleeve.

Nicolás visited regularly at the Peterson house. The second weekend in March he and Marcos split Cole's winter supply of firewood, and that earned the Serrano boys a standing invitation to Friday night pizza and chocolate cake with our family. After supper, the guys disappeared into Cole's study for a while and did something Linda termed "discipleship"—a Bible class of some sort, I gathered. Nicolás appeared to gobble that up almost as much as the pizza.

"I still cannot get over it," Miriam whispered at a church youth meeting. "You people did *something* to those Serrano boys out in Chauquelín this summer. If you had only known Nicolás last year, Melissa."

"I thought he came to youth group then."

"Oh, I guess he did, a few times." She giggled. "I thought it was for the ping-pong tournament."

My involvement did *not* extend beyond a social level at the church. I attended all the services out of courtesy to Cole and Linda—I granted them that. If they asked me, I even played the guitar or sang occasionally. But I dodged any more participation. When Linda asked me to help in her Saturday afternoon children's Bible club, I countered with an offer to babysit Keli instead.

"I appreciate that," Linda said. "But you show a knack for teaching, yourself. You could develop your own gifts."

I snorted. "When did I ever teach anything in my life? And what's more, when did you ever hear me?"

"I hear you read stories to Reba every night."

"That's different."

"What about a verse every night on Chauquelín?"

I jerked away toward a window and glared down at the patchwork of roofs through the silky curtain of a rain shower. Just because I'd been in a good mood on the island and let Linda talk me into her scheme, didn't mean that she could suck me in further with flattery now. Goodness knew, I resented sitting on the shelf sometimes, but a Bible class wasn't my idea of giving back to the world.

"Please... *don't*, Linda," I said. "Don't go there. It's not my thing at all."

"Or it's out of your comfort zone?"

"Maybe it is. I'm not like you."

"Bless me, as Grandma Rose would say, you have no idea." But my sister took the hint and backed off.

# 18

*Mellehue to Chauquelín*

*Month 3 – April*

*In mid-April, the school's boarding students, including the Serranos, scattered to their homes throughout the archipelago for Holy Week...*

"I hate to be the raincloud on your travel plans, 'cause I'm all for it." I poured out mugs of tea for the family on a bleak Palm Sunday evening. "But isn't it pretty damp and cold now for camping?"

"We can sleep on the launch." Linda smiled. "Not very spacious or glamorous, but we've managed before."

"Yeah, and we really should take advantage of the break." Cole bit into a ham-and-avocado sandwich. "We haven't been back to Chauquelín since the meetings in February. I need to visit some of the other islands, too, but..."

"But those new believers in Chauquelín right now," Linda said. "From what Nicolás tells us, they're not having an easy time of it."

Late Monday afternoon, our group of five anchored in the cove in front of the Pérez and Serrano homes. So different from our arrival in the summer. Then, Ramón and Gina and their children had scrambled to the beach to greet us, and the whole landscape beckoned with rich colors and fragrances and tantalizing promises.

Today, no welcoming committee met us. No welcoming air. Instead, the island's friendly summer face now warned, even threatened. Through a screen of drizzle, the deserted shore looked forbidding. Forlorn, yellow-leaved scrub dripped and drooped at its edge. Cold gray rocks huddled, ready to pounce.

I shivered, trying to shake the sense of impending doom. Silly. Days of dreary weather were bound to depress a person. *And of course, no one's expecting us this time, either.*

It was too wet and too late in the day to venture far, but we zipped into rain slickers and rowed ashore. Ominous clouds hung across the sky, obscuring what little light remained of the day. Fog collected in pockets of white wool along the beach, like something out of Dickens. Definitely more sinister than any *Gilligan's Island* episode I ever watched after school.

Unexpectedly, we came upon Nicolás as we trudged south along the shore road toward the Pérezes'. The dark figure on horseback materialized out of the swirling mist like one of the legendary creatures of the Chilote mythology I'd heard about. He sported a wool hat and sweater, knit in a disarray of gray, olive, and rust. An enormous sack of flour, strapped over the foaming chestnut flanks of the mare, had powdered him from head to foot.

"You look like you're in your natural habitat, Nicolás." Cole's smile gleamed in the dusk.

He swung off the horse and gave the back of his jeans a swipe. "I'm on my way home from the mill with our last load of wheat ground. Sure did not expect you folks here this week, but believe me, it's a relief to see a cheerful face for a change."

"What's the matter?" I asked.

Nicolás shrugged. "Everyone is scared of their own shadow. There's a story going around that evil spirits are causing this bad weather, remember? Sometimes I wonder if my grandmother started it."

"Goodness, they're making a big deal over what's quite normal in Chiloé for this time of year." Linda shook her head.

"Could just be an El Niño season, too," Nicolás said. "But another family sold out to Don Juan Bórquez and left the island last week. Bórquez has been pressuring Don Ramón again to sell. And the Garridos—what little they have left. You remember they trusted Jesus during the tent meetings, too."

"There's more to this than meets the eye." Cole scratched at his chin. "The guy seems to have his sights on controlling the whole western shore. Why? What's his agenda?"

Nicolás's lips drew to a taut thread. "That's what I want to know. Ramón and Gina are pretty upset. They will be glad to see you." He made to remount his horse, then paused, unwinding the reins. "Don Colin, could I use your rowboat while you're at the Pérezes'? I'd like to go over to Dolphin Bay after I drop off this sack of flour."

Right, he'd sold his own boat to pay off Bórquez.

Cole nodded. "It's calm right now in spite of the rain. Going to see your dolphin friends?"

"I'm going to try, but it may be for nothing."

"What do you mean?"

"I've been there—on shore—for the past three nights and they have not come." Nicolás fidgeted with the worn leather straps in his hands. "I only saw them once, on Saturday, and then just a glimpse. They would not come in close."

"That's a bummer," I said. *He must be sick with disappointment.* I was, myself. "You think it's because you've been away?"

"Maybe. But I thought I could go out farther in a rowboat, anyway."

Nicolás rode off into the creeping dusk. The Petersons and I plodded on. The miserable evening was chilly but windless, as Cole had observed. Rain fell in a steady drip. Shrouds of mist drifted beside the path. *Spooky.* Even the fickle sea reflected the leaden gray of the sky—dull, motionless. No longer sparkling turquoise.

Ramón and Gina received us with characteristic hospitality. They draped our beaded jackets on a wire strung over the wood stove and served strong hot coffee with *chapalele,* a bread patty cooked in boiling water, heavier than a dumpling. I grimaced at the rubbery texture and slipped it into my hoodie pocket, but nobody noticed, least of all the Pérezes, distracted as they were by recent events on the island.

Conversation was anything but merry. Every few minutes Ramón bent over the stove to refill his mate cup. Then he paced the bare kitchen floor, trademark brown wool hat tipped over his left ear.

"Bórquez thinks his every whim is law." He took a quick sip through the metal straw. "At first he badgered poor Angélica all the time. Now he is on everyone, especially…everyone who had anything to do with the tent meetings last summer."

In the flicker of the candles—the only light in the dim room—Linda's eyes narrowed in concern. "Do you think that's significant?"

Gina's voice laced with tears. "When he came here, he accused us of breaking the unity of the island. He said he would make us sorry we ever invited you here."

"Break the unity of the island, indeed. Sí, señor, we were *united* before—drinking together, fighting together, crawling together—" Ramón thumped the kettle onto the stove again and straightened up, leaner and more solid than the chimney pipe. "No importa, we will not let Bórquez intimidate us. Pastor Colin, I think his complaint against the evangelicals is only because he fears he cannot manipulate us so easily. Most of the others have given in fast enough."

The talk droned on for a long time. I listened in intermittent stretches until I grew sleepy, feeling like part of a vaguely foreboding dream. The children ran in and out of the room as they played and threw quivering shadows on the walls. The relentless patter of the rain on the tin roof increased to a drum roll that reverberated in my ears like a thousand soldiers marching to their doom.

When we finally headed back to the launch by flashlight, a thick fog blanketed everything. I kept glancing over my shoulder. Was a stealthy figure lurking in the gloom behind us? Once, I jumped, but it was only a dead eucalyptus twig fluttering over the sand. I shook myself. *Chill, girl.* I was getting paranoid.

Our rowboat was tied in its customary spot. Had Nicolás paddled to the north cove? And if so, had he seen his dolphins?

I awoke to the thrum of more falling rain and a more nagging sense of dread. Linda and Cole rowed into shore to visit some other island families while I tidied the cabin of the launch and read stories to Reba and Keli.

Even my nieces pinged off the walls, restless. I tore paper from my science notebook and set them to drawing pictures, while I tried to concentrate on memorizing biology terms in Spanish. In vain. Wasn't it nearly lunchtime?

The *Ambassador's* guardrail chains jangled. A thud followed at the starboard side. I cleared the vapor from the cabin windows and saw Nicolás lurch onto the deck. He leaped over the ropes coiled in the bow and jerked open the cabin door, his face as pale as ashes beneath his tan.

"Nicolás! What's wrong?"

"There's been an accident," he said in a low voice. "Can you come out on deck a minute? I do not want the little girls to hear this."

I grabbed a rain slicker to shield my head and joined him outside. "What? Linda—Cole?"

"No. Bucha, sorry, didn't mean to startle you like that." He took a hoarse breath, gripping the edge of the cabin roof until his knuckles turned bone-white. "It's Jaime Garrido. Our neighbor to the north on Dolphin Bay. You know—their place is right next to Bórquez's. Jaime is...dead. The body just washed up on shore."

## 19

A gasp snagged in my throat. Blood rushed hot and cold through my chest. "D—drowned then? That's awful! How did—?"

"Jaime went fishing last night with Lucho Riveros, and—"

"What! Ramón uuld —" I clutched Nicolás's soaked sleeve. "Ramón was planning to go out with Lucho. Guess he changed his mind after we arrived."

"I know." His voice sounded as hollow as a tomb vault. "Lucho made it to shore. One of the neighbors found him dazed and half dead from exposure on the beach this morning. You should hear what he is blubbering. Says they were chased by the *Caleuche*—you know, Chiloé's ghost ship. Then their rowboat capsized."

"But it was so calm last night. Though super foggy and black... I suppose a guy could imagine anything, or make a mistake." I'd reacted to the *Grimm's Fairy Tales* set myself.

"But upset the boat?" Nicolás's tone bordered on incredulous.

"Well, if they were scared and rushing away... Come on inside. Keli's wailing, and you need to get warmed up."

He shook his head, spinning a shower of moisture off his wool poncho. "No, no, I'm not cold. I actually came to get you and the kids. Don Colin and your sister headed to Garridos' with Ramón and Gina—Jaime was Ramón's cousin. But Don Colin does not want you girls here alone. My mamá invited you to our house for the day."

"Whatever will your grandmother say?" I wiggled my eyebrows.

Our eyes locked.

"We'll find out, no?" Nicolás said. "My mother isn't always so meek, you know. In a crisis, she can show her spirit."

At lunchtime, I discovered a dog-eared paperback on island mythology on the shelf in the Serranos' living room. That afternoon, I skimmed it while I helped Nicolás and Marcos make cider in their apple shed. Helped in theory. After mainly getting in the way, I found an observation post on a chunk of luma wood beside the woven baskets overflowing with beaten fruit pulp.

"'Brilliantly lit up, the *Caleuche* navigates the island channels whenever there is fog,'" I read aloud in Spanish. "'Beautiful party music, the most wonderful ever heard, drifts over the water from the ballroom on board. The ship can travel at a great speed,' etc. Oh, and it says, 'She outfits herself with a crew by attracting sailors or shipwrecked men with her melodious orchestra. Fishing or digging shellfish when it's foggy also runs the risk of having the *Caleuche* seize you for her crew.' Well!"

I looked up. The giant cider press, handmade of wood dark and glossy with age, reminded me of an enormous ironing board with a screw-on plank cover. Thick golden juice poured along a center trough into a bucket as Nicolás clamped the lid down over another basket of apple mash. Marcos emptied the bucket's contents into a wooden barrel on the opposite side of the shed. The air hung heavily with a sweet, ripe odor.

"Well," I said again, hunched on my stump stool. "So this is what Lucho Riveros claims chased him and Jaime Garrido to their deaths? Or at least Jaime's. Do you guys believe in this ghost ship?"

Nicolás grunted. "Of course not."

"It's just an old Chilote superstition." Marcos shrugged.

"Then what? Is this Lucho lying?"

"No." His expression grim, Nicolás fitted the last of the flexible apple baskets into the press. "I saw his face when he told us what happened. I don't think a guy could look like that and be making it up."

"There *is* such a thing as a sea mirage," Marcos said. "You know, like in the desert. Probably what started the legend in the first place."

"Very likely." Nicolás grunted as he tightened the screw.

I lifted the book again. "'The *Caleuche* may disappear suddenly and without warning, becoming invisible or trans-forming herself into a sea lion, a dolphin, or even a trunk of luma. All that remains of the ship is the echo of a mesmerizing melody.' It's a shapeshifter, huh? Maybe that's what happened to your dolphins, Nicolás." I tried to lighten the mood.

"What, they turned into the *Caleuche*?" He straightened up. "It's possible, though… I mean, not the dolphins, but what if this thing Lucho saw really was a ship? It would not be hard to rig up. A few ragged sails, some speakers and strings of lights."

Marcos's rain-gray eyes widened to silver dollars. "Cahuel, you don't mean someone deliberately scared them?"

"Just occurs to me it's not impossible, that's all."

"With everything else going on here," I said, "you get the feeling anything could happen."

Frowning, Marcos picked up two brimming buckets of fresh cider and headed across the soggy yard to the house. I laid the book down and wandered to the half-open doorway, staring after him. It was like peering into a steamed-up mirror.

A powerful north wind had kicked up during the afternoon and whipped the rain into frosty whirls that surged from all directions. The shed's ancient timbers groaned. Its lone window rattled every few minutes, like loose bones of a skeleton. Goose pimples popped on my arms. Was it the chill or my gruesome thoughts?

Could a phantom ship like the *Caleuche* really exist in Chiloé?

I stepped back into the shelter of the shed. "It's sure different here now from the summer." Not so peaceful as I thought. "Doesn't it bother you?"

"Not unless it's planting or harvest time." Nicolás grinned and gave a final effortless crank on the clamp handle. "Rain doesn't affect my mood much. I'm part fish, remember?"

Yep, apparently totally Chilote in his wool hat and sweater and knee-high black rubber boots, elbow-deep in mashed apples. "Sometimes I wonder if you're not a fish out of water," I said.

"What do you mean?"

"I've never known any other guy your age who concerned himself with planting and harvest. It's like you get right into being an island boy." I spoke slowly, groping for words. "Do you…really feel at home here, or is it sort of a role you play?"

Hands on hips, Nicolás said quietly, "I really *am* an island boy, Melissa."

"But you seem…somehow…different on Chauquelín than you do in Mellehue. What were you like in Santiago?"

"Pretty much the same, I daresay."

"But you aren't a bit like anyone else, even here in Chiloé." I crossed my arms and leaned against the doorframe. Rain dripped from the eaves. "I said that to your grandmother in Santiago. She said you were like your father, and he was no Chilote. Who's the *real* Nicolás Serrano?"

I kept my tone light, but my curiosity had been mounting for weeks. We'd clicked that first night in Dolphin Bay, almost instantly. Yet, now that I knew Nicolás better, he was still an enigma. I sensed a complexity, a sort of contradiction, in his character that intrigued me. *Talk about a split personality.* Only it wasn't a psychotic, unbalanced thing, not at all. More like he possessed the privileges of dual citizenship. Like the dolphins, a creature of both air and water.

He didn't answer me right away, just scraped the remaining fruit pulp along the wooden trough and into the pail. "I suppose," he said finally, "that I'm different because I wasn't *born* to Chilote life. I *chose* it. I've come to appreciate the people here. They are tough, independent…they work hard. Somehow they manage to survive in the face of all the odds, even enjoy life. Maybe I'm not like them, but I want to be."

"Wasn't Chiloé a shock to you after growing up in Santiago?"

"I'm not blind, you know. There are negatives here too, I'll admit that. Poverty, superstition, ignorance—incredible ignorance." He paused to empty the last bucket of cider into an open barrel. He fit the wooden lid on and grabbed up a hammer to nail it in place. "When I first came here, almost three years ago now, blending the two ways of life was a challenge. But this is my home now."

I watched him give the nail head a passionate thwack and wondered if he were trying harder to convince me or himself. "Do you have to wash this press out or something?"

"Marc will bring a couple pails of water from the spring." He flashed a wry grin. "I guess this is a long way from Maryland, USA, Melissa Travis. Like going back a hundred years in time, no?"

"Well…"

"You're not adjusting too badly, considering. When I saw you that first afternoon at Don Ramón's, sitting on the fence with that look of disgust—"

"Disgust! No." My cheeks felt warm.

"Ah, sí, señorita, your face is an open book. But I said to myself, 'I'm going to make that girl fall in love with Chiloé in spite of herself.'"

His candor sometimes caught me off guard. I gave him the flicker of a smile. "Then I guess you did that, Nicolás. I was hooked before the end of my first day here."

"The dolphins won you over." He stepped across the shed to stand beside me in the doorway and gazed out at the dismal yard. "And maybe, you were just *meant* to be here right now. Like me. Do you believe in destiny, Melissa?"

"I don't know… You mean, like fate, karma, something like that?"

"Oh, nothing so mystical, not that. Just the combination of circumstances that only God can pull together."

"I—I guess so."

"I begin to realize that God wanted me here. Truthfully, it was *not* easy, being transplanted to Chiloé. But in Santiago I never thought about needing God, might never have come to know Him. So what can I say? Sure, plenty of things here I would like to change. Anybody would. But somehow, over it all, I am sure God has a purpose for putting me in this place, at this time. And you, too."

"Uh-huh." I felt as gloomy as the day. If Nicolás only knew why I was *really* here… Whatever *God* had to do with it, He never meant it as a blessing in disguise. He'd messed with my life for His own agenda. I leaned my head against the doorpost and closed my burning eyes—eyes that apparently betrayed too much.

"There's always a reason, or a lesson, Don Colin says. No blind chess move of fate." Nicolás glanced at me. "You all right?"

*I'd be fine if you'd drop the sermonizing.* "Oh yeah, I—I just think I'll go inside and warm up. And see how your poor mother and Valeria are managing with that herd of kids. Here comes Marc with the water."

# 20

A sprig of eucalyptus simmered in a kettle at the back of the stove and infused the air with a clear, sharp aroma, but the atmosphere in the house was as dense as the fog.

Nicolás's Grandmother Luisa had endured us canuto guests at the noon meal, glaring from her birdlike eyes and making disgruntled clicking noises with her tongue. Afterwards she'd hobbled to her bedroom off the kitchen. Now she refused to come out at all for tea.

I tossed my head. *She's worse than a spoiled child.* If the old queen bee wanted to sulk alone, better for the rest of us.

Señora Angélica didn't share my unconcern, however. She served the Peterson and Pérez children with a nurse's tenderness, but her hands trembled as she spread apple butter on a *sopaipilla* for Keli. Uneasily, she glanced toward the bedroom door. Did she expect Señora Luisa might fly out on a broomstick in a fit of rage at any moment?

Once again, I noticed how striking Nicolás's mother was—her dainty hands and deft movements, her flawless features and dusky complexion. Deanna Troi in Princess Leia hairstyles. I was mixing my movie metaphors again, but seriously... No lack of fashionable clothes or cosmetics could diminish that woman's kind of beauty. Even the mall chicks back home would've envied her. No wonder the young lieutenant, David Serrano Larraín, had defied his family and risked his future to marry her.

Hard to imagine this shrinking violet with enough nerve to face the disapproval of prospective in-laws, though. Now, terror of her elderly mother's displeasure about *anything* paralyzed María Angélica De la Cruz. Almost enslaved her.

I smacked my lips over a glass of the tart, fresh cider. The older kids and I carried our biscuits into the living-dining room and roasted chestnuts and *choritos*—tiny mussels—in the glowing embers of the fireplace, a built-up stone hearth under a hammered-copper chimney hood. The faint cinnamon scent of the luma wood mingled with the shellfish and the smoking chestnut skins.

Outside, the storm raged on. The windowpanes shivered in their thin jackets. The roof shook under the beat of the rain on its back. Still, it felt warm and snug inside as Nicolás and Marcos and Valeria and I, with the five smaller children, huddled around the fire. After the meal, we sipped hot mate. Unbelievable, but I'd grown to like the herbal brew, at least the social aspect of it.

The coziness lasted until Grandmother Luisa tottered, huffing and puffing, into the room on Señora Angélica's arm.

"Abuela, are you having another attack?" Valeria jumped up and dashed to the old woman's other side. Señora Luisa did look sick, her face flushed and her dark eyes glassy.

Señora Angélica rubbed her hands together. "Nicolás, you are going to the wake at Garridos' this evening, dear?"

"Thought I'd go over for a while as soon as Don Ramón and Don Colin get back."

Señora Luisa's voice grated out, harsh as a rusty hinge. "Then I want you to get Juan Bórquez while you are out. He told me last week to call him for a healing liturgy whenever I had trouble again."

Nicolás's eyebrows shot up. "Really, Abuela. I will be glad to go into the village and ask the paramedic to come if it's that serious."

"Indeed you will not! The medic does nothing, only drugs me. Juan has promised me some help that is worthwhile, and I am going to try it."

*Charming lady—not.* She stung more like a wasp than a queen bee.

Señora Angélica licked her lips. "Of course, the herbs are helpful, Mamá. But I think you may have a gall bladder condition, and the medic agrees. You need surgery."

"There, you see, Abuelita," —Valeria patted her arm— "you need to go to Mellehue with us kids next week."

"I have no more use for modern medicine." The old woman shook off her little granddaughter's hand. "Everything that has gone wrong in the island lately is a direct punishment on us for leaving the old customs and the old saints, make no doubt about it."

Nicolás snorted and turned away to poke a batch of scorched chestnuts out of the coals. Marcos chuckled into the mate cup.

"Boys, please." Señora Angélica seemed a little embarrassed by their disregard of Abuela Luisa's opinions. "Nico, don't you think...?"

Nicolás straightened up and stood silent a moment. "Mamá, you know I'd go all over Chiloé for you or Abuela," he said gently. "But a magic ceremony? It's a bunch of superstition. Useless at best—evil, maybe. I cannot see that his rituals have done much good elsewhere, and Don Juan Bórquez is certainly no friend of this house."

Señora Angélica licked her lips, her face like putty. Even if she agreed with her son—and maybe she did—she'd never dare to say so.

Señora Luisa jerked her arm from Angélica and brandished both bird-claw fists. "The devil take you—you canuto, Nicolás Serrano! You will not act so high and mighty when I die in my bed of neglect. And you had better take care you do not follow Jaime Garrido to the grave."

Valeria and I gasped in unison. I inched across the floor and clung to the back of a chair. What a venomous old witch, cursing her own grandson.

"Maybe so, Abuela." Nicolás's voice softened even more, so quiet that I heard a damp log sizzle in the fireplace. He didn't sound angry or afraid, only sad. "But if I follow Jaime to the grave, I'll go to God like him, too. I wish you had that peace."

Señora Luisa spat with the force of a water pistol on her daughter's impeccable waxed floor. "Bah, canuto talk! They have brought all this trouble on themselves, and on the rest of us. Our entire family is put under a curse because of you, Nico."

"Lots of troubles come in life," Nicolás said. "Accidents, sickness, bad weather. That's the world we live in, Abuela. But should not those things lead us to *trust* God, instead of blame Him and turn our backs on Him—" He broke off as a quartet of drenched figures trudged by the living room windows and knocked at the back door.

Grandmother Luisa wheeled around faster than I would've imagined possible and hobbled through the kitchen, muttering. She cast a malevolent glance at Ramón and Gina Pérez, her neighbors for years, before slamming the door of her bedroom.

"Thank you for keeping the children, Angélica." Gina panted, wiping at the water that ran down her face. "Señora Luisa probably hasn't been very gracious about your offer."

Still pale, Señora Angélica nodded and passed the ladies flour-sack towels. "How are Vanessa and the children? I'll go over tomorrow morning."

"Good." Linda blotted her streaming auburn hair. I'd never seen her look so weary. "She's going to need friends, poor woman. She's completely distraught, and those pathetic children..."

"Their situation is indecent at the best of times." Angélica's husky voice quavered. She turned away to crumble herbs into a ceramic pot.

"And now they will suffer even more, hosting this big wake." Ramón accepted a gourd of mate. "It is nothing more than a death cult, sometimes I think."

*A death cult?* Had I understood him right?

Nicolás blinked. "You mean, Pastor Colin isn't doing the funeral?"

"I haven't been asked," Cole said simply.

"But... Jaime was a believer."

"Vanessa claimed to be, too," Ramón said. "When push comes to shove, I guess you find out where people really stand."

"Oh, the pressure from family and neighbors was just too much, I suppose." Gina sighed. "They are going all out—slaughtering the livestock for the feast, the nine-day prayer *novena*, everything."

"What gets me" —Ramón gave Nicolás and his mother a significant look— "is that Bórquez wasted no time trying to grab up what he could not wangle out of Jaime before. Hounding that grieving woman to sell the rest of their land to pay for extra rosaries and such."

"Don Ramón, it could have been you out there with Lucho last night," Nicolás said.

"I know." Ramón looked grave as he drained the mate. "At least, I hope my wife would have more sense. You going over now, Nico?"

"Síp." Nicolás slid into his tall boots again and lifted a thick gray poncho from a hook by the back door.

I surged forward. "Take me with you. For company."

He tilted his head toward Linda and Colo. "I'd love to, amiga, but it's a wild night. Marcos can go with me."

"Actually, if you don't mind this weather, Meli, it wouldn't be a bad idea," Linda said. "Vanessa asked about you today, in all the commotion. She might appreciate your visit."

*Vanessa?* I could barely conjure an image of her face.

## 21

Nicolás had his horse saddled and waiting at the back door before the water had boiled for the late arrivals' tea. Over my raincoat, Señora Angélica slipped a hooded poncho, a virtual work of art handwoven of pure white wool and embroidered in a kaleidoscope of blues and violets. "Wool sheds rain almost as well as rubber." She gave me a weak smile. "And it's much warmer."

With a thick black mane and tail, the chestnut mare was stout and small like most Chilote horses, but even so, Nicolás had to hoist me onto her back behind him. The saddle, a skimpy leather pad topped with a sheepskin, didn't encourage long rides.

The last feeble vestiges of daylight fled as we clopped onto the shell-paved western shore road. No dusk held off the deepening darkness this evening. The storm that had lasted all day grew steadily worse. The tormented sea thrashed the couple of launches anchored in the cove, including Cole's. How could we sleep on board tonight? Would the *Ambassador* be jerked off its moorings?

"Look at the seahorses galloping in," Nicolás said.

I'd never heard surf compared to a stampede before, but I got it. The huge, white-crested waves charged into shore, like… inescapable destiny toward me.

Wind whipped our ponchos into knots and shredded the yellow leaves from the trees beside the path. Rain drove into our faces in sharp sheets, but I bowed my head in the lee of Nicolás's back and avoided the brunt of it. On horseback with him, I didn't feel as nervous as I had last night, walking along the same path. Yet my spine tingled. As if anticipating some strange adventure.

We talked little on the short ride to the Garridos' house. The wind's roar almost cut out conversation anyway. Once, after we crossed the peninsula and emerged onto the open part of the road bordering Dolphin Bay, I poked my head from behind Nicolás's shoulder. "So no dolphins last night, either?"

"No." He sounded glum.

"Do they, like, migrate in the winter? Or could it be the storm?"

"Maybe. We'll find out when it stops." His shrug didn't convince me of his nonchalance.

A blast of wind pelted my cheeks, and I ducked again.

Located at the far northern end of the crescent of Dolphin Bay, the Garrido place cowered in the shadow of Bórquez's mansion. While Nicolás tethered the horse to a derelict fence, I shifted my boots to keep them from sinking into the deep muck. So this was what Linda meant when she'd countered my comments that first afternoon last summer. *You should see some of the other places.* Even in the murk, I could tell this cottage sagged in disrepair, strangled in vines. Garbage littered about my feet. It made Ramón and Gina's yard seem tidy.

Within the shabby little house, a chorus of shrill wails and moans interrupted the monotone of chanting. Hair raising on my neck, I froze before the door.

"It's just the *lloronas*." Nicolás took my arm. "Paid mourners and prayer reciters."

I'd worried about being conspicuous, but only a handful of people even noticed us enter. They murmured, "*Buenas tardes*," in flat voices. Islanders—relatives and neighbors of the Garridos—crammed wall-to-wall, some sitting on benches, most standing. The dirt and disorder of the shack's interior matched its exterior. Of course, the family *was* in the middle of a funeral wake, I reminded myself.

After a languid "Ameeeen," the place exploded with activity. People jostled for space near a brazier in the center of the dingy, smoke-filled room or milled past the rough-hewn pine box propped across two sawhorses in one corner. Jaime Garrido's once-spare frame stretched, stiffly bloated, in its coffin. *Open!* Totally macabre. I pressed a hand to my mouth as my stomach contents shifted.

"We got here at a good time," Nicolás said. "Looks like they just ended a round of prayers."

Señora Vanessa de Garrido and her mother-in-law labored, flush-faced, over the hot stove, handing out plates of boiled potatoes and roast mutton to all who had piled in on them for the evening. A young woman, maybe not yet thirty, Vanessa might once have been attractive. Now she looked old and worn out, even compared to my fuzzy memories of her from the summer. She wore a tacky, pilled black skirt, adjusted to size by a crooked row of rusty safety pins. A black shawl slung carelessly around her shoulders. Her dark hair had been tucked up under a black kerchief, but now hung like damp mop strings around her sweat-glazed face. Eyes red-rimmed and swollen, she served visitors nonstop, while her four children roamed through the crowd, whimpering and filthy.

It was like a bizarre dream.

Turning down the food, Nicolás drew Vanessa aside and spoke with her for several minutes. Then he motioned to me.

I took the old young woman's hand. "I'm so sorry for your loss, señora," I said with all the sincerity I could muster.

Vanessa heaved a shudder. "Thank you for coming, Señorita Melissa." Her eyes flickered and swept the crowd. What was she afraid of? In a croak, she said, "God forgive me, I could not stop this. Don Juan said he would not permit us to use the cemetery if Don Colin had anything to do with the funeral. He said if we broke the traditions, it would go badly for us too, and that Jaime—Jaime's spirit would not—" Her voice cracked, and her face crumpled into her work-reddened hands.

"But Vanessa, you know that's not true," Nicolás said. *Scolded, more like.*

She lifted tear-filled eyes. "I—I know, but—I just could not do that to Jaime's mother right now. And the children…if anything should happen to— Oh, *Señor mío,* I do not know." Her chin quivered as she bowed over the stove again. "Sure you will not have supper?"

"No thanks, we'll get on our way soon. Got to go into North Head. Abuela Luisa needs the medic."

Vanessa flinched and swallowed. "Of course."

"Well, maybe just a cup of coffee then," Nicolás said.

Crowded into a corner by the stove, I gulped down the over-sweetened Nescafé from a chipped cup and watched the scene with rising revulsion. The *lloronas* reigned in black-clad dignity from a bench near the coffin, but most of the other mourners flocked around the iron brazier, chatting and eating with relish. *As if they were at a neighborhood block party.* As far as my limited Spanish could decipher, they were avidly discussing the appearance of the corpse and the strange details of the drowning, which was *terrible* and *muy raro.* Just like those hunchbacked buzzards that roosted on the church roof back in Mellehue, hungry for the treat of a grisly tale.

But nobody paid much attention to the haggard young widow and her wretched children.

The prayer vigil kicked off again, an unbroken chant of recitation, unintelligible, meaningless, to my ears. And to God? Had I ever felt so ambivalent in my life? The atmosphere of grief and gloom, combined with almost a fiesta mood, mixed like oil and water.

I clutched Nicolás's arm as the wailing spiked to a frenzied pitch.

"Vamos," he said. "Don't want you to freak out. I already spent a good part of the morning here, anyway."

Slipping away as discreetly as possible, we bid Vanessa good-bye and edged toward the door. Our stay at the wake had been token-brief, but I was shaky with relief. I'd rather face the storm's battering than this—this horror film.

As I squeezed past the two smallest Garrido kids, I hesitated. More than the grimy faces and snarled hair, the children's bewildered expressions stabbed like daggers in my chest, twisting with a sickening pain. I had no comb or facecloth, nothing of the sort. Fishing in my raincoat pocket beneath the poncho, I found a package of tissues and some caramel tubes. I thrust the candy into their grubby hands and followed Nicolás outside.

"Those pitiful children!" Anger poured out of me like the torrents of rain. "Doesn't anyone care about them? Doesn't anyone even notice that poor Vanessa's about to collapse? Or is it all just a big party, a free meal?"

"It's the island way." Nicolás pulled a plastic tarp off his horse's back and boosted me up once again. "I'd never say their wakes are one of their more admirable customs, *amiga mía*. You heard Don Ramón call it a death cult. Strong words, but sometimes that's what it amounts to. Though I can hardly believe a born Chilote would say that."

"What did she mean about Juan Bórquez? What does he have to do with Jaime's funeral?"

"Oh, he has wormed an appointment as the *fiscal* for the island, sort of a lay leader within the local brand of Catholicism. We have not had a full-time priest here for a century, yet the Diocese of Chiloé has dug its fingers deep in Chauquelín because of a famous—infamous—religious festival they hold here every winter." He nudged the mare onto the path to the village, now a flowing river. "That makes Bórquez the church big shot now, see."

"So he's calling the shots on this funeral and getting away with it."

Nicolás snorted. "Not only that, but profiting from it, if Vanessa goes ahead and sells the rest of the Garrido property to him, like Don Ramón mentioned. Of course, besides the church connection, he's known as a *machi* too, like I told you before."

"A witch—or witch-doctor. How does he justify that unholy matrimony?"

"*That's* what terrorizes people like Vanessa more than anything else." His voice tightened with controlled fury. "I tell you,

I never believed in the devil before I came to Chiloé. It did not take long to change my mind."

"But you're not superstitious, you said."

"No. But a struggle is going on here between darkness and light, between truth and lies, good and evil. It's real. I have always felt it, but now more than ever."

"You'd never realize it just to visit here. I mean, last summer I…I never imagined everything lurking below the surface."

He'd warned me that very first evening at Dolphin Bay, though, hadn't he? But then it seemed like a story, a myth like the *Caleuche*, even his own suspicions run wild…

A sharp whistle, like Nicolás's ocarina flute, keened on the wind. Maybe it *was* only the wind. I shivered.

He swung around on the makeshift saddle. "Melissa? Don't mean to scare you. Chauquelín has its charm, too. I'm just thinking out loud, I guess."

"I know, it's okay. Wish I could do something to help besides just being a sounding board."

"Well, that's something. It does help."

But I couldn't help, and I realized it, though Nicolás might not. I had nothing much to give him. If I'd floundered talking about God, then I was beyond over my head dealing with diabolical spiritual forces. I had zero weapons to fight a battle against something that wasn't even flesh and blood. The unbearable, intangible tension mounted, and I felt absolutely powerless.

"I feel so frustrated sometimes." Nicolás echoed my thoughts. *Uncanny.* "I mean, it's a pack of lies what Bórquez and his cronies have told Vanessa about not being allowed to bury Jaime in the island cemetery and bringing bad luck to the family if they break the traditions. She's not thinking rationally. But what can I do? Pressure a poor widow, the same as everyone else?" He shook his head, spraying raindrops from his wool hat into my already wet face. "Does not seem right just now. She has had enough stress for one day. But Bórquez and the devil win this round, I'd say."

"Maybe you or Ramón and Gina can talk to her later."

"That will help her personally, yes, but don't you understand? *Tonight* is when the whole island watches to see if we canutos are serious, or if we just go on the same as always, like everyone else. Tonight people are getting the idea that when a crisis comes, faith in Christ—the Christ of the Bible—makes no real difference. Means little or nothing." An edge of dejection, almost desperation, sharpened his voice.

Abruptly, his zeal for Vanessa de Garrido's religious convictions needled me. Why was it so important anyway? For pity's sake, couldn't the woman change her mind and do what she wanted—whatever was less hassle, at this point—without it becoming a crime, a-a mortal sin?

"Don't get so bent out of shape," I said. "It'll work out in the end. Live and let live, that's my philosophy."

A blast of wind tore the wool hood back from my face as Nicolás whirled to glare at me. In the grayness, I felt, rather than saw, the blaze in his eyes. "Live and let live!" He snorted, contempt palpable. "Bucha, what's wrong with you? You mean, die and let die. Because *that's* how it will work out in the end. The strong man wins, and the rest of the islanders take the slow boat to hell."

I fought an urge to slap him. But still, I cringed beneath his scorching words and gaze. "Geez, Nicolás... it's only a funeral."

"*Sí-po*, only heaven or hell, only God or the devil, right. Come on, amiga. God is light, God is love and life. Did you see *anything* pure or beautiful back there at the Garridos'? One drop of hope?"

"No, but..." *God is light, and in Him is no darkness at all.* The words of a verse, memorized back in what seemed like another lifetime, rose from my subconscious. Why did that come to my mind?

And what on earth had Nicolás been *doing* in Cole's study for the past six weeks? Soaking up the Bible like a sponge? *Oh, please...*

Icy rain trickled down my back. "Whatever you say, hothead." I tugged my hood back up.

As we left the partial shelter of the woods, a new cloudburst dumped an even heavier torrent of rain on us. The horse slogged on. Our path now wound down a boulder-strewn crag to the cluster of quavering lights that was the island's main village, North Head. A river the color of creamed coffee rushed down the hill under the mare's hooves. Cold, wet, and irritated, I shrank behind Nicolás's shoulders. The boisterous wind made talking impossible here, but an awkward silence hung between us anyway—a curtain thicker than the mist.

# 22

We clomped into town. It took only a few minutes to locate the paramedic's cottage, annexed to the island medical outpost, and discover the note, dated yesterday, tacked to the door: GONE TO MELLEHUE ACCOMPANYING EMERGENCY CASE.

Nicolás groaned. "Why now, of all times?"

"Will you consider getting Juan Bórquez then?" I asked. Not that I liked the skunk either, but we had to do *something*.

"Never. At least, *I* won't—Mamá might be bullied into it, I suppose." He guided the horse back up the steep hill out of the village. "I don't trust the guy, Melissa, and he's not going to hang around our house if I can help it."

"Third cousin or not, huh?"

"Look, I'm sorry to sound so harsh. But for some reason—whatever his agenda is—Bórquez is pushing these old customs, like healing rituals, and it's not *just* Chilote culture—it's related to spirit worship. It is not innocent, it's poison. We cannot just be neutral."

"But what about your grandmother then? You don't think she's really ill?" Sure, Señora Luisa was a spiteful crank, but she *was* old.

He threw me a grin. *"You're* going to be really ill by tomorrow. What a night to be out."

"Seriously." I liked the Nicolás who teased instead of preached.

"Sí, Abuela's sick—sometimes. Her gall bladder trouble seems to get worse. But other times, she has these spells when she wants to manipulate my mother—control her, you know, to get her own way about something."

"I can sort of see that." I bit my lip.

He sighed. "Mamá never used to be like that. I guess after Papá's death, and everything else that happened in Santiago then, she could not cope. She has no will to resist my Abuela Luisa's domineering, too. But whatever the case, Bórquez has no legitimate medical help to offer Abuela. Not much we can do except pray."

"Nicolás! What's that up at the top of the hill?" Under the trees ahead of us and to the left of the path, the orange light of a bonfire pierced the gloom, casting eerie shadows. Showers of sparks shot upwards.

"Who—who is it?" I repeated. Excited voices resonated, though muffled by the rain.

Nicolás made his unique rumble of disgust and reined the horse a moment. "We'd better go carefully here. I never imagined they would start this early."

"Are they drunk?"

"Oh, they will be drunk no doubt before it's over, but that's not all." His voice dropped to a ragged whisper as he took a deep breath. "It's a *tropón* dance. I heard some of the men at

Garridos' say Don Juan Bórquez had organized it for tonight with the North Head elders. I did not realize they would hold it by the road, though. We must have just missed them earlier."

"What's a tropón dance? Never heard of it."

"It's another kind of magic ceremony performed by machis like Juan Bórquez. An appeal to the spirits for sunshine and good weather."

"Oh, the reverse version of the North American rain dance." I was tempted to snicker. "They can't be serious about this?"

"Dead serious, I'm afraid," Nicolás said soberly. "It has not been done for half a century in the Big Island, I suppose. Probably many years here too—I've never seen one before. But you know Bórquez and his revival."

My giggle slid to hysteria. This evening adventure was turning into more of a nightmare than a novelty. The whole island gave me the creeps.

Suddenly I felt chilled to the bone, tired and soaked and sick to my stomach. My ribcage ached. My knees were knobs of ice. My backside had numbed a while back too, though that had nothing to do with cold. "So why don't we just ride past this bunch of loonies and go home? You can't be thinking of stopping them."

"No, but I might try if you weren't with me." His grim voice told me his jaw was clamped, though I could barely make out the outline of his head in front of me. "Our passing by might be challenged, is all. But what else can we do? Vamos."

The storm and the boisterous crowd muted our winding approach up the crag. From the horse's back, we could see dark forms flit back and forth in front of a string of bonfires, silhouettes on a floodlit stage. But none of the motley participants in the tropón dance noticed *us*. At least a hundred people had gathered—half the village's population. Age and sex blended, indistinguishable in the shadows.

Except for the notorious Don Juan Bórquez himself. Nicolás pointed him out as we neared the final curve before clearing the summit. "That's him on the stump by the eucalyptus tree. Directing the show."

With all I'd heard about the man, I half expected horns and a pitchfork. But Juan Bórquez looked as ordinary and unimpressive as I'd first seen him. He was so short that the stump raised him only slightly above the crowd as he waved his stubby arms and shouted. Rain dribbled in streams through the steel-wool beard covering his face. A ratty wool sweater stuck to his barrel chest.

"Looks like that ugly mountain goblin, the Trauco, that I read about in your book today." I didn't feel flippant—not at all—but it helped loosen the apprehension knotted in my chest.

Nicolás chuckled. "How flattering. He does at that."

The event got underway in earnest now. A squad of men dragged a brazier into the center of the gathering and heaped it with shovelfuls of blazing coals from the fires. Slowly—he believed in drama—Bórquez drew a gray-white ball of dough, the size of a skull, from a gummy plastic bag. He kneaded it in his sausage-like fingers.

"That's the tropón, the top," Nicolás said. "It's made from a special concoction of potato starch and salt. Watch, he will throw it into the coals. If it jumps up and down in the fire, that's supposed to mean the weather will clear."

I gawked in morbid fascination, repelled by the whole primitive affair, yet unable to tear my gaze away. As Bórquez's bellow carried through the swathes of mist, the flesh on my arms crawled. My grip on Nicolás tensed.

"Lift your *clamor* together with me, neighbors and brothers, to our Dios-mundo, the god of this world!" Bórquez brandished the potato dough ball over his head as if it were a potent grenade instead of a limp lump of paste. "Let us unite and beseech him to rid our island of the outsiders who seek to destroy us and our ancient traditions. We want no change! We must respect and cling to the good customs passed down from our elders. Refuse the new ways. They leave us weak against the evil forces that cause such misfortunes as we have seen on our island recently. *Ayyyyy*, let us beg our Dios-mundo to return the sun to our land! He has great power, powerrrr!"

His rabid speech climaxed in gibberish. The crowd responded with a rhythmic recitation.

"What's he saying now?" I wriggled on the seat pad.

"Don't know exactly, but it sounds like the old Huilliche language. Probably an incantation of some kind."

Like a druid offering a sacrifice on an altar, Bórquez heaved the tropón into the waiting brazier. The crowd's chanting rose to a crescendo and then fell silent as the ball sizzled. Smoke smarted in my eyes.

A few seconds later, the crowd gasped and then roared. I inhaled sharply too. The spinning top of potato starch, now encased in a sooty brown crust, leaped several feet into the air. It continued to bob up and down amid berserk cheering. People popped jug and bottle corks and guzzled without restraint.

"How—how does it do that?" My breath was trapped in my throat.

Nicolás shrugged. "Some say it's the salt reacting in the heat. Whatever. People believe what they want to believe. They don't make a difference between what's natural and what's satanic."

All at once, the crowd started to sway and whirl in unison.

"The so-called tropón dance," Nicolás said. "Imitating the top in the fire."

His eyes bulging in the smoky firelight, Bórquez hopped down from his stump platform. He caught the ball in his bare hands. Tearing off the outer layer of crisply cooked dough, he presented pieces of it to two men standing nearby. Then he tossed it back to bounce again in the coals.

"Saint Peter and the keys to the kingdom," I murmured.

Nicolás nudged his mare. "Now's as good a time as any to ride past this. Vamos, maybe we will not be noticed in the commotion."

*Wishful thinking.* Almost as soon as we emerged from our hiding place in the curve, Bórquez spotted us. While most of the crowd were too immersed in their chanting and dancing, his shifty red eyes missed nothing.

He stalked like a bulldog into the path and hailed us. "*Vaya*, Nicolás Serrano has come to join us. Welcome, my son."

*Oh, that was sly.*

"I am not your son," Nicolás said through gritted teeth. Was he aware of Bórquez's malicious lie and its aftermath of turmoil in his family?

"No offense, boy. Why not stop and get in on the fiesta?" Bórquez eyeballed me. "Who is the little lady with you this evening?"

He hadn't even acknowledged my existence during our previous run-ins, but he must know who I was by now. Some of the dancers broke away from the circle around the brazier and straggled over to flock around their leader. If I'd been alone, I would've bolted in panic. My chest ached from holding my breath.

His chin high, Nicolás prodded the horse forward. "She is a friend. And I am not here to join in your fiesta, Don Juan. I have been on an errand for my mother and am on my way home. If you would let us pass?"

"I am sure my *tía* Luisa would be happier to know you were here with me rather than squandering your youth in canuto meetings." Bórquez kept his bulky frame planted in the middle of the path. Was he determined to provoke Nicolás? "You tell her you saw the tropón dance and that we are confident Dios-mundo will soon end the storm. That will please the old lady."

"I won't tell her I had anything to do with this cheap theatrical." Nicolás's even voice still managed to penetrate the deadening shroud of rain. "You might believe your tropón dance will stop the rain, but all these things are under God's control, God's alone."

Whatever happened to the idea of low-key and discreet? I tightened my grip on his arm. The crazy guy was cruising toward all-out confrontation.

"Why don't you people trust in the one true God, the Creator?" he said. "The heavenly Father, instead of these... these myths?"

Bórquez's mouth worked, chewing steel wool, as he spun to face his horde of followers. "He dares to mock the traditions of our fathers!" he cried above the wind's bluster. "Just as

I told you, these people who want to change the old ways are sneaking in here, too. *This* is why we have tragedies like Jaime Garrido's drowning. We must put a stop to these attitudes of rebellion."

An indignant rumble swept through the throng as Bórquez kindled their idle curiosity into definite hostility. He was a propaganda expert, I gave him that. Violence crackled in the air.

Nicolás was too perceptive not to sense it, too. Yet, as I shrank behind him, he sat straight as an iron rod in the saddle and stared Bórquez down. "You insist on practicing these things that defy the God of the Bible, and you think that's not rebellion? You're supposed to be a *fiscal*, Don Juan. Do you know what Saint Peter says? That the blood of Christ has freed us from the vain traditions handed down from our forefathers."

I gasped aloud at his audacity. Along with a dozen other people.

"You insolent puppy!" Bórquez shook his pudgy fist in the air. "Smart aleck, eh? Guess I know as much about God and the Bible as any cocky canuto brat."

"Then do you obey Him? Because if you really believed the Bible, you would turn from these dark rituals and—"

"You babble about things you don't understand, boy. You don't know what you are getting into, who you deal with—"

Nicolás snorted. "Believe me, I know enough."

"You want to throw away our whole Chilote culture for this canuto garbage. Don't you realize that these poor people need—"

"What, we *need* drunken brawls and demon worship?"

Nicolás was bold as a puma if not exactly tactful, but a wild whoop from the fringe of the crowd interrupted him then. Men and women screamed in excitement and pointed frantically across the wooded central ridge toward the eastern shore of the island. There, in three separate places, fluorescent blue and scarlet flames glinted through a haze of smoke and drizzle.

"What now?" I said. The diversion bought Nicolás a respite, at least.

"I don't know, but it's sure strange, since no one lives on that side of the island."

"Vamos, then! What are we waiting for, *compadres*?" One man's thunderous bass boomed above the tumult. "Let us mark the spots before the fires die out, and tomorrow we are rich."

A woman squealed, "The flames are red! That means the treasure is gold!"

"The blue means silver."

"Do we need to take anything?"

"That's later when we dig, imbecile!"

"Why can we not dig tonight?"

Nicolás slapped his forehead and slumped. "Oh, bucha, it's another old myth. They're saying those fires on the deserted side of the island show the location of buried treasure." I felt him trembling now that this new foolishness had distracted from his clash with Juan Bórquez. "Oh, come on, neighbors, *think*."

"But what about the evil spirits that guard the place?" Another voice, slurred with booze, spoke up.

"Aw, Don Juan will pray to the Virgin and she will protect us." Rowdy laughter of approval met that suggestion. "Or maybe he should lead the way."

Bórquez again mounted his stump in the epicenter of the chaos and screwed his grizzled lips into a smile. "I must stay here to finish the tropón dance. But I will call upon Dios-mundo for your success, *vecinos*. Not Christ or the Virgin, but our Dios-mundo owns the riches of this world."

"What blasphemy," Nicolás muttered.

Bórquez led his fan club in a repeat of their weird chant. To drunken cheers, a horde of men struck out eastward down the dark ridge.

"Vamos." Nicolás turned his horse with such a jerk that the poor animal stumbled and nearly lost her footing.

But it was *not* Nicolás's tug on the reins that sent the mare reeling. The ground beneath her hooves, already coursing with water, became a heaving sea. Rocks in the rugged face of the hillside dislodged, rolled down the path, crashed into the ocean below.

The commotion among Bórquez's sheeplike groupies erupted in full-blown panic now. Tipsy dancers toppled in the press. Others staggered toward the road, shrieking.

"A tremor?" My stupid question needed no answer. I felt like I was rocking in the topsy-turviest ride at a theme park. But I'd already been too frightened to be more so.

As abruptly as it began, the shake was over.

In the seconds of eerie hush that followed, Nicolás urged the horse to a brisk canter southward. We didn't wait to witness what might happen next at the tropón dance. But before we reached the woodsy part of the road, near the entrance to Bórquez's private lane, a flying stone hit the patient mare's hindquarters with a sickening smack.

Only inches from my back. The animal broke into a terrified gallop.

For the first time in the two months since I'd decided to stay in Chile, it crossed my mind that the tame monotony of Baltimore's suburbs had its advantages. This beautiful island was not what it seemed. Evil hid beneath the tourist-brochure allure.

Maybe it was time to rethink my strategy and move on. This was getting just too creepy.

## 23

Overnight, an ever-so-slight shift in the weather confirmed Juan Bórquez's reputation as a powerful machi among the more gullible islanders. The wind switched from north to northwest. The rain relented a little. By late morning, showers alternated with patches of weak sunshine and glimmers of rainbows.

But the mood on the island hardly lightened at all.

I volunteered to babysit my nieces and the three Pérez children while Linda and Cole accompanied Ramón and Gina to the noon burial of Jaime Garrido. They returned to the cottage at teatime in damp clothes *and* spirits.

"Folks aren't as friendly as last summer," Cole said. "I don't know if it's us or the drowning accident or what."

"Bórquez is behind it, you can bet on that. People have been warned against you, Pastor Colin." Ramón poured a fresh gourd of mate and took a long sip. "Not everybody goes along with him deep down, but most are too afraid to stand up to him openly."

"Nobody except Nicolás. That boy has more nerve than an *loco* poacher." Gina punched at a mound of rising dough in a wooden tray. "The rest of us could use a share."

"I shudder to think what could've happened to you two last night." Linda shivered and shook her head. "Nearly hit with a rock. I never dreamed of such danger here."

"How did the funeral go?" I asked, to change the subject. My sister blamed herself far too much for our run-in with Bórquez last night. Yeah, it was scary all right, but no point freaking over it now. I didn't want her mother-hen clucking.

"We didn't go into the mass," Linda said. "But we waited and walked with the family to the graveside. The Serrano boys helped with the shoveling."

"Truth is, hardly anyone was there except the old circuit priest from Quenao." Gina sniffed. "All their hype about island solidarity, and where in everyone when we have a real tragedy? Digging for buried treasure in the woods. Buried treasure!"

It did sound like a corny fairy tale. "They're really off on this wild goose chase, are they?"

"Síp, headed out this morning." Ramón passed Cole the mate cup. "Armed with picks, spades, and a host of good luck charms."

"But what will they find?" I asked incredulously.

"Nothing. Mud and stones. Tonight they will return whining about evil spirits and cursing the canutos."

"Ramón, would it be all right to hold our Bible study this evening?" Cole said. "We didn't plan to leave here until Friday, but after what's happened, I think we'd better let the uproar settle and come back to visit another time. This afternoon Nicolás asked me to take his grandmother out to the hospital when we go, so that clinched it for me."

"Seems Señora Luisa is doing quite poorly today," Linda said.

"She has her bad spells." Gina patted two round loaves of bread onto a metal pan. "But if Nicolás can actually persuade her to go to the Castro hospital, or even Mellehue, it will be a miracle. I bet she has not left the island in twenty years."

"I should let them know our plans have changed then," Cole said.

"We can invite the boys to the study tonight too, if they can come," Ramón said. "I'll run over to the De la Cruzes' as soon as we have tea."

"I'll go." I hopped up. "Have to return the mythology book I borrowed yesterday, anyway."

"Don't come back alone after dark, Meli." Linda shivered again. "This island doesn't feel safe anymore."

I took advantage of a break between showers to make the ten-minute walk to the Serrano-De la Cruz home by way of the shore road. Late afternoon gloom already gathered over a misty, rain-drenched world as I knocked on their back door and eased it open.

I totally did not expect the scene I found there. Don Juan Bórquez himself stood at the stove, stirring a panful of wet ashes. He looked every bit as sinister in the dying daylight as he had last night in the dark. His swarthy, bearded face bent over the metal basin in concentration, his thick body swaying with the swirls of the wooden spoon.

Loud groans and grunts came from Señora Luisa's bedroom. Angélica slumped in the doorway, weeping mutely. Marcos and Valeria clutched each other, wide-eyed, in the shadows of the hall. And like an enraged lumberjack, Nicolás stood fists-on-hips in the center of the room, still wearing boots and a striped gray poncho beaded with moisture, as if he'd only just arrived from the village.

*Whoa.* In a startled split second, I recognized the awkward situation I'd stumbled into and made to duck out again.

But Nicolás saw me and waved his hand. "Melissa."

"Uh, sorry, bad timing," I said. "I'm out of here."

"Don't go. I need your help."

"My...my h-help?"

"I'm trying to convince Mamá and Abuela that we need a doctor here more than magic." Despite his calm voice, a twitching muscle in his right cheek betrayed agitation.

Her hands fluttering, Señora Angélica glided across the kitchen. "My dear, would you like a cup of tea?" She crumbled a sprig of dried mint into a china teacup, poured hot water over the leaves, and drew me to the table. "Of course Mamá must go to the doctor in Mellehue too, Nico. But she is so set on giving this a try that I thought it could not hurt. Please, darling, she is *so* sick and if Juan can help at all—"

"How many times must I tell you, my dear Gela," Bórquez said without glancing up, "that doctors do not understand this type of sickness. Only a machi can cure the *empacho* your mother has. A trip to Mellehue would be useless."

"How can you lead the church and participate in this—this *sorcery*?" Nicolás said. "Instead of all the hocus-pocus, why don't you just pray for her in Jesus's name?"

Bórquez looked up then, a ring of angry scarlet wrapping his bulldog neck. He really did remind me of the Trauco, the grotesque troll character the Chilote mythology book blamed for out-of-wedlock pregnancies. No wonder Angélica had fled from Chauquelín the first chance she got as a teenager.

And this guy fantasized that he was a candidate for David Serrano's replacement? *Seriously?* Nicolás once remarked that Marcos resembled their father. At only thirteen, sturdy, angel-faced Marcos was taller than Bórquez already. *And mega-cute*—certainly showed every promise of becoming a more-than-attractive man. I couldn't imagine two people more different, and never mind the looks. His dubious intentions made Bórquez a black-hearted creep.

It didn't seem to matter whether Angélica accepted or rejected him, however. He forced himself on the whole household anyway. I cringed as Bórquez narrowed his eyes on me now, as if he'd noticed my presence for the first time.

"Eh, saw you last night at the tropón dance, señorita." Calculating malice lurked behind his leer. "You're not from around here."

*Uh, definitely not.* "No, I—" My voice came out as parched and quivery as a leaf in a dust storm. I swallowed and tried again. "I'm a visitor here, but—"

"Leave her alone," Nicolás said.

"Ah, the *canuta* girlfriend." Bórquez returned to stirring the ashes, as though he dismissed the entire subject of Nicolás and me, God and religion in general. "Our fathers' ways are more ancient than even the Church," he said. "Only the old tongue is used for healing rituals. The name of Jesus would hinder, I think. Angélica, can you not do something about your boy's impertinence?"

She lifted her delicate hands in helpless appeal to them both.

Nicolás wasn't giving an inch, though. "The name of Jesus is a hindrance? Bucha, then what you do is from Satan's power, not from God."

"Opinions of a foolish youngster who spends too much time with the canutos." Bórquez's mouth twisted, but his tone was bored. Now that he'd won the argument over Señora Luisa's illness, last night's belligerent aggression faded to gruff disinterest.

I sat and gulped my tea. I almost liked this herbal stuff now, and maybe it would settle the butterflies. I'd left the Pérezes' before Gina's bread emerged from the oven, so I was starved. Except for this terrible foreboding in my stomach. I shouldn't be here; there was nothing *I* could do.

Bórquez lumbered toward the bedroom door with the bowl of pasty ashes. "If Señora Luisa is ready, we will begin the ritual bath now. Come along, Angélica, you will see this truly works. Tomorrow your mother will be better, and in two more days—miraculous."

"What does that prove?" Nicolás shot after him. "She usually gets better within a couple of days. So you will brainwash her into believing it's because of *you*?"

Tomblike stillness hovered over the kitchen. I licked my lips. "Nicolás, I, uh, came to—"

A guttural croon, like the yowl of a wounded animal, shattered the momentary quiet. I jumped and dropped the book from my hands. Dear God, did that unearthly noise tear from the grandmother or her shaman healer? Marcos and Valeria vanished like ghosts seeking a less haunted house.

Nicolás sprang to pick up the book. "You finished this already? I'm sorry to drag you in here and put you on the spot. I just thought…a bit of moral support…"

"I—I want to help you, but—" I really did. I'd never told him the unvarnished truth about my life back home, maybe because I didn't want him to know my ugly side. Part of why I liked Nicolás so much was because he seemed to think of *me* so highly. Put me on a pedestal, for once in my life.

So I wanted to pay back the favor—help him as he'd helped me. Get off the shelf and do something that mattered, also for once in my life. Make a difference in his life. God knew it wasn't easy for him.

"It's not easy," he said.

*Do I hear that echo again?* "But I can't, amigo—I've never been good at this spiritual—"

"I can't convince Abuela that all this dark, mystical stuff has nothing to do with God. Even Mamá, with her upbringing here in the islands... Sometimes I wonder if they'll ever change." His expression sagged.

I could hardly focus on what he was saying above the rise and fall of Bórquez's rasping chant in the next room. The cadence of the Huilliche incantation pulsated in hypnotic waves through my ears, into my chest. Cold prickles pierced my body all over.

"I'm sorry," I said. "I wish I could do more. But I'm not a missionary like my sister."

Wasn't that what everybody said to me? "Why can't you be more like Linda or Jenny?" Not that I wanted to be. My worst fear was that I'd end up a preachy-prude clone of my siblings.

Still, they had talents I didn't. I was the carefree baby sister, the doted-on family pet, but... Somehow I always elicited a *but*. But—I was too thoughtless, too naïve, just too young to be of any use.

*Qué será, será. Right, Mom?* Certainly too silly and immature to change the world. Especially a treacherous world like this one.

I drained my teacup and bit my lip, trying to fight off a tide of inexplicable panic. "He's right, I'm not from here. I don't belong, I don't understand—"

"No, but you belong to God. You understand the truth—"

Bórquez clomped out to the kitchen again. "Next we make up a purge of *huinque* herbs. You know, you could learn to prepare this yourself, Gela, and save me the time."

"I brewed some *bailahuén*." Señora Angélica trailed behind him like an ethereal shadow. "That's good for—"

"Bah, you know nothing." He snatched a leafy branch, a sort of fern, off the oilcloth-covered table and froze. "Is this your cup, señorita?"

"Ye-es, why?" The empty teacup, gold-rimmed aqua with pink roses, perched on its saucer beside me. "I mean, it's Señora Angélica's. I just drank—"

He grabbed the cup and waved it under my nose. "I read tea leaves. Fortunes, *sabe?* And—" He smirked through his bushy, gray-streaked beard as he ogled me. "So sorry, but you should know. You will die here. In the island."

"You lying devil!" His face dark as a thundercloud, Nicolás draped his arm around me. "Don't listen to him, Melissa."

I shook my head. "Of course not. I don't believe in that hogwash." *Do I?*

"The leaves do not lie, children." Waving the *huinque* branch at us, Bórquez clanked the cup back onto the table. "They just do not always tell when or how, see."

Nicolás's blazing eyes sought his mother's. "Cooperating with this sorcery is all wrong, Mamá. The devil only wants to hurt and destroy people in the end, and you know Don Juan isn't the least interested in really helping us, either. He only wants to use us, control us."

"But your grandmother—"The poor woman sobbed like a torture victim now. "Melissa, I am so sorry."

"Please, Mamá, let's trust God instead. He loves us. He promises never to abandon us. Isn't that right, Melissa?"

I gulped and nodded—feebly.

Bórquez chortled. "Bah, you are nothing like the rest of your clan, señorita. Just a puny little girl, like Angélica here. In fact, you—your life—are as flimsy and useless as this teacup of hers." With the flick of a pudgy finger, he nudged the Limoges cup and saucer off the table's edge. "Ooops."

The reverberating tinkle of antique porcelain arrested the players in our drama for a second. I stared at the floral-patterned shards scattered over the wooden planks. Nicolás, too, scowled at the floor, his mouth compressed in a hard line. And his mother literally wrung her hands while silent tears sheeted over her fine-boned cheeks.

A high-pitched wail from the bedroom punctuated the hush. Bórquez turned to the stove with a cackle. "*Ay*, it wasn't a wedding present from the noble Serranos, was it, *querida*?"

"No, it was her great-grandmother's," Nicolás said, his voice strangled. "On the noble De la Cruz side."

I whirled and fled the house. Whether a demon or an angel chased me, I had to get away from here.

# 24

I ran wildly, heedless of the renewed shower, straight down the lane and north onto the road. Ramón and Gina's warm, sane home lay in the opposite direction, but right now I didn't want to see *anyone*. Naturally they'd all ask questions, and I just couldn't face their kindness and concern. I couldn't even spell out to myself the why behind the nameless dread that seized me in the Serrano kitchen. But I couldn't take any more of that horror film.

Finally I sank, sides heaving in painful spasms, onto the boulder loveseat at Dolphin Bay. Here, only a couple of months ago, I'd first watched Nicolás swim with his aquatic pals. The dolphins were gone now, along with the rest of the summer's delights.

Another detail for that all-but-forgotten essay: I'd learned things were *not* what they seemed then. Wretchedness and tragedy nipped at the heels of those happy days. Tension and terror stalked after the simple joys of living. The fiend who owned that cedar-shingled mansion, tucked high on the hillside behind me, had a lot to do with it. I knew he wasn't there right now, but I still couldn't shake the sensation that that Trauco troll peered over my shoulder.

It wasn't only Bórquez, though. Instead of sunshine, this cold, miserable rain battered the island. Would I ever completely dry out again? I stretched my legs in front of me, sneakers and jeans both spattered with mud. Webbing now grew between my toes, I suspected. Impatiently I pushed back the wet blond frizzles that escaped the hood of my rain slicker.

*Yes, Nicolás, I did fall in love with your Chauquelín. But I think it's time to break up.*

Even in yesterday's torrential rain, I'd thrilled to the reckless beauty of the storm—the thrashing sea, the howling wind and swirling fog. Now I rested my head against the rock and watched the mist clumping along the shore again, spreading out like an ermine stole on a lady's shoulders.

Beach scrub quivered and trickled with sparkling teardrops. Blackberry bushes bowed heavy laden under their burden of plump purple fruit. Through the slate-gray curtain of cloud, two brave stars shone while a gull screeched a greeting and winged up to meet them. The steamy fragrance of damp earth and woods and salt permeated the air. I drew a lingering breath. It was still lovely.

But ever since last night's encounter with the darkness, it all felt too bizarre…too desolate. Not that I didn't care about these people—I did—but Chiloé's hideous underbelly was getting to me. And after Bórquez's death threat today, maybe I'd better backpedal home as fast as I could—with or without the dazzling transcripts I aimed for. Of course I didn't believe tea leaves could influence my fate, but that was the drop that overflowed the cup, as Chileans put it.

Back in February I assumed I'd just hang at Linda's until my friends got up the guts to share the blame about the oranges incident. After all, Amanda knew how much the dramatic monologues meant to me—we'd qualified for the next round together. But the date for the competition finals was fast approaching, and it looked like my hope of a winning speech would dwindle into just another letdown for my family of overachievers. Like my maverick choice of the guitar instead of a more highbrow instrument. Or the spelling bee I'd once let Candie Davenport win.

The drama disillusionment aside, I'd figured something bearable might open up in Maryland before the new school year started in September. Until then, I could muddle through at the Mellehue *liceo*.

But the plan wasn't working—I really *would* die if I spent much longer in this looney bin. Maybe my Chilean-island lark was coming to an early end.

Yeah, Mom and Dad, home, church, and whatever school I got stuck with—all had their downside. But compared to this unreal world I found myself in now, Baltimore at least offered sensible familiarity. I could finish the fall trimester in Mellehue for Linda's sake and plan to leave then, about four weeks after Easter.

*Easter.* What meaning did Easter have on the island of Chauquelín? Oh, sure, I believed in the resurrection. But it was hard to grasp that Jesus Christ could be alive and victorious under these leaden skies, in such a godforsaken place. What good did Easter do for a world ruled by death and evil?

Pessimism festered in my thoughts. My skin still crawled as I remembered the scene in the Serrano kitchen. I could easily believe Bórquez *was* the devil's own henchman as he stirred his potion of ashes, mocked Nicolás's earnest arguments, jeered and sneered at us all, smashed Angélica's best china with shameless nonchalance.

But what could *I* do about it? I hated to admit it, but my faith *was* as fragile as porcelain. As weak as a little bird that strays too far from the nest, hurts herself, and loses the strength to make it home. I could barely prop myself up, let alone support anybody else.

My pious performance at the summer tent meetings wasn't the real me. I couldn't help Nicolás, and I knew it if he didn't. That seemed to be my job in life—disappointing everyone. But if I couldn't please *them*, I might as well please myself, right?

Why did Nicolás insist on involving me in his battle to change the world, anyway? It appeared a thankless, impossible task. It irked me because he made me feel so…vulnerable. I was no warrior-maid ready to wrestle against the cosmic forces of the universe.

Sometimes his passion almost made me wish—but no! I'd traveled the religious route all my life. Church was something the Travises did. My body was always present in the pew, no questions asked, but my brain had checked out back in junior high.

So some of my choices hadn't been the wisest. Why had I ever let Amanda and Jared talk me into sneaking out of Grandma Rose's house that night last summer, for example? Sure, it wasn't the first step, or even the last straw in the disaster of my life. But maybe…it was the watershed moment that tainted everything afterwards.

Too late to think things could be different now. *Qué será, será.*

~

How long had I moped here on the beach? A host of timid stars winked along with the frontliners now. On the path at my back, light, rolling footsteps approached. I knew it was Nicolás even before he eased in beside me on the stone bench.

"Thought I might find you here when you weren't at Don Ramón's," he said. "We had some fun times in this spot last summer."

"Yep."

"You remember I told you the legend about the White Lady who wanders along the shore on misty nights. Good thing you're not wearing Mamá's poncho from last night."

"Or you'd mistake me for the ghost?" I tried to brace the wobble in my voice. "Was she murdered by the Trauco?"

"I shouldn't have mentioned that." He took my ice-block hands and warmed them between his heating-pad ones. "Bórquez didn't really spook you with that superstitious bunk of his, did he?"

"Don't you dare tell my sister what he said. She fusses enough already." I stared straight into Nicolás's caramel-taffy eyes. "Is—is the voodoo over? Is he gone?"

"He's gone. Headed off through the woods to rendezvous with his treasure hunters."

"Will they find anything?"

His sober answer matched Ramón's. "I doubt it, but no importa. They will claim the canutos jinxed them. I have an idea it was only a diversion, anyway. A sort of decoy staged for the crowd."

"What do you mean?"

"I saw one of Bórquez's launches drop anchor off Dolphin Bay when we were riding home last night. I don't know—just a gut feeling, maybe—but I don't think Bórquez wanted any witnesses around when that boat—the *Angélica*—came in." He grimaced.

*Right, his mother's name desecrated.* "How's your grandmother doing?"

A reluctant smile tugged at his lips. "Resting peacefully. She will be up spinning wool tomorrow if the power of positive thinking has anything to do with it. I'm sorry it hasn't been a nice visit for you this time, Melissa."

I shuddered, still gripped by the heebie-jeebies. What a jumble of strange events. "You can say that again. I might even be glad to get back to the dull routine at home." My attempt at a casual laugh sounded nervous, instead.

"Come on now, señorita." He joggled my arm. "We still have the Lord, no? He can change this island, even if it takes a while."

"I…I guess so."

We lapsed into a brief silence. Overhead a gull honked as it dove.

"Melissa, are you—" Nicolás hesitated. "Are you a Christian?"

Jolted, I shifted uneasily. "Of course I'm a Christian."

He looked out over the puce-colored sea, instead of at me. "But you—you never want to talk about God. You always act… bored, or something, and change the subject."

"Well, just because I don't go around talking about it all the time… But it would be hard *not* to be a Christian with a family like mine and practically raised in church."

"I've learned these past few months that it's not your family or church that matters." His tone cooled as he turned a penetrating gaze full on my face. "What about *you*? *Your* faith? You asked me yesterday who I really was. So, who is the real Melissa Travis? What is she really like?"

"I—" I opened my mouth for a quick retort, but the words fell short. I glanced away. I couldn't face the magnetism of his eyes and offer a trite reply—he'd see right through me.

Sometimes I didn't know who I was anymore, anyway. Everybody wanted to make me someone different than I was. I felt like a split personality, living in two places at once—drowning in the church, gasping in the world—and never at home in either. That pretty well summed up my life—one big charade. Maybe it was time to quit the acting. Save that for the drama competitions.

My friends in Maryland had said, "Why are you always so serious, just like the rest of your family? Crack the mold. Be yourself, Melissa."

"I've always been myself," I answered.

And snarky Jared hooted. "Sure you have, a good little girl like you. You do just what you're told, never step out of line or break a rule. That's what happens when you're brought up by a bunch of old fogies, I guess."

Spot-on, I'd conformed here in Chile. The ultimate fake. But I'd strayed so far from family expectations before now—and broken Grandma Rose's heart along with her hip—that I hadn't wanted to disappoint Linda and the rest any more than they already were.

"Meli, amiga mía," Nicolás said, "I just wonder where you really are with God. Are you, you know, like you said last summer, just *religious*? Or are you honestly a Christian?"

"Yes." I wasn't even religious if I dared admit the truth. Nothing against Jesus, per se, just all the paraphernalia that went with the whole church gig.

"Sure?"

His terse question made the blood rush loud through my ears. My earliest memory rose up—Mom reading Bible stories to me and my sister Jenny, curled up under a blanket on the couch. Then another memory swung into clear focus: myself as a six-year-old sitting with my mother at our kitchen table after a neighborhood Bible club. On that breezy spring day, the entire world seemed as happy as I'd been to trust Jesus as my Savior.

Absolutely no doubt in my mind about it. No matter what I did, how far I ran, or how hard I tried to ignore God, I knew deep down that I believed in Him and belonged to Him.

A whisper within, as unmistakable as a spoken voice, said, *Yes, my child, you're mine. Even though you shut Me out, even though you don't love Me, I'm always here. Watching and waiting because I promised I will* never *let you go.*

I swallowed hard. A flush burned up from my neck to my cheeks. "Yes, quite sure."

Nicolás was nothing if not annoyingly persistent. "Then why does talking about the Lord upset you? Why does it make you so unhappy?"

"I'm not unhappy about it. Don't be ridiculous."

"You are *not* happy. You're not one bit glad to be a Christian, Melissa."

I lost patience with his probing then. "Hey, what is this, some kind of interrogation? I've been a Christian a long time, Nicolás, a lot longer than you. So I'm not a perfect Christian.

Maybe not even a good one. So be it. I am what I am, and I'm satisfied with that."

"No, you're not."

"Yes, I am! Why can't everybody leave me alone and stop telling me who and what to be?"

"Because you are a child of God and blessed to high heaven, and you—you don't think that's special?"

"Of course, it is." I wrenched myself off the stone seat. If only it were so easy to escape the memories. Grandma Rose's sweet voice echoed in my head now.

*When you're a daughter of the King, you really are a secret princess like Sleeping Beauty, ma chérie. We belong to the royal family of God's invisible kingdom. But remember, our privileged position comes with responsibilities.* Just what I needed to hear, not.

"But I've known all about Jesus ever since I can remember," I said. "I was weaned on the Bible. Seriously, what do you expect me to do, jump around and cheer? I can't see anything to get hysterically excited about."

"Don't you wish you *could?*"

I huffed. "Yeah, yeah. For you, it's great—"

"It's great for *me?*" Nicolás leaped to the top of the boulder and towered above me, his body bristling. "Oh, but for you, it's just so old, no? Boring kindergarten stuff."

I turned my back on him and stomped a few paces away. "You don't understand."

"You are right, I don't. How can you not love God when He has done so much for us?"

I had no answer.

He vaulted down beside me and steered me by the arm towards the path. "We need to get back to the Pérezes'. They are all wondering what on earth happened to you." His voice softened. "Melissa, don't you ever feel…like, *hungry* for God deep down inside, like I did? Have you ever tried to fill up with, whatever…parties, friends, fun…but you still feel empty when it's all over?"

"Oh, yeah, I know what you're saying." As if a viper possessed my tongue, I mimicked him. "Come to Jesus and He'll satisfy your soul. Hungry? Please! I've been sitting at the church banquet table all my life."

Still he was unfazed. "Then, bucha, you have eaten nothing, and you let it get cold and stale. Or else you are so stuffed with junk food that you've lost your appetite for anything nourishing."

"Maybe, but—" I looked him directly in the face. Time for honesty here. "You once said something about finally being on the right road. That's great, I know the road, too. But I've already been there, done that, seen everything there is to see along the way, and…I just can't get that thrilled about it anymore."

He grasped my shoulders, his expression riveting. "But don't you realize how *privileged* you are? How much you take for granted?"

"Oh, shut up!" I twisted free and stormed ahead of him into the peninsula woods.

He caught up with me in an instant. "Now don't be mad, Melissa."

"Here I thought you were my friend."

"What makes you think I'm not? I'm only trying to help you."

"I don't need your help." I tossed my head. Just what I needed—another friend with their own agenda. "And this may come as a surprise, but I can't help you, either. I'm *not* special. I'm so ordinary you wouldn't even notice me in my hometown. I'm not a little angel, and I'm not the china-doll princess you think I am."

Nicolás grunted. Seemed to give up. He made half-hearted conversation the rest of the twilight walk to the Pérezes'.

I muttered vague replies. Now that I'd lost his good opinion, I was grateful for tonight's Bible study for once. It meant no further opportunities to talk with Nicolás alone this evening.

Oh God, how I wished my life *had* some sort of transcendent meaning, like Grandma Rose's princess-incognito pep talk.

But I more resembled a rag doll with dirt on my face.

# 25

*Back in Mellehue*

*Month 3, continued*

*Easter weekend flew by after we returned from Chauquelín, and I didn't get a chance—or work up the courage right away—to tell Linda I was leaving soon...*

While my sister hurried inside the school to speak to Reba's teacher, I dawdled on the sidewalk after Monday music practice, gobbling up the mail my sister had handed me. Finally, a letter from Amanda Ellis.

But what a letter. I was so furious I could spit. Right through the holes in my threadbare friendship quilt.

My older friend was thrilled that I was enjoying Chile, blah-blah-blah, but more exciting things were happening back home—Amanda's trip to Europe with the senior class over spring break, the upcoming graduation parties, the countdown to the drama finals. Amanda aimed to take first prize in the dramatic monologue category.

And no mention of regret—not even a hint—about my personal interest in the competition. No reference to my entry,

"The Blue Cup," that had garnered top marks at the qualifying event in January. Or *why* I'd been disqualified.

So it was high time to face my friends up. Three months ago, I'd felt like they were closer than my own family, but they'd abandoned me to my fate here. They'd sucked me into some questionable stuff—not so terrible in and of itself—but they'd let me take the rap for it alone. Somehow, deep down, I'd had a bad feeling about that all along.

Not that I intended to snitch on them now, either, but I was *so* ditching that group. And giving Amanda a piece of my mind. Believe me, I intended to deliver a speech that might turn *her* blue.

Drawing a breath, I swung around at the bang of the wooden gate. With Keli in the stroller and Reba hanging on the handle, Linda paused to wave toward the waterfront. A rainbow arched over the channel like a suspension bridge, and beneath the glistening curve sauntered a cluster of guys I recognized.

Brother, I *really* wasn't in the mood to debate religious convictions with Nicolás Serrano again.

He hadn't traveled on the *Ambassador* with his ailing grandmother last Thursday, after all. Señora Luisa made a remarkable recovery thanks to Juan Bórquez's magic, as Nicolás predicted, and refused to budge. And when classes re-commenced this morning, the island kids still hadn't arrived. The *Última Esperanza*, the seedy passenger launch, must've just now docked.

Linda greeted Nicolás, Marcos, and the oldest Garrido boy with a sort of group hug. "Welcome! And the girls?"

"Just left them at their boarding house," Marc said. "We're on the way to ours now."

I scuffed my way to the edge of the group, and the guys offered me the obligatory round of kisses. I'd never felt this awkward with Nicolás since the day we met.

"I'm surprised to see *you*, Rodrigo." Linda patted the skinny kid on the head. "Thought your mother would keep you close by for a little while."

He snuffled as he swiped a tatty wool sleeve across his runny nose. "Mamá didn't want us to miss any school, even though the novena isn't over yet."

"The novena?" I asked.

"The nine-day prayer vigil for their papá," Nicolás said.

"Oh, right."

"Why don't you all come up for tea as soon as you're settled? Melissa baked a cake yesterday." Linda winked. "If there's any left."

"Uh, sure." I cracked a weak smile.

"Goodness, I said tea, not torture." My sister frowned, parking a hand on her hip. "What's wrong? You two quarrel or what?"

Nicolás lifted a shoulder. "I have no quarrel. Anything wrong with you, Meli?"

"Not at all." *Get out of my face, Preacher Boy.* My gaze darted away from his. "A bit homesick, maybe. Lin, I—I've been thinking I might just finish this trimester at the school here and then head home."

"Bucha, you were staying until winter vacation," Marcos said.

"Are you sure?" A twinge of confusion crossed Linda's face, accentuating the freckles. "I thought you were enjoying it here."

"I was. I mean, I am," I said. "It's just—well, it's starting to feel like a longer time than I realized. But there's still a few weeks till the trimester ends. May seventeenth. I'll finish it out, Lin, if only to show old Martinet Martin at Mt. W."

A wry smile plucked at Linda's lips. "Is *that* why you've been studying so hard?"

If they wouldn't validate my Chilean studies anywhere back home, then I'd have to suck it up. Not worth trying to recoup anything of the school year at the end of May, anyway. Maybe I could take something by correspondence. Or…didn't City College have a summer program? Not that my parents would likely condescend to that.

I clamped my lips. At any rate, I wasn't going to discuss it in front of the Serranos. They knew nothing of my disgrace.

Reba piped up. "It's spring in Maryland, isn't it, Auntie Melissa?"

"Yep." I spoke with an enthusiasm that rang hollow as I hugged my niece. "Tulips, daffodils, cherry blossoms. Doesn't that sound lovely?"

"Sure, I'll arrange your return flight," Linda said on the way up the hill. "But what's the rush? Is there something I can do to—"

"Bucha, Linda!" *As Nicolás and Marcos would say.* I flailed my hands in the air. "Would you stop trying to solve everything for me? I don't need you to rescue me, or save me from myself."

Not anymore, I wasn't the helpless little sister any longer. I was taking charge of my own life from now on.

Linda pressed her lips together and gave me the laser eye. "You know what? Maybe you don't. What you need is to rescue someone else."

"Like who, your Chilotes here? So they can go back to their hocus-pocus mumbo-jumbo the minute your back is turned or the pressure's on?"

"I should put you in charge of the Garrido girl, helping her. She could use a big sister."

"Huh, like I have a lot of experience there. What could I do for her?"

"My stars, what couldn't you do if you had a mind to, Melissa Travis. Didn't you volunteer or something with Grandma back home?"

"What about it? All I did was help her with story hour at the library."

"But you don't want to teach."

"Bless me, no." The homeless shelter in Upper Fells Point figured into the charities Grandma dragged me to as well, but no way was I letting that out of the bag. I shared my friends' opinion that it was a supremely uncool place. Those people stank like rotten cabbage—and probably had lice. Like some Chilotes.

We clicked open the gate of the picket fence at the Petersons' yard. "Guess I could make a batch of Berger cookies for tea," I said.

*Cookies.* Pretty lame to imagine a few cookies could take away the ache of a loved one's loss. I ought to know.

I studied the timid faces of Jana and Rodrigo Garrido across the mounded plate of chocolate-iced sugar cookies. Woefully poor and neglected hardly began to describe them. Jana wore misery like a second skin. Her matted hair stuck around her head like wisps of winter hay.

Linda to the contrary, what could I do to help? In the few short weeks remaining?

And I *had* to get away from here, I was convinced now. Not only had my Baltimore friends let me down, Nicolás disapproved of me, too. Over the past months, we'd grown so close. I reveled in having at least one friend who understood me. But now that bond was broken as well.

I was embarrassed about who I really was, so I'd put on a sort of style these months. I despised pretense, yet I did it anyway. Nicolás was so serious and committed and genuine about all this faith stuff that I was afraid for him to see my true self. But he really knew me now, and I'd been right—he *didn't* like me anymore.

Oh, no doubt he'd still claim to be my friend. But he saw clean through me. I might as well strip off my church fashions and walk around naked. Not literally, of course, but the point was, I was a fraud, and he knew it.

After Linda and I cleared the crumbs from the big dining room table, I lent Nicolás my tower of notebooks so he could copy out what he'd missed of the day's lessons.

"Vaya, so you're running away," he said beneath the clatter of dishes in the kitchen.

I glared at him, refusing to answer.

"It's not because of Bórquez's threat, is it? Because—"

"Don't be ridiculous."

He tilted his head and tapped a pen against his chin. "Then you're leaving because you're mad at *me*? I begin to wonder what brought you here in the first place. Was Chile just your last resort as a place to *hide*?"

"It's not what you think, Señor Smarty-Britches Serrano. Watch out there, you missed a word. You might lose that big scholarship."

"Meli, amiga mía…" Hurt welled in those golden eyes of his. "I'm going to pray that God will follow you to the end of the earth."

Suddenly I was ashamed of my rudeness. *Oh, drop the bravado.* "Then you're both wasting your time on me. Sorry." I rushed upstairs before he could hear the choke in my voice or notice the hot tears springing to my eyes.

I might have been wrong. Whatever Nicolás thought of me, he *cared.*

# 26

*Month 4 – May*

*Poor Linda made the tedious phone calls to rebook my flight to New York for the twenty-second of May, a few days after the end of the Chilean school year's first trimester...*

At different times, I felt both wistful regret and immense relief.

One afternoon, as the date of my departure neared, Miriam Barrientos sidled up to me on the way out of school. "Would you look who is chasing Nicolás again."

"Delicia-alias-Delilah Treviño?" Yeah, I noticed.

More than noticed, to admit the truth. I missed Nicolás, a lot. Some days I longed to return to the way things were between us. Miriam and I had become genuine friends despite our dissimilarities, but she could never fill the gap. There was *no one* else like Nicolás Serrano De la Cruz in Mellehue. Nobody to really talk and share things with.

On the other hand, I was the one who avoided contact, not Nicolás. I had to keep aloof—his x-ray insight scared me. He understood me too well, made me think too much—and I didn't want that. I'd already made my choices, as I'd told him, and they didn't include God in any great way.

But more and more, anyone who didn't choose to be a radical Jesus follower was bound to squirm around Nicolás. Was he only a smug fanatic like others I knew? No. Nicolás was no poser, I'd give him that. His blend of high spirits and quiet steadiness made an impact at school, was probably the fertilizer for growth in Cole's church youth group that fall. Nicolás didn't believe in doing things halfway. Our classmates wanted to know what made him tick.

He even won skeptical Miriam over. Miracle, that. "Delicia's no good for him, Melissa. I would hate to see the guy ruined now."

"Nicolás seems well able to look out for himself, Miri."

"I'd like to know why you two are suddenly so cool." Miriam slanted a black brow, like a smudge of ink on parchment. "I mean, sí, you are leaving soon, but why throw the poor guy to the lioness ahead of time?"

*She knows.* I laughed and gave my friend a light squeeze. "You're so dramatic. Come on then, let's go watch today's *fútbol* game and ward off the man-eating lioness."

*May 17*
*The final week, I second-guessed my hasty decision more than once, but at last Friday arrived, much more quickly than I'd imagined.*

Spanish class crawled that morning. While the teacher went on about some Nobel Prize–winning poetry, I scribbled a few more lines on "What I Learned in Chile" in my notebook.

Who knew where I stood for readmission to Mt. Washington Christian Academy in the fall? Maybe that was going nowhere, yet I felt compelled to capture my impressions on paper. I'd seen the best and worst of humanity during this time in South America. Maybe I could approach the writing from that angle. The contrasts in the Chilean way of life staggered me—the paradox of squalor and splendor. That point had struck me since my first days in the country.

Why? A lump bobbed in my throat. Why should this place at the end of the world *move* me somehow? Why should it touch and at the same time repel me? *Was* I spoiled and ungrateful, like Nicolás insinuated?

*Scratch that. Not for the essay.*

This visit with my sister was only a trip, an educational experience. And okay, an escape route, as he'd accused and I'd admit. I'd never been sentimental about it. Maybe I was suffering from what they termed culture shock. I was a long way out of my comfort zone, for sure.

But my time here was ending, and I was as much a failure in South America as I was everywhere else. I'd barely seen that pinch-faced mouse of a girl that Linda had suggested taking under my wing. I didn't exactly cross paths with the fifth-graders much, and I hadn't taken time to look Jana up. Not that I was opposed to the idea. Linda was probably right.

To my own surprise, I couldn't dis Linda and Cole's work—ministry, whatever—anymore. As little as I cared about religion for myself, as much as I longed to be myself no matter what, I wouldn't hurt them for the world. I'd never wreck things for them.

But I'd probably been more of a liability than an asset these months. No help at all.

And then...I'd bulldozed one of the best friendships of my life. No small loss.

Nicolás sat ahead of me and to the right. I could tell his mind was as far away as mine from Pablo Neruda's *Ode to the Sea*. The strong lines of his still-tanned face contrasted sharply with the pale light of the late-fall day as he stared out the window, chin tilted.

What was he thinking about? Man, I missed talking with him.

What would I do when I got home anyway? Chills pricked along my arms. Sure, I'd enjoy some time with friends, the old faithfuls. I wouldn't mind a Big Mac and some English television. But would I really be content to return to the same rut again? Maybe I wasn't as ready to face Mom and Dad as I figured.

And I'd never see how things turned out on Chauquelín. Perhaps that's what I minded most about leaving.

Did I really want to find out? Did I even care? And what did it matter, such an insignificant little place? Linda would write me the news. Besides, it would look silly to cancel my plans *now*.

*May 18*
*I never had so many mixed feelings in my life as this last weekend...*

When I walked over to the church Saturday evening for my final youth meeting, I discovered around thirty teens, mostly kids I'd come to know at school and church, gathered for a good-bye party. So it wasn't the snazziest bash I'd ever attended in my life. It didn't matter. It was the kids, not Cole and Linda, who organized the farewell for after the service, and I was touched.

During music time, a brief tremor, the same as half a dozen we'd experienced lately, rolled through the church. *Ha, finally some rock 'n' roll around here.* Only it more resembled a mother rocking her baby. Everybody grinned, shrugged, and kept on singing.

"You've become a real Chilean, Meli," Marcos told me. "You don't even miss a beat with these shakes."

"Chile's waving good-bye to you," Tito Bahamonde, Nicolás's friend, said.

Over our guitars, Nicolás threw me a look I didn't try to interpret.

Cole started his Bible study, somewhere in Ecclesiastes, I heard before tuning him out. My gaze roved around the circle of now-familiar, friendly faces.

Long, lanky Tito was shy, yet down-to-earth and kind. Peach fuzz shaded his upper lip.

The super-sensible Miriam. What could I say in the end? Miriam's loyal heart was as big as her bones.

Baby-faced Marcos. Easygoing, easy on the eyes, and oh, so easy to love.

Nicolás, brown and robust from field labor, his bearing athletic, always self-assured. His expression tonight blew my mind. A complete enigma.

After tonight, good-byes would move to fast-forward. Linda and I would travel by bus to Santiago tomorrow evening. I pressed back a grin. The liceo director had made a special effort to prepare my report card yesterday, and I could hardly wait to see the sour look on Martin's face when I presented it to him with a flourish. My grades averaged a very respectable six-point-five out of seven.

So I had one small triumph, at least, in this season of trouncing. If it mattered at all.

But my lost friendship with Nicolás did matter. I *had* to talk to him again, felt compelled. But how and when? Time was running out. And talk about what? I only knew I couldn't go with so much left unsaid between us. Perhaps after the party, I'd find a chance.

Something in my brother-in-law's talk drew my attention. "Solomon had a great start in a God-pleasing life," Cole said. "But then, he became preoccupied with things that were trivial compared to eternal realities. He looked for satisfaction in education, friends, expensive possessions. He chased fulfillment in projects, money, music, and fun. But in the end, he realized that all those things have little value if our lives aren't anchored in God and His priorities. God's destiny for His children is—"

He paused as another tremor struck. Abnormal, following so closely on the heels of the one twenty minutes previous. This was more like a rock concert than a swaying lullaby, though. We all darted uneasy glances at each other. When it lasted longer than a few seconds, Cole said calmly, "I think we'd better step outside."

A buzz of consternation erupted as we scrambled in rapid exodus to the churchyard. The kids were tense, but no one screamed or stampeded in panic. I figured they'd grown up in this seismic country and knew it would stop soon.

"Aren't you supposed to stand in a doorway?" I asked, heart thudding.

"Maybe in the city," Nicolás said, "where you might be hit by falling objects. But there's plenty of open space here. We're safer outside."

"Can't all fit in the doorway anyway," Tito said.

The shake picked up in intensity. Streetlights at the sidewalk's edge wavered and dimmed as I veered around the corner of the church building. Through the pulsating darkness, we jostled toward the broad meadow at the back of the property, reeling as if on a surfboard. *I* was freaked if the rest weren't. All around me, the other teens staggered, tripped, even sprawled headlong. Then they fumbled up again and raced ahead, hands stretched out.

The sound of a freight train rumbled a few feet away, but there was no train. Lurid light flickered over the yard, like sheet lightning in a thunderstorm, but there was no rain. A strong wind lashed the air. The electric posts creaked and swayed, the cables flapping like whips. Dogs set up a howl. Some of the girls joined in the wail.

No mere tremor, this was a full-fledged earthquake. No doubt about it.

The neighborhood exploded now. Crashes and cries of terror shattered the serenity. Doors banged up and down the street. Windows cracked and burst.

The ground beneath my feet churned so much it was like trying to balance on the swells of an incoming tide. I stumbled and would have plunged flat on my face if Nicolás hadn't grabbed my arm and steadied me. He stayed beside me as we both tottered across the yard. Or tried. I clung to his sleeve, awed into silence by the raw display of the earth's energy. Sweat trickled down my neck despite the frigid air.

Linda wrenched open her front door. Cole rushed, lurching between jolts, to meet her at the gate. He swept from her arms both hysterical children, still dripping from the bathtub and wrapped in nothing but a towel. The door swayed on its hinges. Inside, cupboards flew open, dishes hurtled to the floor, ornaments tumbled and tinkled.

A thunder-like boom reverberated through the crisp night. The Petersons' house rattled off one of its foundational sockets, and the stout wooden post smashed up through the floorboards. It sagged like a tipsy drunk toward that corner.

"Dear God," I gasped.

Nicolás jerked on my sleeve. "Back off, everybody! The hillside's caving in!"

Almost in slow motion, the low-slung bank of earth that had nestled against the far side of the church teetered and then pitched over. With an earsplitting roar like a bomb blast, it crumbled in a landslide and ripped through the wall of the church, dragging with it the neighbors' house from above. A whirlpool of dirt and debris rained over the yard. Wood splintered. Shrieks echoed in every direction. The streetlights convulsed again, flared, and died.

The earth heaved another great shudder, as if it, too, were terrified. Writhed as if in agony, then sank, exhausted, into stillness. As suddenly as it had begun, the quake ended.

Only the odd flailing flashlight dotted an otherwise complete blackness. But the screams resonated all over town. In the distance, engines gunned. Feet slapped along the sidewalk. My legs twitching, I groped along the picket fence toward my sister and brother-in-law.

"You kids need to head home, check in with your families." Cole floundered over to his van, yanked open the side door, and plopped the two little girls inside the vehicle. "There'll be aftershocks coming."

"We've got to get to Valeria, Marc," Nicolás said. "Before the tsunami."

*The tsunami! As in…tidal wave?* And the girls' boarding house perched right on the waterfront. If it still stood.

# 27

"Right, I forgot about the possibility of tsunami." Cole snapped the van radio on and cranked up the volume. "Maybe we should move to higher ground. Certainly no one should go back to the lower level of town."

Nicolás shook his head. "We have to. You folks will be all right here, Don Colin."

"You think?"

"My mother was a little girl here during the 1960 quake. There was a big swell, she says, but not like in the movies. These channel waters don't get the full brunt, on the protected side of the island. Even so…"

"How long do you suppose we have, man?"

"Depends how close the epicenter was. Could be an hour, could be ten minutes."

"Okay, I don't know what to tell you kids then. Those who live on the hills or outside of town, go home. Those from the lower level of the village, you'd best stay here or go over to the gym and wait for your families there. Nico, I'll get you a flashlight."

Party plans forgotten, the rest of the teens scattered into the darkness. Linda hung onto Cole's arm, and they crept back toward the house. Keli sobbed at the top of her lungs, and Reba's decibel level wasn't much lower. No wonder, the air was freezing. I wobbled to the van, slid onto the bench seat beside them, and whipped off my jacket and sweater.

"See about Jana and Rodrigo too, when you go down there," I said to Nicolás as I tried to wrap my nieces up. My teeth chattered like ice cubes in a glass.

"Of course." He paced beside the open door of the van.

In a couple of minutes Cole returned and tossed the boys a flashlight. They bolted off just as Mellehue's fire station siren cranked up a shrill whine. Most people were running up the hill, not down it. A steady parade of cars and pickups ground up the gravel road out of town now, honking nonstop.

Cole handed me fleece pajamas and coats for the girls. "Can you help them get dressed, Meli? Lin's finding some candles and sweeping up the broken glass in the kitchen. I'm gonna go see if the Alvarados got out of their house before that embankment collapsed."

Trembling with adrenaline, I didn't know how I managed to dress the girls. My fingers quivered like icicles. Somehow I got them comforted and warmed, and still comprehended some of the frantic Spanish of the radio broadcast.

"It's an eight-point-eight," I said when Linda came back to the van. "Epicentered in Ancud? That's what I'm hearing."

"The northernmost town in Chiloé Island." Linda sucked in her breath as she hoisted Keli to her hip. "Not fifty miles from here, right on the open Pacific. Oh, Lord."

"And two and a half minutes long? Brutal, it seemed like two hours."

Inside the Petersons' now-lopsided house, Linda set the children at the kitchen counter, lined with a row of flickering candles, and skidded a saucepan of milk to the center of the cookstove. "Cole shoved the stovepipe back in place right away. But Melissa…my china cupboard…"

"Oh, no, Lin." I pressed a fist to my mouth and spun toward the dining nook. The cupboard doors swung open. Some of Linda's collection of exquisite porcelain balanced on the edge of the shelves, but a good many cups and saucers and sugar bowls lay splintered on the floor. Gold sprinkles glittered in the wavering light. Just like at Señora Angélica's that dreadful evening in Chauquelín. Tears stung at the back of my eyes.

"Well, they're just things," Linda said in a weird strangled voice.

"You can have my share of Gran's china." I bit my bottom lip. "I know it means a lot to you."

"I wouldn't think of taking your stuff."

"In the meantime, I'll see what I can rescue here. And put what's not broken in a safer place."

Cole returned with the Alvarados, the neighbor family of five whose home had plummeted into the church. Linda offered them shelter and set to work. I had to admire my sister's composure. I'd long since tossed my opinion of Linda as so heavenly minded she was no earthly good, but that night she was magnificent. She stirred hot chocolate for the children and served the rest of our stunned group coffee and sandwiches by candlelight. Then she settled Reba and Keli underneath the dining table for the night and hunted up bedding for the company.

For a while, the adults took turns hanging out by the car radio. Information was sketchy, at best. The firefighters' siren blared for the first forty-five minutes and then fell into ominous silence. Muted voices still buzzed over the town. Bonfires dotted the fields.

Finally we tried to situate ourselves for the night, mostly propped up around the kitchen floor. We didn't dare venture far from the front door of the crooked house. Aftershocks vibrated at irregular intervals throughout the endless hours. With each one, we jerked awake and sprang to our feet. Not exactly rock-a-bye-baby. Twice, the dangerous intensity of the new tremor forced us to flee the house again.

Maybe the littlest children slept some that night. But the other eight of us, huddled in a ludicrous piggy-pile of blankets and sleeping bags, did not.

The truth was, I hardly closed my eyes at all.

A pale, bleary dawn at last crept over the mountains, threatening rain. Or was it smoke in the air?

Cole tried to get the news again, but the radio only squawked static now. He grunted. "Transmitter in Castro must've gone down in that last aftershock."

Town water mains had apparently broken, too, and no water remained in the kettle for coffee, so Linda warmed more milk while I sliced bread for breakfast for our two families. Afterwards, the Alvarados, dumbstruck and drawn-faced, headed out to see what they could salvage from the rubble that was once their home.

Cole and Linda and I surveyed by daylight the damage done to ours. The entire two-story structure listed toward the northwest corner where the dislodged support post had punctured the floor. Amid a shamble of fractured boards, toppled books, and strewn papers, the post now poked three feet high into Cole's study.

"Maybe I could use it as an extra desk," Cole joked lamely. A shard of glass skittered across the floor as he uprighted a fallen bookshelf.

From the outside, the scene reminded me of Dorothy's Kansas farmhouse crash-landed in Oz. The remaining posts appeared stable enough, though.

"At least the house isn't too precarious," Linda said. "Could be worse."

She never even mentioned the loss of her heirloom china.

"You can probably fix it, huh?" I attempted to be cheerful, too.

"Yeah, a big jack and some new wood should do the trick," Cole said. "But I wouldn't count on getting the manpower to help any time soon."

"I just thank God we still have a roof over our heads," Linda said. "It's more than the Alvarados have."

Cole threw a somber glance across the yard. "We won't be using the church for a while."

"How badly is it damaged?" A frown etched between Linda's brows. "We won't be able to have services?"

"Not today you won't," I said. "Didn't you see it, Lin? The whole hillside just caved into it."

"I'm sure the entire back side got bashed in," Cole said. "Daresay part of the roof's gone too. And as Melissa says, the inside's gonna be a mess."

"How long do you think the power and water will be off?" I asked. "I was kind of planning on a shower this morning."

"Depends how many lines are down and exactly where the mains are broken," Cole answered. "Alvarado said he'd hike up to the town reservoir and bring us a couple buckets of water for washing up and cooking. Think I'll walk down and see what's happened in the rest of the town, and the country."

"Maybe you should check in with the church folks and decide about the service while you're out then," Linda said.

"Why don't you go with him, Lin?" I said. "See if you can get a phone call through to cancel my flight."

"Oh, gracious! I guess we won't be going anywhere today, will we?" Then, inexplicably, Linda wilted against the zinc siding of the house and cried.

After they left, I tidied up the house as well as I could and fixed a pot of soup to simmer on the wood stove while I watched the girls and waited. Even the meaty aroma of *carbonada* didn't dissolve the ball of congealed nerves in my stomach.

When Linda and Cole returned—hours later—Linda's green eyes were red-rimmed and her face blotchy. She sank into a tilting chair. "It's absolutely awful. The lower part of the town is devastated."

"Is anybody…dead?" Sheesh, that was blunt. But anxiety for my friends was killing me.

Cole slumped against the kitchen counter. "Fifty, so far," he said in a low voice. "Up here on the hill, we—we missed the worst of it. The waterfront area's hardest hit, of course. All the fisheries have *some* damage, and most of those old shacks on stilts collapsed. What was left standing after the quake, the tsunami took."

"Thank God for the port captain," Linda sighed. "His timely warning probably saved a lot of lives."

My jaw unhinged. "And the girls' boarding house? Valeria and Jana?"

"That *palafito* fell, all right. Flattened. But Jana's safe at the gym. We talked to the school director and offered to keep the girls from there. I didn't see Valeria, but someone said the boys had taken her to the med-post."

I released a shaky breath.

"We didn't try to go into the *posta*," Cole said. "One wing was damaged, and it's a madhouse with injured people trying to get attention and the staff working around the debris. Thank God, it's on higher ground, though." He shook his head. "Police are busy keeping the looting down. Can you believe how the local hoodlums take advantage of this tragedy? It's almost a *good* thing most of the town's flooded as far up as the school. Part of the south side of Freire Street, too. It'll stay up for a while."

"Smells really good here, Meli." Linda rose and tied an apron on over her denim skirt. "Sorry I didn't get through to Santiago about your flight—the call office is underwater. The only way to communicate right now is via the medical or police radios, and they say the wait's several hours long. I figured I'd better come home and let you go stand in line, since we have people arriving here any minute."

"We changed the service to the afternoon," Cole said.

"Open air?" A smile twitched on my lips. "Or maybe you should set up the Big Top."

"Good idea," he said. "Seriously."

# 28

I only had to walk partway down the hill, not through the most mutilated section of Mellehue. But lured toward the waterfront, I passed the medical post, the police headquarters, and the fire station. Only to be dead-ended at Freire Street, flowing a foot deep in molasses sludge and debris. A gaudy orange rowboat anchored at the bus stop across the river, wedged between the bench and the side of the shelter.

Gone was the island town's picturesque beauty. In its place unfolded a ravaged heap of ruins. Every other building on the south side of Freire lay in rubble, and the rest looked too risky to enter. Aghast, I watched a handful of weeping neighbors wade out of a crumpled house, bearing a body on a makeshift stretcher of dirty ponchos. A torn black shawl and a leathery claw dragged in the mud.

Somebody's grandmother. The family hadn't reached her in time.

A memory washed over me like a tsunami—the paramedics wheeling Grandma Rose out of her Baltimore home on an ambulance gurney. My head swam. I grabbed the *notro* tree at the corner for support.

The poncho-stretcher slipped and uncovered a bloodied face below a shock of white hair. Dear God, wasn't that the old woman who'd sold me a woven tea box and called me "butter head" at the market last summer? I hung my head over the ditch as a wave of nausea swept up my throat.

Hunched over, I wiped my mouth with an old tissue from my pocket and pressed my fingers against my temples. I couldn't take any more. But would I ever forget that grisly sight as long as I lived?

I stepped backward to the sidewalk—and banged into Miriam Barrientos. "Miri!" I gulped. "How are you—your family?"

"They are okay, we're okay." Miriam set down the plastic bucket of water she carried. Her usually pale face was chalk-like, her eyes glazed. "But—our house was destroyed!"

"Oh, no." Not surprising, when only a web of paint flecks and mold had held that string of decaying buildings together. I wrapped my arms around my friend.

She drooped against me. Practical, prudent Miriam... quivered with sobs.

*Now I've seen everything.* I patted her tangled hair. "Why don't you come and stay with us for a few days? Until you can get it fixed back up."

"Fixed up! Did you not understand me? It's demolished—done. Besides, how can we move in with you? We are so many." Sniffling, she scrubbed at her tears. "Last night we camped out around a bonfire in the soccer field. With dozens of other families. I guess the municipality will let some of us live in the gymnasium temporarily."

"Then, what do you need that we can help with? Dishes, blankets? Have you seen the rest of our school gang?"

Miriam's baby-blue eyes grew round. "Tito's father is dead."

"No!" I clutched her arm.

"You know what a drunk he is—was. Guess when the quake hit, he and some of his drinking buddies were at the cantina across from our house, probably too *borracho* even to notice at first. They found" —Miriam's voice cracked— "his body floating in the wreckage this morning."

I squeezed my eyes shut. If only I could hide my face, as I'd done as a child during the scary parts of a television program. Only this was no movie. This day of horrors was all too real.

With a hug and a promise to talk more later, I left Miriam and headed back up Mocopulli.

A stiff north wind had arisen. It cut through the damp air like a knife and stripped the last of the crinkly gold and amber leaves from the trees, but at least cleared the smoke. At the police station, a chaotic line of shivering people desperate to contact loved ones spilled out to the sidewalk.

I spied Nicolás and stole in beside him.

"How did you folks pass the night?" he asked without preamble. Like Miriam, his expression was dull with fatigue, his clothes rumpled and dirty.

"We survived, I guess. You guys found Valeria, right?"

He nodded, his jaw grim. "Took a while. That popsicle-stick shack was one of the first to go down. Some of the girls did not get out in time. Jana is safe, some bruises. Vali was unconscious when we pulled her from the rubble. But at least we got her out just before—the water came in." His deep-set eyes glistened like pools. He bent his head and pawed the ground with the toe of his sneaker. "Bucha, it's hard to see your little sister like that."

236

"I can imagine." I laid a light hand on his arm and bit my lip, unsure of what else to do or say. What calamity would I hear of next? "Is she—what happened to her, Nicolás?" I hardly dared to ask. Those deep maroon splotches on his denim jacket looked like…dried blood.

He flinched as he inched ahead in line. "She will be okay, I think, though she's a bashed-up kid. Broken leg, some broken ribs probably, concussion. We spent the night at the med-post with her."

"So she's staying there?"

"For now, on a cot in the hall," he said. "She was in shock, and they still have to set the leg. Marcos is with her now. But I doubt they will send her to the hospital in Castro, or even keep her long at the *posta* here. So many people with worse injuries."

"Cole and Linda have volunteered to take the girls from that home, so she won't have far to go when they discharge her. How'd your boarding house do in the quake?"

"Part of the stairway buckled, and there's half a meter of water on the bottom floor. But it will be livable again once the water goes down, I think."

"Where will you and Marcos go in the meantime? Surely you don't plan to camp out in the soccer field."

He shrugged. "Lots of people are."

"You guys should come stay with us too," I said. "It's a big house, and I know Linda will make room for you. You guys are practically like family."

"Thanks, maybe we will, at least while Valeria recuperates. But we need to get home to Chauquelín." Nicolás's husky tone betrayed keen emotion. "We don't know how Mamá and

Abuela are, alone out there. I'm trying to get a radio message through to the island now."

"Right. There on the hillside…" My voice trailed away. If an avalanche of earth could pitch into the side of the church, how had the earthquake affected the rest of the country? Chauquelín had probably fared much the same as Mellehue, only it was farther from the reach of emergency assistance.

"We'll pray they're all right." For once in my life, I meant that lame reassurance. "You should let your grandparents in Santiago know you're okay too, while you're here making calls."

"What do they care?" he muttered.

"More than you want to believe. Don't think I haven't noticed the letters that come from them to Cole and Linda's post office box."

He went cool and stone-faced as always when the subject of his Serrano grandparents popped up. "So, you are here to call your parents then?"

Was he turning the tables on me? "Oh, gosh! Linda and I hadn't even thought of that yet. I should at least send a message via the mission in Santiago, I guess. Actually, I'm in line to cancel my Tuesday flight."

"Looks like you have no choice but to stay a little longer." Nicolás grinned faintly. "Some people are so stubborn it takes an earthquake to change their minds. What is the new departure date?"

"I don't even know yet. As soon as possible, I imagine." I gave him a shove. "Wipe that smirk off your face."

My radio call—relayed via the police precinct nearest to Cole and Linda's mission office in the capital—had to achieve several purposes with a single message. By the time I finished and reached the Peterson house again, their afternoon church service had got underway in the big tent.

I was starving, but I trudged across the yard toward the meeting. Muffled by a breaking downpour, a solemn cadence of voices read the Scripture.

"God is our refuge and strength, an ever-present help in trouble. Therefore we will not fear, though the earth gives way and the mountains fall into the heart of the sea, though its waters roar and foam and the mountains quake with their surging. There is a river whose streams make glad the city of God, the holy place where the Most High dwells. God is within her, she will not fall; God will help her at break of day. Nations are in uproar, kingdoms fall; He lifts His voice, the earth melts. The Lord Almighty is with us; the God of Jacob is our fortress..."

I slipped into the back of the tent. Those ancient words buoyed me up, somehow. Wholesome and solid, like a thick slice of bread. Not so mouthwatering as a piece of cake, but... strengthening.

I shut my burning eyes and let the psalm soothe my spirit. It sank like a balm into parched skin. Amazing, the Bible's vivid portrayal of the powerful natural phenomena we'd just witnessed—the toppling mountains, the raging sea. Yet through all the turmoil streamed God's peace.

Maybe that explained why so many villagers flocked to the tent meeting today. Seeking God in the catastrophe. I gazed around at the crowd. Most of the people I recognized, a poor but hard-working lot. Some had lost what little they owned. Others had lost even more—loved ones.

Miriam sat in the front row, accompanied by her mother and sisters—a first. Tito, his thin face haggard, clasped the arm of his newly widowed mother. Marcos, just relieved from his shift beside his little sister, slid onto a bench next to me, his jeans and jacket soaked to the skin. A fat drop of rain plopped from the leaky canvas roof onto his nose. He chuckled as he rubbed it away.

How could these people recite, "The Lord Almighty is with us"? It was more than I could do. Their faces wore a glow of stubborn courage. For the first time, I caught a vision of exactly what Nicolás valued in his islanders.

I couldn't leave now, even if I wanted to. At least not for a while. Nor did I really want to, I realized with a shock. As long as I could do anything to help here, I'd stay and work. *So then, I won't run away, Nicolás.* I made a fist inside my coat pocket and accepted the challenge.

# 29

*Month 4, continued unexpectedly*
*Work I did, as I've never done in my life. The weeks fol-*
*lowing the quake blurred into an unbroken nightmare...*

Rain and mud and cold, flattened houses and crushed bodies,
endless chores, sleepless nights, hopeless wails. Every day new
scenes of horror assaulted me on all sides, until I wanted to
blot them out with a pillow over my head and never leave my
bed again.

But of course, I did, and not that I had much choice—we
almost had to sleep in shifts. Even with the damage, homeless
neighbors packed the Peterson house to its moss-green roof.
Cole and Linda moved their daughters into their own bedroom so they could lend Reba's room to the Alvarado family
and Keli's to Señora Ana, Tito's roly-poly mother who was
the only one short enough to fit the bed. I offered my room
to accommodate Nicolás, Marcos, Tito, little Rodrigo Garrido,
and two other boys who'd been flooded out of their boarding
house. They stretched out on the hardwood floor like macker-
els layered in a tin can.

Downstairs in Reba and Keli's big playroom, Linda set up another dormitory for the seven elementary-age girls the school director sent. I volunteered to supervise. I figured it would be like a winter camp, but I ended up more nanny than counselor. The earthquake had killed two of their companions at the waterfront stilt-house, and those traumatized girls now hovered at the frayed edge of terror.

My nieces came down with severe bronchitis. Being snatched from the bathtub to the frigid outdoor air the evening of the quake probably aggravated the case. For the better part of a week, caring for Reba and Keli occupied most of Linda's energy.

Señora Alvarado tried to share the load, but she also worked long hours with her husband as they whacked together a temporary shanty for their family. And poor sweet Señora Ana...I'd always figured her cornbread wasn't quite done, maybe brain-damaged from her husband's beatings. But now she stared out the window, in a daze for hours on end. The guys helped Cole shovel out the church and repair the house. So for a while, a lot of the household responsibilities fell to guess-who. Regardless of the want of experience on my resumé.

I hauled pail after pail of water from the town reservoir, scrubbed mountains of clothes, peeled bushels of potatoes. With twenty-six people in the house, helping hands never lacked, but the to-do list never ended, either. The rainy days stretched on, packed to the brim.

I didn't mind. Not really. At least I was contributing. Maybe it was the first time in my life anything or anybody had ever depended on me.

But when bedtime rolled around each night, I dropped like a zombie into my bed on the playroom floor. My legs throbbed from standing all day. My arms were bruised from lugging the heavy water buckets. My hands grew rough and ugly, covered with stinging cuts and raw sores. I forgot what a relaxing bath felt like.

Despite the exhaustion, I didn't sleep well. I snapped awake, ready to bolt, with each of the aftershocks, once or twice a night at first. Plucky as they were, my schoolgirls suffered a lot of nightmares too. Their screams tore the stillness of the dark hours. More than once, I wrapped my arms around Jana and hummed until her whimpering subsided.

On the fourth day, Nicolás and Marcos carried their sister, cast and all, up the hill to Linda and Cole's place. Though Valeria was still disoriented, feverish, and in pain, the overwhelmed village medical post couldn't keep her any longer. So I added nursing to my duties.

Vali was an awesome patient, though. Within a few days, once her head cleared, she led that gaggle of girls.

After one pre-dawn tremor, she pointed to the shelves lined with picture books. "Why don't you read us a story?"

"Um, I'd be glad to, but—" *Believe me, I would. Anything to get these kids back to sleep faster.* "I'm pretty sure most of Reba's stuff is in English."

"So? You can translate as you go."

I dragged my eyelids open and glared. "Good thing I like you, Vali."

But it did the trick. My halting Spanish probably bored the girls enough that they drifted off. Unfortunately, it started a nightly ritual. Seriously, like I was back doing the story hour at Enoch Pratt Library, minus Grandma Rose.

"Move Valeria upstairs? Why?" I lifted the lid on Linda's kitchen flour bin one dreary afternoon. *Whoa, almost empty.*

A frown creased my sister's forehead as she measured ingredients for a batch of bread. Ten days after the earthquake, grocery shelves in our small town had emptied. The *panadería* had closed its doors until supply trucks got through again. Linda was scraping the bottom of her own barrel now. "It's warmer in our room, and now that Reba and Keli are on the mend…"

"I doubt that, Lin. It gets pretty cozy with ten of us packed in the sardine can down here." I smiled wryly. "Besides, Nicolás spent the last of his scholarship money on an extra blanket for Vali. What a guy. Anyway, she'd miss us. And you're up enough nights as it is."

"Then we'll leave Valeria there until you're gone. Maybe I could take you to Santiago the end of next week? I hear the bridge that went out on the highway is being repaired and the buses will be running again soon."

"But…but…" I bit my lower lip. "I'm not sure I should go so soon anymore. I mean, how can I desert a sinking ship?"

"We're pulling through this. They say we'll have water and electricity again before the week is out, and with all the boys' help, Cole's ready to jack up the house and put in the new post tomorrow. Things are slowly getting, sort of, back to normal here."

"But—what about these kids?" They'd probably miss me more than Amanda Ellis and her mall peeps. The drama competition was long over now, anyway. *Wave your fool's-gold medal, Mandy.* "Unless…you don't need me anymore…"

"Goodness, on the contrary. How would I have managed without you these days? You've been a marvelous help. But enough with the forced labor. Combine your trimester here and the summer session at City, and you *might*—"

"I could catch up in summer school at home?"

"It's possible, isn't it? I don't want to tie you here, sis." A cup of bubbling yeast poised in midair, Linda studied me. "Your decision, of course."

"Then I'll risk it, stay till July or August. Stick to the original plan." Voice muffled, I yanked my fleece jacket off the hook by the front door.

"Are you sure?" Humor lilted in my sister's tone. "Wiping runny noses and shoveling mud don't make for exciting vacation tales."

"You mean, it's not gonna sound glamorous to my friends back in Baltimore? I'm past caring. You know, Linda..." My voice trailed away.

"What?"

I groped for words that wouldn't sound sappy. "You know I'm not much into church and all that. But I gotta admire what you and Cole do here. At least, it's something worthwhile, something bigger than your own comfort and pleasure...I don't know."

"It's the most challenging job in the world," Linda said softly. "It takes all we've got to give."

"It's not fun. It's not cool, except the temperature." I grimaced and thrust my arms into the jacket sleeves. "Maybe it's not even important in the overall scheme of things, and you can't help everybody, but—"

"It's a very big deal to the person you help."

I sighed as I looped a scarf around my neck. "Lately Maryland seems a long way away. Not the center of the universe anymore, by a long shot. My crowd there was so…so silly, I guess. Like we were a bunch of spoiled brats who had so much we didn't know how to appreciate it. All we ever thought about was trivial stuff, parties and fashions and the latest fads and gadgets. Talk about being consumed with yourself. It's almost embarrassing when I look at people around here."

"Where are you off to now?"

"I'm going to blow my allowance on some clothes for these kids. They get tired of being shut up in the bedroom for a day at a time while I wash their raggedy wardrobe."

"But that's your souvenir money, Meli."

"That's what I'm trying to tell you—it won't hurt me to miss a few trinkets. Valeria and Jana and the others need it more. I'd like to buy Miriam some clothes too, mine are too small for her." I paused, my hand on the doorknob. "Lin, can't we do something about Jana? Her skin's a mess, and she scratches constantly. I checked for lice, but it's not—"

"It's scabies, I think." Linda thumped her mound of dough. "About the worst case I ever saw, too. She probably picked it up in that boarding house."

"The seven-year itch, you mean? Doesn't that last, like, seven years?"

"It does take a fuss to get rid of. But you're right. The other girls might get infected if they're not already."

"Oh, great. I'll go by the pharmacy and ask. Suppose they still have anything? I think you got the last antibiotics in town. And when I get back…"

"Yeah?"

"Could you teach me to make bread, the way they do here?" I stepped onto the muddy porch.

"Sure." Linda smiled. "But you know the kids would rather have the gringo cookies and cupcakes."

"Basics before frills. I'll see if the flour's arrived too."

# 30

*Month 5 – June*

*The tsunami waters that swept into Mellehue ebbed away by the end of the second week after the earthquake. A group of us liceo students volunteered to clean up the school buildings...*

"Classes aren't starting again until August? Why, that's nearly two months away." I leaned against the doorframe of our classroom.

"Even then, the repairs might not be finished." Nicolás scraped a layer of black silt, scrambled with rubbish, from the floor and shoveled it into a nearby bin. Messy work, it meant a hard scrubbing, several days to dry, and a return visit to rub red paste wax onto the bleached wooden floors.

But we were experts now. Nicolás and the guys had done the same job at their boarding house before moving back in the day before. "We already ran on a half-day schedule because of the space problem, you know," he said. "They can't function without the older wing."

"I suppose not."

"Besides, half the students still don't even have a decent place to live. People need to make their homes the priority." He scooped up another load of mucky garbage. "Meli, run down the hall and see if Tito's done with the hose, would you?"

In a minute, I was back with his request. "I'll spray while you sweep."

"*Vale.* So most of your girls have gone home—Melissa! Your hands!" He dropped the broom with a clatter and snatched up my red, swollen hands. "They're covered with chilblains and who knows what else. Bucha, they look awful."

"You're flattering, Señor Serrano." A self-conscious giggle escaped me while I tried to withdraw my hands. I *was* a little embarrassed about them—they looked worse than Vanessa de Garrido's the night of the wake on Chauquelín.

At first I'd dreaded I might have caught the scabies from rubbing down Jana nightly with medicated lotion, but my sister—like Nicolás—had lived long enough in southern Chile to identify the shiny lumps as chilblains. *From exposure to damp and cold,* Linda explained with pressed lips.

"I think it's partly an allergy to the clothes detergent, too," I said. "Now that we have running water and electricity in the house again, I won't have to—"

"You're not used to that kind of work. You should not have carried all those water pails, either. I tried to go as often as I could, but you're so stubborn that—"

"That I might become a good Chilote yet. It's nothing, Nicolás."

"Nothing! If you want to be a Chilote, you should wear a wool hat and gloves, girl." He grunted and picked up the hose along with the broom. "Here, *I* will handle the water if you'll sweep."

I shrugged. "Okay."

He eyed me thoughtfully for a moment. "Melissa, you've been amazing over these weeks."

*High praise from the guy who considers me a total heathen.* We'd hardly had any opportunities to talk, but now that I planned to stay longer, maybe we'd find time to knit the unraveled threads of our friendship back together. A bit, anyway, I hoped. "You guys have been a great help to us, too."

"Thanks for what you've done for Valeria especially."

"She's a feisty little thing, isn't she? How long did the doctor say she has to wear that cast?"

"Probably until the first part of July. Do you think she could stand a trip to Chauquelín?"

"Oh, pretty soon, anyway. Are you thinking of going out there?"

"Might as well." He forced the stream of water from the hose into a spray with his thumb while I swished the broom across the floor. "If the liceo is closed until August, I could do plenty at home in the meantime. And other than just hearing they're safe, I have no idea of Mamá and Abuela's situation. When I think how the hillside just crumbled into the church here…"

I nodded. A steep wooded hill rose just behind his backyard on Chauquelín. "Don't blame you, I guess. You *did* let your grandparents in Santiago know you're all right?"

"No, never got to call. Guess I ought to, eh?"

"Stop dodging." I smacked the seat of his jeans with the wet straw of the broom. "They've written you at least two letters since the quake. They must be going crazy!"

"You'd better watch yourself, señorita." He laughed as he dropped the hose and knocked the broom from my hand. In an agile glide, he pinned my arms to the wall, his face so close that I could smell pungent eucalyptus on his breath and see tiny creases of strain around his compelling golden-brown eyes. "Why do you care so much about them anyway?"

My pulse quickened. "Because I think *you* really care, deep down."

Abruptly his grin faded. He released my arms and rescued the snaking hose. "You said your grandmother died recently," he said quietly.

"It's almost a year ago now. She...she fell and broke her hip and then died in surgery...and I..."

*I should have been there for her.* Last summer I'd offered to keep fragile Grandma Rose company. Better that than serving scones at Tea Reads, my mother's shop. Instead, I made excuses by day and sneaked out by night, chasing cheap thrills. And cheap friends.

"You miss her," Nicolás said. "A lot."

"That doesn't even begin to cover it. I—I should've treated her better." Regret filled my mouth like gravel. Tears boiled at the back of my throat. I clenched my teeth lest it all come spewing out. "Don't...be bitter, Nicolás. It's worth it to make things right with your grandparents, especially since they seem to be trying so hard."

"It's too late for trying, as far as I'm concerned." Every muscle in his face went rigid as he strode down the hall with the hose.

The Serrano guys kept busy with Cole while they waited for Valeria's medical clearance to travel. They repaired the church and put in many hours building a cabin for Tito and his mother. Finally, the voyage to Chauquelín materialized when Cole offered to ferry the Serrano and Garrido kids out on the *Ambassador.*

"He wants to find out how the folks there are," Linda told me. "See what we can do to help."

"Maybe…" I twirled a lock of hair around my finger. My Christmas spirals had washed out to a mess of jumbled waves by this stage of the perm, but at least my hands had healed to almost normal. Either I was restless now, or a sucker for punishment. "Maybe I could tag along for the ride to Chauquelín. I thought I never wanted to see that place again, but for a change of pace."

The number of houseguests in the Peterson home had dwindled. The Alvarado family had moved into their hastily constructed shanty a few days ago, Tito hoped to have his new place finished before long, and the other boys had returned to their boarding house.

"You could use the break," my sister said. "There're only two girls left here now anyway, at least until Miriam's family comes."

"Miriam's family's coming here?"

"I convinced them to stay with us a while. Felt so bad for them, herded into the gym with twenty other families."

"And the roof is so weakened they hardly dare sleep inside. But they're a big family, Lin."

"Seven. We were more than that, growing up, remember?" She smiled. "Besides, we've had three times that lately, and the Barrientos won't be any trouble. Miriam and her sisters are good, conscientious helpers."

"If they're not, Miri will make 'em march." I laughed. "It'll be fun to have her here with us."

Linda pulled three small boxes and some wrapping paper out of the lower china cupboard. "I'll put you in charge of these gifts for the island ladies."

"What!" My eyes widened, probably bulged. "I don't believe what I'm seeing. You're not giving away those cups of Grandma Rose's."

"Not all of them. But last year I started giving teacups as wedding and birthday presents. Most women here just never imagine they'll own anything so beautiful in their entire lifetime. And tea tastes better in china. It *does*, Melissa."

"But—but that's half of what you have left since the earthquake."

My sister shrugged, though her eyelids fluttered over a wet sheen. "These ladies have all lost something important. That Bórquez broke Angélica's china, Vanessa lost her husband. I think God wants me—"

"And Gina, what has she lost?" *Her mop and scrub bucket?* Ouch, I winced at my own cruelty.

"She's lost most of her friends on the island. And she has no family there."

"So you think God's telling you to give your teacups away? If you want to give them gifts, why don't you just send… oranges, or something healthy like that?"

"Your basics-before-frills? I'll do that too, but He's just telling me He has another use for those cups besides collecting dust on my cupboard shelf. 'What I kept, I lost. What I gave, I kept.' Martin Luther."

"You've got bats in your belfry, sister." I swept my limp curls into a long ponytail. "Termites in your teapot."

# 31

*Island of Chauquelín, Chiloé*
*Month 5—June 15*
*The weather mellowed again by the time we traveled to*
*Chauquelín on a Saturday afternoon...*

The air was glacial, to be sure, but what Grandma Rose called bracing. Clearer than in summer, with every color and shape intensified. The icy-bright cobalt of the sky and sea hurt my eyes to look at them long.

A gleaming stretch of snow on the distant Andes slashed through the horizon like a serrated knife. Odd, how I viewed the mountains as enemies. That first voyage in the summer, I'd seen fences, hedges. Linda had seen vistas of eternity.

Like with those stupid teacups. Señora Angélica possessed a bit of culture, but the others? Giving away our grandmother's expensive Lenox and Royal Albert seemed like nothing but a waste to me. Yet Linda thought she was investing.

Well, we'd always been polar opposites.

As the *Ambassador* approached on the azure satin sea, the island came into focus—a gem of emerald meadows, sapphire brooks, and pewter beaches, trimmed with the delicate lace of leafless trees. Its poignant beauty made my throat ache.

But so deceptive. I shivered.

Nicolás and Marcos dropped the anchors while Cole handled the rudder. As they untied the rowboat, the petite figure of a woman darted along the white-shelled path toward the shore.

"Look, it's your mother," I called to the boys. "Wonder what's been happening on the island these days."

Marcos smirked. "If we're lucky, Don Juan Bórquez's house fell into the bay and him along with it."

"No such luck." Nicolás scowled. "I saw the place when we passed by."

"Señora Angélica looks glad to see you guys, anyway," I said.

With the grace of a woodland nymph, the island woman wove a nimble path among the uneven stones of the beach. She wore a seafoam-green dress knit of homespun-and-dyed wool. Her hair was loose for once, coiled around her shoulders like glossy ribbons of dark brown seaweed. She could've been La Pincoya, Chiloé's mythological siren that I'd read about. The Little Mermaid who left the seaside and won the prince. Only now she was back where she'd escaped from.

Beside me on the deck, Valeria waved and wobbled up and down, delighted to arrive home. Between her tears and giggles, her brothers and Cole maneuvered her with the clumsy cast into the smaller boat. Jana and I squeezed in with her, and Nicolás rowed us ashore with quick, smooth strokes. While he returned for the others, Valeria sobbed in her mother's arms.

I gripped Jana's corpse-cold hand. "Your mother probably didn't see us arrive."

By the time the guys landed, the Pérez family reached the beach too.

"Hard to believe it's been a couple of months since we were last here," Cole said.

"Much has happened, for sure." Gina offered me a welcoming hug, but looked thinner and weary. The rose color that always bloomed in her cheeks had faded.

"We haven't heard much news from here," I told her. "Tell us how you've made out since the earthquake."

Ramón frowned. "Our house went down. Part of the hill slid into it. Missed the storage shed, thank God. That's given us a place to live in the meantime."

"I had them stay with us at first," Señora Angélica said, "since we didn't have much damage done. But my mother, unfortunately, made life too miserable for them."

"Nonsense, Angie." Gina's smile, pathetically valiant, didn't quite reach her eyes. "It was just... Our presence there made it too hard for *you* with Doña Luisa."

"You've been rebuilding, I take it, Ramón?" Cole said.

"Sí, though it's a long job, cutting and planing our own lumber. But with everybody needing it and not many launches running right now, we manage the best we can."

"So our house wasn't damaged?" Nicolás asked his mother.

"Only the balcony."

"Oh!" I cried. "That was so pretty."

"But that's *it*?" Nicolás was incredulous. "No landslide, like at Don Ramón's? Our hill's just as steep and even closer to the house."

"But more wooded, maybe more hard-packed," Ramón said.

"God knows the whys and hows," Gina said softly. "We are thankful to be alive and glad that your home at least was spared, Nico."

"Don Colin brought some stuff from Mellehue," Marcos said. "Building supplies and clothes and that. Looks like he won't be hauling them back."

"And Señora Linda sent you each a chocolate cake." Valeria beamed around the group. "That's a guaranteed smile."

"One for Vanessa Garrido and her family too," I said. "And…another little gift for you ladies. How'd Vanessa's house fare?" Its sorry condition made it a candidate for demolition, even before the quake.

Gina clapped her hand to her mouth, staring at the two Garrido children. "Bucha, it's a wreck, but that's not all. Vanessa signed the place over to Juan Bórquez and went to her family in Cocotúe—the Desertores Group—for a while. Two days before the earthquake. I—I thought she'd sent you children a message and that you were just along for the ride today." She patted Jana's shoulder.

Rodrigo began to mewl like a kitten. Jana rocked on her heels, her eyes silent pools. *These children have already shed too many tears.* I wrapped my arms around them both and squeezed. "We'll work something out, kids."

"The message never reached them," Cole said. "That's why we could never get any news of Vanessa from the Chauquelín radio, then."

"I tried several times." Nicolás twisted his lips. "So Vanessa finally sold out to Bórquez, did she?"

"What did you expect?" Ramón shrugged. "He's been harassing your mamá again too."

Nicolás's eyes narrowed to golden slits as he turned toward his mother. "What now?" His jaw tightened.

Señora Angélica combed her dainty fingers through Valeria's nut-brown hair. "Oh, the usual, dear. No importa. It—it's not difficult to refuse his proposals." Spots of crimson burned in her cheeks. "I am worried about his influence on your grandmother, though. Juan badgers her for more rent money on the north field. We cannot possibly pay right now, but she insists it's the least we can give after all he has done for us. I wish—if only—"

"All he's done for us!" Nicolás choked, his face aflame.

"I'd contest Bórquez's claim to that land if I were you," Cole said. "After half a century, even squatters' rights should count for something."

"Why don't you come up to the shelter for a hot drink?" Gina's teeth chattered. Her shoulders shook with cold. "You must see our real Chilote stove, Pastor Colin."

"You are welcome at my home, too," Nicolás's mother said firmly. "Please don't go without at least stopping by. I hardly know how to thank you folks for all your care of my children."

I hunched beside Cole on a rude wooden bench drawn close to the smoking hearth of the Pérezes' temporary home. This miserable hovel—a dilapidated storage shed—upgraded their old place to mansion level. A circle of stones contained the fire, and a steaming pot of water hung over it, suspended from a hook in the soot-blackened roof. I felt like we were extras in a pioneer movie.

"What should we do about Jana and Rodrigo?" I asked. The kids sat across from me, expressionless as stones.

Don Ramón's trademark wool hat flopped from side to side as he shook his head and offered the mate cup to Cole. "Don't know. Vanessa is probably frantic, but if you think it's rustic here, you should visit the Desertores. No regular launch service, no communications at all."

"How did she get out there in the first place?"

"Bórquez's launch. His crew had a fishing trip near there. Probably fleeced her for the fare, too."

"Any possibility they'll make another trip soon? I'd cover it so the children could go out with their mother until school starts again." Cole handed the mate cup back to Ramón. "I mean, we can take them back to Mellehue, and I know Linda would be happy to keep them, but as you say, Vanessa must be worried."

"What about the grandmother?" I said. "You know, Jaime's mother. Doesn't she live somewhere around here?"

"Toward the southern end of the island. But the old lady is in no condition to take the kids. Had to move in with a sister herself since she sold her property to Bórquez last year."

"Oh, Jana and Rigo can stay with us until we locate a launch going to the Desertores." Gina gave the two stone-faced children each a caress and then squatted on the packed-earth floor to slice bread on a slab of wood. "We'll take care of the situation, Pastor Colin. They *are* relatives, you know."

As the grown-ups discussed their fate, the Garrido kids' listless gazes jabbed an acute pain in my chest. *I thought I had no input on my options.* But I'd led a charmed life, comparatively. Maybe I'd never understood that until now.

That weasel Bórquez had practically stolen everything from them—their home, their mother... I wanted to gather them in my arms, cry with them, share their confusion. But I only sat shivering in the fire's feeble, smoky heat and sipping gross tea from a battered plastic cup.

"If only I had the time to go out to Cocotúe myself," Cole said. "But so many are depending on us back in Mellehue, and tomorrow is Sunday—"

"No, Pastor Colin, don't even think of it," Ramón said. "It's another four hours' voyage from here, and you don't know the waters, either. Go in peace, Gina and I will see to the children."

I bit my lip. How could the Pérezes take on extra responsibilities in such circumstances? "Cole, I could stay here," I said impulsively. "Gina doesn't look well, and I'm sure they need to put what energy they have into building the new house while the weather cooperates. I'll help with the kids until they find a boat going to their mother's island."

My brother-in-law blinked his blue eyes at me twice and gulped, I squirmed. He was probably trying in vain to visualize his finicky teenage sister in law surviving for more than a few minutes in this dirt-floored hut.

"Are you—are you serious, Melissa?" His Adam's apple bobbed up and down.

"I've never been more serious in my life. It'll just be until arrangements can be made for the Garrido kids, anyway. Linda can spare me now with Miriam's family there to help. Er, that is…if I won't be in the way here." I flushed and looked toward Gina and Ramón. Brother, I'd stuck my foot in my mouth, again.

"We would welcome your help, my dear," —Gina gave me a closed-mouth smile— "if you don't mind staying in this humble shack."

"But—but what about your clothes, and…" For a preacher, Cole was having a hard time getting his words out.

Did he think I was *that* frivolous? That I couldn't get along without my wardrobe? "Didn't you say something about coming out again with another load of supplies? I'll manage in my jeans until then. Besides, maybe I'd even be going back with you by then."

Half an hour later, I hiked with Cole toward the Serranos' for a brief visit.

"I don't know about this caper, Meli," he said. "What will your parents think? I mean, I'd trust Ramón and Gina with my very life, but it's a pretty crude setup they've got here right now. Even for someone used to roughing it."

"And I'm not, yeah, I know that. And I know I'll be stuck here till further notice." I wouldn't be able to walk away whenever I felt like it. *Qué será...* "I—I just sorta jumped in with both feet."

"Maybe you should've, uh, tested the depth of the water first, sis."

"Maybe that's exactly why I did it this way. No chance to chicken out."

He grunted and then grinned. "Well, as you say, I'll be back soon, if you change your mind."

I wouldn't. I wasn't—I was *not*—too fragile to be useful. Or too worried about my image to get dirty.

# 32

"Vaya, this is kind of a primitive place for a señorita like you, no? Like playing cavewoman."

I glanced up from the bread dough I was kneading in a wooden tray on the floor, surprised to see Nicolás slouched against the doorframe of the Pérezes' shed. Three days of struggling over the open fire had blistered my hands in several spots and stained my single set of clothes beyond redemption, but I'd become an expert housekeeper-in-a-hovel. I'd also kept too busy—lugging water from the spring, peeling potatoes, sweeping ashes and dirt—to socialize with our neighbors during that time.

I countered his grin with a grimace. "It's not the Holiday Inn for sure. I pretend I'm a Girl Scout at wilderness camp. Or maybe a Marine in boot camp."

"Did you not get enough of camping last summer in the tent?"

"Oh, that." I shrugged. "That was just a lark." Did he expect me to whine about the harsh realities of life on Chauquelín? Not even the worst suffering would persuade me to admit any regrets about my spontaneous offer of charity. I wouldn't give him the satisfaction.

Besides, in spite of everything, I wasn't sorry I'd stayed. The Pérezes needed me. Life here wasn't comfortable or convenient. The squalid conditions made simple jobs like cooking and washing herculean. But I was lightening Gina's burden at least a little. That was enough.

Chiloé winters were *not* Chiloé summers, I got that. Biting cold and frosts assaulted every single day. The gloom of night fell early and clung until late.

My only pajamas the same jeans and sweater I wore all day, I'd slept fitfully the first couple of nights and awakened at the first blush of dawn filtering in through the threadbare sheets that Gina had tacked up for curtains in the shed. My bed consisted of a narrow board, a flea-infested mattress, and a few thin scraps of blankets. I'd shuddered imagining mice, and worse vermin, scuttling up the bare wooden walls behind me or—*horrors!*—across my face.

This third morning, I'd resisted as consciousness claimed me for yet another day of slave labor. My cramped limbs ached. My breath hung like frozen fog in an igloo. Shivering, I'd started to drag the moldy blankets over my head in protest, when I caught my breath.

A gossamer of cobwebs dangled from the rafters, glazed with beads of ice. Like prisms suspended on spun-silk thread, they glittered in the sunrise. Dazzled by the unexpected beauty, I pushed aside my self-pity along with the pitiful bedclothes. *You asked for this, Melissa Rose. And there* are *compensations.*

"Well, you don't have to work *all* the time," Nicolás said. "My mamá sent me to invite you to bring your charges over for tea. Actually for *yoco* since she had us kill the fatted pig yesterday."

"In honor of your homecoming? What's *yoco*?"

"Roast pork and *milcao* with cracklings and deep-fried *calzones rotos*—"

"Fried *raggedy underwear*? You've *got* to be kidding."

He laughed. "Everything's good, you'll see. Besides, Valeria is fretting because Jana gets to see you all the time, and she hasn't seen you since we got back here."

"Poor thing, I've neglected her. How's her leg?"

"The leg is mending fine, just the spirits are a bit damp today." He glanced with raised brows at the smooth ball of dough rolling under my hands. "Mamá says, too, that if you're making bread, to come early and use her oven. You must be tired of baking it in the ashes."

I slid my ugly hands beneath the dough and sank back on my haunches. "I've almost begun to like it now that I'm on to not burning most of it. But I'm thankful to your mother for the offer and I'll do that. What did you find out about boats going to the Desertores?"

His shoulders sagged. "Most of the fishermen don't plan to head that way again until abalone season opens the first of August, and it's pretty expensive for them to make a special trip. I even humbled myself and asked Don Juan Bórquez about getting Vanessa's kids out to her." He snorted. "No sympathy there. Wants fifty thousand pesos for the charter, more than anybody else. Otherwise, he says, his launches are occupied elsewhere. And are they occupied. He's made a killing on inflated prices for building supplies from Mellehue."

"Maybe it's a good thing Cole's coming back with more."

"You bet it is. Ramón and Gina have made good progress with that load of lumber Don Colin brought. Marcos and I came here to help for the afternoon. I've been preparing tools and things for spring planting, but we will wait on that and do what we can for Ramón first."

"That's generous of you."

"It is the least we can do." He paused a moment, then said abruptly, "Did I, uh...see you outside *splitting wood* just now?"

"Yeah, we used quite a bit cooking dinner, and I needed more for the bread." I smiled and gave the dough a pat. "But not now, since your mother's offered to bake it for us."

"Melissa, don't—don't do that anymore. Ask Ramón if you need wood, even if you have to interrupt him. He won't mind."

"You think I'm made of glass? Gina chops her own wood."

"So does my mother—sometimes," he retorted. "She grew up doing it, and she's quite capable. But not when I'm around."

"Well, you're not around here. So there."

"Then I will be. Seriously, Meli." A note of concern persisted in his voice, as well as something else I couldn't identify. He took my bruised hands and drew me to my feet, compelling me to look into his eyes. "I'll come every day to split wood, if need be, but do not *you* try it again, *please*. You may chop your foot off or something. Bucha, it—it gave me cold chills. Now, I'll go right to work."

His odd intensity amused, baffled me, sometimes. To the rhythmic percussion of his axe against the chopping block outside, I set the dough to rise beneath a tattered flour-sack cloth. He didn't have to act so machista about it, but still... I was forced to acknowledge that he was ten times more effi-cient at the task than I was.

He made short work of turning several thick trunks into
a neat stack of firewood and then crossed the yard to the
construction in progress. All before I'd banked the fire and
gathered Jana, Rodrigo, and the three Pérez children for the
short walk to the Serranos'.

Jana and I swung a covered basket containing the bread dough
between us. Except for the same mud and the scurrying geese
and hens underfoot, the Pérez yard had changed drastically
since the summer. The remains of their home lay flattened
beneath a heap of tumbled earth, a somber reminder of May's
disaster. Semi-recognizable objects jutted here and there
among the debris—spears of broken glass, splintered teal
boards, crumpled stovepipe.

Ramón and Gina had spent days sifting through the rubble
to salvage what they could. Now they poured their efforts into
a downsized version of their home. For now, Ramón planned
to build a three-room single-pitched structure. When time
and money permitted, he'd complete the other half of what
they called a *media-agua*.

They had most of the frame up now. The Serrano boys'
extra hands would advance the project a lot today. I figured
the least I could do was to spare the Pérezes additional worry
by keeping the five children, aged three to ten, entertained
and out of the way as much as possible.

Both Gina and Nicolás looked up from the sheet of corrugated zinc they were measuring when I lifted five fingers
and pointed in the direction of the shore road. Nicolás waved.
Gina gave a jerky nod.

Gina worked like a man alongside her husband, sawing and slamming nails nonstop. I admired her drive, but I pitied her too. She refused to rest, and she'd lost weight. The strain was obviously taking its toll.

But the clear weather wouldn't last long in Chiloé. They had to take advantage of it.

Gina's little daughter, Anita, clung to my other hand while the three boys raced ahead. I smiled down at Jana's pale face. "Looks like we'll be together for a while yet, kid. We'll be old friends before this is over."

Jana returned a smile as wary as a wounded animal. "That's good, Señorita Melissa."

The bashful girl kept addressing me as *Señorita*, but at least she no longer looked like a neglected scarecrow. With a warm red parka, still-crisp jeans, and a bow in her mousy hair—my purchases in lieu of souvenirs—Jana was better dressed than I was at the moment. She'd responded to my attempts at kindness with puppy-like adoration. That much was gratifying, sort of.

But the hopelessness haunting her eyes gnawed at me. I couldn't scrub it or wipe it away. Some things a trip to the store didn't cure. How could I lift that lead weight of sadness from her heart?

We rounded the bend to full view of the Serrano home, a dark shape that almost blended into the landscape, like an eagle's eyrie clinging to the hillside. In spite of minor earthquake damage, the house was still striking.

"Oh, look!" Jana pointed to the fractured balcony. "It's Doña Luisa!"

Tufts of white hair flapping from her black headscarf in the breeze, Señora Luisa Guzmán tottered on the threshold of the French doors that led from a second-floor bedroom to the balcony. During the quake, the gracefully curved structure had buckled in the middle and pulled away from the main part of the house. Its carved railing had crumbled away like the fragile antique it was.

Nicolás's grandmother was too fragile to hang around the edge of a precarious ruin, either. Alarm skidded through me. What if she stumbled and fell? *Like Grandma Rose...*

Heart thudding, I picked up our pace. "She shouldn't be up there. It's not safe, and she's not steady on her feet at the best of times. I wonder where Señora Angélica went?"

Angélica blanched when we told her. "I just stepped outside to fetch a couple of eggs. I never imagined she was not still lying down in her room." She hastily wiped pastry dough from her hands.

Valeria dozed, stretched out on a pile of cushions in an enormous wicker chair by the wood stove, her gangly cast propped up with another pillow. The kids surrounded and woke her.

"Do you need help?" I asked as Señora Angélica started toward the stairs.

"Maybe."

I trailed her into the hall, as gleaming-gold as ever, and up the staircase. At the top, Señora Angélica paused before a door to the left, slightly ajar. "I'm afraid I might startle her. Not only is the railing down, there's a gap between the house and the balcony floorboards."

"I saw. This room opens onto the balcony? Whose is it?"

"It belonged to my parents until my father died, but it's just a spare bedroom now. Mamá moved downstairs when I came here with the children—her idea. But I sleep with Valeria."

"Your mother likes to look at the cove from here." Spying on the neighbors, I always assumed.

"She loves the view from this room, often climbs up on a fine day. Since the earthquake, it is almost an obsession with her." Señora Angélica took a deep breath and pushed the door open.

Grandmother Luisa didn't react when we entered, although she must have heard us. Seeming oblivious of the gaping space in front of her, she clung to the doors leading to the balcony, swaying in the brisk wind. A black knit shawl billowed around her gaunt shoulders.

"Mamá, you should have told me you wanted to come up here," Señora Angélica said quietly. "It is dangerous for you alone."

The old woman didn't budge, didn't even take her eyes from the scene before her. She trembled like a dry leaf. "Angélica, it must be fixed. Your father built this home when we were newlyweds. I've watched from this balcony for fifty years."

Was she still waiting for her husband's return from a voyage? That sounded almost romantic.

"I know, Mamá." Angélica patted Señora Luisa's scrawny arm and tried to steer her away from the draft and danger of the open doorway. "But we have to be patient. Others have no home at all."

Grandmother Luisa shuffled away from her balcony in silence. Her cracked face quivered like a tidal flat of burrowing clams. She halted when she noticed me. Usually she just ignored me—the unwelcome canuta—but now her sharp tarblack eyes narrowed and locked on mine. After a few seconds, her gaze fluttered to the French windows overlooking the sea again. Her mouth twitched, but she said nothing.

Gosh, the old girl was mourning the damage to her bridal home. A twinge of sympathy stung me. "Nicolás can't repair it, Señora Angélica?"

"Perhaps, but God knows that boy has enough to do. I don't know what we would do without him—" Her voice grew husky and caught for an instant. "And even Nicolás, handy as he is, could not make it like it was. Sometimes I fear we forget he's not yet sixteen. My father was a master craftsman."

Once again Señora Angélica nudged her mother towards the stairs, but the elderly woman planted herself, facing the balcony, and dug her claws into the shawl. Her eyes glittered with moisture.

"Señora Luisa," I said, on a wisp of inspiration, "would you show me how you spin that wool into yarn? I've watched you do it before, and I saw another bag of wool downstairs today."

Some nameless emotion flitted across her dried-apple face. "Come then, señorita." She turned and hobbled downstairs faster than I could've imagined her asthmatic lungs and rheumatic legs allowed.

Señora Angélica watched, speechless, but I was even more dumbfounded. Who knew my spur-of-the-moment brain-wave would prompt Grandmother Luisa's immediate, if gruff, acceptance? I scrambled after her.

Maybe I could use this unexpected bridge to win the old lady's good will. It was worth the try. If even one canuto could gain Luisa Guzmán's confidence, it would benefit the whole Serrano family.

## 33

Splashes of sunlight in the Serrano kitchen created a warm, bright oasis after days of the dim, damp chill of the Pérezes' shed. The first thing Señora Angélica did was hustle me into the tiny bathroom under the stairs and hand me a homespun wool dress like her own. "Pass your things out and I'll wash them while you shower. I think they'll dry before you have to go."

"Señora Angélica, you're an absolute angel. But—what about the kids?"

"Next time. I'm a little short of hot water for everyone."

A bottom-line-basic affair, the real-live water closet contained little more than a three-foot-square enamel shower base, a sink and toilet, and a hammered-copper tub hanging on a nail. But I would've given a month's allowance for the luxury of that hot shower—piped through the kitchen stove, like at Linda's place. The heather-blue dress prickled my skin a little, but even so, I felt like heaven when I emerged into the kitchen again.

Then, while Señora Angélica shaped and fried a huge batch of "raggedy underwear"—twists of sweet squash pastry—and another of the potato patties with pork cracklings they called *milcao*, I filled the oven twice with round, satiny loaves of bread. I was pretty proud of them by this time. The mouthwatering aromas of freshly baked bread and frying meat mingled with the musky smell of raw wool.

Between bakings, I hovered by Grandmother Luisa on the bench behind the stove and observed her spinning the cream-colored virgin wool around a wooden spindle. As swift as a top, she formed a smooth, strong yarn.

Her gnarled fingers worked deftly, never hesitating, but I found the technique tricky. When I tried it by myself, the thread snapped or unraveled in weak spots. Or balled into a cocoon. Humor glinted in the elderly woman's dark eyes as she guided my fumbling hands to gently tug, stretch, and twist the clumps of wool into an even thread and wind it around the spindle.

Even Jana and Valeria showed more skill than the klutzy gringa. *Talk about total humiliation.*

"Don't let Anita try it." I laughed. "It would really be disgraceful to be outdone by a three-year-old."

"Nonsense," Señora Angélica said. "The girls have been spinning since they were little. You do well for a first time, my dear. Does she not, Mamá?"

Señora Luisa grunted, her lips pinched as straight as a pin. Only her eyes betrayed a slight softening. At least, they no longer smoldered like coals at me.

"Then let's do something you're good at, Meli," Valeria said. "A guessing game like we played back in Mellehue. Or...I know. A story! I don't have any storybooks like Reba's, but you could tell us a Bible story. Like Señora Linda does."

I froze with a loaf of bread suspended midair. Swallowing, I carefully lowered the steaming loaf to the tablecloth. *Just go for casual.* "I might be better at spinning than Bible stories, Vali. I'm not a Sunday school teacher like my sister, you know."

"Oh, I bet you could do it anyway." Valeria clasped her hands together and appealed with those kitten-gray eyes of hers. "Vamos, something about Jesus."

My heart thumped, and my mouth went as dry as a ball of wool. "Why don't you ask Nicolás when he comes home? He's a budding preacher."

Oblivious to my sarcasm, Valeria giggled. "Nico can't tell stories. Please, Melissa, *please.*"

Even Jana added her timid voice to the clamor. "It would be like last summer."

How could I refuse them? Jana practically homeless, Valeria sprawled there with her broken leg, both without a father. In desperation, I threw a pleading glance at Señora Angélica. "But your grandmother, Vali…"

"I don't think she'll mind, will you, Mamá?" Angélica shot a nervous smile toward her mother's expressionless face. "It is about Jesus, and Valeria needs a treat, no? She's been so cooped up here."

*Sweet, no backup there.*

The back door into the kitchen slammed as the three little boys raced in from playing in the yard. "How long before tea?" Julio César bellowed.

"We will have story time first." With a regal wave, Valeria wriggled upright on her throne and squished over for me to join her.

Why didn't the kid blow a trumpet and advertise in the village too? On the verge of panic, I racked my brain. What story could I tell when I'd turned a deaf ear to sermons and Bible lessons for years?

In my mind, I shrank to a little girl again, smaller than Valeria and Jana, maybe not much older than Anita. Cuddled up at my mother's side, I listened to her read from the Bible storybook my sister Jennifer dragged out each night. From the dusty oblivion of this long-locked room of my life, I scrounged a narrative or two I could use now.

"One day," I began, "Jesus was teaching in the synagogue—like the Jewish church."

Hushed, expectant attention reigned. Perched on the edge of the big wicker chair beside Valeria and her clumsy cast, I balanced Anita on my lap. The other children lounged on the polished floor around us. Señora Angélica drained the last of the *milcao* from the bubbling fat and leaned against the wall by the stovepipe. Grandmother Luisa continued to sit by the fire and spin, her bent profile carved in wood.

The story of the stooped old woman whom Jesus noticed and healed on the Sabbath was one of my early favorites. But seriously, I felt like a blundering fool—in a dress, no less, though not exactly like Linda's.

"The Pharisees, Jesus's enemies, complained loudly because Jesus had supposedly broken their traditions by healing the poor woman on their day of rest. But He said, 'You're a bunch of hypocrites! Satan has kept her crippled for eighteen years now. Don't you think it's right that she should be freed from her sickness as soon as possible?' So then His enemies were ashamed of their meanness, and the people thanked God for what Jesus had done for her." I ended the tale rather lamely.

"He sure got the best of them, didn't He?" Rodrigo crowed like a rooster.

"Another one," Joelín said.

Valeria tilted her head and batted her thick eyelashes. "Sí, one more. Then we'll have tea."

Resigned, I plunged in again. "Just a few days before Jesus died on the cross, some friends invited him for supper at their home in a village called Bethany…"

Telling these ancient stories wasn't as difficult as I'd feared. This attic corner of my mind, though cobwebby and neglected, had never really been forgotten. Now awakened, vivid memories stirred there. Stories as familiar to me as my own personal history.

I warmed to the subject. "The alabaster jar of perfume Mary brought was very expensive and rare—"

The back door creaked open. Nicolás and Marcos filed in. They stopped short just inside, mute and motionless as statues in their work clothes, as intent as the rest. I felt Nicolás's eyes fixed on me in unconcealed astonishment. A half smile played on his lips.

Now more self-conscious than ever, I floundered on. "Probably she'd saved a long time to buy this perfume and was keeping it for a special occasion. It was her most prized possession. But, without holding back, she broke the jar open and poured it all out on Jesus's feet, every drop, because she figured He was worth it." I drew the story to an awkward conclusion. *The abridged version.*

I bit my bottom lip and slid Anita to her feet. "There now, girls, the boys are home. We'd better quit goofing off and set the table."

"Oh, don't stop for us." Marcos stalked over to snitch a *calzón roto* from the dish on the stovetop. "I wouldn't mind listening a while longer."

His mother frowned at his rubber boots but handed him another pastry twist. "Would you mind picking me a handful of cilantro instead, Marc dear? And bring in the rest of the dahlias. The frost has left a few, I think."

"Come tomorrow for another story hour, Melissa," Valeria said.

I arched my brows at the precocious child. Rolling my eyes, I turned away to gather dishes for the dining room. *You've got high hopes, Vali.*

Nicolás took the stack of saucers from my hands. "You know the Bible so well in your head, amiga," he said in a low murmur. "Why do you try so hard to shut it out of your heart?"

I refused to answer him. Not with a word nor a look. I didn't dare to meet the probing gaze of those bottomless topaz eyes of his.

But I knew exactly what he meant. And no doubt he knew I knew.

# 34

Señora Angélica snipped the stem off a scarlet dahlia and floated it as a table centerpiece in the silver-and-red flowered teacup Linda had sent her. "God bless your sister's thoughtfulness. I will send her a note the next time Don Colin comes."

"Actually," Valeria whispered as she hopped into the dining room, "she cried when she opened the box."

A stab of guilt pierced my conscience. I'd never delivered Linda's gift to Gina, just stuffed it into the plastic bag of extra items I'd scavenged off the *Ambassador* before Cole left. Honestly, Gina didn't even have a decent home at the moment. No cupboards, no shelves, not even a table. I couldn't bear to think of Grandma Rose's precious china smashed in that hovel.

Maybe Gina wasn't as careless as that. But she had no concept of fine things like lace tablecloths and floral centerpieces and silver tea sets. Why waste valuable heirlooms on someone who wouldn't appreciate it?

*Why this waste of perfume?* Judas Iscariot had objected.

Dear God, in my haste I'd skipped that part of the story.

Why this waste of china on worthless Gina? Was that what I really thought? With a fist, I pressed back a groan.

After the lavish tea spread, I changed back into my own clothes, board-stiff but spotless, for a few hours anyway. Señora Angélica packed a plate of *yoco*—a sampler of hog-slaughter delicacies—for the Pérezes and bundled the little ones into their jackets again. She snatched up a length of yarn—one of my spinning rejects, by the clumpy texture—and wound it around an armful of dahlias.

As I ushered the kids out the door, she placed the bouquet on top of the breadbasket. "Something for Gina."

*For Gina.* In the vermillion sunset glow along the shore road, I got an idea. Or maybe a kick in the pants.

I'd patronized my host and hostess long enough. Sure, I'd helped them. But why? Because I wanted to feel important, like some kind of gringa princess doing the Chilote peasants a big favor?

They'd accepted me as if I were their own sister. They shared their meager food, lent me blankets I knew they couldn't spare. But I held them at arm's length. Even Jana, I treated more like a pet dog I'd rescued from the pound.

It was time to move from feel-good charity to spillover love.

"Ramón went to dig a few clams for tomorrow's lunch. Wonderful change tonight, real bread." Bleary-eyed, Gina lifted the lid of the soot-smudged pot hanging over the firepit, checked the contents, and sank to the log bench. "Water's almost boiling."

"Good, because I have another little surprise tonight." I tucked Señora Angélica's rainbow of dahlias into an empty powdered-milk can.

"*Yoco!*" the children shouted in chorus.

Gina brightened. "Oh, I'd love a hot *milcao* with tea right now."

"Your wish is my command, milady." I unpacked the basket and pushed a couple of greasy potato patties into the ashes at the edge of the blaze. They really were as unappetizing when cold as Nicolás's Grandmother Rosalía had declared. The raggedy undies would taste better crisped, too, and…I found a packet of dried leaves. "Um, Señora Angélica sent herbal tea, too. You know what kind this is, Gina?"

"*Cedrón.* Type of lemon verbena. Lovely, relaxes the nerves." Gina tipped a weak smile. "Maybe we all need some. Also called Luisa-herb."

"Really?" I groped inside the flimsy grocery bag I kept my few things in and pulled out the giftwrapped cube. "Gina, this…this is for you, from my sister. I thought you should have it tonight."

Gina staggered up to give me a hug and kiss before even touching the present. Who said she had no culture? Then she opened the box, while the kids crowded around. Wadded-up newspaper dropped to the ground. A gold-rimmed cup and saucer nestled inside.

I knew that set—I'd drunk from it during scores of tea parties with my grandmother. Country Roses, Royal Albert's most famous pattern. Those precious moments shaped the foundation of my life. *She* sure didn't bury her best unused in the cupboard.

Amid the children's oohs and aahs, I lifted the china out and crumbled a couple of *cedrón* leaves into the cup. I poured a dipperful of hot water over it, propelled Gina back to the log seat, and knelt to place it in her hands. *A country rose.*

A spicy citric perfume filled the shed and forced out the mildew and smoke and wood-rot.

"You should be using this cup," Gina said. "I can—"

"Absolutely not. It's meant for you, señora." *Basics before frills, people before porcelain.*

Gina brought the cup to her lips. Tears streamed into the tea.

"Gina, do you have a Bible I can borrow?" I asked after a second afternoon of storytelling recruitment.

"Of course, querida." If Gina considered it an odd request, coming from the missionary's sister, she was too polite to say so.

But since I had to keep doing this, I might as well prepare. I'd run out of raw material today, though I'd discovered I had a flair for telling stories—hadn't Linda said that once? It was *kind* of like the dramatic monologues I enjoyed. The children were a flattering audience, too. Even Señora Angélica paused her work to listen, and Grandmother Luisa listened, if she didn't pause.

So I didn't mind *that* much. Consider it atonement for my sins. Volunteer experience for my college resumé down the line.

Cole returned to the island on the weekend to drop off more building supplies, new stove pipes for the Pérezes, and a welcome dufflebag of clean clothes for me. Underwear never looked so good.

On the beach, I asked him about some flashcard pictures or flannelgraph figures.

His Adam's apple bobbed, probably swallowing shock. "Uh, sure, I'll mention it to Linda. She must have some things you can use. You really want to stay on here for the long haul, though? Sounds like Jana and Rigo could be waiting indefinitely for a launch to their mother's island."

"That's exactly why I need to stay. If I'm here to cook and look after the kids, then Ramón and Gina might be able to move into their house in another week. So unless Linda needs me in Mellehue—"

"It's not that," he said quickly. "Lin's getting along with Miriam and company at the house. I'm just not sure if I'll get out here again very soon."

"I'll be *fine* until you can." *I hope.*

# 35

*Isla Chauquelín (continued)*
*Month 6 – July*
*Cole brought out my notebook, too. Finally I got caught up, but ...*

Two weeks later, I wasn't so sure about my survival. Anita had a cough and stayed behind at the Pérez shed with Gina when we walked over to the "class," as Valeria dubbed it, that day. On the way home, the other four children agreed to race each other along the woods path. I all but snatched at the chance for a moment's solitude in the lavender twilight.

As soon as the kids were out of sight, I ducked through the bamboo thicket to El Mirador, the clearing that overlooked the twin coves below. I shouldn't linger. I'd been out for the better part of the afternoon, and Gina would need my help soon. That was what I was on the island for, not to bask in the sunset or the scenery. But I was desperate for a few minutes alone.

I'd never liked being alone. I got to thinking too much, took things too seriously. Maybe I was just overtired now—oversensitive—but truth told, I'd never experienced so many conflicting emotions in all my fifteen years.

This was getting to me. Oh, not the hardships of island life—the grueling work or the rough living conditions—but my enlistment as the neighborhood Bible teacher. The job of telling Bible stories had stirred up this weird introspective mood.

Why should matters I'd long ago filed away in my mind suddenly distract and fluster me? Why did the things I'd always held important—friends and fun times and freedom—now rate as insignificant, even dull? Everything I'd refused and resented before somehow touched me here.

Why, *why* on earth should the chapter about Jesus and the Samaritan woman bring a slushy lump to my throat? I'd heard all the stories before. I'd never been a sentimental sap. So, how could it move me to read, "Whoever drinks of this water will thirst again, but whoever drinks of the water that I shall give him shall never thirst…"?

*Ridiculous.* I rejected my own reaction, objectively. But inexplicable doubt had snuck up and overtaken me. A whirl of confusion mocked me, whispered that while I wore my badge of disinterest, it was only that—a careful masquerade. *Practiced* indifference.

Tears leaped to blind me. Wasn't it enough that I worked my tail off for these islanders? Now I had to play the missionary on top of it.

It was Valeria's fault, her and her Bible stories. But I didn't have the guts to disappoint the kid.

It was this life in a bubble, where I had nothing better to think about.

And it was definitely Nicolás and his arrogant digs about "head and heart."

I blinked and wiped my stinging eyes. Sure, I'd come to love Chiloé and its warm, sturdy people—I really did. But my goal to encourage them in this difficult time had gone too far. Lend a helping hand? Gladly. But shake up the bedrock of my whole life? Enough already. My willingness to sacrifice had a limit.

A familiar iron fist squeezed my chest as I moped at the towering edge of El Mirador. The winter sunset made a vibrant garden painting. Flower hues of lilac and rose, tiger lily and leaf green, bloomed in the sky like a giant bouquet. Drifting petals of color brushed land and sea. So achingly beautiful.

The islanders claimed that each year they enjoyed a couple of weeks of perfect weather around the time of the winter solstice. St. John's summer, they called it. Back home, it was midsummer now, but this was more like Indian summer in the fall. Perfect it certainly was, breathtaking, in fact. Was that why I was trembling?

Or was it because caring about people, about things I couldn't see or understand or control, made me feel as vulnerable as a molting crab? I didn't want to care, but I did. I wanted to be hip and snarky like my friends—*make that ex-friends*—but hadn't that kind of free-spirit sophistication turned out to be just an act? The more I tried to pose as that version of myself, the more I imitated everybody else.

In trying so hard to take a different path from my family, I'd lost my way. No, I didn't have to be a clone of my sisters. But I didn't have to be cookie-cutter cool either. Who was I, really? What was my place, my purpose, in the world?

Wasn't it time to live my real story? Be honest, face the good, the bad, and the ugly? Happiness is within you, Amanda Ellis always parroted. That was *so* not true. When I looked inside myself, I found…well, not much happiness, for sure. Was such an elusive goal even possible?

And wasn't part of the dread I felt because I wouldn't let myself bolt again? Then Nicolás would know his words had penetrated the weak spots in my armor like well-aimed arrows. I admitted it—yeah, I'd tried to run away earlier, before the earthquake in May. That was my life MO—hiding, as he'd seen—lest anything should breach the fortress of my heart.

All this brooding made me nervous. It couldn't lead anywhere safe. But—I clenched my cold hands—I wouldn't retreat this time, even if I could. I'd prove him wrong. He expected me to run, if not from the inconveniences of island life, then definitely from…God.

There! I dared to bring the long-avoided, long-imprisoned phantom presence out into the open courtyard of my mind.

I could blame my inner turmoil on whatever or whomever I liked. Blame my family or school, my current circumstances, or other people, including Nicolás. But at the end of my rant, I knew it was God Himself who disturbed me.

He invaded my thoughts and upset my life. I couldn't escape Him. The more I tried to shut Him up and shut Him out, the more relentlessly He called and chased me. He would not let me go.

Most astounding of all, instead of finding His pursuit irritating, as I imagined, I was intrigued, ever so reluctantly allured. Could Jesus Christ truly want Melissa Rose Travis?

His Spirit within me seemed to leap up with intense yearning. The paths I had once walked with Him, overgrown with neglect, now beckoned to a meadow filled with joy and light. Mysterious doors enticed me to secret soul-rooms I'd never entered before.

Could my empty wells, parched with pride and clogged with—yeah, garbage—spring to life again? I was so cold and hungry inside. Now that I felt drawn to the table, was a banquet really waiting?

I inhaled the blade-sharp air. Hadn't I told the parable of God the Father's party invitation only this afternoon? *"Everything is ready. Come to the...banquet." But they paid no attention and went off...*

So He had my attention. What next?

Absently I watched the sky blossoms wither and fade in the dusk. Then two brilliant objects glided from the north into Dolphin Bay. In a moment, they swung into unmistakable focus—boats about the size of local fishing launches. One sported wraithlike sails and glittered with lights that would've rivaled Baltimore's city Christmas tree.

Rooted to the spot, I clapped a hand to my pulsating throat. Was it the *Caleuche*? I remembered with blood-chilling clarity what I'd read in Nicolás's mythology book about the dazzling Chilote ghost ship. The black horror of the day following Jaime Garrido's death in the bay engulfed me all over again.

I sucked in a tremulous breath. *Use common sense, girl.* Of course this floating Christmas tree had some logical explanation. Hadn't Nicolás once remarked that anyone could stage a *Caleuche* show with the right equipment? But *who*? And for what despicable intent? To intimidate people? To *kill* them?

*Nicolás. I gotta tell him right away.* Forcing my paralyzed limbs into action, I tore off through the shadowy woods.

# 36

Thank God, the Serrano guys still lingered at the Pérezes', storing Don Ramón's tools for the night. Clutching my heaving side, I described what I'd seen from El Mirador. "I don't think I'm crazy—or hallucinating. Can we check it out?"

The boys pawed the ground, eager to set out at once, but Ramón hesitated. "*Chuta.*" He scratched his stubbled chin. "Shucks."

"Ramón is sapped," Gina said from the open door of the shed. "I think he's caught the same miserable cold Anita has. Maybe you kids could go down and tell us what you find?"

"Be careful." Despite his lack of energy, Ramón wagged a stern finger. "Don't go out into the bay."

"Not to worry." Marcos smirked. "We don't have a rowboat anymore, and not even Cahuel's likely to go swimming this time of year."

We three teenagers scrambled down to the shore road. At the Serrano home, Marcos dashed inside to let his mother know our plans while Nicolás and I waited. The honey glow from the house outlined the skeleton of the damaged balcony.

"You don't think you can rebuild it?" I asked.

He paced the path beside me. "I'll give it a try, eventually. Not a top priority, though. We don't use that room much. So many more pressing needs right now."

I touched the denim sleeve of his jacket. "You know something? I'd make it a priority if I were you. It means a lot to your grandmother."

He glanced at me with a sly smile. "I think you have grown to like Abuela. Truth is, she likes you, too. Oh, she doesn't say much—just chuckles every night over your practice with the spindle."

"My fumbling, you mean. I'm determined to master that before I leave here. She hasn't had any more of those attacks since Easter, has she?"

"I guess not. She has her sulks, though, which are almost as bad as the real thing. At least for Mamá."

"But if she really has gall bladder trouble, won't it keep getting worse?"

"Maybe, but Mamá watches her diet pretty carefully. And for now, Abuela has convinced herself that Medicine Man Bórquez healed her. The machi can do no wrong in her eyes."

Marcos slipped onto the path again, and we resumed our hike over ground already furring with frost. Darkness settled in for the night, but even through the peninsula's thick wooded canopy, a huge amber disc of a moon dominated the speckled carpet of stars.

"I just hope those launches are still in the bay after all this fuss," I said.

"Me too," Nicolás said grimly. "And not because I doubt you, but I'd sure like to get to the bottom of this."

Even before we emerged from the woods, I heard the strains of music, the seesawing lilt of a traditional island melody, played by guitar and recorder. My pulse quickened. Locking elbows with the two boys, I gaped as we stumbled onto the stony beach of Dolphin Bay.

For an instant, the blaze of multicolored lights on the bigger launch nearly blinded us. Another craft, more sparsely lit, hugged its starboard flank.

"Vaya, if it isn't the *Caleuche* herself—lights, music, and all." A smirk spread across Marcos's face.

Nicolás stiffened. "And look, the smaller one's Bórquez's *Angélica*. I'd know that launch anywhere."

We stared, too dazed to take in all the implications of our discovery. Why was Juan Bórquez's fishing boat joined at the hip with a ship outfitted to resemble the infamous *Caleuche*? In plain sight and completely tangible, the two vessels now moved as one from the calm waters inshore toward the rugged string of shoals off the peninsula.

A gear in my memory clicked into place: that first day in Chiloé, Bórquez banging into me on the Mellehue dock, his arms laden with boxes of Christmas lights. I sank onto the familiar rock bench and expelled a long breath. "Well! Either the *Angélica's* a ghost ship, or—"

"Or the *Caleuche's* not." Marcos grunted. "Chu, you were right, Cahuel. This whole business is just a floating stage show. And Bórquez is in it up to his neck."

"I had my suspicions," Nicolás said. "Can't figure out the motive behind it, but one man has already died because of this foolishness, and I—look!"

He pointed at the illuminated deck of the *Caleuche*. Beneath the crossbar of a mast festooned with shreds of sailcloth and strips of eucalyptus bark, two figures in baggy slicker-yellow overalls and Spanish morion helmets trudged from the cabin to the stern. *What a crazy costume.* They lifted a bulging sack and heaved it over the handrail of the launch. In a geyser of spray, it plummeted beneath the surface. On the *Angélica*, another rubber-suited team did the same. The bay churned as six more dishwater-gray bags dropped into the sea.

"Well!" I said again, too astonished to play nonchalant. "What on earth are they doing?"

"Hard to be one-hundred-percent sure from this distance," Nicolás said, "but I'd guess... What do you bet, Marc?"

"Sí, señor." His brother flashed a knowing grin. "Bórquez is running abalone."

"They could be butterfly clams, for all we know. But why all the secrecy, this convoluted scheme to frighten people off? And there's only one way to find out."

"What's abalone? And what's wrong with it?" I asked.

"You're *not* diving around out there, Cahuel," Marcos said.

"Don't tempt me."

"No boat, no wet suit, and it's the middle of the winter. You have a death wish? Besides, we promised Don Ramón and I promised Mamá."

"Looks like a couple of the goons are rowing in, anyway. Let's see who they are."

"Do you—do you think we should hide?" I stood up, lacing my fingers together. Hadn't Bórquez warned that I'd die on this island? "And *what is* abalone?"

"Relax, it's a public beach. Let *them* explain themselves." Nicolás pulled me down beside him on the bench while Marcos patrolled the coarse sand in front of us. "Abalone—locos—are a shellfish, bigger than clams or mussels, and kind of spiral shaped. They're exposed on one end, like a snail, so they usually attach to rocks or gravelly bottoms for protection."

"Rocks, like the Dragon's Back out there?"

"We used to find them there at low tide, but abalone are scarce around this island now. But they're still very popular for their white meat—it's delicious—and for the mother-of-pearl lining of their shells. People use it to make jewelry. So abalone are *the* big cash catch for the fishermen of Chiloé."

"Seriously, the way you guys reacted, I thought it was a cocaine haul."

"Believe me, it's almost as valuable. *And* just as illegal right now."

"So why did those men dump all the bags into the ocean if they're worth so much?"

"That's the point," he said. "They are not supposed to *have* abalone now. The season doesn't open for another month or so, around the first of August. They probably found a huge bank somewhere, dug them illegally, and brought them here to stockpile for a quick lift on opening day."

"Oh!" It all made sense now. "And the *Caleuche* getup's a scare tactic to keep people from getting too close to their poaching operation."

"That's the way it looks to me. Here come those guys."

Yammering louder than a pair of squabbling gulls and intent on their clandestine activities, the two fishermen didn't even appear to notice us in the shadows of the shore. I shrank into the overhang of the stone bench and tried to make myself invisible anyway. In spite of Nicolás's boldness, I had the icy feeling that the abalone runners wouldn't exactly welcome three teens spying on their shady activities.

Now minus the wacko conquistador helmets, the men sloshed through the shallows in knee-high rubber boots, dragging their rowboat behind them onto the beach. The crunch of Marcos's footsteps alerted their attention. One thug froze for a second, then grabbed his buddy's arm, raking the darkness with a glare.

"Hey, who is there?" he called in a gritty voice. "Come out and show yourself, you sneaking devil."

"Stay here, Melissa." Shoulder to shoulder with Marcos, Nicolás stepped towards the men. "It's the Serrano brothers. Who are you?"

"What are you urchins doing snooping around here?" the man growled.

"Might ask you the same question," Nicolás said. "You're not from around here, and that's some strange-looking launch you got."

"Mind your own business, kid, or you will regret it." The second man, shorter and stouter and even surlier than the first, thrust beefy palms against the boys' chests and sent them reeling.

Nicolás steadied himself, but Marcos toppled to the ground in a tangle of long limbs. I screamed and sprang to his side. But the men ignored us now. Gravel-Mouth tied the rowboat to a boulder while the pudgy one plodded toward the shore path.

"Bórquez was supposed to take care of things on this end," Pudgy grumbled. "Keep the coast clear and all. You'd think that windbag could do a better job."

His crony snorted and spat on the hard-packed road leading toward the Bórquez mansion and North Head. "*Cálmate, gordo.* They are only a couple of runny-nosed brats."

"You okay, Marc?" Nicolás hoisted his brother to his feet.

Marcos brushed damp sand from his jacket sleeve. "You heard that, eh? Bórquez *is* involved in this hot little racket. What should we do, Cahuel?"

"Tell Don Ramón for now, I guess." He shrugged. "When I think this *Caleuche* scheme was responsible for Jaime Garrido's death—"

"It makes you sick and gives you goosebumps at the same time." I glowered after the rubber-suited pair now ambling by the deserted cottage that had belonged to the Garridos. *Speaking of goosebumps...* Even partly cloaked behind a jungle of vegetation, that rundown hovel spooked me.

"Hey, you guys, there's a bonfire up on the headland again." I spun around. Several small blazes dotted the soaring black-green hills above the shore. "Another tropón dance? More buried treasure?"

"Vaya, I get it," Marcos said. "If Don Juan can lure everybody off on a treasure hunt, he keeps them away from his operation here in the bay."

Nicolás nodded and steered us toward the southward path. "His gang's getting overconfident. We were never meant to witness them caching those bags in Dolphin Bay."

A shiver skittered across my shoulders as the gloom of the peninsula woods enveloped us. "*Mind your business,*" the pudgy fisherman had ordered. "*Or you'll be sorry.*" What if those hoods reported our presence on the beach tonight to their boss? We sure didn't have the excuse of playing with dolphins anymore.

"Wait a minute," I said. "What if Bórquez's scare tactics aren't only aimed at *people*? This all started about the same time that—"

"That the dolphins disappeared." I couldn't see Nicolás's frown, but I heard it in his voice.

# 37

Near the end of that week, the Pérezes finished their *media-agua*. Just three rooms, the tiny makeshift house would do until they could afford to build the other half, perhaps in the summer. But after the cramped, smoke-filled, earthen-floored shed, I felt like we'd moved into a palace.

On my knees the fourth morning, I rubbed yet another coat of ruby-red wax onto the raw pine floorboards. "My brother-in-law should visit again before long," I said to Gina. "Wasn't he bringing the glass panes for your windows?"

"Ramón gave him the measurements last time." Even in the putty-colored light from the plastic-tacked window frames, Gina looked paler and more worn out than when I arrived three weeks ago. But she'd taken over most of the household duties again and was peeling potatoes at Energizer Bunny speed. "I am more concerned about that abalone operation of Bórquez's. You and the boys have done well keeping watch at Dolphin Bay, but Pastor Colin will know what to do with the information."

"The passenger launch might even pass by first." I spoke with more optimism than I felt. "Maybe you could get a message out?"

Gina whittled a knobby potato as if it whirled on a lathe. "We just don't know who we can trust anymore."

"Yeah, tough being that bully's only opposition on the whole island." I scoured hard with my rag. If only I could grind some mud into Bórquez's face. "It's like these people are blind and bewitched."

"And those who are not, are too intimidated to be of any help."

Months before, three families on Chauquelín's western shore, as well as the young teacher, Señorita Marisol, and the Garridos of course, had all capitulated to fear and abandoned their homes. Now, according to Ramón and Gina, Bórquez had used his sneaky traditions revival to worm his way into the confidence of the *mayores*, the community elders of North Head.

I bit my lip. I was *not* afraid of that phony-baloney anymore. Regret it or not, I wasn't going to run away from his threats ever again. "Well, you have my help. For what it's worth."

"What it's worth! More than we can ever repay, that much is certain." Gina tucked back a stray curl and smiled. "It has not been a walk in the park for you here. At least now we can heat bath water, and you will not have to go to the Serranos' for that anymore."

"It's nice to have an oven here again, too." I didn't much care for *chapalele*, the dumpling-like bread boiled in water. Not that I'd admit it, but… "You never appreciate such simple things until you have to do without them for a while."

Ramón had sanded down the old cookstove and installed it, with the new chimney pipes Cole had brought earlier, in the center of the kitchen. Our menu didn't vary much from the same brown bread and potatoes—boiled potatoes, fried potatoes, mashed potatoes, potato soup—but at least the stove's blazing heat quickly took off the chill each morning. And we could bake now—potatoes as well as bread.

"I'm sure you miss the electric lights and automatic washer," Gina said. "Not to speak of a proper bathroom."

I *was* totally sick of the smelly kerosene lanterns most islanders used. I could've hugged a Maytag, and I would've given my last dollar for a real bath. But weeks had passed since I'd thought of television—the Pérezes' battery-operated set was smashed in the earthquake, along with so much else.

I returned Gina's smile. "Never mind. It's a sure bet I'll never take any of those things for granted again." Or Gina either, for that matter. Underneath those mismatched fashions shone a cheerful woman I'd come to appreciate almost as much as my own sister these weeks. Gina even resembled Linda today, in a hunter green sweater. Since retiring from the construction crew, she'd ditched most of her ragbag wardrobe in favor of Linda's donations.

"Gina, would it be okay," I said, "if we alternate between your house and the Serranos' for the Bible class from now on?"

"Querida, I wanted to suggest that, but Valeria?"

"Nicolás takes her into the med-post in North Head to get her cast off today." I gave the last corner a vigorous swab with my rag. "They'll go in the oxcart, of course, but in a few days she'll try walking this far. She wants to see your new house, and I thought it might give Señora Angélica a break from having us all the time."

"Her mother, too."

"Ummm, maybe. Señora Luisa didn't look that well yes-terday. Though she actually smiled when Nicolás told her he'd repair the balcony as soon as he gets his winter wheat sown."

Gina sighed. "That will take a while. The boys should have worked on their own home instead of ours. I hate to say it, but we cannot pay them, as good as they have been to us."

"Oh, they don't expect to be paid. Your need was more urgent, anyway." I bounced to my feet and squeezed Gina's shoulders—bony, compared to a few months ago. "You'd be more exhausted than you are now if the guys hadn't helped."

"Now that we are settled again, I will bounce back quickly."

"Right. So don't you get discouraged, señora. The worst of this is behind us."

I wondered about that when I arrived at the Serranos' in the afternoon. Grandmother Luisa had forsaken her post behind the stove and taken to her bed.

Señora Angélica led me and the troop of children into the living room for our class so that the elderly woman's moans wouldn't disturb us. Or vice versa. Valeria wobbled across the floor to demonstrate her mended leg, weak but apparently straight.

"The doctor in Mellehue did a good job of setting the bone, *gracias a Dios*." Señora Angélica dabbed a handkerchief at her brimming eyes. "Now if I only knew what to do about Mamá."

"Maybe you could convince her to go into Mellehue whenever my brother-in-law returns," I said.

"Nico spoke to the paramedic in North Head this morn-ing." She wrung the handkerchief in her delicate hands. "All he can really do is give her a sedative. Some relief, but it's no permanent solution. She wanted me to get Juan Bórquez again, but I—I just couldn't this time."

"You mean…you *refused*?" I could hardly believe it.

"Sí, I did." Despite her emphatic words, her hands betrayed her. Pathetically nervous. "Whatever Juan did before, perhaps it helped her some. But the trouble is back, and I can see it is the same old ailment. She ate some cold *milcao* yesterday before I noticed."

"I bet the tea *you* gave her that other time did as much as anything."

"Possibly. So it comes and it goes, as always. What kind of magic cure is that?"

I nodded. "Black magic, maybe. That scumbag only does the devil's work, I've got that clear. Reminds me of the first Bible story I told here—"

Señora Angélica laid a gentle hand on my arm. "We all thank you for your willingness to share the stories with the children. It has encouraged Valeria so much to look forward to that every day. I—I have thought much about your Bible lessons… I heard some of this long ago when I went to school in Castro. And even Mamá has enjoyed it."

"You think?"

"Sí, she—" Señora Angélica smiled at the tug on her sleeve. "Very well, Julio, I will let your teacher get on with the class and talk afterwards."

Three-quarters of an hour later, I ended the story time with a song. Above the chime of the children's voices, a rap sounded at the kitchen door. A man's voice, gratingly familiar, boomed. Juan Bórquez had arrived uninvited to attend his patient. His victim, more like.

My heart did a flip-flop. "You kids play quietly a few minutes."

I'd rather have stayed safely in the closed room too. Hide away in blissful ignorance. Yet I felt compelled to join Señora Angélica. She needed the moral support right now.

"Sí, Mamá's gall bladder is troubling her again," Señora Angélica said as I eased the parlor door shut behind me. "But the paramedic will see her this evening. No need to trouble yourself, Juan."

"No trouble at all, my dear Gela." He made a mocking bow and lumbered bear-like across the room. He shoved a clipping of silver-green fern leaves into her hands. "Here, make up the *huinque* herbal while I look at the old lady."

Without waiting for a response, he pushed Señora Luisa's bedroom door open with a square paw. He shot a brazen glance backward, as if defying anyone to stop him, and then bulldozed into the room.

Señora Angélica's face flushed, then drained to a ghastly pallor. She knotted her long slim fingers while conflicting emotions tumbled across her tormented features. "Melissa, can you—" she began.

The back door banged open. Nicolás and Marcos stamped in, scraped their rubber boots, and slid them off.

"We have both fields ready for planting." Nicolás's dark hair was wind-tousled, his face burnished with color. "Looks like this spell of clear weather is about over, though. Wind's up, we'll get rain soon. Think I'll try to—What's wrong?"

I thumbed toward the bedroom. "Your grandmother has company."

He stiffened.

Marcos rolled his eyes. "Uh-oh, here we go again. Round three...or four?"

"I did not ask him to come, Nico. He just appeared at the door." His mother sounded a trifle defensive.

"Bad news travels fast on Chauquelín." Nicolás's voice hardened.

Juan Bórquez's squat form wedged through the bedroom door again. "*Buenas tardes*, boys." He smirked. "Preparing for planting, are we?"

Nicolás grunted and gave him a flinty stare.

"I may have to raise the rent on that north field this year." Bórquez's eyes glinted beneath their shaggy brows. "Not sure you folks want to lease it at my price."

"Why, you—!" Nicolás surged toward him, then stopped short and sagged. The muscle in his right cheek quivered while his fists clenched and unclenched. But he said no more, only closed his eyes. Was he praying, or...?

*Oh, no, Nicolás, don't give up!*

Bórquez thrust his grizzled chin at Angélica. "Haven't you made that *huinque* purge yet?"

"No." She held the leafy branch away from her, as if it were poisonous. "I am not going to."

"Get on with it, Angélica! I have not got all day. Here, I will prepare the ashes myself." He yanked a metal bowl from its hook on the wall and stalked toward the stove.

His arrogant presumption fired a nerve in me. "Leave her alone! How dare you barge in here giving orders and treating people like dirt? Señora Angélica didn't ask you to come. And she said she's not making this witch's brew or whatever it is. So there."

Bórquez flicked me a contemptuous glance, as though I were a cockroach he'd spied on the floor. "You are that little snippet of a gringa canuta here again, no? Chu, I did not think you had it in you."

A shiver slithered down my backbone, but I steeled myself against those leering fish-eyes. "Yes, and I probably know more about you than you do about me," I said coolly.

"Is that so?" He sneered. "Then for your information, Señorita Canuta, I do not *need* Angélica's permission to come here, as she well knows. Doña Luisa wants me here and that is *suficiente*—in *these* parts."

"Angélica!" the old lady shrilled from the bedroom.

"Just a minute, Mamá," Señora Angélica said, as assertive as I'd ever heard her. "Melissa, what were you going to say about that Bible story a few minutes ago?"

*Duh.* I gawked at her. "What? Oh, you mean…in the other room."

"Sí, you said the first story. The one about the woman with the crippled back, was it not? I have often thought about that one, too."

Suddenly it was like she and I were alone in the room. Marcos slouched against the back door, wearing his devil-may-care grin. Nicolás straightened up, brows knit together. Bórquez appeared stunned into silence for once. But I was so focused on our discussion that I was only vaguely aware of the others.

"Remember how the Pharisees—Jesus's enemies—complained when He healed her on the Sabbath?" I said slowly. "They made a big deal about all their traditions and stuff, but it was mostly just a pious front for their own agenda. In reality, they didn't give a flying fig about that old woman. But Jesus showed her genuine compassion."

"He was different." Señora Angélica nodded. "I—I've been reading on my own, and the more I read, the more I realize how amazing He was. He didn't just talk religion, He lived it."

"But He was despised for that," I said. "The religious leaders hated Him because He cared more for people than for traditions. He exposed them for what they really were—"

"Just like some of the so-called religious leaders these days," Nicolás spoke up. Such an odd combination of gentleness and fierceness blended in his tone that I gaped at him.

Angry and dejected a moment before, his face now glowed. Hope snapped in his golden eyes and told me he was back in the battle.

"Angélica!" Grandmother Luisa's reedy call came again, more urgent this time.

Bórquez cleared his throat as though coming to himself. "Canuto nonsense." He picked up the iron stove poker to scrape some ashes into the bowl.

In a quick, graceful movement, Angélica snatched the poker from him, lifted one of the stove's round lids, and crammed the *huinque* branch into the hungry belly of the fire. Bórquez spat at her in a tobacco-brown stream that splattered and sizzled on the stovetop. Seizing her hand, he twisted the poker away. She cried out as he brandished it over her head.

Her two sons flashed to her side. So swift, I barely saw them.

I wouldn't have liked to be Juan Bórquez under Nicolás Serrano's unblinking scowl at that instant. Burly, barrel-chested Bórquez was built like an ox, but he literally shrank beneath Nicolás's knifelike glare. Though Nicolás was tall for a Chilean teenager, he now towered straighter and broader than I'd ever seen him. His eyes, like sunlit chips off a glacier, bored into Bórquez's.

"Put that poker down—and leave this house—right now." His words cracked off in frozen chunks.

Bórquez flung down the poker with a clatter and backed away.

Nicolás slipped his arm through his mother's. Warmth returned to his tone. "Mamá, two forces are at war in this room. One is Satan and everything he can throw to deceive or destroy us, and the other—"

"Or terrorize, control us, like you said once. I...I figured out a long time ago, son, that these mysterious rituals...are only meant to mislead us into believing there's some spiritual connection."

"But the greater force is Jesus Christ and His love."

"Then in that I will rest my soul." She sighed and stepped toward the bedroom door. "And my case with your grandmother."

"You people better watch out." Bórquez snarled like a cornered wolf. "I can rock your little boat yet, canutos."

"Threats," Nicolás said.

"For the first time in my life, Juan, I feel perfectly safe." Her head tilted high, Señora Angélica looked anything but helpless and fragile.

Bórquez slammed out.

While the guys and I hung in Grandmother Luisa's doorway, Angélica smoothed the rumpled bedding and took her mother's tiny, restless hand. Only the old woman's dark birdlike eyes showed up against the white of the pillows.

"Mamá, I sent Juan away."

"I may be sick," Señora Luisa retorted, "but deaf I am not."

"I'm sorry, but I had to." Angélica licked her lips. "The medic should get here in another hour, and I think we should trust God to—"

"I know what you think. I heard it all myself." Señora Luisa's eyes narrowed to sparkling slits. "So. If this is true, why does Nico not pray for me?"

"I will then, Abuela." A smile tugged at the corners of his mouth.

"And the girl. May-lee-sa."

"I will too...Abuela."

# 38

Two days later, Marcos walked Valeria over to the Pérezes' for her first outing. Total success. Nicolás came to fetch her home again after our Bible class and asked me to do sentinel duty at Dolphin Bay with him.

"The wind is strong north," he told Gina. "It's a good bet Bórquez's *Angélica* and her *Caleuche* sidekick might try to make port tonight."

We three set off down the hill. The dry ground crunched beneath our feet. "It's almost like old times in the summer," I said.

"Only a lot colder." Valeria shivered.

"Let's get you home," Nicolás said. "It hasn't rained for weeks, but I guarantee it will be raining this time tomorrow. I can smell it in the air."

"You can *smell* rain?" I laughed.

"Sure, can't you?" He grinned. "The air is moister or something."

At the lane leading to the Serranos' house, Nicolás knelt to hoist his sister up piggyback style.

"I'll wait here," I said. "Give your mother a break from my face today. How's your abuela, by the way?"

"Lots better." Valeria waved good-bye. "Mamá's *bailahuén* tea did the trick."

"Abuela figures our prayers did as much as Don Juan's hocus-pocus," Nicolás said. "We even got her to let the medic give her a pain killer. Truth is, I think she perked up as soon as she heard my hammer on the balcony yesterday morning."

"Oh, I'm glad you've started that project," I said.

"I didn't realize it meant so much to her until you mentioned it. Be right back."

I meandered a few paces along the shore road and studied the cove. No sign of a launch anywhere on the horizon, but dusk was still an hour or so away. Someone from the Serrano or Pérez household—I'd taken my turns—had maintained a regular watch on the bay at twilight for ten days now. Bórquez's launches had made three other suspected abalone drops during that period. Tonight might be time for another.

The brisk wind swept masses of purple clouds across the drab-gray sky. Nicolás was right, a storm brewed over the Pacific. I had the feeling some change lurked, just out of sight, in my own future, too. Not disaster, as in Bórquez's menacing tea-leaf prediction, no. But something… revolutionary.

For too long, I'd stood on the sidelines of my life—leaning on the fence, as Nicolás once remarked. After what happened at the Serranos' the day before yesterday, I was finally fully engaged here. This island life made me a useful part of something bigger than myself. The simple mundane tasks filled my cup to the brim with happiness. Who would've guessed?

But hauling water and wood in this back-of-beyond were incidental details. I wasn't aiming to score brownie points with my parents or my school anymore. Being a blessing to the others mattered far more now.

"I'm praying that God will make you hungry for some real food, that He'll chase you and not let you go your own way," Nicolás had said, months ago.

Nicolás might be—*was*—cocky and candid to the point of brashness. But he was also genuine, perhaps the best friend I'd ever had.

He never argued around my excuses. Instead he made a direct assault on the façade I showed the world. My defenses never daunted him. Scaling the crusty walls of my heart, ignoring the taunts I threw at him, he'd dared me to face myself. *Where are you with God,* amiga mía? *Why are you afraid to tell me who you really are? Because I want to know you.*

Under fire from his radiant friendship, my resistance had cracked—and melted. I didn't—couldn't—resent what he'd said any longer. He was only a catalyst, his bold words a bugle call from God.

Now that I was listening, a life with Jesus beckoned rather than repulsed me. What would it be like to turn around and run back into His arms? Could I give up my independence for some elusive adventure with God?

In the meantime, I had to mend fences with Nicolás. Sure, we talked. We'd picked up the pieces, declared a truce in the aftermath of the earthquake. But he'd risked rejection to be authentic with me back in April—and he'd got it, by the earful. Now I had to go back and apologize before I could move on.

Nicolás's feet pounded down the lane from his house. He took my hand and wound along the rocky beach toward the peninsula. "It's a little early. We can catch up over tea." He swung a Thermos and a bag of sandwiches in his other hand.

"You Chilotes and your sacred teatime."

He laughed and squeezed my hand.

I returned the squeeze. Maybe he *didn't* hold my old spitefulness against me. "I'm with you, you know," I said. "In this fight against Bórquez, I mean. Come what may."

"I knew you were," he said, "when you prayed with us the other day."

"The least I could do."

"Are you kidding? It was a lot."

"Yeah, my big preaching debut, spouting off everything I know, right? Not."

"Bucha, Meli, you weren't spouting off. That was incredible, what you did, standing up to Bórquez like that. You shocked me—pleasantly, of course."

I shrugged. "He didn't pay any attention to me."

"Maybe *he* didn't, but the important thing is, it helped Mamá—you don't know how much." A smile lit his brown face. "I have talked to her so many times before. I didn't know what else to do, nothing more I could say. She's an intelligent woman, she understood, she believed, but…she could not bring herself to act on what she knew was the truth. Until you spoke up."

"I finally couldn't *shut* up. You—you were right. It's the devil who wants us to sit passively at the back of the shelf. Your mother saw it too. She's a great lady, Nicolás."

"I had no idea she had been talking to you."

"I'm sure she has plenty of reasons for her hesitance, her lack of faith. I can't say I have any excuses." I squirmed, a bit ashamed. *Frankness is sure brutal on the ego.* "I—I have some things I need to tell you. The kids' Bible stories have—helped me too, I guess."

"Thought you were on dangerous ground there for a girl determined to avoid God."

"I couldn't seem to get out of it gracefully. But I admit I didn't want anything to do with that, at first."

"Look what happened to me when I started reading the Bible. At your suggestion, remember. You said if I wanted to know the truth about Jesus, I should read the Bible."

"I remember," I said. *Do I ever.*

"It changed my life. You must have known the Bible is powerful stuff."

"Yeah, and it scared me half to death." I'd got to the point of no secrets, no matter how humiliating. "I knew all the answers. And rejected them for myself, as you know well enough now."

"The Bible ought to have a warning. 'This Book may turn your life upside down. Hazardous to your indifference.'"

"Like an earthquake, huh?" I gave a little laugh and then sobered. "To be honest, I hadn't read the Bible for…oh, probably three years…*really* read it, I mean."

"I was glad when you started teaching the kids."

I gazed over into his deep-set amber eyes. "You mean, you thought if I could once get a taste of good bread, I'd give up the junk food I was living on?"

He opened his mouth to answer, but I hurried on, needing to spill it all into the open. "You were right, that evening back in April. I guess I—I *was* sort of a spiritual anorexic. I never knew how starved I was until you came along and tantalized me with a hint of something delicious. You—like, you triggered hunger pangs. Though mostly, at that moment, I was just mad that you seemed to sense exactly where I was."

"You almost went home because of that."

"Partly, yeah. I was afraid, Nicolás. Afraid to open up to you or anyone else—to let you see me as I really was. And I was afraid of the weird things going on here in Chauquelín. It made me feel helpless." My hand in his slipped, sweaty in spite of the chill, but he didn't let go. "But I was even more afraid to trust the only One who *can* help. So where could I go? But circumstances sort of ganged up on me."

"God doesn't send many people an earthquake to get their attention," he teased.

"Just the stubborn ones, like you said." I smiled wryly.

Out the other side of the peninsula, Nicolás led the way to a wooded knoll that commanded a panoramic view of Dolphin Bay. The lush evergreens camouflaged us from any incoming launches while we bunkered down to watch and wait.

He poured a cup of herbal tea from the Thermos and passed it to me with a couple slices of bread slathered with apple butter. "Warm your innards."

I sipped the mint brew. I loved the mint now, but Linda was dead-on about the taste gap between plastic and china. "Do you honestly believe God sent that earthquake? I mean, I know He's in control, but..."

Arms tucked behind his neck, Nicolás stretched out beneath a bushy *mañío* tree. Weak sunlight slanted in long uphill strips through the trees. "Coincidence, we call it," he said. "Or luck, good or bad. Yet...I think more things than we imagine are God's direct intervention. His destiny, His purposes for us, are more dependable than any coincidence. How else did either of us even get to this moment in the first place?"

"It *is* awesome." I flicked a shriveled brown leaf from the knee of my jeans. "You from your world, me from mine.

Together in this place, this time, for something God's obviously doing."

The bittersweet lump that had throbbed inside for days choked me. I pushed the plastic cup back into Nicolás's hands and hugged my knees to my chest. "Look at me. Who am I that God would go to so much trouble for me? Nobody special, yet He's chased me to the end of the earth, until I finally *want* to be caught."

The tense ball in my heart burst in a flood-release of sobs and giggles. "I can't believe myself. I'm sure I've never talked like this to anyone in my whole life."

"It's okay, maybe you needed to." Nicolás sat up, poured himself tea, and said nothing more for several minutes while he drank it and I sniffled like a toddler.

But somehow the tears rinsed away the pressures, the pretense, the rebellions and resentments of months and years. Yeah, being so vulnerable was excruciating. Yet profound peace—relief—cascaded through me. I felt...clean and fresh. But no longer empty.

I shifted my position in the carpet of pine needles and decaying leaves and leaned into the writhing cinnamon trunk of a myrtle tree. Swallowing a hiccup, I drew in a shaky breath. "I—I wanted to tell you before. I had a fair start in the Christian life—every advantage, you might say. I trusted Jesus as my Savior when I was in kindergarten, I really did."

"I believe you. You know so much."

"Including how to play the part to perfection, to a certain point. After I was thirteen or so, nothing satisfied me anymore. It sounds so cliché, but I—I turned away from God, went searching for something—happiness, I guess—in all the wrong places. A new crowd of friends—the old ones were too square. Thrills, freedom, whatever."

"I understand, amiga. Don't think I don't." He reached for a fallen eucalyptus limb, stripped a handful of the white-coated blue-green leaves, and kneaded them.

"But my whole life was about *me*, wrapped up in trivial, worthless things," I said. "I was miserable as sin if I ever dared to think about it. Which you can be sure I didn't too often because I always came back around to God. Then last summer—"

I couldn't go on. A whiff of the pungent eucalyptus rushed up my nostrils, pricked my eyes, stabbed my chest, like the mentholated ointment my grandmother smeared me with whenever I had a childhood cold. Last summer's trag- edy—Grandma Rose's untimely death—was the last locked door in my life of sham and shame. My darkest secret, my worst sin. God knew how sorry I was. And I had to confess.

But I couldn't parade that whole sordid mess out before Nicolás.

Hot tears scalded my cheeks again, not a gush this time but a slow trickle. Licking the salty wetness from my lips, I pounded the ground with my fist. "Oh, Nicolás, I haven't—I can't tell you everything. My life back home, my parents, the trouble at school. You can't imagine—"

"Oh, but I can, amiga mía." A half smile played on his lips as he nibbled on a eucalyptus leaf. His golden eyes gleamed.

I laughed, a choked giggle really. "Yeah, I guess you prob- ably can. Remembering how suspicious Miriam was when she heard you'd trusted Jesus."

"How could you be afraid of my opinion, after Miri informed you of all my *pecadillos*?"

"But you changed. And I didn't want to. Then." My voice cracked. "I've disappointed everyone my whole life. I figured if you really knew me—knew everything—you'd hate me."

"Hate you! You make my day." He handed me a wild rhubarb leaf the size of a bath towel. "Need a handkerchief? Melissa, you are *not* and never have been a disappointment to me."

"I'm not—not a perfect saint, like my sister. Bórquez was right about that much."

"Neither am I. So what if you're not just like everybody else? You're you, you're unique. Bucha, that very first day, I figured you for spunky *and* kind."

"Among other things." My lips twisted down.

"Sí-po, like amazing." He scuttled like a crab closer to me. "More so every day."

"If I could only go back and erase the past."

"I have been an independent brat all my life, too, you know," he said. "Captain of my own ship. It's no exaggeration to say I was headed for shipwreck when I met Jesus in February, and I'm not telling you everything I'm ashamed of, either. But I realized then that my life was in for some big changes. Maybe I didn't comprehend everything, but one thing I saw right away. My ship had a new Master."

"I wish" —I sighed— "that I could do this past year over again. Two years, even. I'd sure make a few changes."

"New Year's resolutions?" Nicolás slanted a grin at me. "Why just wish for a do-over? You know God lets us *start* over again any time. He forgives us. We can begin a new life *today*."

My eyes glazed over with tears again. "There'll probably be times when I'll want to go back on Him," I whispered. "I'm weak and, you know, stubborn."

"So? He is strong and patient, right?"

I blinked. "Nicolás Serrano, I've never known another guy like you in my entire life. How did you change...grow...so radically in, what, five months?"

"God is the one who makes the changes. And..." He shrugged sheepishly. "I never do things halfway. Everything has to be different now. I'll never be the same as before, and I want everybody else to know Jesus, too. I...I want to change the world, at least my world."

"Don't you think the islanders hate you for that?"

"Bórquez sure does. But I'm willing to risk *that*. Where it's hard is at home, with my own family. But Mamá and I had a long talk last night. She's with me now, one hundred percent."

"I'm so glad. I have a feeling your grandmother's changing some, too."

"It's not easy at her age, but Abuela Luisa is sharp as a spindle." Nicolás toyed with another long, razor-thin eucalyptus leaf before chomping it between his teeth. "I think she finally sees that Don Juan's motives aren't to help her, or even to revive the old customs. He just uses her for his own program, like he does everyone. Pestering her about this land issue may bring his downfall yet. Sort of a blessing in disguise."

I nudged him and snatched the eucalyptus leaf. "Would you quit chewing on these things! Isn't this what the koalas in Australia eat?"

"I daresay I've been called worse than a koala. I like the taste and smell of them."

He tried to grasp my hand, but I slithered down the slope on a slide of leaves and needles. He somersaulted after me and wrested the leaf from me in a playful tussle. I laughed, wheezing, on the ground, while he stood and waved it in triumph over his head like a pale sea-green banner.

"I think you get some kind of high from them," I said.

"Chu, a country-bumpkin high." His eyes narrowed on the bay, suddenly alert as a deer. "Look, there's a launch coming in. With her lights on."

We glued our gaze to the boat as it chugged closer. The final rays of the sun brushed Dolphin Bay with metallic blue stripes.

"That's Don Colin!" He broke into a downhill sprint. "It's not Bórquez's launch, it's the *Ambassador*—and headed for the south cove."

We raced back across the peninsula and waited while Cole's launch anchored. I hopped up and down on the carpet of gravel. We hadn't seen anyone from civilization for more than two weeks.

Frowning, Nicolás eyed the man who helped Cole lower the rowboat into the water. "Who's that other guy? Not dressed like anyone from Mellehue."

That much was obvious, even in the murk of twilight. Definitely not an average island fisherman, the stranger carried himself stiffly, as if he felt out of place in this setting. His salt-and-pepper hair was trimmed to precision, and his clothes sported an air of designer-tailored-for-casual-wear.

As he handed down two large tan suitcases to Cole, a woman emerged from the cabin. Tall and slender, she wore a thigh-length chocolate parka and beige slacks. A tangerine scarf, draping a fluff of buttercream hair, fluttered in the breeze. The distinguished gentleman assisted her into the rowboat, then clambered in himself.

"Maybe it's the governor of Chiloé and his wife," I said, "inspecting earthquake damage in the island. You know, disaster area or something."

When Nicolás didn't respond with a chuckle, I glanced at him sharply. He stared at the couple in Cole's rowboat in disbelief, almost aghast. Every vestige of color drained from his face, leaving it as chalky white as the day he'd rowed out to break the news of his neighbor Jaime Garrido's death.

I waggled his arm. "What's wrong? Who are they?"

He spun towards the woods and covered his eyes with his hands, a gesture so foreign to him that poignant pain clutched my throat. What was going on?

"*Ay*, this is a nightmare come to life." His voice croaked out, so clotted with emotion it barely resembled his normal tone. "Don't you—don't you recognize my Grandmother Serrano from Santiago? It's *them*."

Of course he was right. Without warning, his two worlds were about to collide.

# 39

Even though three years had passed since he'd last seen them, Nicolás recognized his grandparents instantly. I realized that, for him, it was like having them come back from the dead, because he always separated the two lives he'd known before and after his father's death.

An impassable gulf stretched between those worlds. Centuries instead of years, a universe instead of a thousand miles. He'd been forced to exchange the glitter of privileged Santiago for the rugged beauty and simplicity—and challenges—of the islands of Chiloé. I understood his nightmare, sensed his anguish.

Though I didn't blame him for feeling conflicted, I gripped his arm and wheeled him around. "Amigo, I know this is hard for you. But you have to greet them. They've come so far to see you."

No more time to coax him. The arrivals pulled up to shore, calling out hellos.

Cole leaped from the rowboat. "You asked me to consult a lawyer for you, buddy, so I've brought one on site."

Nicolás managed a weak smile as he helped Cole drag the boat out of the water.

His bearing erect as an admiral, Don Manuel Ignacio Serrano stepped onto the rocky shore. He clapped his long arms around Nicolás in an awkward hug. "Glad to help any way we can, son." He cleared his throat.

The men lifted Señora Rosalía to terra firma. The elegant woman couldn't stop crying, babbling, and gazing in delight at her grandson. "And Melissa, a pleasure to see you again."

"Charmed too, señora." This blue-blooded society woman remembered me? *Well.*

She linked a slim arm through Nicolás's on one side and mine on the other. Cole and Don Manuel followed as we strolled toward the house.

Señora Rosalía chattered nonstop. "Three years makes a tremendous difference at your age, does it not? You left Santiago a boy, Nico, and now I find you practically a man. I do believe you will be as tall as your papá. My, it's been too long. I can hardly wait to see the other children. And, ah, your mother too, of course. How is dear Angélica?"

"She's well." Nicolás grunted. "Thank you." He went through the protocols of courtesy, recited the pleasantries demanded by his culture. He was, after all, a well-brought-up Chilean.

But his distant politeness sounded automated, like a droid on remote control. Uneasy, I peered at him through the dusk. His face was still cold and rigid as a tombstone, but his vacant eyes betrayed no trace of emotion now.

*Shoot.* I tried to compensate for his lack of response to his grandmother's efforts. "So you decided to visit Chauquelín, Señora Rosalía. Don't you think it's lovely?"

"Fabulous, my dear. We should have come years ago, but I was always such a chicken about traveling to these remote areas." Her voice caught. "Since the quake, we have been so anxious for news of the family that we finally decided to come. What a relief to hear from your sister and brother-in-law that everyone is safe."

"How long ago did you arrive in Mellehue?" I asked.

"Three days. We planned to continue on here immediately, but no passenger launches were running. Your dear sister kindly extended hospitality to us, even though they already have a full house. Don Colin finally insisted on bringing us out. The poor man feels a little under the weather, I think—and no wonder with all he has to do—but he said he had to make the trip anyway and that it looks like a storm before long."

"So you and your husband will stay for a while then?"

"Sí…er, well, we hope to." Señora Rosalía glanced uncertainly at Nicolás. Her hand on my arm trembled. "If Angélica can find room for us, that is."

"Of course, Abuela," Nicolás said in his robot voice.

As they turned up the lane toward the Serrano house, I drew him aside for a second. "Chill, will you? Whatever they did or didn't do in the past, right now they've sacrificed to travel here. You can at least meet them halfway."

"Don't you and Ramón forget to tell Don Colin about Bórquez's launches and the abalone," was his only answer.

Cole drained his mug of mint tea in the Pérezes' new kitchen. "So how many times have you seen these bags dumped into Dolphin Bay from the *Angélica* and this *Caleuche* look-alike?"

"Four times now," Ramón said. "I only witnessed it once myself. The boys and Melissa have been more the patrol."

"We've got it figured that they usually come on Fridays, and sometimes between," I said.

"Seems like a pretty well-organized poaching outfit," Cole said, "especially since Bórquez himself spends most of his time here on the island, right? He's got the details down to a science. Hard to believe, yet it all fits—Lucho Riveros's *Caleuche* story, the customs revival as a diversion on their dumping nights, the intimidation of the neighbors..." He shook his head. "Bórquez must stand to make a fair pile of money on that stash of abalone, or it'd hardly be worth so much trouble."

Ramón snorted as he refilled his mate cup. "Oh, it is worth it. He will turn millions of pesos' profit the first few days of the season if he can pull it off and get the abalone out of here unnoticed. And other diving crews will make chickenfeed if he's cleaned out the cream ahead of time."

"When does the season open?" Cole asked.

"I heard they set Monday, July twenty-ninth, this year. Give or take a few days. Sometimes Fisheries Service moves the date at the last minute."

*July twenty-ninth.* A chill pebbled over my body. The first anniversary of Grandma Rose's death. Would that date always foreshadow calamity for me? Like some fatal conjunction of evil forces...

"Then that gives us a little over two weeks," Cole said. "I'll try to get somebody with authority out here before then. In the meantime, best lie low and not give Bórquez reason to suspect you're on to him."

"Let him make his bed good and tidy before we drag him out of it." Ramón slapped his thigh, grinning.

Cole rubbed his forehead and stood up. "I've got to head back soon, folks, so we'd better get the launch unloaded. The Garrido children are still here, I see."

"Nobody traveling to the Desertores these days," Gina said. "But Jana and Rodrigo can stay here as long as necessary. Now that we are in a house again, it is no extra trouble."

"I made radio contact with Vanessa in Cocotúe last week."

"You did!" we all exclaimed.

"Poor gal's been worried sick about her kids. But she's stuck there too, until some launch happens by. I think she'd like to come into Mellehue to work. At any rate, the kids can return to school when you do, Meli." His blue eyes crinkled at the corners. "Unless you're coming with me now?"

I stared at him blankly. *No way.* I hadn't anticipated any such thing. "Wasn't thinking of it. That is…if it's okay with Gina and Ramón, I'll stay until you come back next time anyway. School won't start until then."

"You're welcome to stay as long as you like." Gina gave me a warm smile. "She more than earns her keep, Pastor Colin. Vaya, she's practically an islander herself now."

"I see." Cole winked.

"You…you brought my Bible lessons, didn't you?" I asked him.

"Wouldn't forget. Lin sent you some other stuff, too."

"I'll hike down to the *Ambassador* with you now."

Don Ramón rushed to hitch up his ox team for the load of glass, lumber, and other stuff Cole had brought, while he and I headed for the shore again. It was dark now, an ink-concentrate blackness that blotted out moon and stars. The north wind lashed at my face, trying to drive me back.

"So you're an island girl now, Meli," Cole said.

I laughed. Yep, I modeled the whole getup these days—chapped hands, ragged fingernails, and hopelessly stained clothing. "Not sure what Gina meant by that, except I've done my share and I'm no glamor girl at present. Life here kind of grows on you, though."

"Well, roughing it seems to agree with you, sis. You look happy and healthy." He caught my arm as I stumbled on the path and hung on. "I'll give Lin a good report. She's been a bit concerned about you out here alone."

"Alone? Hardly. But why?"

"Bórquez on this island's enough to make anybody edgy. Don't know if I should even let her know about this latest incident. But that's not what's worrying her." He hesitated a moment. "I guess she doesn't want you to feel pressured to do this. She knows Chauquelín's a tough assignment for a gal who came to Chile for a vacation."

"I came for a change as much as anything. And I got *that*, all right." Suddenly I wanted to share my feelings with him, but it was all still so newborn-wobbly that I held back. "What about Nicolás's grandparents? What are they doing here?"

"Bad timing, I'll agree," Cole said. "I was as surprised as anybody when they sent us a telegram out of the blue, trying to locate their grandkids. The kids had already left for Chauquelín, so they arrived determined to get out here. The *pensiones* in Mellehue were filled up—you have an idea what those places are like, anyway. So bottom line, they ended up spending a few days at our house. Must've been a humble enough hotel for them, too."

I made a face. "They're *cuicos*, Cole. That's what Nicolás calls them. High-class snobs."

"Yeah, that's what I always understood, but…did you know Don Manuel Ignacio Serrano has been a criminal court judge for over ten years?"

"Nicolás never mentioned that."

"His grandfather's a highly respected and—I imagine— very busy man in Santiago. It can't have been easy for him to get away."

"Don't suppose."

"Of course, his wife is the socialite, I suspect, but—" He broke off in a fit of coughing.

"You better take care of yourself, Cole."

"I'll be fine, bit of a cold coming on. I was gonna say that a few times, I think, I caught a glimpse of a little more depth in Señora Rosalía than appears on the surface. Hope the family can reconcile, despite the bad blood."

As we trudged by the Serrano home—the De la Cruz place, as the islanders called it—I glanced up and shivered. What was happening within those walls right now? Eerie lamplight glimmered through the gathering fog from the parlor windows and from the large bedroom off the balcony. "Doesn't seem likely, the way Nicolás feels about them. I mean, he didn't even want to say hello."

"Yeah, cool welcome, I know." Cole sighed and shook his head. "I'd hate to see him destroyed through unforgiveness. He has so much potential, but hanging on to a grudge will just sap that passionate spirit of his."

"I think you're right." I threw another backward look at the house. Light quivered and disappeared from the balcony room upstairs. "Still, I doubt if anyone in the family exactly rolled out the red carpet for Mr. and Mrs. Serrano. Guess I'll find out when I go there for Bible class tomorrow."

"That reminds me, Linda sent you a Bible, too. Said it belonged to your grandmother."

"What! I brought it down to *her* in February."

"She thinks you should have it instead."

I bit my lip. "What else did she send—teacups?"

"Two five-kilo bags of oranges."

*Very funny, Lin.*

# 40

Underneath a wool blanket that was more like a rug, I hunkered on the bench close to the snapping warmth of the fire. The Pérezes had turned in for the night, the adults to the right-hand bedroom and the children packed like a box of dolls on the living room floor to the left. The old sheets still hung in ragged strips for privacy. It wasn't much, but at least now I could read awhile in the evening before bunking down on my mattress in front of the stove.

Until the candle guttered out, whenever that was. Maybe sooner than later tonight, if that gale-force wind tore off the rattling plastic at the windows. With the impending storm hanging like a bat, it was a good thing Ramón would have the glass installed by this time tomorrow.

I brushed my fingers over the cover of Grandma Rose's Bible. Was the worn leather's original color black or mahogany? Hard to tell in this light. The binding was broken, the dog-eared pages loose. Maybe it was Gran's first Bible. Surely she hadn't carried this brittle antique to church in recent years.

And Linda had entrusted it to *me*? I hadn't given it more than a cursory glance when I delivered it months ago. Gran's handwriting, a delicate, loopy sprawl, lined both flyleaves and most of the blank pages at beginning and end. Horizontal, vertical, diagonal. I'd dismissed it as way too much bother to read earlier.

Doubly challenging now, in the flickering light from the candle and the gaps in the stovetop. God had a sense of humor sometimes. Still, I intended to decipher it all. Grandma might speak to me here. Grandma, who'd gazed up at me from the fishbone-parquet floor with agony darkening her emerald eyes but never a whisper of reproach for not being there when she fell.

"*Chérie*, everything will be fine now. Don't you blame yourself," were Gran's last words as the paramedics rolled the gurney out of her Mt. Vernon home to the ambulance. Her last words to me before she died in surgery.

No, it wasn't my fault Grandma Rose broke her hip. I recognized that in theory, of course. But if I hadn't skipped out that night with my worthless party-friends, I'd have come running the moment Gran fell. I could've called for help so much sooner. Instead, the one person who'd always been there for me had lain, alone and in pain, in the dark for over an hour.

My tears dripped on the open flyleaf like the pitter-patter starting on the zinc roof. *Not again.* Would I never get done blubbing? I blotted the puddle with the ball of my palm and read the blurred line: *I have seen the face of Jesus—Tell me not of aught beside.*

Wow, it sounded ancient. *Aught*—was that even English? Intrigued, I drove on: *I have heard the voice of Jesus—And my soul is satisfied.*

It was a poem, maybe a hymn. Framed in curlicues on the crowded page, like a jewel crammed into a chest of trinkets.

The voice of Jesus? Grandma heard Jesus calling, too? I longed to hear my grandmother's voice again. Could this Bible contain a message from both God and Grandma?

I leaned back and studied the ceiling. The plain pine boards, shrouded in velvet gloom, revealed nothing. No mysterious light, no glow-in-the-dark presence. Definitely no voice. I peered back at the rest of the poem:

> *In the radiance of His glory,*
> *First I saw His blessed face,*
> *And forever shall that glory*
> *Be my home, my dwelling place.*
> *Others in the summer sunshine*
> *Wearily may journey on.*
> *I have seen a light from heaven*
> *Past the brightness of the sun.*

My vibrant French-Canadian grandmother had met Jesus later in life. Ever after, Rose-Françoise Michaud Calvert radiated Him, not like the moon reflects the sun, but like a star aflame from an internal source. "By the grace of God, I am what I am," she'd often quoted. "His beloved daughter, by His mercy."

Grandma had tried *so* hard to convince me I was special. And yeah, sure, I knew I was God's child. *For God so loved the world...*

Maybe my sense of being lost in the crowd began with those mission trips my family took when I was small. I was always shuffled aside, never old enough to participate. The one time they'd planned to take me along, in the end they left me behind with Grandma—again. They didn't include me in their activities, so after a while I excluded myself. So as not to feel left out.

Only I'd lost sight of Jesus, too, strayed from the warmth of the fire. Fingers plugging my ears, I'd turned my back on Him. Amazing that somehow I knew He still loved me. I wanted to stop running and fling myself into His arms. Begin the journey again, as I'd said to Nicolás earlier today.

But still I dillydallied at this crossroads of my life, as I had for weeks. Because if I chose Jesus, I'd have to deal with my parents. Forgive—and ask forgiveness.

I glanced back down at the crazy-quilt page. My own name leaped out at me, in a tiny note squeezed perpendicular to the left of the poem.

*24 Juin 81–Melissa broke out definite pox today, fever 102.*
*25 Juin–M. quite sick, Susanne called again.*
*27 Juin – Melie much better, Susanne so relieved.*

*Chickenpox* was the reason I'd stayed behind? Six at the time the rest of my family traveled to Bolivia, I must've come down with it shortly before our flight. Why on earth my grandmother tracked the progress of a childhood illness in her Bible was a conundrum, but…

Evidently my mom had phoned several times to check on me. At maybe a hundred dollars a pop in those days. *Wow.* Somehow Mom was persuaded to go ahead with the long-anticipated plans, but she'd feared dragging her sick baby—me—off to that remote jungle. Grandma Rose to the rescue.

Only, my parents hadn't exactly dumped and forgotten me. It sounded like Mom hovered over a Bolivian phone for days. And…it was after that she turned down her dream job at Johns Hopkins and opened the tea-and-books shop in our home's front porch. Claimed she treasured being around for her younger kids more than the university library anyway. Though I'd assumed it merely gave Mom an excuse to tighten the apron strings.

The smoky wax in the air smarted my eyes. "Oh God, I am so sorry for my attitude," I whispered.

Sure, my parents made mistakes, of course they did. But maybe I'd misjudged them sometimes. God had placed me in the family I had for a reason. My home, my position as the last-born, even my ancestors…were no random accident. They all were part of His design to make me who I was.

I *was* one of them, a Travis. A little laugh bubbled at my lips. Could it be I wasn't cursed with this family—but blessed?

And could it be that my Heavenly Father wanted me, not because I was a carbon copy of the others, but because I was the beloved daughter He desired a *personal* relationship with?

I wanted that, too, with all my heart. I opened my hands, palms up, on top of Grandma Rose's Bible. Satan had crippled me with doubts, teased me with mirages, too long. I didn't care anymore about being myself, only finding—and doing—whatever Jesus wanted of me.

*Lord, change me. Make me different. And let me make a difference.* If I followed Him, mirrored Him—only Him—then He had something for me to do, I felt it. Something no one else could do.

Rain stamped on the roof as the hour marched on. The candle stub sputtered in a pool of melted wax. I needed to find a story for tomorrow's lesson quickly. What about Jesus washing His disciples' feet? Didn't it come soon after the incident with Mary's perfume?

Flicking through the yellowed pages with icicle fingers, I located John thirteen and read it over. Man, I loved to tell these stories about Jesus now.

*Dear Lord, that's a hymn, too*—"the story of unseen things above, of Jesus and His glory, of Jesus and His love." His mind-boggling love for immature John, blowhard Peter, even treacherous Judas.

Verse seventeen slapped me like a dash of water in my face: "If you know these things, happy are you if you do them."

*If you know.* I'd figured I knew all about Jesus, and yet I wasn't happy.

*If you do.* How could I have been anything *but* miserable, knowing all I did, yet not willing to obey?

God sent happiness in the strangest of places.

Grandma's poem was right. Even in this dark winter exile, I didn't need the summer sun if I had Jesus.

## 41

The following day, I hiked alone to the Serranos'. It was the Pérez-Garrido clan's turn to walk over, but the rainstorm finally unleashed its fury. Gina wanted to keep her chicks inside, now that she had a dry, cozy place. She and I had aided Ramón in speed window glass installation that morning.

"I cannot believe we had so much clear weather this past month," she said. "It has been dreadfully cold, of course, but a miracle we could raise the house so quickly. God is good."

When I arrived for story time with Valeria, most of the family gathered in the kitchen—an odd company that drab afternoon. Grandmother Luisa, sallow and scrawny but otherwise improved, perched in her customary spot behind the stove. Her little bird claws worked the spindle, dark bird eyes never wavering. But I knew the old woman was far from oblivious.

Her Santiago counterpart, Grandmother Rosalía, replaced Valeria in the big wicker chair. She fiddled with a piece of needlework, too, but completed no more than a few stitches during the lesson. Her hands fluttered up and down in her lap while her gaze darted about the spotless kitchen, mostly toward the door. At first she sat poker-straight. Then she sank into the support of the cushions. Then up again.

Don Manuel Serrano withdrew to the living-dining room with a thick book. Marcos scuffed in with an armload of wood, poked at the kettle of eucalyptus leaves simmering on the back of the stove, and then prowled from window to window while he listened.

At the table Señora Angélica filled pastry turnovers with chopped *choritos*, the sweet island mussels. A stunning Chilote ballerina in soft raspberry wool and a sleek chignon, she was more reserved than she'd been a couple of days before. Her forlorn expression bordered on…worried?

The dynamics in that house had switched to squally, like the wind. It was as if…they all waited, waited for something to happen, and nobody knew what or when. Tension stretched like an elastic cord, ready to snap. Though everyone pretended that Manuel and Rosalía Serrano's appearance on Chauquelín was an ordinary family visit, I sensed a time bomb, ticking relentlessly toward some explosive clash.

After I finished the story of the day, Valeria twirled around the room, her nut-brown hair tumbling in waves about her rosy face. "Melissa, we have a surprise for you."

"What?" I asked, intrigued.

"Two surprises really." Señora Angélica put on a brave smile. "First, can you stay for tea? My mother-in-law has brought a marzipan torte from Santiago. A special treat in our family."

"And the other is…this!" Valeria popped like a jack-in-the-box in and out of her Grandmother Luisa's bedroom. In her hands she flapped a hooded Chilote poncho, woven from handspun wool. Like the one Señora Angélica had lent me the stormy evening of the wake in April, its blue-on-cream embroidery featured the shades of nature from pale sky to deep sea.

My mouth dropped. "Oooh!" I ducked as Vali placed the exquisite handwork over my head and arranged it. "Why, thank you. It's lovely. You made it, Señora Angélica?"

She bowed her head. "I did the piecing and embroidery. Mamá always weaves the material. It was her idea, really."

Señora Luisa responded to my smile with a slight softening of her prim mouth and went on with her spinning.

"Just what you need today, Meli." Marcos wrinkled his nose as he stared out the window at the pelting rain. "Looks like they finished it just in time."

Señora Rosalía examined the poncho's colorful edging. "What an excellent piece of work, Angélica. The color is perfect for you, too, my dear. You look a picture."

"Now, about tea," Señora Angélica said. "If you think it will be too late, Nicolás could walk you back after—"

"Where *is* Nicolás?" I asked. "Hard at it on the balcony?"

"He's practicing his guitar in the apple shed." Valeria's carefree tone contradicted the cryptic explanation.

"He's *what?*"

"You know he does weird things sometimes, Melissa." Marcos's gaze, unusually sober, bored into me like steel. Depression descended on the room again like a wet blanket.

I bit my lip. "I, uh…I could go call him for tea. If you're almost ready."

Señora Angélica nodded, her eyes grateful.

Between cloudbursts, I dashed across the yard. Puddles reflected a double rainbow that arched over the garden gate. The door of the apple shed hung ajar, and I slipped in unnoticed at first.

His back to me, Nicolás hunched over his guitar on a stump of luma wood. He sang a haunting melody in a voice so low yet clear, it reminded me of the silvery ripple of a summer stream. Straining to listen, I caught the repeated phrases of the chorus, something about change and pain and love for his people.

I padded across the spongy earthen floor and leaned against the great cider press in front of him. "It's beautiful. But sort of sad."

He didn't seem surprised to see me. "It's one of my favorites. We did it at the Folkloric Festival last year."

"I'd like to learn it sometime."

"I see they gave you the poncho." He laid the guitar aside on a barrel. "Suits you, Meli. Even if you don't look too Chilote. Mamá worked on it evenings for weeks."

"I'll cherish it as an heirloom. A wonderful, special gift." I forced a bright smile. "You coming in for the rest of the party? I hear there's even your favorite, marzipan cake."

When he didn't answer, I hoisted myself atop the other remaining barrel of cider. The spicy scent of ripe apples still clung to the room, flooding my mind with memories of our last rain-drenched afternoon spent here. "You wanna tell me what's going on? You've been here brooding all afternoon. Sulking or something."

His head jerked up. A spark kindled in his eyes. "What do you think is going on? I could have described the whole scenario before it ever happened."

"Well, tell me."

"They walk in, gushing compliments and gifts. Apologize for their neglect, they have been so busy, but so terribly concerned since the earthquake. Blah, blah, blah. Grandmother Rosalía cries, and so does my mother, though not for the same reason. Vali is delighted to see them. She's the only one."

"Did it ever occur to you, amigo, that your grandparents might honestly regret what happened in the past?"

"Oh, I don't know." His jaw clenched, his right cheek twitched. His hands between his knees gripped each other in a white-knuckled ball. "But what do they expect? They cannot just barge back into our lives whenever *they* feel like it and find everything is sweet again."

His anger matched my own, too painfully familiar. We both tended to heavy-duty overthink. But, closing my eyes a second, I felt compelled to probe. "So what, you think you need to punish them a bit first? Blow them off, hurt them, the same as you've been hurt?"

Nicolás bristled. He opened his mouth to retort, then clamped it shut, scowling at me with blazing eyes. Finally he said, "I guess that's just exactly what I do think about it."

Deep down, I'd wanted to punish my family, too. But nothing—*nothing*—they'd done could justify how I'd deserted my grandmother last summer. Yet Grandma had forgiven me without reservation.

Slowly, I went on, thinking aloud. "You can't trust God and then run your own life, Nicolás. Not and be happy, that is."

He grunted. "What do you mean?"

"It's like the song, you know, 'Trust and Obey.' In this case—don't be mad at me—the *obey* means *forgive*."

"You don't understand. I can't just change the way I feel. It's been too much, too long." His fierce expression relaxed, but his eyes glassed over.

"But that's just what we were saying last night. We *can* change. Or better said, *God* can change us. But your point was, everything's different now. I know your grandparents have ignored you, maybe mistreated you—"

He snorted. "*Maybe?*"

"And I do understand it's hard to overlook that. But—" I leaned forward, dead earnest. "You've got to let go of those old hurts and wrongs and forgive them, or the bitterness is gonna eat you alive. Ruin your life."

Nicolás shuffled to the door, cracked it open a few more inches, and glowered out at the gray screen of rain. "Melissa, I really thought you were my friend," he said in a dull, faraway voice.

I winced. Sliding off the barrel, I closed the space between us and joggled his arm. "Now don't you shut *me* out too, Nicolás Serrano! It's *because* I'm your friend that I'm talking to you so tough."

His eyes locked with mine in a surly glare.

"Like you did to me when I needed it," I said. "I didn't like it much, either, but that's what friends do. If I live to be a hundred, I'll be telling my great-grandchildren that I once knew a guy who was enough of a real Christian to make me hungry for God. And enough of a real friend to make me face it."

In different moods, Nicolás could be defiant, intense, even maddeningly self-assured. Sometimes he wore his untouchable aloofness like a suit of armor, but no longer. His guard crumbled. The Nicolás I'd known before—always in control, always confident of what to do and what to say—now vanished, replaced by a tormented boy, suddenly incredibly vulnerable. A single tear slashed a glistening trail down one brown cheek.

His lips trembled as he smiled. "So it's my turn to need…a confrontation, is it? Maybe you're right." His voice got that husky quality it had when he was moved.

I looped my arm through his. He gripped my hand. We stood for several long minutes in the sheltered doorway of the shed. The silence felt like a refuge, comfortable and warm. The air was as fresh as clean laundry, and I took deep breaths, waiting while he mulled.

I prayed too, a novelty for me. Nicolás the maverick, the daredevil Dolphin Boy, had exposed his heart to me. I wanted to treat his secrets with tenderness. *But Lord, what do I say next? Help me to speak honestly and still be kind.* Spiritual truth was alien territory, to say the least.

*Finish sharing your story.*

My breath came in a sharp gulp. *Everything, Lord?*

*You know the part I mean.*

What good would *that* do—to expose my worst sin, my lowest moment, to the friend who thought most highly of me? Humbling myself hardly equaled a do-over. My heart hammered corks into my throat. But…secrets could fester. Doing the hard thing might mean step one in a start-over. For both of us.

"I—I mentioned about my grandmother's death, didn't I?" Shame scorched my face, in spite of the damp nip.

"Sí, and I get you think I should reconcile with my grandmother before it's too late."

"That's true, but—there's more to it."

He shifted to look at me, curiosity glimmering in his eyes. "She fell, you said. That wasn't your fault, Melissa."

"Not directly."

"You had a quarrel?"

"Oh, not with Gran. I had a quarrel with the world—and with God." The wool poncho weighed a thousand pounds. My forehead oozed moisture. "She'd been sick—and I was supposed to stay with her—but I snuck out to a party that night. I should've been there when she got hurt, but I wasn't, and—" I cleared my clogged throat and spit out the rest like a disgusting bit of rotten apple. "I've never told a living soul except you."

"Oh, Meli." He loosed my hand and draped his arm around my shoulders. "You've carried this around a long time."

"Yeah, and I need to level with my parents now."

"But you can't forgive yourself, can you?"

"I couldn't for a long time. But *she* forgave me, from the floor—" I pressed a sob back with my fist. "Bucha, I'm *not* going to cry again. This story's as happy as it is sad."

"I suspect," he said, "that it sort of set in motion a whole house of cards that eventually led you here."

"And...to God. You once told me—right here in this shed, remember, that dreadful day Jaime died? You said that even though bad things happen, we have to trust that God has a good purpose in it." I drew a piercing breath. "Don't you think that applies to your situation now, too?"

For a moment, he froze. Had I stepped too far? Then he tilted his head against the doorjamb and blurted, "Melissa, I do know in my heart that forgiving is the right thing to do. But it's hard. And it—it feels like a betrayal."

I was puzzled. "A betrayal?"

"When I first came to Chiloé, I was just a scared, lonely kid, you know. I was! My papá, my hero, had been *murdered* only a few months before. My mamá walked like the living dead, in a fog of despair, and here Papá's last words to me were, 'Take care of your mother.' I didn't know what to do. But—"

"You were only twelve years old, Nicolás."

"True, but listen. When we landed on Chauquelín, the island—the people here—welcomed us—me. I was nobody and had nothing and belonged nowhere, but they made me one of them. Somehow I survived, even thrived. I'm proud to be a Chilote. And I'm not going to throw all that away, as if it means nothing to me." A resolute tone iron-edged his voice.

"No, how could you? But I don't understand. What makes you think you have to reject the island to accept your grandparents?"

Or...maybe I *should* understand. I'd rejected my family to find myself. I'd even rejected God to chase the devil's carrots.

"The two don't mix." He shrugged, a look of misery creeping into his face again. "They're too different, two completely opposite worlds. I ask myself, would my grandparents even be interested in me if they knew me as I really am now—just a country kid, with no desire to change that?"

"You'll never find out unless you give them a chance to *get* to know you."

"But that—"

"I know," I said softly, "that means taking a risk. Forgiveness does sort of open up the possibility of being hurt again." Even more softly, I said, "On the other hand, it could also open some doors you might not want to miss."

"I'm not so sure about that."

340

"What about your mother and Marcos? What do they think of all this with your grandparents now?"

"They don't know what to think."

"You know what? I think they're watching and waiting… for *you*, amigo. Take Marc, for instance. He always acts like he doesn't have a care in the world. But he idolizes you. He'll follow *your* lead."

Nicolás groaned. "I do not need *that* on my conscience."

"And your mother. She probably feels a lot like you. This idea of giving every problem to the Lord is new to her. Maybe she needs to see if—if you're just going to handle this your own way, or if Jesus is really all you claim He is to you."

"I think she can see that from our dealings with Bórquez."

"Fighting his kind of blatant evil is important, yeah. But don't you think forgiving your grandparents will touch her even more?"

Nicolás fell quiet for a few minutes before squaring his shoulders. "I can't say I have worked through this yet. But I promise I'll think and pray about it some more."

Abruptly he noticed that he still held his arm around me. He colored and released me. "Your hands look a lot better," he mumbled.

He turned to stuff his guitar into an empty flour sack. "Ready to run for the house before it rains harder? I can smell Mamá's empanadas from clear across the yard."

42

Rain poured all that night and all the next day. In fact, it rained one way or another—sprinkle, shower, stream, bucket, and torrent—every day for the next week. It became hard to tell when one storm ended and the next began. Voices keened in the wind. Drafts stirred the curtains and swirled along the floor. I feared Ramón and Gina's new roof would get ripped right off.

The undercurrent of anxiety on Chauquelín felt unbearable at times, though escape no longer even crossed my mind. I was committed with the Pérezes and the Serranos to the end, whatever the end might be, come what may in the struggle against Juan Bórquez's bid to control the island. Somehow God had entwined my life with theirs.

How long, though, before the smoldering tensions burst into flame? Every day we hoped and watched for Cole to return with some arm of the law.

"Why, oh why, doesn't he come?" I griped to Gina one dreary morning more than a week later. Sighing, I wiped condensation off the kitchen window with my sleeve and scanned the battleship-gray horizon. Only foaming breakers rushed toward the shore of the cove below. "He said he'd get the authorities as soon as possible, and he knew time was crucial."

"You look outside and ask why?" Gina smiled. "We have had only stormy weather since Don Colin was last here. You have never traveled in these rough seas, Melissa. It is dangerous even for a bigger launch than Don Colin's. Only a fool would try it. No." She shook her black ringlets. "Even Bórquez's boats have not come in this week, you know."

"But I'll bet he has them anchored somewhere close, waiting for the big day. If nobody catches him before the twenty-ninth, it'll be too late to do anything about it."

Gina shoved another red luma log into the stove. "Sí, querida, I know." Her calm unnerved me. "But I am sure Don Colin is doing all he can. We must trust it with God and be patient."

*That's easier said than done.* Every hour I waited, my patience stretched a little thinner. But...stretching exercises were supposed to be a good thing.

"I should tell Noah and the flood for this afternoon's story." I laughed.

"How about Jonah and the whale?" Gina grinned back.

Later that morning the steady rains relented to a drizzle. Nicolás stopped by the Pérez house to invite Jana and me for tea after the Bible class.

"It's Valeria's eleventh birthday." He shifted in his mud-caked boots at the door of the house. "I'm headed to check out the north field right now. Grandfather's suggestion. He thinks we may as well go ahead and plant it. It's our best field, and now's the time to do it, if the rain would just let up."

To his credit, Nicolás had resigned himself to his grandparents' visit. He'd made an effort to ease the strain in his home. He and Marcos even worked together with their grandfather, Don Manuel, for several long days repairing the balcony. But I knew the Serranos' presence still smarted like vinegar in my friend's open wound.

"So if Bórquez wants to make something of it, he'll have to take it to court," I said, hands on hips.

"Grandfather doesn't think he has much legal claim, for all he may technically own the title."

"That's gotta be a relief to you guys. I think God sent your grandpa along at just the right time. Not only for the legal advice, but having another man around to back you up."

He let out a tight breath. "Síp."

"Have you…have you told Don Manuel about the abalone?"

"No,"

"You have to trust him. Tell him, Nico. You might need his help if Cole doesn't get back here soon."

His face a blank, Nicolás grunted and swung away towards the hill. I turned inside, shaking my head. *Dear God, please do something.*

# 43

The mood at Valeria's party was surprisingly festive. The Serrano table boasted golden fried *milcao* and chunks of smoked pork, crisp *sopaipillas*, and a choice of apple butter, *ulmo* honey, or a spicy salsa made of chopped onions, chilies, and cilantro from Señora Angélica's herb garden. The last of the hoarded marzipan cake from Santiago reigned from a plate of honor.

Valeria's other gifts—a variegated wool sweater knit by her mother and a denim skirt and jacket showing off a boutique label from Santiago—more or less dwarfed the Sahne-Nuss chocolate bar her brothers and I chipped in to pick up at a North Head shop. Still, she was delighted with her birthday bash. Even Señora Rosalía expressed pleasure in the tea treats and admitted that the *milcao* wasn't so bad.

"You don't know how I dreaded the possibility of being served these potato-patty things." She gave an embarrassed twitter. "But they really are quite good. Perhaps it depends on the cook."

Señora Angélica blushed and smiled.

As the adults finished a second cup of mint tea and the kids passed around the mate, a knock reverberated at the front door. Nicolás rose from the table to answer it. When he didn't return right away, his mother followed him. An unintelligible conversation rumbled in the hall.

Then a man's indignant bark pierced the paneled pine walls. "I demand to see Doña Luisa! This household has always contributed generously to the Fiesta of Cabildos."

Scowling like a nettled hen, the old doña hobbled toward the hallway. I exchanged an uneasy glance with Señora Rosalía and then raised an eyebrow at Marcos. "Guess the party's over—calm before the storm?"

He shrugged. "The celebration for the island's patron saint. Must be about that time of year. The *cabildo*—the festival committee—has come to collect our quota for the expenses, I guess."

"But this contribution is voluntary, no?" Don Manuel frowned.

Almost as if in reply, an irate voice scraped out. "Nobody is asking what you *prefer*, Angélica. As a responsible member of this community, you are *required* to participate."

"That's Bórquez!" Marcos bounded to his feet. "Bucha, the guy's like a barnacle here."

I jumped up too. For a second, I kneaded the chair back, trying to calm the trembling in my hands. Then I trailed Marcos through the kitchen to the wide doorway looking into the entry hall. The grandparents and the two little girls joined our gawking parade.

Bulging in his usual grubby sweater, Bórquez filled the front door like a potbellied stove. His face shone raw-liver red underneath the grizzle of his unkempt beard. Two older men, also flushed with annoyance, flanked him. They looked vaguely familiar. Shopkeepers from the village?

The one on Bórquez's right scolded Nicolás. "Here you have a position on the cabildo, young man, and you have not attended even one meeting this year. Plain irresponsible. You were brought up better than that. I am certain you received last week's notice."

"I did," Nicolás said evenly. "But I also gave in my resignation months ago. Whether your committee accepted it or not, I cannot say. But I am a follower of Jesus now, Don Alfonso… not the image. I cannot in good conscience take part in the festival."

"Your good conscience! Lies and hypocrisy!" Bórquez bellowed. "You try to turn your whole family against the traditions of our people—mock our island ways. Chu, what else could we expect of an uppity *nortino* brat, son of a filthy butchering city cop? Too high and mighty for the likes of us here, the impudent Serrano spawn."

The insult to his father triggered Nicolás's leap. He sprang forward, his arm drawn back taut as an arrow in a bow. The same glare of steel-cold fury that had compelled Bórquez to stand down last week flashed from Nicolás's face.

I really thought he was going to punch the bully.

Bórquez and his cronies edged a step backwards. Señora Angélica tucked a restraining hand at her son's elbow. Don Manuel Ignacio Serrano strode down the hall and clapped Nicolás's shoulder.

"Well, now, Señor Bórquez, I am happy to hear you call Nicolás the son of a Santiago cop." Anger and amusement mixed in Don Manuel's cool voice. "Strange, though, that is not what you told us about the boy fifteen years ago."

Nicolás sucked in his breath as though struck. He jerked around to gape at his grandfather's enigmatic remark.

Across Bórquez's piggish eyes flickered stunned recognition. Even fear? Was it possible he hadn't heard of the Serranos' arrival on the island?

Nicolás's rigid jaw slackened. Confusion clouded his eyes. Had he ever asked his mother to explain Señora Rosalía's reference to Bórquez's troublemaking in Santiago? Likely not, since he appeared completely bewildered.

But I grasped the significance of Don Manuel's barbed words. So did Bórquez—he'd just been snared in his own trap. The old lie had circled back to bite him.

The weasel recovered his swagger quickly enough, though. He cleared his throat and nodded to Don Manuel. "Why, good afternoon, Your Honor. Never thought to see you swells in these parts."

I couldn't believe it. The slippery eel ignored Nicolás's grandfather's subtle accusation and bent the conversation to his own advantage.

"Bit too little too late, eh, Gela?" Bórquez simpered. "I still say you should throw in your luck with me. Forget your purse-proud aristocrats, querida."

Señora Angélica skewered him with a frosty stare.

He swallowed back the forced hee-haw at his own feeble joke. "No importa, we have not come to dig up the family quarrels. About the fiesta, surely as an islander born and bred, you recognize the great privilege and importance of your contribution."

"And the saint will bless you," the man on the left said.

Señora Angélica clasped and unclasped her hands, graceful head bowed so that a loosened strand of glossy hair veiled her cheek. "Again, señores, I must decline this year. My son and I are united in this. My mother, of course, will do as she pleases with her own goods."

All eyes riveted toward the old lady. Señora Luisa gripped the carved cedar banister of the staircase for support. How would she respond?

I suspected her sympathy for Juan Bórquez had shrunk drastically of late. But in Chiloé, ancient ties and traditions weren't that easily forsaken. Even the family matriarch's growing disgust for her nephew—cousin, whatever—probably wouldn't make her ditch this customary island festival he represented.

The old woman's black eyes glittered. "I have two remaining barrels of cider I would be glad to get rid of."

"Thank you, Doña Luisa," the man on the right said. "What a relief that not everyone in this family has turned traitor. But…other years, you have given a dozen lambs as well."

"So I have, Don Alfonso," the old doña agreed. "Perhaps you did not know we had to sell more than half our flock in the summer to pay the rent on some land? We have no yearlings left, and the old ewes have not started to lamb yet."

Don Alfonso's mouth dropped open. "Of course not yet," he mumbled, beet-faced. "I—I do remember hearing about that misunderstanding a while back."

I almost laughed out loud. Señora Luisa had managed to twist her agreement into a sly denunciation. *Shrewd old bird.*

"*Pérdonennos*, then. We have nothing else to offer." Señora Luisa's gaze stabbed Bórquez's meaty face. "We slaughtered our pig in June when the children came. Other than that, we have only the oxen and a couple of heifers we must keep for emergencies."

Bórquez glowered back at her. "Such as rent on the north field again? I saw the boys tramping in it today, so I presume your payment is forthcoming."

Nicolás shook his head, teeth gritted. "More lambs for the wolf."

"Now see here, Bórquez," Don Manuel broke in, "you had best leave these two ladies alone. Their claim to the land in question might be as valid as yours. So unless you want to test my theory in a court of law, I advise you to desist the harassment."

Bórquez's face grew mottled-pink-and-gray, like a roll of rotten baloney. He looked daggers at Don Manuel but made no reply.

Don Alfonso elbowed him and squeaked, "Vamos, Juan, we have finished our business here. Other places to stop yet, Doña Luisa, my team will pass by tomorrow to collect your cider donation."

The heavy double doors slammed behind the foiled fiesta committee.

"Grandfather, would you walk with me down to the bay?" Down the length of the hall, Nicolás's eyes met mine. "I want to show you something while there's this break in the weather."

*Finally, thank God.* I gave him a thumbs-up. He grinned and winked.

Bórquez had crashed our party…and unleashed more than a storm of confetti on his head. On the other hand, Manuel Serrano was a judge, not a commando. I sighed. Would all of us end up losers in this game of Pin the Loot on the Donkey?

# 44

The next morning dawned gray and cheerless, though mild as a dove. With the respite from the rain, I watched expectantly between chores for Cole's *Ambassador* to chug into the cove. No go.

As we dished up my new favorite lunch, a seafood soup called *paila marina*, a quick, light rap sounded at the door.

Nicolás burst in, panting. "Where are Jana and Rodrigo? Your mamá's here, kids! Came in from Cocotúe on a fishing launch."

Before he finished speaking, the two Garrido children flew out the door, wearing neither coats nor boots. I smiled so wide that tears stung my eyes. "What d'ya know? A happy day, after all. Let's all go welcome her." I reached for little Anita's parka.

"Vanessa's not staying," Nicolás said. "I ran on ahead, so I didn't hear her whole story, but I did get she's only here to fetch the children on her way to Mellehue. My grandfather is going in too, to contact the police."

"I can't imagine what's holding up Cole," I said.

"Me neither," Nicolás said, "but last evening when I took *Abuelo* to watch Dolphin Bay from the woods, Bórquez's *Angélica* sailed in about dusk—along with the *Caleuche* all aglow. Abuelo about freaked, same as we did at first. Then they unloaded those big sacks, like they always do, but this time one broke. And it sure looked like abalone spilling out."

"But you've never seen Bórquez anywhere around?" Ramón asked as we half ran, half skated down the slick path toward the shore road.

"He makes himself scarce when the launches come in." Nicolás grimaced. "The crew usually heads up to his place after they dump their contraband, though. Or to the bars."

"Bórquez was busy soliciting for that festival yesterday anyway, remember," I said. "No wonder he's so big on this Cabildos Fiesta thing if it'll keep people occupied in North Head all weekend. Gives him the perfect cover to load the abalone again just as the season opens."

"Bucha, you're right, the fiesta's this coming weekend, right before season opening next Monday." Nicolás picked up his pace. "It's a good thing Abuelo is going to Mellehue today. Let's hurry and help Vanessa and the kids get ready."

Gina stopped short. "The children need their things, then. We should pack a bag for them so the launch does not have to wait."

The Pérezes wheeled back toward the house.

I said quietly, "Is everything okay between you and your grandparents now, Nicolás?"

His glance rested on the murky waters of the cove. The sea was as dead and motionless as a stone, the sky still bloated with rain. "I had a long talk with Abuelo on the hillside last night," he said. "We—both of us—discovered things we never knew before, and…I suppose we have both learned some hard lessons over the past three years."

"Yeah?"

He looked back at me, golden-brown eyes misted, but the somber shadow that always curtained his face whenever we spoke of his grandparents had lifted. "I'll tell you about it sometime, amiga."

"If you want to."

"I do." His smile dazzled like the sun. "So, sí, everything's okay. Is it not all insignificant anyway, when God has forgiven me so much? He rescued me from the pit of desperation, as the Bible says, and turned my life around. No matter what my human reason—or the devil—tells me about how I came to be in Chiloé, the bottom line is, it was part of God's plan."

My heart swelled. Somehow, he dared to defy the bleakness in the air and raise a flag to the God of impossible hope. Of victory against all odds.

I returned his smile. "I think God had His eye on you all along, Nicolás."

No time to say more. Past the Serranos' house, we rounded the curve in the shore path just in time to witness Jana and Rodrigo race into their mother's outstretched arms.

"And look!" I cried. "It's a sign."

A tenuous rainbow shimmered over the bay, arching from the neighboring island of Quenao into the wooded hinterlands of Chauquelín. Beneath it, the Garrido family clung together, reunited.

Maybe…maybe all the miracles we'd witnessed thus far were only a prelude to whatever drama God was about to unfold here. He'd transformed my apathy into love. He'd drawn Nicolás's bitter spirit to the release of forgiveness. He could certainly break Juan Bórquez's dark stranglehold on the island.

# 45

The dismal week crawled by. We waited. And waited some more.

The skies wedged in a solid wall of cloud unmoved by the bluster of the wind. At least the drizzle was only sporadic. No reason why Don Manuel or Cole—or *somebody*—couldn't pop out to Chauquelín. But not a sign of them, even since Nicolás's grandfather had departed on his mission for police assistance in Mellehue on the same launch as the Garridos.

I ping-ponged between resentment and mounting concern. Had *everyone* failed us? Or else, what could be holding them up? By Saturday, Tuesday's surge of confidence had dwindled away.

Nicolás and Marcos accompanied Valeria to the Pérezes for our Bible lesson that afternoon and stayed for tea afterwards. Discouragement drooped on my shoulders like a waterlogged poncho as I listened absently to the islanders' crop-talk around the stove.

"We gave up before noon today. Just too wet yet." Frowning, Nicolás stirred a spoonful of sugar into a steaming mug of tea. "So I rode into North Head for some groceries for Mamá."

I'd hardly seen the Serrano guys the entire draggy week. Sowing winter wheat in barely dried fields would challenge a brawny man, let alone a couple of teenagers, but they were pushing to finish the job before heading back to the liceo. Don Juan Bórquez hadn't even shown his face to oppose them.

Cole *would* eventually return, I was gloomily certain. After all, school classes were scheduled to resume next week. The question was, would he arrive in time to catch Bórquez and his crew in their abalone poaching? After Monday, the twenty-ninth of July, we could forget pinning anything on them.

"Stupid timing, I guess—I stumbled into the middle of the Fiesta of Cabildos," Nicolás said. "Bórquez is sure putting on a spectacle this weekend, Don Ramón. I mean, I've been at the festival before—know you have, too, of course—but man, this beats all."

"I heard a lot of visitors made it from Quenao and Meuluy." Ramón's wool hat wobbled as he chuckled into his mate. "Meaning, more disorder. More booze."

"And more images in the plaza than I could even count," Nicolás said. "People were crawling on their hands and knees across the esplanade to where they had their saint set up in a pool of water. Bórquez was there, snipping off pieces of the Santo's old robe and selling them as lucky charms."

Agape with morbid curiosity, I squirmed between the boys on the stove bench. "I still have half a roll of film in my camera."

"You don't want pictures of that, believe me, querida," Gina said. "Chuta, I'm not even sure it's safe. After the religious duties, most of those guys only care about getting drunk and picking up a woman for the night."

"No, I mean—" I leaned forward. "Not a soul on the island's likely to go near Dolphin Bay this evening. Bet you anything Bórquez's gang will make their move tonight, to load up the abalone they've cached in the bay."

"Take photos of that?" Nicolás grinned. "It may be pretty dark by then, but we could give it a try. Anything is better than nothing at this point."

Ramón took a long sip of mate and nodded. "Guess you're right. It's a last-ditch long shot in the dark, but it can't hurt."

At dusk Nicolás, Marcos, and I settled into sentry duty on a eucalyptus log in the woods that overlooked Dolphin Bay. Another storm brewed behind clouds as thick and black as coffee sludge. Like the sun, the moon, too, had been exiled from Chauquelín for weeks.

Rain began to pelt down. Vicious gusts of wind bit through to the skin even though I wore the embroidered wool poncho Señora Angélica had recently given me. Waterproof it might be, but I was still thankful for the canopy of spicy trees.

"It was a dark and stormy night." I laughed and shivered at the same time. "Photography's kind of a boring activity for such a dramatic occasion, isn't it?"

"The suspense is killing me," Marcos said, grinning.

We didn't have long to wait. As I'd predicted, Bórquez's two fishing boats once again materialized on the oil-spill horizon. The bigger launch, the one we dubbed the *Caleuche*, sparkled like a fantastic marine castle. The smaller *Angélica* glided in its vaporous glow. Chimes tinkled across the water.

A tingle shot up my spine. If this wasn't a ghost ship, then somebody was dead serious about keeping people away.

Arm in arm with the guys, I observed the next minutes with bated breath. The darkness deepened but, as easy to spot as actors on a brightly lit stage, two men in wetsuits climbed over the railing of the *Caleuche*. They slid beneath the choppy waves while a third man in shiny raingear remained on deck.

The divers broke the surface again. Between them, they hoisted a glossy grayish sack and attached it to a hook and chain. The deckhand cranked it up and into the launch's hold while the diving team plunged back underwater. Soon they emerged with another bulky sack and fastened it onto the makeshift winch. Then a third.

"Hard work," I said. "How many bags do you think they've got hidden in the bay?"

"Depends how long they've been stockpiling," Nicolás said. "I've seen them dump twenty-five or thirty over the past month myself."

I handed him the camera. With stealthy grace, he tiptoed across the road and slithered into the low scrub that straggled down to the edge of the beach. Though we could see the scene almost as well as if it were daylight, I doubted whether film could capture much of it. My camera wasn't exactly high-tech. But surely that blaze of lights would show up in any photo and prove *something*.

Nicolás snapped several shots of the two launches and then crept back to Marcos and me in the woods. "Wish I could get a close-up of what's inside those bags."

"We're witnesses, at least," I said, "even if the pictures aren't worth much."

In spellbound silence, we watched the divers dredge up sacks, presumably of abalone, for almost an hour. After Marcos's tally reached thirty-five, the men halted and struggled with a bag over to the *Angélica*. There another crew member waited to operate the deck setup.

The divers loaded about twenty sacks onto the *Angélica* and then clambered back onto the *Caleuche*. Dripping and glistening, they disappeared into the hold of the launch.

"You think they'll come ashore tonight?" Marcos asked.

"Usually do, making their report to Bórquez," Nicolás said.

"Doubt if he's home yet. Probably still running the fiesta in the village."

"I know. Let's hang around a bit longer."

"You're not gonna try to take *their* picture when they come in." I was incredulous. "They'll notice the flash at this close range."

"I guess. And what we don't want is to tangle with them or scare them off tonight. Let them believe Bórquez has lured the entire island population to the fiesta."

Soon the four crewmen, all now in hooded yellow slickers, shoved their rowboat over the rocky beach and tied it up. One of the company cackled and crowed, silly with booze. The others attempted to shush him. But he only roared, more boisterous than before, as he staggered up the path toward North Head.

"What's with you guys?" The slurred voice shrilled over the whipping wind and rain. "We celebrate now, eh? The job's done, the goods on board. Five million pesos in our pocket."

Marcos grunted. "It has to be abalone, all right. No other cargo would bring that price around here."

"What's five million pesos in dollars?" I said.

"Don't know," Nicolás said, "but it's a small fortune in Chiloé."

Marcos stood and tugged his wool hat down over his ears. "Looks like the show's over for tonight, gang."

"Wait." Nicolás eyed the last of the divers straggling up and around the curve in the northbound path. He took a deep breath. "I bet we could get some good photos on board. Think I'll row out in their boat for a few minutes."

I gasped. "What on earth are you thinking? What if someone sees you—or catches you? There're still lights and music going on the *Caleuche*."

He gave me a roguish grin. I could tell his mind was already made up. "Aw, those barflies will not return for a while. I think they only left the *Caleuche* set up to discourage visitors. I'll stop at the *Angélica* first, anyway. You up for it, Marc?"

"Oh sure, Cahuel."

"Vamos, then. Melissa, can you stand watch here just a little longer? If we're not back in half an hour, you'll know the *Caleuche* turned us into dolphins and shanghaied us to join her crew."

"Not funny." I dashed after the boys. "You're not leaving me here on guard duty. I'll go with you."

Nicolás turned a dubious frown on me. "The bay looks rough tonight."

"So I know you can handle a rowboat like a pro. Besides, I can swim."

"I would not like to see you try it in *this* water. And…we really could use a lookout," he said lamely.

"I'm going! It's about time we did something besides sit around and watch and wait."

"How about you watch and pray, then?"

We glowered at each other a minute before he grinned and shook his head in defeat. "Is this so you can tell your grandkids, too?"

"She wins!" Marcos hooted. "What a girl. I can't believe it."

Our reckless scheme started off without a hitch. Like silent wraiths, we stole through a steadily increasing torrent of rain to the boulder where the dingy rowboat was fastened. In two deft flicks of the rope, Nicolás had it untied. He and Marcos scraped it over the ice-slick gravel of the beach to the water. The harsh grinding, loud enough to wake the dead, let alone any guard, bristled the hair on my scalp.

But it honestly seemed we were the only living creatures for miles.

In the boat, no one spoke. The wild surf creamed and sawed around us. Nicolás manned the oars, avoiding a direct route out to the anchored launches. Instead he rowed in the overhanging shelter of the moss-and-myrtle woods along the peninsula arm of the bay. When we were almost opposite the *Angélica*, he struck out toward the tubby little fishing launch.

Dolphin Bay had never seemed eerie or menacing before. I'd spent so many peaceful evenings here, bathed in moonlight, humming the music of the universe. Now the bay convulsed with swells under the *Caleuche*'s lurid glare, rocked by a cacophonous duet of canned music and screeching wind.

I put on a brave front to the boys, but my muscles cricked with tension. Was I the only one who remembered that the crooks and spooks on this *Caleuche* had pursued Jaime Garrido to his death? Of course, the guys and I would hardly fly into a panic over a supposed ghost ship now, but what if Bórquez's henchmen saw us in their rowboat and lay in wait on shore? Not a comforting possibility, to say the least.

The rowboat bumped the starboard side of the *Angélica.* Thankfully, the wind's wail and the thunder of waves crashing over the Dragon's Back off the peninsula muffled our noise. Nicolás handed the oars to Marcos and mouthed, "You stay here, okay?"

He gripped the iron rail with a fist and swung himself up to the deck. Then after looping the rowboat's rope over the rail, he gave a hand to me. I stepped aboard the *Angélica.*

We headed straight to our purpose. Nicolás peered in the salt-spattered window of the cabin. It proved empty. So far, so good. We edged along the deck to the entrance of the hold in the stern.

"Watch this door be locked from the inside," he muttered.

But it wasn't. The slide-bolt, though rusty and stiff, yielded to his touch. The door sagged open. He vaulted into the dim hole. I crouched at the top while my eyes adjusted to the darkness of a low, dank chamber. My nose scrunched at the odor of rotting wood, salt water, and fish.

Nicolás pointed out the rustic ladder hanging from the threshold and helped me clamber down. The air was too close, almost claustrophobic.

He grunted as he grazed his knuckles over the pale, bulging lumps that lined both walls of the hold. "Right shape. Chuta, I left the light with Marc."

I fumbled in the pocket of my poncho and pulled out a tiny keychain flashlight. "Does this help?"

"Knew I brought you for something." A smile sounded in his voice.

Under the glimmer of my flashlight, he broke open the reed-sewn top closure of one of the bags and drew out a sample of its contents. Balancing it in his palm, he gave a suppressed whistle. "There's an abalone for you, Melissa." *Triumph*.

The large cone-shaped mollusk had a grainy white shell, like coarse stucco. At the wide end, it spiraled to reveal gleaming ivory flesh and a flash of rainbow color. In other circumstances, I would've examined it more closely and admired the mother-of-pearl layer.

But now we didn't linger. I took a few quick photos while Nicolás trained the light on the shellfish and then on the slit sack.

Only a few minutes passed, at most, but I was relieved to escape the stifling place. A blast of fresh cold and rain hit us at the top. It felt good.

We hustled back along the deck and dropped with a thump into the rowboat.

Marcos waited, his eyes alert. "You saw the loot?"

Nicolás grinned, thumbs up.

"You want to drop in on the *Caleuche* too? Haven't seen any signs of life over there."

Nicolás reached for the oars. "Okay then, vamos."

We inched out from the shadowed side of the *Angélica* into the dazzle surrounding the *Caleuche*. A stout figure burst from the cabin and gave an eardrum-bursting squeal.

"Trespassers, eh? Snoops and thieves! Well, I can fix your little boat fast enough, same as we did to that Garrido fool." The man I'd named Pudgy a few weeks ago snatched open the *Caleuche*'s cabin door again and disappeared inside.

Instantly—as instantly as possible in the heavy chop—Nicolás swung the rowboat around in a beeline toward shore. My skin prickled. Between chattering teeth, I said, "He—he said something about Jaime Garrido. What's he gonna do?"

As though in answer to my question, the large inboard motor of the *Caleuche* snarled to life.

"He can't chase us far," Marcos said. "We'll reach shore long before he can even lift the anchors on that launch."

But Nicolás heaved at the oars, his face grim. "He can do enough harm without bothering with the anchors."

The *Caleuche* slammed into gear and mowed a path through the water at right angles to the rowboat. Just as it tugged at its anchors, the malicious sailor threw the engine into reverse. The launch sliced back to its original position.

Back and forth the *Caleuche* lurched, never more than a few yards in either direction. Still, the movement stirred up a virtual tsunami of frothing swells. Violent rollers rose, writhing like a sea monster, and threatened to sweep the rowboat upside down into the bay.

Our small open craft rocked, clung precariously to the surface. Danger loomed, I knew it. The boys knew it, too.

A wave smashed over the rowboat. Somehow Nicolás managed to keep it upright. Again and again. As I'd glibly said, he *was* a skilled oarsman. His jaw locked, rigid with concentration.

Marcos, wide-eyed behind him in the stern, braced himself against either side with his sturdy arms and legs. Frozen and drenched, I dug my nails into the sodden plank of my seat in the bow. With every rush of the breakers, I held my breath. *Oh, God...*

Finally, we pulled near the south shore of the bay. Off course, too far out to sea, too close to the Dragon's Back of boulders scattered from the tip of the peninsula. But almost to safety. My shoulders relaxed. I released a sigh.

At that moment, another wave seethed and washed over my legs. The camera in my lap spun away. Frantically I snatched for the precious cargo.

The next surge pitched me overboard and flung me into a whirlpool of frosty foam. The frigid temperature tore my breath away. I gasped as the sea swallowed me.

I flailed in a nightmare. Brutal waves slapped and plunged me under like a rag on a scrub-board. Churned back to the surface, I sucked in saltwater and choked. I could barely gulp air or pump my arms, let alone swim. And still minus the camera. Icy bands clamped my ribcage. The soaked poncho dragged at my shoulders like a fishing net.

Desperate, I twisted my head around. Where were the guys—the boat? I blinked water from my eyes to search, but another billow knocked me over and under again. My forehead struck something hard and sharp beneath the water.

Blackness engulfed me.

## 46

Strong hands at my armpits wrenched me from the clutches of the sea. Nicolás's voice barked, breathless and hoarse as a dolphin. "Are you all right? Melissa! Breathe!"

I could only force out a croak, then gagged. He eased me onto a bed of pebbled sand and turned me over on my side. For an awful moment, I strangled and retched and hacked up mouthfuls of salt water. Finally, I snagged a breath. My throat and nose stung.

"My head…I hit my head," I whimpered. Gingerly I patted the lump burning at my temple. My hand came away sticky.

"Marc, she's bleeding," Nicolás shouted into the dark. "Here, help me with the boat. Then I'd better get her to the house fast."

He disappeared. I heard the rowboat grating over the gravel. Through the haze in my head, I was vaguely aware when the *Caleuche*'s engine died, though its lights still glared across the bay.

In the woods above the shore, a luminous wisp of white fluttered downhill. Nicolás's white-gowned Lady of

Chauquelín? But before I could squeak, the White Lady vanished.

A handkerchief, a flour sack? A signal from Bórquez…or a trick of my vision, who knew?

I forgot it when Nicolás knelt at my side again a few seconds later. His clothes hung as stiff and wet as my own. In the *Caleuche*'s garish reflection, his ashen face betrayed anxiety and…something else unfamiliar.

He moved to carry me, but I teetered to my feet. "I think I can walk."

Brusquely he swooped me into his arms anyway. "How can you walk? The ground is rough, and you have lost both boots. You're not much bigger than a *chorito* anyway."

My body quivered like a blob of seaweed. Suddenly limp, I slumped against him. "Nicolás, you saved my life, didn't you?" I shuddered. "Did—did you get the camera?"

"No, it's gone. Doesn't matter." His voice caught as his arms tightened. "I got you, Melissa."

Marcos galloped ahead to raise the alarm at the Serranos' home. Nicolás stripped off my poncho and wrapped Marc's slightly less waterlogged one around me—his own poncho seemed missing in action. Even so, I was shivering uncontrollably by the time he deposited me in the wicker armchair by his mother's kitchen stove amid mega commotion.

Señora Rosalía immediately offered the balcony bedroom. Between the boys, they carried me upstairs and then all the women of the family set about clucking. I'd have been embarrassed if I wasn't so fuzzy around the edges. My head throbbed.

In the golden light of a kerosene lantern, they peeled off my soggy clothes, wrapped me in flannels, stacked piles of thick wool throws over me, and tucked a hot water bottle at each side. Valeria held a cup of hot tea to my cold lips while Señora Angélica daubed at the gash oozing on my forehead. She peered into my eyes and scurried out of the room.

She returned with some sort of cool herbal brew, dipped a cloth in it, and applied it to the injury. "I have no ice." Her lips compressed. "Nicolás says you lost consciousness?"

"I…maybe for a minute."

"He's already changed into dry clothes and saddled the mare. As soon as he drinks a mug of coffee, he will try to get the medic from North Head." She frowned. "And I pray Don Alberto is around, because you need stitches, my dear, or you're going to have an ugly scar. *Please God*, let there be fine sutures available."

I shifted under the weight of blankets. "And…Gina—"

"I'll dispatch Marcos to the Pérezes'" —she patted my shoulder— "to let them know you will spend the night here. I am concerned about concussion. *And* hypothermia."

I babbled another question, but Señora Angélica shushed me. My head pounded. I let my eyelids droop.

Maybe I slept. At best, the hours blurred together. I might have vomited once—or twice.

At some point, Chauquelín's bachelor paramedic arrived. He rubbed his stubbled chin at the sight of my split brow and quickly went to work stitching. I barely felt the needles. A local anesthetic, probably an antibiotic, too.

"Keep her quiet a day or two," he said.

The morning brought relief, a returned sense of normality. I took my meals in the big antique carved bed and visited with each of my nurses in turn. *I'm the queen of Chauquelín, charmed.*

"Sure, it's nice to be the center of attention," I said to Nicolás after lunch. "Everyone's been great—your mother's been *wonderful*. But she has plenty to do besides look after me."

"Nonsense, she loves it," he said. "My mamá *is* almost a nurse, you know. She was starting her fourth year of studies when…Papá was killed."

I cocked my head. "I didn't know, but I'm not surprised. She—well, it fits, know what I mean?"

"I do. She's a born nurse. She should have finished her course, but… Anyway, you don't need to feel in the way."

"Thanks, but I *do* feel silly about the whole thing. Everybody's making such a fuss. When it was my own fault."

"It was *my* fault." Nicolás shuffled over to the French doors that opened onto the newly rebuilt balcony. His voice tensed. "I was wrong to take any of us out there, and I have confessed and apologized to Mamá and Don Ramón. Bucha, if anything serious had happened to you, just because I was so obsessed with trapping Bórquez—"

"Come on, you can't blame yourself." I'd award him a medal for shouldering the responsibility for the fiasco—unlike my so-called friends in Baltimore—but I'd insisted on going with him, and the photos were my idea in the first place. "I'm just as eager as you are to see that weasel get caught. Too bad I had to lose the evidence."

He stared out the doors toward the cove, heavily banked with clouds. "It's okay. We can report what we saw." But his mood, somber and sagging as the sky, contradicted his words.

"Cole or your grandfather will surely bring the police by this evening," I said. "The weather's calmed off again, hasn't it? And we're supposed to start school tomorrow."

Nicolás shrugged. "Doesn't matter that much anymore. Bórquez's launches are long gone, along with the abalone, of course. That guy on the *Caleuche* probably told him everything. Both the *Caleuche* and the *Angélica* lifted anchor before day-break this morning."

"Oh, no!" I bolted upright in bed. "Does that mean Bórquez won't ever get caught now?"

"Makes it harder to pin anything on him, for sure."

I fidgeted beneath my layers of blankets. "I'm gonna get up and head home to Ramón and Gina's."

"What! You're supposed to have strict bed rest, señorita."

"I'm fine now," I said. "Your grandmother can move back in here. Can't be too comfortable with your whole family crammed into two bedrooms. Besides, I need to get my things packed for Mellehue."

"How do you figure on getting there? Another swim?" Amusement and pessimism mixed in his wry grin.

I smiled back at him. "No swimming, please." But inex-plicable peace flooded me. "I just really believe that Cole or your grandfather, or somebody, will come today. I know it seems unlikely. But is it too hard for God? Do you think He's brought us this far to dump us now?"

For a long minute, our eyes met in cool challenge.

Finally Nicolás's expression thawed. "All right," he said gruffly. "So maybe God will not work things out my way. I'll trust Him anyway, to do things *His* way."

"Good. Now, would you go ask Vali to bring up my clothes if they're dry?"

"I'll talk to Mamá about it." He squatted at the bedside. "You want to pray with me first, amiga? Because I...I need it."

I bowed my head, a lump in my throat. "Dear God, please intervene here in this little corner of Your Earth. We confess we feel helpless. But I know *You're* not limited by time or place, by bad weather or evil men..."

Six months ago, who would have believed I'd join hands with a Chilean guy to *pray*? The twist of fate that teleported me to this alien universe was really God's destiny. I thought He'd messed up my life. Instead He'd snatched me from my mundane existence to bless me with an extraordinary adventure. I assumed my blundering choices had brought me here, but everything formed part of a plan. He'd provoked an earthquake—not the May eighteenth one, but a seismic shift in my heart.

Here I was with Nicolás. The gringa and the Chilote islander, two people who would never have been together, except for God. From totally different worlds, yet we met on common ground, understood one another.

He took up where I trailed off. "My God, You are not delayed by accident. There are no coincidences or calamities with You..."

I would never forget the power of this moment of prayer as long as I lived.

47

Of course, Señora Angélica objected—strenuously—to my proposal. I expected she would.

"Look at you, black eye and all." She eased off the bandage and passed me a hand mirror. "You should not exert yourself yet."

The tug at the stitches hurt when I grimaced at my reflection. Sure, it was livid, puffy and bruised from my hairline through my left eyebrow. But it was slit clean—probably the impact with the boulder—and neatly repaired.

"I could make her a bed in the oxcart and take her over," Nicolás said.

"Oh, thanks, pal. Not the oxcart, my brains will be completely scrambled. But horseback I'd do."

"And straight to bed at the Pérezes'." Señora Angélica smiled as she tacked the gauze back into place. "After tea."

"I'll need to borrow some shoes," I said.

We started out toward the shore road on the chestnut mare. Along the western horizon, the thin light of the lackluster day

372

seeped into the sea, leaving the sky the color of cold pea soup. No rainbows today. But, as I'd noted from my bed, the stormy wind had sunk to a whisper. The rain dwindled to sporadic drizzle.

"It's dreary, but there's a hint of hope." I tried to paste on a cheerful face. "Couldn't we take the path through the woods? Then we could stop a minute and look over Dolphin Bay from El Mirador."

"Don Colin always anchors here in the south cove, you know." He grinned. "Which we can see perfectly from the road."

A few minutes later we nudged aside the foliage of the thicket tunnel to El Mirador lookout. Nicolás shot up in the saddle in front of me. "Melissa, a launch of some kind *is* coming in there! I can hardly believe it, though I guess I should."

"Yeah, you should."

"It looks like...like a police patrol!"

He snapped the poor mare around and urged her back down the way we'd come at a pace she'd probably seldom matched in her life. I clung to Nicolás's waist as we thudded along the familiar shell-packed road and then across the peninsula. Apparently he'd forgotten about my head injury for the moment.

When we dismounted at Dolphin Bay, a spruce green tender-dinghy with an outboard motor had just reached the rock-strewn beach. Two of the passengers wore the olive uniform of police officers. A third had salt-and-pepper hair and a starched posture that I recognized this time.

"It's Abuelo." The genuine warmth in Nicolás's tone differed vastly from his reaction the first time his grandparents appeared in the island.

I couldn't help smiling to myself in the growing dusk. "I still wonder what happened to Cole."

"Are you two always on duty as the official greeters?" Don Manuel called as he stepped ashore. He introduced the two carabineros. "What a time I had. Bet you thought we had let you down, Nico."

He shrugged, evading his grandfather's eyes. "The weather's been uncooperative."

Don Manuel grunted. "Not only that." He turned to me. "Your brother-in-law came down with typhoid just after he dropped us off here. He has been one sick fellow."

"Oh, no!"

"Do not be alarmed, my girl, he is better now. And the rest of your family is fine. Doctor believes Don Colin picked up the typhoid from drinking water while working on some widow's home the other side of town—"

"The Bahamondes," Nicolás and I said in unison.

"Sí, before the water mains were fixed there, folks used river water that must have been contaminated. There has been a minor epidemic in that neighborhood." He paused and stretched his arm, stiff as a stick, across his grandson's back. "Don Colin felt bad about failing you, my boy. Another problem was the police have been tied in port too. Their patrol cutter was out in the Desertores, dropping off supplies for quake victims while they investigated a rumor about a gang of abalone runners."

"But that's just—" Nicolás broke into a wide grin. "Sí? And did they find anything?"

"Nothing." The police captain took up the tale. "All we had to go on was a vague tip from some other fishermen. They complained of a couple of launches hanging around the sand bar north off Cocotúe Island. But we never saw them, though we made two trips out and several locals confirmed the report. When we arrived back in Mellehue Friday night, we had given up the search. Then your grandfather came to us on Saturday."

"But the storm was on the rise by that time," Don Manuel said. "We sailed as soon as it calmed off this morning. Would you believe we met Bórquez's two launches dropping anchor an hour or so out of Mellehue? Place called Flamingo Beach. The captain and his men boarded them, and sure enough, the hold was full of contraband abalone. Just as you suspected, Nico."

Nicolás looked at me and laughed, whistled, and nodded. "Beautiful, they sailed straight to you."

"So we assisted the *Angélica* and the *Akina*—alias the *Caleuche*—back to custody in Mellehue. Crew, contraband, and all." The corners of the captain's eyes crinkled. "Now we are looking for the mastermind of the operation. Hope you can help us with that."

"Can I!" Nicolás's topaz eyes glowed. Quickly he recounted our previous evening's escapade.

Don Manuel shook his silver-and-sable head, though a smile curved his lips. "You are as daring and impulsive as your father, my boy."

"Reckless and desperate is more like it." Nicolás gave me a sheepish glance. "Thank God it didn't end in tragedy, as it well could have. That's Bórquez's house up on the hill behind us, *mi capitán*. But I'm pretty sure you will find him front and center at the Festival of Cabildos in North Head right now.

This is the final night. Just let me deliver Melissa home, and I'll show you the way."

"Dream on, amigo. I'm not missing this." I propped my hands on my hips.

"Melissa Travis, you're the most exasperating girl. Look what happened last night when you would not stay put."

"Yeah, I lost the camera. What if we lose Bórquez while you're babysitting me now?"

# 48

After a brief, hot argument, Nicolás boosted me once again onto the horse. Halter in hand, he led Don Manuel and the captain toward North Head on foot. The other carabinero returned to the patrol launch to move it the short distance north along the shore to the village dock.

From the crest of the steep hill overlooking the town, precisely where Bórquez held his tropón dance three months before, I made out the twinkling strand of a procession of lights, draped like a gaudy rhinestone necklace around the village plaza. Only slightly muffled by the damp night air, the festival music drifted up. Accordions and guitars droned out a monotonous tune, more melancholic than an organ prelude at a funeral. A clamshell moon quivered over the town, its face shrouded behind a veil of mist. I suppressed a shiver—a blend of nerves and anticipation.

"You say Bórquez is the church *fiscal* on the island?" the captain asked skeptically. "Bit of a hypocrite, no? Seems a shame to interrupt a religious festival, though. When is it over?"

"Probably not until late tonight," Nicolás said, "by the time they finish all the parading and partying."

The captain shrugged. "No help for it then. We cannot wait that long."

"What will you do?" Don Manuel asked as we started into the town.

"Not sure yet, señor. Arrest him, of course, though I hate to set the whole town in an uproar. I have no idea how this fellow Bórquez will react."

The tiny hamlet of North Head swarmed with people, swollen to three times its normal population by pilgrims from all over Chauquelín and the neighboring islands. Stragglers weaved in and out of cheap cantinas or haggled over greasy, lukewarm empanadas at vending carts set up in the muddy alleys or in the dubious shelter of shop eaves. Under one hut's leaky roof, a swarthy señora shushed a wailing baby while she fried *milcao*.

Most people, however, congregated in the center of town, either watching or participating in the intricate procession of images. The plaza had become an encampment of moldy tents. A whirling forest of totem-pole figures nearly overwhelmed the long green esplanade that ran at an incline between the plaza and the church on the bluff.

I slid off the horse and clutched Nicolás's arm. Clammy mist slithered about our ankles. I'd expected a carnival atmosphere, but I was wrong. Except for the drunks, the mood struck me as anything but merry.

Sure, the banners and the gaily colored robes of the images waved about the esplanade like a field full of flowers—wilted ones, anyway. But the pious crowd who carried them only trudged along, bedraggled and listless, intoning their litany of gloom and doom over and over.

A score of wretched penitents crawled on their knees across the soupy ground to the focal point of the pageant. There the principal image—called the Saint of Chauquelín—dominated the scene from a low platform of stumps and boughs. *This is supposed to be their…what, god?* The regally arrayed wood-and-plaster figure, tortured and pinned to a weathered cross, looked rather grimy beneath its tawdry tunic and crown.

In a haze of smoking candles, three young girls in frilly pastel dresses and a dozen men and boys in Chilote hats and ponchos formed a sort of court of honor nearby. Wicker-clad demijohn wine jugs swung from their hands or parked at their feet.

"That's the cabildo," Nicolás told me. "The committee that hosts the fiesta."

Yeah, Nicolás used to be part of the festival cabildo, I remembered. Even though the islanders attached a lot of importance to this fiesta, he recognized it wasn't the same as faith in Jesus. No wonder Cole had described the system as Christopaganism—a thousand-piece puzzle of Christian religion, *mestizo* culture, and primitive spiritism. Despite the effort and expense it demanded, somehow it bound these people together…in unthinking delusion, slavery, even dread.

The spectacle seared itself into my consciousness like so many other sights of the past months. Only this time, I was unafraid. No thought of turning tail and fleeing.

What I did feel was helplessness at the people's hopelessness. Their moaning filled my ears—a cry for help, a groan after liberty and joy and peace. Maybe they didn't even know what else.

The chant of misery echoed deep. Tears stung my eyes in the murky light. Yearning for them all to know Jesus—the real Jesus—burst into a poignant ache in my chest.

Maybe scenes like this had first planted the seed of desire to know God in Nicolás's heart. A loving and living God, beyond the hollow form of religion and the shroud of mystery.

The police captain's aide rejoined our group at one corner of the plaza. The five of us threaded our way through the throng. Even in the crisscross of flickering light and shadow, mist and smoke, it was difficult to be inconspicuous, especially with the horse in rein. Juan Bórquez, at the head of the concourse with the rest of the cabildo, couldn't help but notice us.

Still, I froze when his grating voice boomed. "Eh, Nicolás Serrano, what are you doing here, you young devil? Come to join us after all? Or just snooping as usual?"

"Neither, Don Juan," Nicolás said quietly.

"Ha! I don't believe that, you lying—" His tirade choked off as his scowl fell on the two crisp uniforms standing behind Nicolás. The familiar angry red collar wrapped his bulldog neck.

"Señor Bórquez?" The captain marched forward at once. "Could we have a private word with you?"

If the captain expected Bórquez would retreat compliantly from center stage, he was mistaken. Like a gargoyle, Bórquez bared his teeth at Nicolás. "This is your doing, no? *Demonios*, I will make certain it is the last time you meddle here."

He pivoted and flung himself at the grotesque figure on the cross. Hanging on its berry-purple robe, he appealed to the crowd, his features contorted and his eyes gleaming with an eerie fire. Was he on some herbal drug?

"Neighbors, why are we gathered here tonight?" he screamed. "Is it not so the world may know that we in this island keep and defend the traditions of our fathers? Each year at the Fiesta of Cabildos, we kneel once again at the feet of our divine Santo of Chauquelín and pay him homage. For those who remain loyal to the legacy of our forefathers, the Saint drives away evil spirits and disgrace."

"That is so," someone said. "The harvests do poorly unless we keep the fiesta."

A man behind me said to someone else, "The Saint cured my uncle's horse of a lame foot when he led it in the procession last year."

The public shifted uneasily. Voices swirled in confusion. A knot tightened in my stomach as Bórquez rampaged on, inciting fear…hostility.

"And this Serrano trash" —he jabbed a stubby finger— "has caused trouble here for months, as some here know. He has abandoned, he has *scorned* our time-honored customs—and persuaded others to do the same. Even as you see tonight, he has dragged carabineros here to harass me, your leader. To spoil our fiesta."

A wave of outrage rolled through the crowd. Nicolás stiffened beside me, but made no defense. I slid my hand into his and squeezed. His tall grandfather laid hands on his shoulders. In my wildest dreams of this showdown, I'd never imagined our moment of truth would backfire into this frenzy of twisted accusations and slurs against my friend. More than a petty human power play was at work here. I could feel the crackle of hatred in the air. *Oh, Lord Jesus…*

Bórquez spat and ranted again. "Serrano's claims are nothing but juvenile fantasy—"

"Stop it!" I spun and flapped my arms. "Nicolás loves this island. He loves you people and so many of your customs. But he hates for you to be deceived by Satan, or by this man—this fraud—who's been scaring and cheating you and stealing for his own profit—"

"You, gringa—neither of you are Chilotes." Bórquez sneered. "Just conceited canuto scum—"

The captain slipped a shiny object from his pocket. For a second, I thought it was a gun, until he blew, long and shrill, on a traffic whistle.

Unnerved, the rabble hushed at once. Only Bórquez opened his mouth, but the captain silenced him with a stern glare. "Enough, señor. You've had your say."

Then he shouldered his way to the front and addressed the fiesta gathering, his tone brisk. "I know nothing about the young man's religious beliefs, but I certainly consider Nicolás Serrano De la Cruz to be a conscientious citizen. He hardly deserves this kind of insult and abuse. Nor would I term 'juvenile fantasy' what I have recently discovered of Señor Bórquez's illegal activities. In fact, I am here to place him under arrest."

A buzz of questions and exclamations erupted, but the captain held up his hand. "You wonder, of course, what the charges are. His launches, the *Angélica* and the *Akina*, have been detained. You don't know the *Akina*? Perhaps you have seen her here outfitted as the *Caleuche*. We confiscated these two ships off Flamingo Beach earlier today, along with their respective crews and over four tons of illegally extracted abalone."

"You see, neighbors?" Grabbing a corner of the Santo's robe, Bórquez wiped at the hideous coat of spittle that swathed his beard. "These *pacos* will believe any nonsense story the spoiled brat tells them."

"The *Caleuche*—that killed Garrido—is *yours?*" Don Alfonso, one of the cabildo members who had accompanied Bórquez on his house calls soliciting fiesta donations, pushed through to the carabineros as a collective gasp arose from the crowd. "I have wondered... doubted his motives for some time."

"How can you say that?" a woman's voice squawked. "He's done a lot for us here. What about the tropón dance, the healings—"

"Don't you believe it. He's a con, like the girl says. He's passed himself off as a religious fanatic to distract us."

"Then chuta, he's made fools of us all. Used us to hide his pirating."

"I think that's an accurate assessment of the situation," the captain said. "Señor Bórquez and his gang of poachers have evidently used this island as a base of operations from which to rob honest fishermen of their chance of a good season. Several other charges are pending, among them a possible accessory in the drowning of Jaime Garrido whom, I believe, many of you knew—"

Another gasp followed. Bórquez slunk out of the spotlight and into the dark of the pressing throng.

"Stop him!" I said to the other policeman. "He's trying to get away!"

The aide wheeled toward Bórquez. The fickle mob—five minutes before his staunch supporters—bellowed and locked together to seal off any avenue of escape.

"Here he is, sergeant!" Don Alfonso shouted.

Bórquez veered back toward the platform. He ducked behind the Santo and tried to shove the image in the path of his pursuers, but tripped on the robe he himself had half tugged off. *Way beyond bizarre.* He crashed to the boards in a tangle of gold-trimmed purple wool and splintered wood.

In stunned silence, the crowd staggered apart to let the policemen through. But far from squelched, Bórquez crab-scuttled off the back of the platform. It took both officers, their billysticks, and a scuffle in the mud to handcuff him.

"Señor Bórquez will be taken to provincial justice." The captain panted as they towed him toward the dock. "I will submit a full report of the affair to the elders here. Beg pardon for disrupting your fiesta. By all means, feel free to continue."

Chauquelín's bogus machi still thrashed and blustered about "trumped-up charges" and "corrupt *pacos.*" Judge Serrano shook his head in disgust. I tucked my arm through Nicolás's as he led the mare away. Behind us, the ranks closed again in chaos. The islanders surged to rescue their toppled Santo. *Sure, on with the show…anticlimactic or what?*

The bandage on my forehead flopped, limp and loose. I squashed it into place, giggling. "I never saw people change their minds so fast in all my life." My brain still reeled with the melodrama.

"Most Chileans respect authority," Don Manuel said.

"Some of them already suspected what was going on, anyway," Nicolás said. "Like Don Alfonso. He's not that superstitious *or* that stupid. He just didn't want to believe his gut, until he had to." He sighed. "Their *hearts* haven't really changed much."

I got it. For the first time, I understood his compulsion to fight the darkness in this depressing place. As he'd said months ago, merely taking down dictators, political or religious, wouldn't save the world when people's need went deeper. *But...*

"It's a start, isn't it? Not all in one day, okay?" I batted him on the back. "Tonight *we* should celebrate more than them."

"Sí-po." He split the air with a whoop, grabbed my hand, and pumped it over our heads. The loose side of my bandage flipped off again. "And what a night for a girl recovering from concussion. Get up on the old mare and I'll take you to Don Ramón's. Now!"

# 49

*Mellehue, Chiloé*

*Month 7—July 29–August 8*

*As soon as they escorted Bórquez to the <u>tenencia</u> jail in Mellehue, the police dispatched the <u>Última Esperanza</u> to pick us school kids up the next day.*

After seven weeks in rustic Chauquelín, Mellehue should have seemed like a modern and fast-paced metropolis. Instead, at first, it felt flat and dull.

Though maybe that was a good thing.

Señora Angélica accompanied her mother into Mellehue along with us students. To our amazement, the stubborn dame finally agreed to see a doctor about her gall bladder complaints. Linda invited the two ladies to stay at the Peterson home. Grandmother Luisa put on her tough-old-bird face, but leaving the island meant a traumatic step for her. Waiting for major surgery couldn't be easy, either.

Two days into classes, I came down with a terrible chest cold. The fever and cough hit both the Serrano boys too.

"It is not to be wondered at, the three of you and that awful night in the bay." Señora Angélica clicked her tongue. "You should lie low this time and forget the excitement, my dear."

The tenderest of nurses, Nicolás's mother rotated from me to the boys at their boarding house and back to Señora Luisa. My fever ebbed after about a week, but between my sister and my nurse, they practically tied me to the bed.

While I recuperated, Señora Luisa crept into my room to sit and knit for a couple of hours each morning. We both soaked up the sun as it warmed the eastern windows and reflected from the honey-gold pine walls.

"What are you making?" I asked one day.

"A pair of Chilote socks for you." The old woman's finely wrinkled hands worked the creamy wool as tirelessly as ever. "If you must traipse about in the rain and the sea, you need proper clothing around here. Look at you, almost got pneumonia from that dousing."

"I bet Nicolás was wearing wool socks that night, and he's sick, too." I pressed back a wicked grin.

His grandmother snorted and kept the needles clacking.

"But I'll wear them," I said. "Know what I'd really like you to make me?"

Señora Luisa's bright black eyes looked up with a glint of interest.

"A wool dress like Señora Angélica's. They look so warm and elegant. Would you? I'll pay you for it."

"Certainly not. What color do you like?"

I figured her refusal referred to the payment, not to the knitting project, and tilted my head. "Maybe periwinkle blue with that dusty rose you make from the blackberries. If you have the wool here, that is."

"I can get it before I go into the hospital," she said.

"Oh, Señora Luisa, I'm sorry. Please don't feel pressured, with your surgery coming up. Next week, right?"

"So it is, and don't you forget to pray for me, señorita." Her eyes twinkled. "Now that I've converted you into a Chilote, you may convert me into a canuta yet."

"Glad to see you're on the mend," Linda said that afternoon when she brought me a tray of lemon ginger tea and crusty buns. "And with the stitches out now, even that scar on your forehead looks pretty good."

"How's Cole doing?"

"He's up and about today. Okay if he doesn't overdo."

I sipped tea from a rose-flowered china cup. "Linda, you must be exhausted. So many people in the house all these months, then Cole crashes with typhoid. You should have sent for me to come home." Remorse speared me. "And when I finally get here, I'm just another burden."

"Nonsense, I've had plenty of help. Miriam and her sisters are very efficient. They only moved into their own place just before you arrived, you know." That was my big sister, upbeat and unruffled as ever. She only *looked* weary and gaunt as she spread mashed avocado on my bread. "I wouldn't have called you back here for the world, Meli. From what Cole told me, I had the feeling something special was happening in Chauquelín. Not only the Bórquez situation, but with *you*—in your heart."

*Somehow, she knows.* "Something *was* happening." I spoke slowly, softly. "I'm different. I know you and Cole have prayed for me, and—you probably can't believe I'm saying this, I can't myself. But there it is. Being here in Chiloé these months has changed my life. My own personal earthquake, sort of. As if God had designed it all."

"What happened, then?" Linda asked, smiling.

"Oh, drat and bucha, as Nicolás says, I can't quite explain it, but—"With a deep gulp, I tried to steel the shaking of my voice, the racing of my heart. Absurd that I should feel so awkward, but I did. "All my life I've known—and *believed*—that Jesus died for me, and I appreciated that in a vague sort of way. But never enough to give Him my life. After a while, I—I turned my back on Him. I'd heard so much about God that He didn't seem...well, very real or here-and-now."

"Uh-huh, sort of stale and not terribly exciting. I understand." Linda nodded. "It's a rut you fall into sometimes. Maybe even a spell the devil puts on you."

I glanced at my sister and caught a curving grin on her lips. *Huh.* Maybe my model sister, and likely my brother-in-law as well, had made their own odysseys to faith and commitment. Hard to imagine Linda—Ginger—muddled and messy.

Yet she could never possess that uncanny perception unless she'd been there herself. She always gave me the benefit of the doubt, always expected the best of me. Ever so subtly offered me opportunities to see the world from a different perspective, to figure out who I really was.

And now that I'd climbed out of the rut and broken the spell, so to speak, I realized I *was* a Travis daughter after all. And *God's* daughter.

"Exactly." I tossed my reserve aside. "Coming to Chiloé was sort of a catalyst for me. Sometimes I loved it here, sometimes I hated it. It attracted and repelled me at the same time. It frightened me, forced me to realize how empty I was inside. For all I thought I'd been overdosed, I had nothing to give anyone." I met Linda's sparkling eyes. "But then in Chauquelín, just reading over the Bible stories I was telling the kids, I started to feel like…thirsty. Fascinated. Like I suddenly wanted to *know* Jesus for the first time in my life."

"Then you've got a marvelous road of discovery ahead," Linda said.

~

## Month 7, continued

*Nicolás's Serrano grandparents lodged in a one-star pensión near the kids' boarding houses for ten days, until they had to return to Santiago. Who knew, maybe Mellehue looked impressive after Chauquelín?*

They stopped by to say their farewells at the Peterson house before heading to Castro, the island's capital city, accompanied by their three grandchildren.

"Now that the boys are better, Manny really has to get back." Señora Rosalía bent to kiss me good-bye. "We will bus to the mainland and from there a plane to Santiago. You *must* visit us on your way back to the States, I insist."

"I'd be charmed. Seriously. I'll plan on it." I needed all the grandmothers I could adopt.

"So glad to see your head healing and color in your face again, querida. You were dreadfully pale for a few days. But that pretty island bloom is back."

"Isn't Chiloé a great place?"

Señora Rosalía gazed at me with her wide, gray-velvet eyes and nodded. "I'm grateful you encouraged me, my dear. I should have come years ago, instead of being such a coward. Now the boys have promised to visit *us* this coming summer."

"Is that to prove *you're* not a coward?" I turned a teasing grin toward Nicolás as he slouched in the doorway of my room.

"That's right." He shot me a glance that brimmed with emotion. "Hurry up and get well, Meli. The provincial music competition is next week."

"Is it even worth going back to school?" I hoisted up the familiar overstuffed book bag on a glacial Monday morning. "With only two weeks left in Chiloé?"

My rescheduled flight to New York was set for September third. I didn't know whether I dreaded or looked forward to it.

"You have been gone practically all winter," Miriam said as we sauntered down the Peterson lane. "Of course, it is worth it. I'm sure our classmates will not hear of your doing otherwise."

"Except Delicia, I bet." I paused on the sidewalk and surveyed the frosted roofs of the town.

"Never mind her. She will have plenty of time to chase Tito and Nicolás after you are gone." Miriam tugged on my arm. "It was not fair of them to keep you out in Chauquelín so long, though I guess it worked out for the best in the end. But let's not lose this last bit of time together."

"You're a gem, Miri. Maybe you could come with us to Santiago to see me off."

She snorted. "What, so I can play the violin?"

"What are you talking about? You know, more than one person has mentioned violins to me, and I have no idea—"

"It means play chaperone. Two's company, three's a crowd."

"Oh." Heat—in the cold air—crept along my cheekbones. "But it's just me and Linda. No need for you to feel like that."

"Won't Nicolás be going?"

"Oh, I don't think so. They hope Señora Luisa will be recovered enough from her surgery to travel home to the island that weekend. Nicolás says he needs to check on his wheat crop." Ramón had ended up planting it for him.

Miriam laughed. "That guy! For all he acts like such a sophisticated dude, sometimes I think he's just a Chilote farmer after all."

While I packed my bags, my friends packed my remaining time with activities. The school and the entire town, it seemed, tried to make up for the months lost to cleanup and reconstruction following May's earthquake.

The classrooms showed the ravaging effects of mud and salt water, the repairs on the old wing slapdash at best. But the studies plodded on. The students looked forward to spring, counted the weeks until the end of the long winter. For me, though, the time was like the final slice of a delicious cake. I savored every mouthful, relished even the falling crumbs, wished it could only last longer.

Each event took on special significance. My last rainy-day tea with *sopaipillas*. My last stroll to the bakery. My last pizza and storybook night with Reba and Keli, sneaking them caramel nuggets under the blanket. My *first* class at Linda's Bible club.

During those unforgettable days, I completed the essay, "What I Learned in Chile." It grew from random diary notes into a regular thesis paper in the process. I hadn't written much over the winter, but I'd never stopped learning. How to survive an earthquake, how to keep house in a hut, how to be happy...

With shaky hands and a cotton ball mouth, I stuffed it into an envelope addressed to Principal Martin at Mt. Washington Christian Academy and mailed it. Up to God which way the wind blew there. Maybe the most important thing I'd learned in Chile was that I was not only willing to turn over a new leaf at school, I *wanted* to—for Jesus's sake.

Still croaking and coughing some, I sang along with the school's folkloric music ensemble, Choros y Locos, at the competition in Castro. I finally grasped the clever play on words that was our group name. *Choros* and *locos*—mussels and abalone—were both shellfish, but the words carried a secondary meaning.

"Cool and crazy, yep, that's us." I laughed.

Our third-place finish came as no surprise to anyone, considering the lack of practice, the rampant colds—and the explosion of snickers when gangly Tito Bahamonde stumbled and sprawled out on the stairs en route to the stage. But it was fun anyway.

Nicolás sang part of one of the classic numbers as a solo. We all wore Chilote wool costumes, but he looked just the same as I'd seen him almost every day for the past two months in Chauquelín. He gazed, not at the audience or the judges, but directly at me as he performed.

> *"On the beach is a beautiful girl,*
> *Her lovely figure shines.*
> *She drives all the sailors a little bit crazy,*
> *And even the captain has lost his mind.*
> *Oh, what joy..."*

"La Bella Lola" was the first song he'd ever played for me, that long-ago afternoon in the orchard. I knew he was dedicating it to me now. The melody resonated, vibrated deep inside me, more haunting than anything that blared from the deck of the *Caleuche*. A strange choice, it seemed more like a welcome-home than a good-bye song.

But my time in Chile was racing to its end. Maryland loomed ahead like a mountain of doom, and I shrank from it. The only reason I managed to choke back the tears was because all the Choros and Locos were watching me.

Nicolás went on to the second verse:

> *"After a year…I made home port and saw*
> *The only one my heart adored…"*

Whatever meaning it held for him, "La Bella Lola" would always sound like a homing signal to me from now on. Like the sweet clay flute that called Nicolás's dolphins to their playground in the bay, the music echoed. Pleasure mixed with pain. It lingered in my memory and beckoned toward the future.

The round of farewells commenced. I accompanied Linda and Señora Angélica to visit Vanessa de Garrido and her children. They'd settled into a few rented rooms on the Mellehue waterfront. Vanessa was taking laundry and housecleaning jobs to support them. I knew Linda would follow up.

I made a couple of trips to the Castro hospital to visit Señora Luisa after her operation. She made remarkable progress—and resumed knitting. One afternoon I took my protégés, Valeria and Jana, along, too, and spent the last of my cash on clothes and candy and trinkets for them.

I cheered the Mellehue soccer team to two more victories. After school Friday, my last day of classes, I organized the girls to play once more and even combined efforts with Delicia Treviño to put in a goal. Dazzling Delicia made herself conspicuously agreeable now that my days in Chile were numbered. *Honestly.* We could've been friends. *Maybe.*

After the game, I hustled home to get ready for the church youth meeting that evening. The group had reorganized the party abandoned on the fateful night of the earthquake. I planned to debut the wool dress Grandmother Luisa had just finished. *Yeah, a dress.* I couldn't help chuckling to myself.

Linda met me at the door with two letters. At a glance, I saw that one was from my old friend, Candie Davenport. The other, with a typewritten address, came from Mt. Washington Christian Academy.

I looked swiftly at Linda. "It's too soon for a reply to my essay. You know anything about this?"

"Possibly, I'm not sure. I wrote to Seth Martin back in July." She met my gaze with a quirky smile. "Well, open it."

Bracing the tremble in my hands, I did. Principal Martin—my sister's friend—wrote a cool, straightforward note. He'd recently received information that allowed the school board to reconsider me as a student at Mt. W.C.A. He expected me in his office for an interview as soon as I returned from Chile.

I threw my arms around my sister and burst into sobs. Then I dashed up the stairs, two at a time.

# 50

*Destiny Island (AKA Chauquelín)*

*Day 212, August 31*

*On the last Saturday afternoon in August—the day before Linda, Miriam, and I would board the overnight bus to Santiago—Cole transported the Serrano family in the <u>Ambassador</u> back to Chauquelín.*

I went along for the ride again. "Just for old times' sake," I promised my sister. "I won't decide to stay."

Though I was tempted. The day, hazy and mild, reminded me of my first voyage out, eight months to the day before. Though winter still squeezed Chiloé in its grip, a tantalizing whiff of spring perfumed the air.

Gina and Ramón Pérez met the launch on the shore of the south cove. *Shades of déjà vu.* I grinned and hugged them. This time they'd already brought their oxcart to carry Señora Luisa home. In the Serrano yard, the doleful bleats of three lambs, wobbling beside the old ewes, greeted us.

"Oh!" I tried to get close enough to pet the skittish newborns. "Aren't they darling?"

Nicolás hopped into the pen and caught one up in his arms. "We can build up the flock again, now that we won't have to sell them off to pay Bórquez."

"I made a fire, and your teakettle should be boiling, Angie," Gina said. "Pastor Colin, Melissa, come over for mate?"

Nicolás dropped the lamb. "Do…do you want mate right now?"

"How long can we stay, Cole?" I asked.

"I've got to head back soon. An hour maybe."

"Then I'll skip the mate today, Gina, if you don't mind, and take one last ramble around here with Nicolás."

Halfway back down the path to the shore road, he laid a hand on my arm. "This better *not* be your last ramble around here, Señorita Melissa Travis."

"Well, it is for now. Though you have no idea how much I hate to say that." I bit my bottom lip as a tangle of emotions swelled in my chest.

"Want to take Don Colin's rowboat out?" he said with a faint smile. "We can loop by the orchard and El Mirador on the way to Pérezes, but we started this at Dolphin Bay, remember? The common island guy trying to impress the pretty blond gringa."

"Nicolás Serrano, you are anything but common." The vehemence of my tone startled even me.

He was so many things—the efficient skipper, the perceptive "professor," the upper-crust heir, the fun pal. But "common" just wasn't a label that suited. I scrambled into the boat; he pushed it off. For a few minutes, we didn't talk. I only listened to the rhythmic swish of the oars and the whisper of the wind in my ears. Talking wasn't necessary with Nicolás anyway, but I couldn't speak past the block in my throat.

Now that the final moments had arrived, saying good-bye was agony. The unique friendship between us had sprung up so easily, grown so close, so natural. It was hard to think of going our separate ways again. I almost couldn't imagine a world, a life, that didn't include Nicolás and his family anymore.

We rounded the wooded peninsula that separated the twin coves, skirting the razor-edged gravel bar at the point. The sight of the Dragon's Back made me shiver and pucker the scar on my brow. *Ouch, still tight.*

But I forgot the trauma of my near-fatal plunge as we drifted into Dolphin Bay. The oval glass bowl shone like translucent aquamarine today, fringed by the newest of lacy green and gold along the shore.

I broke the silence. "The dolphins never came back, did they? Just sort of disappeared after the summer."

"I talked to Captain De la Rosa—the port captain in Mellehue, you know—about that this past week. He thinks they might have a seasonal migration period." A wistful shadow flitted across his face. "But I still wonder if Bórquez hurt them, or poisoned them, to keep them away from his abalone cache, like you mentioned once."

"Or turned them into the *Caleuche*, like your mythology book told about."

"Now that the *Caleuche* has vanished, maybe they'll appear again?" He grinned. "At any rate, Bórquez will not make trouble around here for a while."

"Yeah, Cole told me about the sentencing yesterday. Eighteen months in prison, huh?"

"And a huge fine. They presented our written testimonies to the judge, but the police evidence clinched the case, of course."

"What'll happen to his big house now, do you suppose?" I glanced up at the gingerbread castle peeping through the forest of the bay's north shore.

He shrugged. "Serve him right if he has to sell it to pay the fine. He'd have no reason to come back here bothering us then, would he?"

"It must be a tremendous relief to your mother."

"Though I think it's still a shock to Abuela Luisa. He's her sort of grandnephew, after all. Hard to take from her own kin. But she's a tough lady, and sharp enough to figure out what was going on." He paused, seemed to debate his next words. "Nice dress she knit for you, Meli."

"I love it. And Vali drew me some really nice pictures. She's got talent."

He fished in the breast pocket of his denim jacket and withdrew a tiny package of white tissue paper. "I—well, I have a little remembrance from Chiloé I wanted to give you, too."

"Oh, Nicolás. You know, I tried more than once to find something for you, but nothing I saw seemed quite right, or special enough." I was flustered with pleasure.

"No importa. I have an idea what you can give me. But now, open it."

I released a contented sigh and slipped the wrapping from Nicolás's gift. A small metal pendant in the shape of a leaping dolphin fell into my palm. Inlaid with thin, shimmery flakes, the intricate charm hung on a long silver chain.

"How...totally lovely." I caught my breath at the striking craftsmanship. "What's it made of?"

"The mother-of-pearl layer inside abalone shells, of course." He grinned. "After the fisheries make a fortune on the meat, the jewelers move in for their cut. Our tech teacher had con-nections, I guess."

My eyes widened. "You mean, you made this *yourself* in tech class at school? That's awesome."

"Thought it would be the perfect keepsake for you." His smile softened, almost faltered, as he rubbed the back of his neck. "Seeing as…the dolphins first made us click."

I bent my neck to fasten the clasp, licking salt from my lips. "I—I'll think of you, amigo, and of Chauquelín, every time I wear it."

"That's the idea." His deep copper-flecked eyes bored into me.

A flutter rippled across my belly. Would he kiss me? I kind of wished he would. On the other hand, would it spoil our friendship somehow, ratchet it to another level that was no longer pure and simple?

But if a good-bye kiss crossed his mind, he refrained. Despite my twinge of disappointment, I thought more of him for it. "Now, what can I send you from the States?"

"Only a message."

"A message?"

"Let me hear from you," he said. "Don't just drop out of my life and forget me, *vale*? I would like to think we are friends for life."

"Me, too."

"I'll want to know how you're doing. If you go on teaching the Bible, if you are still loving God, if you keep filling up on bread from heaven instead of meringue. I know you're going back to—well, another world really, and even the best memo-ries…fade. So, whenever you think of your friend back in this corner of the earth, news is what I'd most like to have from you, Melissa."

"Then I'll keep in touch often. I—I'm a little afraid to go back, you know."

"Afraid, why?"

"I was miserable there, deep down. Here I've found something special, something *different*, and I don't want to lose it. I'll never be the same person again, but…my friends won't understand."

"I see. Believe me, I do." Nicolás nodded and shifted his glance over my head toward the rolling hills that bordered the beach.

He took the oars again and plowed a straight furrow across the clear, calm water of the bay. "See those flowers?" He pointed out the clusters of showy buttercup-yellow blossoms scattered through the evergreen thickets.

"Yeah, they've sprung up all over the place. You can even see them way across the channel. What are they?"

"Just gigantic weeds. The gorse bushes that grow wild around here."

"You're kidding."

"No. The flowers are pretty gaudy in the spring, and up close they have this funky coconut smell. But the worst of them is the thorns, you know?" He stretched back, draped his arm along the edge of the skiff. "When I first came here to Chauquelín, they had invaded half of Abuela's land. I tried everything—chopping, burning, pulling them out by the roots. And would you believe those things kept coming back."

"Bucha, *qué lata*." I smiled. "I have the feeling you're trying to tell me, like, a story—a parable."

"I am. Remember the beginning of the school year when Marc and I would go to your house on Friday nights and have Bible study with your brother-in-law in his office?"

I laughed. "Ah-hah, you mean now I get to hear all your secrets? I was sure you guys were up to something in there."

"It wasn't a private man cave," he said slyly. "We would have welcomed you, too."

"You couldn't have dragged me in, at that point. But I admit I was dying of curiosity."

"Well, it was revolutionary, all right. Half the reason I went was to avoid the boozing invitations around town. I asked Don Colin one day how I could ever change my—my reputation, I guess. I mean, everybody in Mellehue knew me for a scoundrel, and God knows I was. And Don Colin just leaned back in his chair and started talking about those thorn bushes."

"Cole talked about *thorn bushes*?"

"I told him I had a bit of experience with them, and he asked me how I finally got rid of them. I said Don Ramón helped me. He said the only thing that really works is to plant something else in their place. Don Colin kept rocking in his chair and grinning. Said, 'Ramón was right, wasn't he? You plant something else in their place. You can't change the past. But this is a new year, and you can always sow a different crop.'"

In the moment of crystal silence, the rich scent of new grass and turned earth flowed down off the hills. I drew in a deep breath of it. "So…like you said before, God lets us begin a new life any time, right?"

"Not only begin, but go on," Nicolás said with his quick candor. "Plant something else over the past when you go home to Maryland. It will take time, sure, but if you're willing to *be* different, then God will *make* you different. Don't be afraid, be brave."

Tears—happy ones—stung my eyes and spilled over onto my cheeks. "That sounds like 'don't be a coward.'"

His chin shot up, but a grin tugged at the corners of his lips. "We both have room for improvement. Thorny spots to work on, you might say, before we can change the world."

"Change the world, huh? How do you plan to do that, dreamer?"

"One person at a time." His grin deepened.

"Starting with me?"

"Starting with *me*."

"I'm so glad you're going to your grandparents' in Santiago in the summer."

"We've had a lot of misunderstandings, made a lot of mistakes," he said. "No importa. Like Joseph in the Bible, I accept that God meant it all for good."

*God meant it for good.* Whatever hurts we'd experienced—whatever hurts we'd caused—our lives were ruled by more than freak accidents or random leaves in a cup. Even if I couldn't see it all yet, He was weaving the details—my family, my school, my talents and interests—into a glorious design. What I did would matter for eternity—and I would *not* be bored.

"Now I just have to figure out how to integrate these two worlds," Nicolás said. "The city and the country, you know. Without feeling schizophrenic."

I gazed at him in amazement. "I don't think you need to figure it out at all."

He wore a smart denim jacket trimmed with black suede, over a shaggy hand-knit sweater. He sprawled out in Cole's rowboat as comfortably as if he sat in a yacht lounge, discussing the fine points of island farming like an agriculture instructor. His smooth accent was a medley of Chilote music, clipped with Santiago military precision.

He loved the woods and the sea, swam like a dolphin, handled a boat like a skipper, and yet played soccer with club-trained finesse. He munched eucalyptus leaves but favored elegant marzipan tortes.

No doubt in my mind. In Nicolás Serrano, the capital city and the rustic island met and melded into a single personality. Whatever future God had destined for him, that dual legacy he'd inherited would surely play a role.

I shook my head. "You've been blending those two worlds perfectly ever since I've known you, Nicolás. Like your dolphins, air and water."

The pleased surprise in his face at my words sharpened to open-mouthed astonishment. He stared beyond me. "Melissa! Could it be? Could it be the dolphins?"

I swiveled and focused on the azure horizon. *Yes!* I made out the flashing silver shapes leap-frogging into the bay. They formed a shooting fountain as they closed the distance between themselves and our boat. "Look, there's a baby with them! *Two* little minnows."

"Calves, Meli." He stood and whistled, a grin nearly splitting his face in two. "The whole pod's swimming circles around the babies."

"Aren't we going to jump in and greet them, Dolphin Boy? Meet the family?"

His laugh rang out across the water. "I think *you* especially had better wait until summer for another dip in Dolphin Bay."

"Bummer I won't be here in the summer." Chiloé wasn't my home. And yet now it was. I'd learned to love this place. Like the dolphins—like Nicolás—I was a dual citizen. I was meant to come here.

I'd learned I could be myself—and still part of something much bigger than me. The three-hour tour had turned into the voyage of a lifetime. And maybe this was only my first port of call.

"You'll be back someday," Nicolás said. "I'll play my flute."

# A NOTE FROM THE AUTHOR:

My family and I lived in the Chiloé Islands of Chile for eight years during the turbulent 1980s and early '90s. The world has changed since then, even in Chiloé, but my hope is that *Destiny at Dolphin Bay* gives a fair view of those times, retaining the flavor of historical integrity, while offering a glimpse of their "what-if" possibilities.

As far as Chilean geography, I've maintained the names of many of the larger towns and cities but renamed and reinvented some smaller towns and islands as composites that reflect the reality. And, as the usual disclaimer goes, references to actual historical events, people, and places is intended only to ground the fictional setting in reality. Other names, characters, and incidents are grown from the seed plot of the author's imagination. Any resemblance to real-life counterparts is coincidental.

Thankfully, there was never a *real* major earthquake and tsunami in Chile in 1990. I based my account here in large part on the tales I heard of the 1960 earthquake in southern Chile, at 9.5 the most powerful in recorded history. But, for story fodder, nothing beats my personal experiences—in the aftershocks of 1985, the 8.8 of 2010, and the devastating effects of the Coquimbo tsunami in 2015. Living with tremors of varied magnitude nearly every day, we know a "big one" could happen anytime.

Also based completely on fact for this series are the amazing hospitality I've enjoyed over the years from countless Chilotes and the model of loving sacrifice by many missionary mentors and colleagues. They're all here, albeit wearing different colors, authentic if not real.

# ACKNOWLEDGMENTS:

Thanks to my husband as always for everything and for being my "Nicolás" in so many ways.

Thanks to my publisher, Lisa Norman of Heart Ally Books, for your kindness and courage in taking a chance on a new writer and for your unflagging support and encouragement. Thanks to my editor, Lori Brown, for your longsuffering attention to detail. The teamwork has made the dream work.

Thanks to my early readers: Mom, the Archer clan, Debbie Gibbons, Seanna Michaud, David and Susan Smith, Ruth Snyder, and Becky Scott. You bravely waded through a really rough draft.

Thanks also to the later beta readers: Joy Rozelle, Gayle Kramer, Cheryl Nurmi, Jan Armstrong, Seanna Michaud Johnson, Kasey Giard Hesher, Colleen Shine Phillips, and the ACFW Genesis Contest judges who chose *Destiny at Dolphin Bay* as a finalist in 2016. All of your feedback has been invaluable in the final crafting of the book.

Thanks, Seanna, for loving it enough to read it *twice*. Thanks, Debbie, for reading *everything*. Thanks, Colleen, for tea and "beach"-storming. And thanks to the Stewardship

Writers' Club for Saturday morning waffles and wordsmithing. The vision is bigger than we are, so…

Deepest thanks to my Lord Jesus for the joy of serving with keyboard, quill, and quiver. May even one sentence touch the target and make a difference.

*"I write for the King…"* –Ps. 45:1

# ABOUT THE AUTHOR:

Diana Delacruz writes under a pen name to keep her ongoing missionary service low-key. In *Destiny at Dolphin Bay*, the opening book in the Desert Island Diaries, she draws on her almost 40 years of experience as a teacher, speaker, and writer in Chile. Diana and her husband work in the city of Coquimbo at present. They have three grown daughters and five grandchildren.

Diana grew up in the state of Maine and has never lived more than an hour or two distant from the ocean. You can learn more about Diana and her Seaglass Sagas at www.dianadelacruz.com.